MOLLY IZZARD

Molly Izzard is the widow of Ralph Izzard, OBE, for many years one of the leading British journalists commenting on and living in the Middle East. Born in St. Ives, Cornwall, she has been connected with the Arab world since 1950 and has known the Gulf, and Bahrain in particular, since 1966, writing about the area in THE GULF (1976). In SMELLING THE BREEZES (1959) and A PRIVATE LIFE (1963) she has written about her experiences in the Lebanon, Egypt, India and Turkish Cyprus.

She served for three years as a FANY driver during the War before being commissioned for intelligence duties. She has four children and three grandchildren, and lives in Tunbridge Wells.

D1396396

Molly Izzard

FREYA STARK

A Biography

Copyright © Molly Izzard 1993

First published in Great Britain in 1993 by Hodder and Stoughton Ltd

A Sceptre paperback 1993

Sceptre is an imprint of Hodder and Stoughton Paperbacks, a division of Hodder Headline PLC

British Library C.I.P.

Izzard, Molly
  Freya Stark: a biography
  I. Title
  910.4092

ISBN 0 340 59779 8

10 9 8 7 6 5 4 3

Printed and bound in Great Britain for Hodder and Stoughton Paperbacks, a division of Hodder Headline PLC., 338 Euston Road, London NW1 3BH by Cox & Wyman Ltd., Reading, Berkshire. Photoset by Rowland Phototypesetting Ltd, Bury St Edmunds, Suffolk.

CONTENTS

LIST OF ILLUSTRATIONS

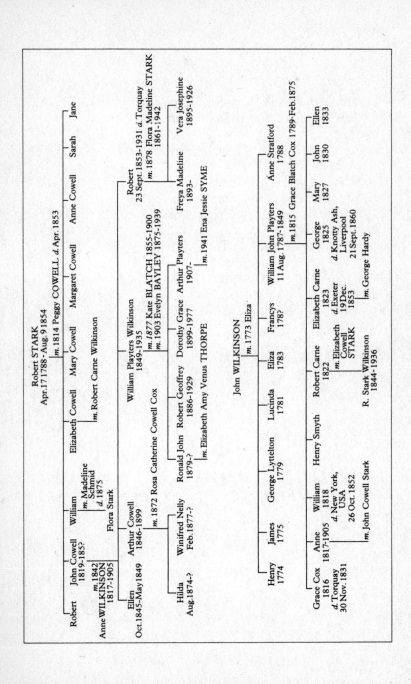

ACKNOWLEDGMENTS

This book has had a long gestation, and thirteen years have passed since I first began in 1979 to explore Freya's personality. Many of the people whom I consulted then, and with whom I discussed my findings, have since died, and I record them with regret: Elizabeth Monroe, Mme Hilda Besse, John and Josie Brinton, Gerald de Gaury, Christopher Scaife, Wilfrid Blunt, Art Stark, Terence Davies, Stewart Perowne, Lord Evans of Hungershall, Ronald Lewin, Peter Tamlyn.

There are many others to whom I owe valuable insights or practical help. I hope that over this long period I have not forgotten any, and that I do not appear casual or ungrateful to anyone. Often only the slightest hint, the merest detail, can round out the picture, or untangle the puzzle for the biographer, and such unanticipated bonuses are very welcome. I am particularly grateful to the late Wilfrid Blunt, biographer of Sir Sydney Cockerell, for access to some 500 letters written by Freya to Cockerell from their first meeting in 1933 until his death. Included in the large package passed to me and described by Blunt as 'Starkiana' were also photographs, letters from Freya's mother Flora, and from family friends of the 1920s in Italy, as well as copies of Cockerell's own letters to Freya and to Gertrude Caton Thompson regarding their vexatious Wakefield archaeological expedition to Hadhramaut in 1937–8.

I should also like to thank Gordon Anderson, Gerald de Gaury's executor, for letting me read the large bundle of Freya's letters to Gerald, and for the complimentary copies of her travel books, and her autobiographies, dedicated by her, and annotated by him. He was among the first of the British community in Iraq to befriend her when she first arrived there in 1930, and put her in touch with the Lur community in Baghdad, which led to her travels in Luristan and recognition by the Royal Geographical Society.

Mrs Doreen Ingrams, the Arabist and explorer of the wadi systems of Hadhramaut, has been generous both with her time and with her knowledge of Hadhramaut in the 1930s, and of the British community in Aden on which Freya impinged at that period and in the first year of the war, and of the personalities involved. I would like to record my gratitude for the friendly sympathy with which she and her daughter Leila have followed the fortunes of this work.

To Malise Ruthven, the son of Freya's wartime assistant Pamela Hore-Ruthven, and one of Freya's ten godchildren, I am indebted for the invaluable introduction to Arthur Playters Stark, Freya's Canadian first cousin. Art Stark, as he preferred to be known, until his death maintained a correspondence with me, and at leisurely intervals sent me items from his father's papers which he felt would interest me. He also supplied me with a family tree, a memoir of his and Freya's great-grandfather, and a short history of the association of his and her father as nurserymen, Stark Bros of Chagford, Devon, and their eventual emigration to Canada between 1910 and 1912, where both are buried.

I should like to thank Hilary Spurling who generously looked through her files on her Ivy Compton-Burnett biography, and produced a letter and diary entries which opened up a hitherto unrecorded area of Freya's development in the World War I period, and of the influences at work on her. I should also like to thank the following for giving time and thought to my enquiries: Mrs Hackforth-Jones (formerly Peggy Drower), Mrs Derek Cooper (formerly Pamela Hore-Ruthven), Professor Albert Hourani, Professor Seton Lloyd, Mrs Evelyn Forbes, Hugh Leach, Caroline Moorehead, Desmond O'Meara, Lady Bingham, Sir Bernard Burroughs, the late John and Josie Brinton, Mrs Theo Larsson (formerly B. Sanders), the Princess Osmanoglu (formerly Lulie Abu'l Huda), Guy Nevill, Mr and Mrs John G. Murray and their family, Mrs Elizabeth Hallett, Mrs G. Davies (widow of Reginald Davies), Dr Francis

Edmunds, Margaret Crosland, Sir John Walker, Lady Holman, Lady Peake, Miss Jacintha Buddicom and sister, Richard Waller, Lady Kelly, Mr and Mrs Colin Colahan (of La Mortola), Mr and Mrs N. M. Archdale, the Hon. Sir Stephen Runciman, Lady Furness, Jonathan Westphal, Stephen Gardiner, and Christina Tuohy for researches in the Torquay and the Exeter reference library.

I should like to record the help I received from the staff of the following institutions: The Public Record Office, Kew (Middle East section), for information on the Brotherhood of Freedom; the County Archivist, Clwyd County Council, for information on the Buddicom estate; the Archivist, Duchy of Cornwall, Buckingham Gate, London, for information on the Ford Park estate, Chagford, Devon; the Librarian, University College Library, London, for W. P. Ker's papers.

Finally, on a more personal note, I should like to thank Antony Daniells, Evelyn Nightingale, Gillian Warr and Nicolas van den Branden for long sustained interest and support, my daughter Sabrina Izzard for much practical assistance, and Roger Hudson and Pamela Norris who with unfailing good humour and patience have edited and supported this book, and to whom I am truly grateful.

7 October 1992

FOREWORD

The difficulty in talking about Freya is that there is so much material it is hard to know where to begin. She was a prolific letter writer, and as well as four volumes of autobiography, eighteen books of travel and belles-lettres, there are bundles of correspondence spanning her entire adult life kept by family and friends obedient to her instructions to preserve them for future reference. There are literally millions of words to digest. Such an embarrassment of riches makes for difficulty. Even the little pasteboard cards, sent out by her mother Flora with her own card to announce the infant's birth in a Paris studio on 31 January 1893, survive, with their twist of pink silk to identify the sex and inscribed in meticulous tiny copperplate with her names, Freya Madeline Stark.[1]

All that was best in Freya's talent came to the fore as a letter writer. She could sketch in a scene or an individual with brilliant economy, a landscape artist assembling detail to be worked up in the studio to a finished composition. These are the passages she herself enjoyed most, scenes recreated in tranquillity from material dashed off at wayside halts, or resting in a variety of temporary accommodations, Levantine *pensions*, shabby Persian hotels, the harems of Arab notables, grand English country houses, viceregal lodges and government houses. It was as if the act of deliberate composition was difficult for her; she wrote best from personal observation and experience. She never seriously attempted fiction. The liberating impulse to communicate came most easily when she was addressing herself to a particular individual; keeping a diary or journal was tedious. She was unembarrassed by the use to which she put her friends.[2] She loved things that simplified procedure. Letters of introduction, personal recommendations, the kindly intervention at high level of well-placed acquaintances, were all aids she solicited and used with remorseless efficiency. She once showed me the writing pads she used on her later travels. Each sheet duplicated itself automatically under the pressure of pen and pencil. It saved so much trouble, she explained contentedly, no worry about carbons or copies, you just wrote what you felt, put it in an envelope, and away it went, and there was the copy, safe to hand.

As so many of her letters were written in out-of-the-way places, one can understand the satisfying practicality of such an invention. Yet it implied an element of forethought. What to the recipient might be simply a gage of affection, or of shared interests, in actuality was a prudent storing away of impressions and a record of days, glowing embers that at leisure could be blown up into a fine blaze. Very often several letters are written on the same day to different friends, describing the same event or scene, each subtly tailored to the recipient's individuality. Vivid, entertaining, direct, touched with poetic sensibility and full of fun, they are never dull. To the biographer they are a fascinating insight into the creative instinct at work, the fugitive impressions recorded, the alphabet from which the printed book will be formed.

Such hoarded treasure-troves were the source from which much of her published work was extracted, and recycled. Read in the original the letters are surprisingly loose in construction, hurriedly knocked together and preoccupied with business, gossip, plans and arrangements. The brilliant descriptive passages are imbedded in a mass of ephemeral concerns which have been edited out of the printed material to produce the elegant literary style which so impressed her admirers.

When, in the 1960s, Freya finally conceded that rough cross-country travel on the model of her earliest adventures was now impractical for a woman of her age and on her own, she turned back to a project she had been turning over in her mind for some considerable time. This was to reclaim as many as she could of her letters from the people to whom they had been written, and to publish them in their entirety. She saw her project in grandiose terms, a great sweep of history mediated through her own experiences and the events she had witnessed. The letters, when eventually assembled, ran into thousands of pages, and were 'tidied' by Freya herself before being typed under her supervision prior to being handed to Lucy Moorehead, the wife of the war correspondent and writer Alan Moorehead, to edit. The Mooreheads were part of a circle of younger friends, dating from the war years, who escaped the dreariness of post-war Britain by settling in Italy. Lucy Moorehead was Freya's own choice (after difficulties with her publishers, John Murray, about how the work was to be presented) to edit the typescript; this appeared between 1974 and 1982 as eight volumes of collected letters, published at Freya's own expense. The material dealing with the break-up of her brief marriage to her wartime colleague Stewart Perowne was ditched when he threatened to sue if she made use of their private correspondence on the matter.[3] Disappointingly, the selected letters begin only in 1914 when Freya was already twenty-one, and thus effectively inhibit access to her formative years. For that one has only her own interpretation, *Traveller's Prelude*, published by John Murray in 1950, when she was fifty-seven; it formed the first of four volumes of autobiography, and it seems that in 1948, while she was sifting through her mother's accumulation of letters in preparation for this work, she threw out a mass of material from the period of her childhood and adolescence.[4]

The story that Freya told in 1950 of her troubled growing-up and ultimate emergence into acclaim as an explorer was poignant and satisfying where it related directly to herself, but complex and mystifying where her relations with others were concerned. When I first became professionally interested in Freya at the end of the 1970s this story was the sole source of such biographic information as existed, and was later the foundation on which younger protégés such as Caroline Moorehead and Malise Ruthven, the children of wartime friends and associates, built their accounts of their parents' distinguished friend, the famous explorer Dame Freya Stark.

What no-one to date had attempted was to look beyond the

achievement to the motivating force. Ambition was undoubtedly a spur, but was there more to it than that? Did the need for self-justification enter into it? And if so, why? This was what interested me, and once the factual chronology of her life was understood, it is what guided my exploration of her personality.

Such an approach presents problems for both writer and reader, for instead of advancing to the climax of the life the story is going backwards, as it were, from an already formulated legend to its source. Fame effectively masks the build-up of the public identity. Freya's childhood upbringing at the turn of the century by parents who were both artists was mildly bohemian, imprinted with the Art for Art's sake ethos of their own youth in and around the studios of South Kensington and St John's Wood during the 1870s and 1880s. This set her somewhat apart from the people who were her associates in her successful middle years, and contributed to her reputation for originality in their eyes. Her educational formation – such as there was – was liberal and progressive, rather than socially or intellectually disciplined, but she was never a bohemian; she had no taste for artistic low life and improvidence, and disliked anything raffish or extreme.[5] Throughout her life her friends were drawn from the well-to-do upper classes, people to whom personal loyalty was important. Anyone accepted into their society was automatically credited with their own standards, and Freya benefited from this. That she herself might not always abide by this understanding was glossed over, but it contributed to the gossip and surmise surrounding her personality, and to the feeling that she was 'different from others', and as an artist unique in herself. This was something Freya in any case was conditioned by upbringing to believe; it was the mainspring of her parents' youth and early days of parenthood.

It was as I listened to people's views of Freya that a reverse image, as in some shadowy mirror, slowly emerged from the vagueness and imprecision of their accounts. What was difficult to overcome was not so much the complexities of her nature as the investment of others in her legend. She was a brilliant reporter, but she used the techniques of the novelist to shape her own story, cutting out or rejigging aspects of a situation.

Both in talk and writing her method was impressionistic, rearranging surface facts and ignoring other witnesses. She carried this approach into history, always prepared to use imagination to get the effect she desired.

The first puzzle I ran into when researching Freya's antecedents was the discrepancy between the pre-war experiences and the post-war fame. The early adventures are by no means conventional success stories. They usually end in arrest and deportation to the nearest frontier, or illness and failure to achieve her objective. The facts and the fame do not correspond. Despite the proliferation of awards she received from the geographic societies, and her literary acclaim, a shadow of doubt was cast on her right to be considered a 'serious' explorer by men whose own record was unassailable. This alerted me to possible discrepancies in the legend.

I came to the conclusion that the earlier reputation in the 1930s was overtaken and then inflated by wartime notoriety as a propagandist in the Middle East. The first identity was a stepping stone to the second, and the modest but enterprising traveller who wrote so charmingly of her adventures was absorbed in the flamboyant public-relations expert. By the end of the war Freya's public persona as a shrewd and experienced expert on Arab affairs was fully established, so that when in 1950 she began publishing her autobiography she was already a celebrity in Middle East circles, and her name was familiar to many people who only knew of her in the context of the war. By this time almost no-one, except an Italian niece, her dead sister's surviving child, remained alive of her immediate family and their friends, and nothing was known of her antecedents prior to her arrival on the London literary scene in 1934, except what she told them.

Was it the wartime search for solutions, and her readiness to take a chance, that produced the manipulative skill that so impressed all who had to do with her then, and gave a boost to the self-deluding, sociopathic element in her personality? No-one seemed too sure whether her rapid rise to prominence was due to her achievements as an explorer, as a writer, as a secret intelligence agent, or as a philosopher and seer. Most people settled for a mixture of all these elements. Whatever Freya might be, it was clear she had the ability to fascinate, and was persuasive and convincing. What I was getting in my enquiries was a looking-glass reflection of the image she projected of herself in her autobiographic writing. This is where confusion arose. What I found when I stepped through the mirror to the other side is what this book is about.

Molly Izzard
Tunbridge Wells, Kent

Caricature by Gerald de Gaury, 1960s.

PART ONE

IMAGE OR REALITY?

ONE

AN ENORMOUS REPUTATION

When we arrived in Egypt in January 1950, I had neither read Freya, nor had I heard of her. My husband was a foreign correspondent, and after war service in the forces for both of us, he was now assigned to Cairo as Middle East correspondent for his paper, following postings first to New Delhi and then to Washington DC at war's end. The story now was the crumbling of the British position in the Middle East, already detectable in the protracted Anglo-Egyptian negotiations over the future of Britain's military base and stores in the Canal Zone, and Egypt's determination to get rid of them.

It was not until October that year that I took the first of many similar sea trips on a small passenger steamer from Alexandria to Cyprus. I thus entered the Levantine world from which Freya in 1927 had made her first steps towards fame, and where even now she was preparing for the series of journeys in Turkey that were to produce the last uprush of her literary talent, four books of travel in which she traced Alexander the Great's footsteps in Asia as he moved towards his death in the East. Perhaps there was already something symbolic in her choice of subject; like Alexander, she may have felt the lack of more worlds to conquer.

Several people wrote about the eastern Mediterranean in the 1950s. It was coming into focus as a playground for the literary imagination, whose dazzling evocations of decaying societies projected wealthy Levantine life to newcomers who had never known it. Like cat's-paws of wind darkening the surface of glittering seas, intimations of loss often shadow the preoccupations of the novelists' fictional personalities. In 1950 these Cassandra-like cries were still inaudible.

For us newcomers to the Middle East, the 1950s ushered in a more casual, less self-conscious lifestyle than the outgoing generation's. There was an unbuttoned quality about it that differentiated it from that of garrison troops and colonial officials, and the personnel of the big commercial enterprises, banks and oil companies, still locked in attitudes of fictitious permanence in the face of great movements for their rejection gathering force in the native populations. There was, in the early 1950s, a sort of hush, a holding of the breath, over the area of the eastern Mediterranean. The transition from Ottoman to French and British Mandate administration in the 1920s had had little effect on the interior, domestic life of the people. They were simple, friendly, hospitable. Old habits, old manners persisted; the economic realities of the post-1945 world were still just around the corner, while the blood feud was endemic.

Freya in these surroundings was an elusive presence, as she flitted through the upper echelons of local British society. The 1950s were her period of greatest productivity as a writer, and this enhanced her topicality as a subject of gossip among people who had been associated with her in wartime. The first volume of her autobiography, *Traveller's Prelude*, appeared in 1950, and was followed by two further volumes in 1951 and 1953. These were *Beyond Euphrates* and *The Coast of Incense*, and the three dealt consecutively with her upbringing in pre-1914 Italy, her arrival in Syria in the late 1920s, her travels in Persia, Iraq and southern Arabia in the 1930s, and the literary acclaim that accompanied the publication of four books of pre-war travel. An uplifting account of her wartime experience, *East is West*, had been published in 1945 as a public-relations exercise directed at the Americans. It aimed to counter Zionist propaganda on the Palestine issue, and was a popular success in its English edition.

I soon heard about her, of course – you couldn't be in the Middle East after the war and not hear about her – but it was as a traveller as much as a literary figure. People spoke about her with a strange mixture of indulgent deprecation and gratified awe. An echo of Browning's Waring clung to the rumour of her doings, as if she had indeed given everyday life the slip and was engrossed in mysterious occupations of her own, descending on old friends and former colleagues for assistance with transport and accommodation, when not holed up in small Levantine *pensions* or journeying around the country by bus and service taxi.

Sightings were reported, as of some rare migrant bird, of her wrapped in rugs on deck, or quietly embroidering in the saloons of the small steamers making their fixed points of call from Egypt to Cyprus, Lebanon, Syria, Turkey, as they plugged their way home to Piraeus or the Adriatic. To the post-imperial Britons in their oil-company compounds and parochial local communities, her resourcefulness and enterprise set her apart from themselves, a distinction emphasised when, led by her writings, they failed to achieve that particular illumination which the sight of historic landscapes triggered in her sensibility. Freya's response to the numinosity of place was a particular literary asset.

The poetic density of her later style may have had something to do with this. She seemed to inhabit a world of rarer sensibility and easier empathy than ordinary people, who were often led to feel themselves deficient in the finer feelings. This daunted the inexperienced. Her reported distinctions between travellers and tourists fostered a notion of exclusivity, a private world into which the mundane and the commonplace did not intrude. Tougher spirits rebelled at this.

The pinch of salt was most evident among those with previous experience of the Levant, or a ringside view of recent events in India, where the rundown of empire had started in 1947. For these the belief in the special relationship of the Englishman with the East was over: 'Quit India' and stone-throwing nationalist mobs had seen to that. But young men sent by the Foreign Office to the Lebanon to study Arabic in the 1950s were urged to read Freya, so as to learn how to enter into human relationships with the people around them. 'There's no-one like Freya,' they were told, 'for getting under the skin of people . . .' Getting under people's skin, getting them to talk about themselves, and so gaining insight into their aspirations, was her speciality, something on which she prided herself. It was the skill from which her wartime career as a propagandist and public-relations expert developed, and on which her reputation as a pundit on the peoples of the Middle East was founded. Tact, and friendliness, it seemed, were now enforceable, learned behaviour, no longer merely fortunate personal attributes. This was perhaps Freya's most significant legacy to the promoters of her country's policies in the concluding stages of empire.

My personal recollection of the Levant in the 1950s is less of a political arena than of a playground, a beautiful, neglected pastoral world where men rose before dawn to plough the red earth, and winnowed chaff on the village threshing floors by moonlight. It was a sea world too, of empty coastlines and warm, sunbaked rocky clefts and promontories, and enticing pools of emerald green among the reefs, where children could float suspended like fish, basking in the translucent element. Here the restlessness of the immediate post-war years was assuaged, the sense of being pressured to sameness and tameness put aside. No wonder I didn't read Freya then. Who needs one's responses programmed by another's sensibility, when one is doing it naturally for oneself? I see from their flyleaves that I bought *Ionia, A Quest* in Cairo in 1954, and *The Lycian Shore* in Beirut in 1956. These were the first two of the four books of travel that she wrote in the 1950s and 60s. But I never got into them. The gossamer evocations of Time and Place that so delighted her reviewers appeared sketchy and insubstantial in the context of everyday living. Other people's imaginations are wonderful when they trigger some new perception in one's own, but much of Freya's material was a reworking of already familiar themes, at a leisurely pace that lacked the astringency of daily life. Practical information was what we sought then. The promised reissue of the French *Guide Bleu* was awaited eagerly. I still have my copy, stained and loosened by damp, its contents secured by a rubber band, its pages smudged by sweaty hands as it was pushed into picnic baskets on seacoast trips, or wedged into donkey panniers while tramping through the high Lebanon.

So at least it seems now as I look back at the history of my involvement with her work. I read her reviews, wondered at and sometimes envied the apparent ease with which she arranged her expeditions. Freya in the 1950s was resuming her identity as a travel writer but, unperceived as yet by me, it was her wartime role as a valued public-relations expert that was the bridge between her travels in the 1930s and her prestige in the 1950s. Official secrecy still shrouded these activities and I was not involved enough to probe further. We didn't talk about the war years very much in the 1950s. They were slipping into the background, something put aside, a tax levied on our generation, and now being forgotten. Private life was far more interesting. By the time we had moved to Beirut in 1954, Freya's wartime relations with the Arabs, when they cropped up, tended to be passed over as something quaint, amusing and irrelevant to the present situation. 'Oh, Freya's tea-parties . . .' people said, and laughed and changed the subject. Israel existed, and so did the Palestine refugee problem; Cyprus was erupting into the EOKA disorders that heralded the eventual partition of the island. In Egypt the Nasserite revolution was established. Everywhere in the area the British were being prised out of their old strategic bases, their authority undermined, their status diminished. The American influence was in the ascendant; the days of British imperial rule were coming to a close and everyone except us seemed to know it.

I can't pretend I had any particular insights into what was happening around me. The sight of great mobs of people flooding through city streets, the sullen roar of a demonstration responding to the rhythmic exhortations of its cheerleaders, baton charges by police, the reverberating crash of rifle fire in narrow bazaar alleyways were already familiar from India, the opening phases of a running story on the abdication of empire which was to occupy my husband's attention as a foreign correspondent for the next fifteen years. Nowadays when I see documentary film of the events of this period, I am struck by the theatricality of the British behaviour. The envoys from London arrive and depart, descend from and climb into aeroplanes, and are piped off and on a variety of naval craft. The ceremonies that attend them diminish as the pace of withdrawal hastens, from the solemn pomp and large-scale parades of India in 1947, which I witnessed, to the time when no ceremony attends the departure, and Aden is abandoned in an undignified scramble.

This passionate attachment, in the last days of empire, to the forms and appearances of military competence, in the face of political realities that rendered the whole thing a charade, became increasingly embarrassing. It was like the pretend games of children, played for their own benefit. There was a reluctance, perhaps even an inability, to accept that people were tired of us, and wanted us to go. How could it ever have been assumed that the individualistic, energetic peoples of the Levant would fit tamely into schemes designed over their heads by self-appointed guardians? Such prefectorial assumptions did seem very naive and conceited.

It was not until twenty years later in the 1970s that my casual interest in Freya sharpened into the particular. Out from England on a visit to my husband, and housebound in one of Bahrain's rare winter storms, I found a copy of *The Valleys of the Assassins* in our bookshelves, and read it, entranced, through the afternoon and on into the night.

Perhaps the setting had something to do with the excitement of the discovery. Outside the palm trees thrashed their leaves, and the rickety wooden shutters I had closed against the rain rattled and flapped in the storm. Wrapped in a rug against the damp chill of a leaking mud roof and sodden walls, I read on into the dusk, transported to a world which for all its strangeness was familiar and recognisable. Our house was an enclosed, rambling structure, built around courtyards where trees grew, and with tall windtowers which, in the days before air conditioning, funnelled the cooler air into rooms dug out of the ground to afford some relief from the humid heat of the summer. It lay between two mosques, one Sunni, one Shi'a. The sonorous voices of the *muezzins*, electrically amplified but unsynchron-

ised, creaked and groaned their way slowly into full volume
several times a day, and joined briefly before entering the competitive babel of sound ascending from Manama's other
mosques, their melodious clamour fading gradually into individual voices, and then silence.

This was the first time I really read Freya, and I was bowled
over by how good she was. Previously I had been resistant to
her; now I closed the book with regret, I wanted more. The
charm of her early writing was in the sense of familiarity it
conveyed, and I was attuned to this. She took the reader along
with her in her adventures, the scenes unfolded easily and com-
panionably, there was no message or purpose, only the shared
intimacy of the experience. To anyone who had known, in however limited a way, the life of undeveloped eastern lands,
Freya's adventures were a happy continuation of their own:
early-morning rides in the cool dawn, before the sun's rays hit
over the horizon, treks through foothills and up river valleys,
over mountain passes and through rocky defiles, in company
with muleteers and *shikaris*, hunters who could show sport with
rod and gun, villagers who knew of ancient graveyards, abandoned watch towers, the histories of ruin and displacement
among scantily recorded races, overrun and obliterated by in-
vading armies.

It was a jolt, not very long after this, to hear Freya's achievements fiercely dismissed by Wilfred Thesiger, who passed
through Bahrain and took tea with us one afternoon. Nothing
Freya had done, I was told, exceeded what any moderately
enterprising Embassy secretary could have managed. If any
one woman was to be thought of as a serious traveller, it had
to be Gertrude Bell. There was nothing else in the same class
as the last arduous and dangerous three-month camel journey
she made in December 1913, across the Nejd desert from
Damascus to Hail, then over the Euphrates to Baghdad and a
return crossing of the desert to Damascus. It was derogatory
even to think of a person like Freya as being in the same
category.

I was ruffled that my enthusiasm should receive such a

putdown. It seemed a monstrously unfair dismissal, and one too that took no account of the sheer tenacity, the almost heroic persistence, needed by Freya to achieve what she did. Gertrude Bell was a rich woman, she travelled *en prince*, as did Lady Ann Blunt, Lady Hester Stanhope, Lady Mary Wortley Montagu, even Lady Jane Digby, married to an Arab sheikh, and resident in Damascus. These aristocratic Englishwomen started from a position of hereditary wealth and family influence. They were born in the purple, so to speak, as indeed was Thesiger himself, whereas Freya had to make her own way from obscure beginnings.

Thesiger's intemperance, aggravated by the fatigues of air travel and the changes that had overtaken the scenes of his own adventures, once discharged, could be soothed by cups of Earl Grey tea, and a detective story to distract an hour or so of rest. My nagging sense of dissatisfaction, however, remained, lodged at a deeper level. Of course Freya was not in the same league as men like Arnold Wilson and Soane in Persia, or Philby, Bertram Thomas, Thesiger himself in Arabia. Theirs were punishing ordeals of many weeks', even months' duration, often in company with surly and inimical companions, disdainful of the Unbeliever. Freya's modest episodes of travel were slight in comparison, but surely the courage to undertake the venture, the deliberate relinquishing of familiarity in favour of the unknown, were characteristics that sprang from some common temperamental source, and it was this that was recognised and applauded by *aficionados* of the genre? So I argued inwardly, affronted but uneasy. Yet, uninitiated though I was, I became aware that something, somewhere, about Freya was offensive to men whose own records of adventurous travel were unassailable, and I wondered why. A puzzling recollection, put aside, and till now discounted, was twitched by Thesiger's dismissal of claims made on her behalf by publicists and admirers.

Some time between 1959 and 1960 my husband was asked to follow up a story that had received some publicity: a schoolmaster taking parties of public-school boys on vacation trips to explore the legendary strongholds of the Assassins in the Elburz mountains of north-west Persia. There in the Alamut district of Mazanderan province, the eleventh-century Old Man of the Mountains, the Grand Master of the sect, had given a new word to the vocabulary of terrorism by brainwashing his adherents with the systematic use of hashish, and sending them out on individual missions to murder his political opponents.

The Alamut was where Freya's reputation began. Her first book, *The Valleys of the Assassins* published in 1934, was her account of treks in Mazanderan and Luristan between 1930 and 1932, when she got her routes from the French archaeologists who updated the revised *Guide Bleu du Moyen Orient* of 1932 to include visits to the Alamut valley and the Assassins' strongholds as part of their itinerary of touristic excursions from Qasvin. Freya's book rekindled interest in a now infrequently visited area of north-west Persia, its old identity as the post route from the seacoast to Teheran and a royal hunting ground lost in the upheavals following the overthrow of the Qajar dynasty in 1925. The traditional passes through the mountain massif were now used only by the local population, peaceful folk cultivating the valleys for absentee landlords, and carrying goods on regular mule trains between Qasvin and the Caspian littoral when the passes were open.

In the summer of 1961, as a spin-off from the schoolboy expeditions of 1959 and 1960, a television team making films for the BBC's Travel & Exploration programme brought out the climber Joe Brown to scale the rock wall of what was believed to be the Assassins' castle of Maymun Diz. The use of a well-known climber to enter the inaccessible upper galleries of the cliff was an adventurous stunt with marginal pretensions to historical research. It made exciting television viewing as the entrance was 150 feet above an accumulated boulder scree, under the overhang of a cliff almost 1000 feet high.

My husband was a moving spirit in this venture. *The Valleys of the Assassins* was read by the TV team not as literature but as a guide to potential television material. This was a mistake. Freya's inspection of sites on that first journey, it was found, must have been cursory in the extreme. Even allowing for the use of Land-Rovers and a scrambler motor cycle instead of mules, it was difficult to equate her schedule in 1930 – nine days from Qasvin to Resht on the Caspian – with any detailed exploration of the valley.

She took four days to reach the Alamut river, in whose side valleys are concealed the ruins of the Assassin castles captured and razed by the Mongols in 1256, and a further two days to reach her muleteer's home at Garmrud, taking in on the way the huge bald boilerplate of pedestal rock – the Rock of Alamut – on which had stood the castle of Qasir Khan. Three days later she had trekked on muleback out of the valley by the Salambar pass and was on her way down from the roadhead to the sea-coast in a service taxi. She had collected as much information regarding sites as she was able to extract from the people of the valley, and noted names.

Thesiger's deflating remarks in Bahrain and my own recollection of the television incident provoked me to look at Freya's career rather more closely. The dates were the first surprise. She was born on 31 January 1893, so she was in her forty-first year when recognition was first extended to her by the Royal Geographical Society in June 1933, with the award of the Back Memorial Grant for her journeys in Persia in 1931 and 1932.[1] She had thus made some sort of a mark as a 'serious' traveller before literary fame descended on her, with the publication by Murray's of *The Valleys of the Assassins* in May 1934.

The bare facts of her career are ascertainable in any public reference library; it is an impressive record. She received honorary doctorates from Durham and Glasgow Universities, was given medals and awards by the Royal Geographical Society as well as the Scottish Royal Geographical Society, the Royal Asian Society, the Central Asian Society, the Red Cross and the Ladies' Alpine Club, while in 1953 she was made a Companion, and in 1972 a Dame of the British Empire. In her old age, the publication of her *Letters*, in eight volumes, which began in 1974 and continued until 1982, revived interest in her personality, and led to two BBC television travel programmes, built around it. The circumstances surrounding the publication of the letters, however, did illuminate something of Freya's character. They occasioned a temporary breach in her friendly relations with the firm of John Murray, her publishers since the start of her literary career.

The firm's reluctance to publish her letters in the form she desired produced a notable explosion. With some justification, it was pointed out that many of the letters were already in print or had been used to provide material for her reminiscences. Freya, in her capacity as much admired celebrity, wanted the job done on a grand scale, and eventually she published them at her own expense – it cost her £3000 a year to do so, she told me indignantly – and though her obstinacy produced in turn difficulties with their publisher, Michael Russell, these were eventually overcome and the series concluded in 1982.[2]

Freya's resentment of both men's unwillingness to publish her letters as she would have liked them was loudly advertised in her circle of intimates. A graphologist was consulted, to analyse Jock Murray's handwriting and explain his defection. This was something copied from Antonin Besse, the millionaire French Red Sea trader, who befriended her in the 1930s. He regularly made use of such assistance when deciding whether or not to keep an employee who had offended or disappointed the fiery Besse temperament. In the end the storm blew over, the bonds of friendship with the Murrays were too well established, and the family continued to look after her, to protect her interests and to deal good-humouredly with her eccentricities. A winnowing of her letters, edited by Lucy Moorehead's daughter Caroline, was published by Murrays in 1988, under the title *Over the Rim of the World*.

Perhaps it was the recollection of this searing episode that produced the slight air of consternation that I detected in Jock Murray when I first expressed my interest as a biographer in his famous author's personality. This was in 1977. 'But nobody reads Freya now!' he exclaimed. 'She's quite out of fashion; she means nothing to the modern reader!' Two years later the suggestion of a direct approach to the subject herself generated an atmosphere of nervous trepidation at the John Murray offices in Albemarle Street. Freya, it appeared, required kid-glove treatment. Experienced handlers tended to be wary of tackling her, lest they be drawn into the administration of a

strong-minded old woman's caprices, unlikely to reach any practical outcome.

Freya's exploitation of her publishers' goodwill had entered
publishing legend. 'Oh, Jock's long ago earned his halo, coping
with Freya,' I was told. Her visits to London, it was rumoured,
entailed a secretary's full-time attention. The nonchalant ease
with which she dismissed any suggestion of difficulty about her
plans had something of the dandy's repudiation of conventional
effort. It was an effect achieved at the expense of other people.
Freya's descents on 50 Albemarle Street, which she treated
as an amalgam of travel agency, parcel office, shop window,
telephone exchange, appointments diary and social club, were
a test of stamina for her host. Yet such was the potency of her
fame and the magnetism of her personality that she never lacked
people prepared to put themselves out on her behalf.

By the time I had read all four of Freya's early books on her
pre-war travels in Persia and in southern Arabia and the letters
relating to these exploits, I began to understand the rationale
of Thesiger's debunking remarks. It was when I got down to
detail, counted the days on the march, analysed her achievement in relation to other travellers in the area, that enlighten-
ment came. Freya's contribution was more humanistic than
scientific. She wrote charmingly of the people she encountered
on her wanderings, and at a period when medical missionaries
were almost the only foreigners to enter the harems, she was
unusual in devoting as much space to the interior, domestic life
of the women, as to the more public political life of the men.
This gave her work its particular femininity, a piquant and lighthearted variation on the standard male approach to travel.

Ivy Compton-Burnett, discussing Freya with Robin Fedden
in the 1950s, remarked that Freya was more a woman of letters
than an explorer, and would have achieved the same success
'exploring Irish villages or Scottish hamlets'.[3] Freya used her
knowledge of Moslem social attitudes to women to align herself
with what was tolerated as insignificant and harmless. There
was nothing in her approach to raise hackles or offend propriety.
She took care to learn the conventional phrases which in social

encounters serve as indicators of piety and politeness, and give everyone time to sum up a stranger. Her androgynous appearance in hat, divided skirt or breeches might arouse doubt as to her sex, but she was clever at enlisting the harem's interest, and by identifying with it, she tapped into a virtually unexploited source of tradition and an intimate view of domestic life which few outsiders had hitherto achieved. Nothing was more useful, she found, for a woman traveller than an interest in dress; it gained her an acceptance in the harems which resulted in her being given presents of garments, and leisurely instructions in social etiquette, make-up and medicine. It also gave her the chance to acquire local jewellery and dresses to add to her collections of ethnic costume at home in Italy. She was ahead of her time in the adoption of such finery for her own adornment, long before the fashion for it surfaced in the flower-child culture of the 1960s.

My interest once aroused, I continued to think and to ask around about Freya in the intervals of other preoccupations. I was still troubled by Thesiger's remarks. Perhaps some latent instinct of feminine solidarity made me keen to see his judgment overthrown. Was it a feeling for fair play? Or perhaps merely my own affronted vanity? The passive acceptance of hearsay about Freya which I often encountered on the part of people who, on the evidence of her published letters, had once been close to her, puzzled me. Their absence of curiosity suggested either impenetrable self-conceit, or an imbalance in the relationship which was not easily explained. Was there condescension somewhere in it, rather than intimacy? Did she kiss, and they hold the cheek? It was a disturbing thought; it put her whole presentation in doubt.

My enquiries produced nothing very concrete. There was this enormous reputation, people dined out on Freya. Some hailed her as the last of the Romantic Travellers, others thought she was bogus. Most commended her enterprise as a famous pre-war explorer; few seemed able to answer a direct question about her. Something of the White Rabbit's nervousness when threatened with the Duchess overcame Jock Murray at the thought of my approaching her. At any moment, I felt, he would mutter, 'Oh my paws and whiskers,' and disappear down the rabbit-hole.

I knew I was being obtuse and that there was a missing element somewhere which I could not identify. Otherwise the story didn't make sense. I used to watch Le Carré's 'Smiley' on the television and wonder, half seriously, if I had wandered into some such enigmatic situation where every utterance had an interior meaning. Was Jock 'Control'? The atmosphere of uncertainty and reserved judgment made me nervous. I was being forced back into an examination of my own motives. Why was I interested in Freya? Had she any real significance? Was there really something odd about the discrepancy between the more than lifesize legend and the absence of testifying witnesses? Perhaps she illuminated larger issues: the devices of people under threat to prop up tottering institutions; the strange incapacity of those self-appointed to mould the destinies of others, to hear the music of that invisible choir of whom Cavafy wrote, the noisy Alexandrian party passing in the night through the city the God is abandoning, and which is about to be lost?[4] I agonised over such conundrums.

The history of the *Letters* indicated a certain waspishness in Freya, not anticipated in one who wrote so glowingly of friendship, and her own capacity to attract it. This was an aspect of herself on which she dwelt a good deal in her autobiographical writing, as if a belief in her own lovability was a talisman, to be taken out and pored over secretly. It wasn't what I expected, and it sharpened my interest. What was it in Freya that polarised opinions for and against her to such a degree? And why was this so? Nobody seemed able to tell me.

TWO

VISITS TO FREYA

It wasn't until the end of January 1979 that, balked by lack of progress from the London end, I decided to take Freya by storm at home in Asolo, a small Italian town in the foothills of the Dolomites, behind Venice. I was to spend some weeks with friends on Elba, so made up my mind to stop brooding over other people's anxious hesitations, and to see for myself what sort of person she was. Then I could decide whether to tackle her on the subject of a biography or not. My host, Tony Daniells, volunteered to drive me. So on 30 January we got up early and caught the 7.40 a.m. boat to Piombino.

Deciding how to approach Freya caused me some anxiety. I had a letter of introduction from Murrays, and I had packed offerings of Earl Grey tea and Floris soap among my things before I left England, sops to the unknown Cerberus I was about to approach. But was it enough? As gifts, they seemed rather staid for the legendary personality. Tony added a jar of home-made marmalade, but as a last-minute thought late the night before we had gathered whole armfuls of mimosa and almond blossom and bunches of the sweet-smelling tazza narcissus that grows wild at this season along the island's ditches and banks; they frame the squares and rectangles of red plough-land with green. We had wrapped the mimosa carefully in wet newspaper and packed it into the boot of the car along with the almond blossom. How delicate it smelt as we fitted the boughs into the space and covered them carefully! And the narcissus!

The honey-sweet smell hung on the air as we prepared them for their journey north.

We reached Bassano del Grappa on the afternoon of the next day and put up at the Stella d'Oro. By an unforeseen coincidence it was Freya's birthday and rather than wait till the morning we drove immediately to Asolo to deliver our freight. I felt rather nervous. What sort of reception would I get? She could be cuttingly rude, I had been told, if she took against something or someone. I had really no idea of what to expect. Freya's personality had now assumed almost threatening proportions in my mind, a species of sacred monster hedged about with Establishment grandeur. I dreaded a cool negative encounter.

A late sunshine faded rapidly to a rosy glow on the snowy crests of the mountains as we went along. Dusk had already fallen as we drove up the steep bends of the approach to Asolo's ramparts. In the central piazza the townsfolk were moving about, and men were roasting chestnuts on the street corners, while the stars emerged very bright overhead in the big frosty night sky. We found the Via Canova, a steep downward slope flanked by stone buildings with little shops and doorways abutting on to the narrow width of the pavement; a dangerous place, especially when the buses come grinding up the hill, filling the roadway. We identified the Casa Gennaro. A card, Freya Stark, in Roman bold, was above its appropriate button.

I rang the bell and waited, my arms full of almond and mimosa. I was committed now, and felt relieved. It would be a sell if she wasn't here, after all this. Then a voice squawked in Italian from the box. It seemed to think we were a taxi. 'No, no,' I answered in some confusion. '*Noi siamo amici di Londra. Di Londra,*' repeated more energetically as I sensed confusion above. There was a pause, then the door clicked, a firm-fleshed, ruddy-haired maid stood before us, gesturing us to enter. I quickly thrust a bundle of blossom into her arms, and turned to the car for more. It was already sharp and cold outside, and as we entered the hallway and went up the stone stairs, the protection of the house and the sense of having ventured and won sent us laughing and elated through the doorway and into the apartment.

Freya was standing there waiting for us, looking understandably flustered as we piled more and more mimosa into the arms of her maid. Already the sweet insidious scent of the narcissi was expanding into the warmth of the rooms; we had brought the Mediterranean spring with us to these frosty northern regions.

'It's my eighty-sixth birthday!' she cried excitedly, in a high fluting tone, as we came in. 'I can't stay, I'm going out to dinner with my landlord, and he's promised me all the things my doctor normally says I can't have . . .'

Her appearance was a surprise. There was nothing of the weather-beaten, travel-hardened explorer about this well-groomed little worldling. Small and plump, rouged, mascaraed, lipsticked, a dress of filmy, discreetly patterned black and white print floating about her, she would not have been out of place at a smart Roman cocktail party, or even in a Fellini film. A jaunty black velvet tricorne, lightly veiled, was perched coquettishly on one side of her head, diamanté buckles decorated her feet. Around her neck was a double row of pearls, and diamond clasps and rings glittered about her person. Out of the rosy smiling face, with its heavy features, darted a roguish, almost piratical glance from small, bright foxy-brown eyes.

She looked in robust health. Perhaps it was the hat and the shoe buckles that made me think of a jolly old buccaneer, ready to receive boarders at the top of her gangway. Later I thought more about her, and then she seemed like some woodland creature, caught on its own ground, whose unwinking gaze, fixed on an intruder, allows it time to assemble its thoughts and decide what to do.

We hastened to explain ourselves. This was not a formal visit; we first wanted to deliver the flowers safely on this, the auspicious day. By now the maid was fussing to get her launched downstairs, where the taxi had arrived.

'I don't know who you are,' Freya cried, as we began to detach ourselves, 'but come to lunch tomorrow.'

'Write it down,' said Floriana implacably, handing her mistress a desk diary. 'You know you'll forget it otherwise.'

Next day we arrived punctually, at a quarter to one. Freya

was waiting for us, neat, hatted, pleasantly suave in manner. Her voice had changed, it was slower, deeper and rather throaty. Floriana hovered about, while we looked at the paintings that covered the walls of the entrance hall and which competed with the tall bookcases for the wallspace of the sitting-room. Four portraits dominated the oil and watercolour landscapes of the 1880s that filled the room: Freya's father and her English grandmother, chalk drawings by her mother Flora; Edwin Bale's watercolour of Flora as a young girl at the piano; and an oil of Freya by Herbert Olivier, painted in 1923.[1] Her father, Robert Stark, was represented by a large watercolour of what appeared to be a view down from the edge of Dartmoor. It was crisp, clean and professionally skilled.

As soon as we were settled, Floriana went to the telephone and dialled a number and then gave the instrument to Freya. There were a few words of conversation before we started down the stairs in a group, Floriana taking Freya's arm. 'I fell on the stone stairs of the British Institute in Florence last year, very dark, one couldn't really see . . .' she explained. Once outside, she seemed firm enough on her legs. The three of us walked slowly down what I thought of as the passage perilous, fortunately empty of traffic, and at the turn of the road, a few buildings down, entered the Hotel Cipriani.

'I eat here on most days,' Freya explained, rather grandly. 'So convenient, you know, I don't have to bother with housekeeping.'

We were greeted by a deferential manager, and led to the best table in the right-hand corner of the glassed-in terrace, with far-reaching views over the plain below, glimmering in the milky Venetian light. Freya, small, upright, dignified, was in complete control. There was no hanging about. We were served immediately, delicious food, brought by careful young waiters in spotless white jackets. A dish of creamy risotto came first, pulsating gently from the flame. Then we had roast turkey, followed by ice cream and little biscuits. Freya ate everything. We drank a pleasant soft Merlot wine of the district, and made general conversation, talking about mutual friends, and about our journey, and asking about the Palladian villas we hoped to see. Conversation was no trouble at all, it flowed pleasantly, easily, passing unmemorably from one topic to another without strain or contrivance.

Bowed out by the polite, smiling staff, under the interested gaze of the other guests, we progressed through the hall. Freya bestowed a few words of appreciation as we passed the desk. It was a regal performance.

Outside, she took my arm, and we crawled slowly up the hill. 'What is it,' she said suddenly after a small pause, 'that everyone carries through life, individual to him?'

This stumped me. Perhaps there was some test in this, some conundrum I was too dull-witted to perceive. My mind felt fog-bound. Freya's little eyes were turned up smiling towards me. 'I can't think,' I replied with desperate honesty. 'What is it? I'll buy . . .'

'The Horizon,' she answered complacently, and we reached the door.

It was the only moment of personal impact so far achieved in our meeting, and I felt a miasmic uncertainty closing around me. But it was a momentary thing, and in an instant we were back in the clear light of practical planning. We were to go off and look at the Villa Maser, and then return for tea. Freya preferred not to accompany us, but was to get a nice neighbour, Shirley Guittand, who lived above, to meet us. She knew all about Palladian villas, and was preparing a book on them.

Tea was animated and jolly. The light was going as we returned, and the apartment was warm and inviting, a fire lit in the sitting-room, and the curtains drawn. Freya sat, quietly attentive, on a sofa covered in a pale silky material, and dispensed tea in white bone-china teacups with a restrained green pattern around the rim.

'My grandmother's,' she explained, as the plates and teacups were handed around. It was an Edwardian scene, the silver tray heavy with a gleaming silver tea-service, the firelight flickering on gilded picture frames and the spines of books, the light from the shaded lamps soft and becoming. Freya and her neighbour now concentrated their attention on us.

'What sort of travellers are you?' asked Freya. 'Are you rich ones, or poor ones?' It emerged that my fellow-traveller was a painter. 'Oh,' responded Freya eagerly, 'and have you come walking over the passes, like my father did, with your easel on your back?' Slightly nonplussed, Tony explained that though his father too had been a painter, the studio easel which he had inherited was rather cumbersome for the type of excursion Freya had in mind.

The attention of both women was now firmly fixed upon him, and I was free to observe the scene. It was rich in content. Photographs of friends – Field-Marshal Lord Wavell and her honorary 'godfather' Professor W. P. Ker were prominent on a shelf by the fireplace – and a Christmas card from the Queen Mother was propped on the chimneypiece, the signature Elizabeth R clearly displayed.

Searching questions as to aspirations, attitudes and influences were now being directed at my companion. There was a touch of the schoolmistress in the tone. I thought of the old joke, 'You be Frank, and I'll be Ernest', as the interrogation went on, until Tony remarked that his parents had been friends of Lucy Beach, the well-to-do American who in 1925 had revived the silk-weaving *tessoria* or workshop in Asolo, which was developed by Freya's mother Flora, and which Freya later inherited. Indeed, he added, the family had known Flora Stark in California, after her rescue in 1941 from wartime Italy by the Beaches. His father had been one of the pall-bearers at her funeral, and Flora's account of her imprisonment by the Fascists was among the family books.

I was surprised – we both were – at how flat this piece of information fell. Freya was manifestly not to be drawn, was not even interested. It received only a perfunctory acknowledgment, then the talk continued. It was the persistence of the aged, steering a familiar course, marked by well-rehearsed anecdotes, a performance rather than a conversation. We admired the apartment, 'Fortunately I can make up my mind; I took it at once'; and heard of the routing of would-be burglars at her former villa at Montoria, 'I had a gun, they had not'. There was a lapidary quality about these utterances that underlay the easy friendliness; the small figure seemed monumentally self-assured.

Next day we were to take tea with Freya again, to say good-bye, and arrived after a muddy day touring around villas and filling our plastic containers with local wine. Freya was waiting attentively by the tea table. Punctuality seemed important. We had a cordial reception. More about books, flowers, gardens, the *Iliad*, mutual friends; the mixture as before. We were starting next morning for Arezzo, we mentioned, to look up a friend from our Lebanon days, Christopher Scaife.

'Why, Christopher's one of my dearest friends!' exclaimed Freya. 'We meet on the governing board of the British Institute, I attend once a year, and never utter a word . . .' I felt surprised, I hadn't connected the two.

As we were preparing to leave, she drew me aside and murmured hesitantly that she believed Jock Murray had written to her about me. This was presumably the letter I had delivered on the evening of our arrival, and which had joined the stack of letters awaiting attention on her writing-table. I wondered how much of her correspondence she really read. 'Yes,' I answered, but perhaps I could write from England? I would like to talk about her wartime Brotherhood, the secret network of pro-British Arab sympathisers she had initiated in Cairo in 1940. This seemed to me to be the essential link between the modest traveller of the pre-war years and the self-assured *grande dame* of public renown.

We received a charming goodbye, and a warm invitation to return and use the tower across the way that she kept for guests. A soft pink cheek was held up for a farewell kiss. I felt warmed and encouraged, though I wondered whether the vagaries of the hither memory would wipe away all recollection of this interlude. The early memory was sound, it appeared, and she liked to muse about her past life. According to her neighbour, old lovers were a favourite topic.

To us, she had seemed eminently worldly, and self-possessed. Talking over old love-affairs rather diminished this view. I remembered uneasily that Elizabeth Monroe, the historian and economist, who was Freya's London link at the

wartime Ministry of Information, had warned me of a peculiarity in Freya; she was always convinced that people were in
love with her. Was this really so? It was a disturbing thought.

Arriving next day at Christopher's rambling, untidy old Tus-
can farmhouse, I received another jolt. Mention of Freya
immediately produced that snort of patronising amusement that
I remembered from Beirut. 'Oh dear, why does mention of poor
Freya always produce this uncharitable reaction! One does try
to be a Christian, yet she always brings it out! *That Woman!*
How does she do it? No, don't tell me, *not* the Queen Mother
now!!!' Uproarious laughter precluded further discussion. 'Look
at us,' he added, 'one thing you can count on: where two or
three are gathered who know Freya, they are sure to be talking
about her.' It was an accurate observation and would probably
have pleased her.

The news that Christopher – hitherto identified only as a
post-war professor of English literature at the American University of Beirut – was associated with Freya's wartime activities
took me time to digest. It was difficult to reassign the delightful
elderly aesthete – a poet, a singer of madrigals, an enthusiastic
participant in the productions of amateur dramatic and operatic
societies – to a role in the sub-culture of the wartime intelligence
community, into which Freya had so resolutely steered her
way.

I found myself rethinking my first impressions of Freya's
candour in Asolo. She knew I was interested in her wartime
Brotherhood, I had been quite frank about this; I wondered
why she had not told me then that Christopher was the person
who succeeded her in 1943 as overall Controller of the organisation; it was under his administration that the Brotherhood in
Egypt and Iraq was expanded into the extraordinary network
of pro-British sympathisers it became.[2] He himself, in response
to my surprised enquiry, was discreet about its activities, and
modest about himself. He was more ready to discuss Freya's
acceptance of his friend Stewart Perowne's proposal of marriage
in 1947. Here he candidly acknowledged his stunned bewilderment on receipt of the news, and explained his subsequent
rationalisation of the event. Only in each other, he decided,

could two such egotisms find a matching partner, and a fitting consort. 'Is Freya a Boojum? That is the question!' he wrote to me when I got home. It was a shrewd indicator. The reader familiar with Lewis Carroll's 'Hunting of the Snark' will recall that the Boojum was a legendary creature with whom it was dangerous to meddle, on pain of a sudden and inexplicable disappearance.

I was to be in Elba again in October, so in August I wrote to Asolo proposing myself for a visit, and received a cordial invitation by return.

I would indeed be happy to have my little Brotherhood known: it was my own solution, with much cogitation, of the problem set before me by our 'Public Relations' in Cairo, who explained that they had a good person for the Press and another one for the Pashas, and would like me to take on the rest of the people. I asked what the population of Egypt was and was told 'about 15 million'.

It was a long letter, five pages of two sides in a full, flowing hand, with many underlinings, dashes and exclamations. On the subject of biography she was cautious.

I have a feeling that, with about 70 years of my life's letters getting published and a lot of autobiographical stuff besides, a 'biography' is not wanted! and it would only be a true one if it were not so much a modern picture as a piece of that procession of an ancient and fundamental world which has been with me all my life, ever since a German governess made me read the tales of *Iliad* and *Odyssey* transformed into German for children – at eight years old. I think I have always walked in that procession, and it is still what shines to me in the modern world. But the 'Brothers of Freedom' were truly part of that enduring world and it made their success; a little book of their story might be a foot-print because it did explore and prove one or two of the secrets of what was not propaganda but persuasion – too little known by us. Anyway, I

hope to see you when I get back in October and we can
investigate the idea?

This time I came to Asolo alone, but no longer so deliberately
open to impression. I had sampled the personality, so to speak,
on the first visit, and found it human and approachable, friendly
and engaging in its apparent simplicity. Only one question had
really interested me at that stage. How had she managed her
legendary journeys – not the actual business of moving from one
place to another, and traversing a piece of country in between –
but the far more difficult one of escaping well-meaning official
obstruction, and the zeal with which all private off-beat travel
was discouraged by the British missions.

I waited my opportunity on the first visit, and managed to
put the question to her during a momentary lull. Quick as a
flash came her response. 'Start well away from them and don't
ask for anything!' It was the only real question I put to her,
and it confirmed my own experience.

For this second visit I had done some homework. I took
Elizabeth Monroe's advice and entered into contact with the
family of Sir Antonin Besse, the French Red Sea merchant
and trader who aided Freya's travels in the 1930s and founded
St Antony's College in Oxford. Prior to departing from France
for Elba, I was driven through the Côte des Maures to Cavalaire, to lunch with Anton Besse's widow and her son Peter
and his wife.

This was the private world of the millionaire Frenchman's
south of France. Cavalaire lay below us on the coast, sparkling
and neat and clean like an expensive Bond Street shop, as we
turned up a long approach through pinewoods to Le Paradou,
a complex of large villas with verandahs and terraces, swimming
pool, guest-houses, maids, guard dogs, scattered on different
levels of the forested hillside. A delicious French lunch was
served at a big table on a verandah overlooking a sea misty and
dulled by fleeting showers of fine rain. It was a very godlike
view.

Hilda Besse was tall and, despite age, still supple and graceful
in her movements. She was a warm, intelligent, handsome

Scotswoman, interesting about Freya's mother, Flora, whom she admired, and found sympathetic, as well as clever and able. Both Flora and Freya had stayed at Le Paradou, in her husband's time, and Freya convalesced there after her return in 1935 from her first trip to Hadhramaut. The daughter, she said, was eclipsed in her mother's presence, and they were not always in agreement. She had been surprised, she remarked, at the closeness of the relationship revealed by the publication of Freya's *Letters*. It had not been the impression received from Freya at the time. This observation chimed with a remark made to me by Sir Julian Huxley's widow, Juliette, on the same subject. 'Flora,' she said, apropos of Freya's account of her parent, 'appears to have been rehabilitated by death in her daughter's eyes. In life it had been a different story.'

A copy of Flora's account of her imprisonment by the Italians in 1940 was shown me, the book mentioned by Tony Daniells on our visit to Freya. It was a small slight volume, with a portrait photograph dedicated in a strong, slanting foreign hand pasted into it. Peter Besse's comments about the daughter were more tinged with Gallic realism. 'She used people. Why not, if they accept it?' She would have found her journeys in southern Arabia very much harder to accomplish, he added, without the support of his father, whose network of commercial contacts throughout the area was utilised to the full.

'You should talk to my sister Meryem about her. She accompanied Freya home to Asolo after her illness in 1935, and was dismissed with a thank-you and a small silk scarf.' This was Freya's standard present to young women who had been helpful to her in one capacity or another. The handwoven scarves were the product of the Asolo *tessoria*.

I came to Asolo to talk with Freya about her Brotherhood and found her well prepared and eager to present her story. The surprise was her identification with British officialdom and her anxious insistence on the disinterested superiority of the pre-war British colonial system to all others; its unquestioning support, she claimed, was hers on all occasions. From one whose post-war reputation as an amusing thorn in the official flesh was widely promoted by her friends, the claim to be the

darling of Authority came as a surprise. Freya, however, was
insistent, and evidently set great store on this interpretation of
her career. She was always most conscious of the delicacy of
her position vis-à-vis the political officers in the field, she told
me, and was careful to consult them whenever she toured their
districts. She *never* embarrassed them, as flamboyant personalities like the traveller Rosita Forbes did on occasion.

This was a conversation that was repeated several times
during my visit. It was evidently important to her; the ideas
were fixed now by long repetition. I wondered why she was
so insistent on establishing her credentials in this way. The
adventurous traveller of the pre-war decade appeared to have
been engulfed by the Establishment figure – at least for the
public record – and was lost in an ethical approach rather at
variance with the private report.

As I became more familiar with Freya's habits of mind I
noticed little was asserted outside an underlying orchestral
motif. She followed her own publicity carefully, and was protective of her record. A critical reviewer was likely to get an
intemperate letter setting him straight about a particular aspect
of his interpretation, while even her oldest friends could be
dropped if they hinted disapproval of her conduct.

'The British Empire, as far as empires go, was the best rule
of life after Christianity,' she assured me. 'Christianity teaches
love your brother as yourself; the Mandate says you rule and
teach a people to rule itself, then give it its freedom. That is
practical Christianity. The Empire has practised this, and given
freedom to about twenty countries, and in doing so has carried
out Christian precepts. It was a Christian empire, with the
minimum of human beings running it, a very closely knit band
of brotherhood . . .'

What could one say? Did she really believe this? I thought of
all I had witnessed since 1945: the angry nationalist demon-
strations, the communal disorders, the eighteen-year-old
National Servicemen taught to shoot other eighteen-year-olds
of a different race and colour. I thought of the old 'sahib's' life,
and of the complacent aloofness of its manners and ways. I
thought too of raw young men handing down sentences of death

and exile to men old enough to be their fathers, of 'Blacks ruled by Blues', and all the other self-congratulatory celebrations of racial superiority which formed the ideological basis of our fitness to rule.

What had happened, I wondered, to transform the high-spirited young woman of the early adventures into such a seeming anachronism? Was this senility? Freya's mind seemed to have telescoped different aspects of her experience into a very foreshortened view of events, as if the past was subsumed in the more recent experience, made over in a new light.

Where was the watershed, I asked myself, between the nimble and entertaining adventurer, shinning up the greasy pole of success, and this doling out of platitudes? If this was the sum of her spiritual discoveries how could anyone ever have taken her seriously? It was a question which was to occupy my mind for a good time yet to come.

Freya off her hobby-horse was more entertaining than when on it, and once the benefits of British imperialism were set aside, we slipped gradually into general conversation and personalities. She had a sly way of drawing one out. Speaking of recent books, we touched on *The Raj Quartet* and its author, Paul Scott. 'I knew him,' she said. 'Such a pity he died, just when it was all coming right for him . . .' A reflective pause, and then, innocently, 'Do you not think he puts Englishwomen in rather a bad light? I mean, surely nowadays a well-brought-up English girl isn't expected to – er – just jump into bed with a man after dinner?'

This threw me. An enormous gap seemed to extend between the realities of present-day life and her idea of it, and I hesitated to disillusion her. But I found myself blurting out that nowadays a girl would be lucky to get the dinner. To my relief Freya gave a hearty snort of laughter, and we settled to a pleasurable discussion of her marriage, and the homosexual personality. She seemed to enjoy this and the talk ranged comfortably over her youth and shattered hopes of an earlier marriage.

She did not hesitate to talk about her disappointment in 1916 with the fiasco of her engagement to an Italian bacteriologist, Dr Guido Ruata, and his marriage to an earlier flame. 'It took

me ten years to get over it,' she remarked, but she had kept
herself informed about him. The marriage had not been an
unqualified success, it seemed. 'I was regretted, you know,'
she added with a certain satisfaction.

It was late when I got to bed, in a small room filled with
heavy Victorian furniture. Thick curtains were drawn, and the
turned-down bed piled with large pillows and bolsters gleamed
in white linen. On the dressing-table was a finicky oval mirror
and matching lamps, wreathed in white daisies, blown in
Venetian glass. One of Freya's favourite Venini pieces, I supposed, coyly out of place in this crowded cell.

I woke the next morning in muffled darkness. Faintly dis-
orientated, I got out of bed to open the curtains, and caught
my foot in a tangle of wires. It brought the flimsy goblet of
yellow glass which acted as a bedside lamp toppling to the
ground where it smashed. O Lucky Jim! I was appalled! Passionate hatred of Venetian glass, Italian wiring, and constricted
movement flared within me. What a beginning! What should I
do? I got up, and went down the passage to look for Floriana.
She wasn't in the kitchen and, stepping through the hall into
the sitting-room, I saw her through the open door to Freya's
bedroom, standing behind Freya, seated before a mirror at a
table crowded with pots of make-up. They didn't see me. They
were engrossed in studying Freya's reflection, and in the slow
business of arranging her meshes of greying hair across a white
oval patch of bare skin on the side of her small head.

I left them to it. There was a hieratic quality about the scene:
the buxom, ruddy tirewoman patiently preparing her mistress
for her public appearance, both women rapt in concentration
before the tall mirror, in the big, crowded room. Afterwards I
thought of Freya's own description of her English grandmother's levee in *Traveller's Prelude*, and traced the analogy
to its source.

I retreated to my room, and into bed. My breakfast came
shortly after, borne by Floriana. It was overpowering. An enormous silver tray, silver coffee-pot, sugar, milk, two eggs, fruit,
toast, butter, crisp clean napkin. I felt I was being enmeshed
in a totally artificial situation, whose stately proprieties were

more suited to some silver-fork romance than to the practicalities of the traveller's life.

I indicated the shattered remnants of the vase to Floriana.
'What shall I do? Shall I tell her? I don't want to upset her . . .'
She was sturdy in her response.

'Tell her, she won't mind. She's quite decent about things
like that . . .'

She was right. Freya took it on the chin. 'Not the
dressing-table . . . ?' was her sole hint of weakness. We
hastened to reassure her and show her the casualty. The incident was dismissed with superb indifference, and we settled
down to a recapitulation of the previous day's discussion of
Freya's relations with officialdom, and the support her Brotherhood had received from both civil and military authorities.

I soon felt entrapped. Freya's manner when speaking of her
achievements was detached and reflective. We were talking of
events long done away with and embalmed in the written word,
something already outside herself. It was only when we touched
on the war years and the work of her mysterious Brotherhood
of Freedom that her manner changed. One could feel a Purpose
take hold. I began to wonder what I was in for. The pensive
nature of her tone, her seriousness, recalled the concern of
adults showing the right path to wayward adolescents. Nothing
very concrete emerged. Perhaps something might be worked
out between us? Collaboration was hinted at; perhaps a
reformulation of the idea behind the scheme, something that
would indicate to a new generation the value of her approach?

I felt uneasy. The puzzling contradictions between legend and
actuality were already troubling me and it would be dishonest to
pretend otherwise. Much of her argument had already been
formulated in *Dust in the Lion's Paw*, the final volume of her
autobiography which appeared in 1961 and dealt discreetly with
her wartime experience. Instinct told me to back off. Freya
was adept at harnessing the energy of others to her own ends.
Schemes might be discussed which led to exciting prospects of
television documentaries, journeys and joint literary productions; these did not always come off.

Freya's Brotherhood, she claimed, had been a spiritual thing, a communion of hearts rather than minds. The distinction was important, she emphasised. People should be prepared to make their ideological choices without reference to the source. The purveyor of doctrine was apart from the doctrine itself, merely a medium for the passing of ideas from one set of people to another. No responsibility attached to the introducing agent on whose sympathetic manner and willingness to show others how to help themselves rested the whole weight of her scheme. It seemed an oddly truncated view, but then I recalled her aesthetic antipathy, confided to her journal in 1929, to the existence of any ethical aim in creative activity.

She insisted on her 'amateur' status and the informality of the concept. Propaganda is an inaccurate word, she said, commonly used to bring people over to one's point of view. That wasn't her object. She felt one had to find out what people themselves wanted, and then show them how to achieve this. In this way their confidence was gained, and that was the important thing. The responsibility for the acceptance or refusal of the doctrine lay with themselves. Nothing was forced on them.

The necessity to gain the confidence of the native Sudanese had been the chief recommendation of Kitchener in 1899, when he formed the nucleus of what became the Sudan Political Service from young men recruited from the public schools and universities of Britain. They were to take over from the military as governors and inspectors of the Sudanese provinces after the defeat of Mahdism. His advice to them was not to trust in laws, regulations or proclamations, which could effect little. 'It is to the individual action of British officers, working independently but with a common purpose, on the individual natives whose confidence they have gained, that we must look for the moral and industrial regeneration of the Sudan . . .' Forty years later this view was still part of the intellectual baggage of men seconded from the Sudan Political Service for wartime advisory employment in Cairo, and in 1940 it predisposed some of them in favour of Freya's approach.

But she improved on Kitchener's recommendation and corrupted it in the process. She believed 'that the benefit to the listener and the belief of the gospeller in his own gospel were

two of the three essentials of persuasion. The third was to
implant the idea in the target's mind in such a way that he
believes he has arrived at it himself; this gives his promotion
authority, and automatically validates the argument.'

In later life Freya herself claimed her wartime achievement
was to help save the Middle East for Democracy. There was
a sublime grandiosity about this statement, so modestly pro-
pounded, that silenced any question. Her age, her honours, her
appearance and something childlike, confiding and affectionate
in her manner ensured a delighted, protective recognition on
the part of her interviewers of 'a genuine English eccentric'.
The actuality of her achievement was outweighed by her willingness to be interviewed. It was not publicity for herself that she
sought so much as recognition of the efficacy of her method.
Always keen on self-justification, she overrode any hint that
her analysis of Egyptian and Iraqi aspirations might have been
inaccurate and that the Adviserate system of 'guidance by
advice' as a means of retaining influence, under which her own
reputation as a propagandist had been made, was no longer
welcome, let alone enforceable.

Freya's talk had a lulling effect, yet I was worried. What was
the matter with me that I could not enter into this friendly and
self-congratulatory world she was so deftly portraying, where
elder brothers guided younger brothers and no-one thought of
self? 'Am I stupid?' I find written into my notes at this point.
The effort to understand, to reconcile the inconsistencies was
exhausting. I felt like a wasp wearily attempting to extricate
itself from the smear of honey on the breakfast plate.

Freya advanced her story with a mild persistence that did
not detract from its determination. One was not expected to
ask questions. My feelings of oppression intensified. Anthony
Powell's borrowing from Wesley came to mind: 'So in every
possible case; He that is not free is not an *Agent*, but a *Patient*.'
Was this to be me, one who is acted on, rather than one who
acts? Was this the secret of Freya's spellbinding? Her tactics,
it seemed, at the combatant level were aggressive. The pre-
emptive strike was temperamentally congenial. Was what I was
receiving a reprise of previous convictions elaborated some

thirty years ago and embalmed in a retentive memory while she was still at the height of her powers? Freya's assumption of straightforward decency and concurrence on the part of her audience was hard to withstand. She was bland, persuasive, sure of herself. Not to accept her argument, proffered with such friendly goodwill, was to align oneself with all that was backward, hopeless, unprogressive. Have the courage to accept the helping hand being offered, and all would be well!

It was all very imprecise; I was no nearer any understanding of what she actually did, or how the movement got going. When I pressed for factual detail, she suggested I see her former assistants in Cairo and Baghdad, Pamela Hore-Ruthven and Peggy Drower. Peggy Drower was the one most in tune with her ideas, she said; having been brought up as a child in Iraq, she had the advantage of speaking fluent Arabic. They could explain the nuts and bolts of the Brotherhood of Freedom in its early beginnings in Egypt and Iraq. Freya's own role, she indicated, was spiritual guidance rather than political management, while she was firm in disclaiming any responsibility for whatever change took place in the direction of the Brotherhood, following her departure from the Middle East in 1943. It had become over-intellectualised, she said rather sourly, appealing to a narrow range of educated people. It smacked of do-gooding, of which she did not approve. Hers had been a combating on the spiritual level of the Nazi evil, an affirmation to the broad mass of simple people of the power of goodness and sanity to overcome wickedness and the perversion of truth. This Manichean view of events had a lofty simplicity that reminded me of Lady Hester Stanhope at Djoun, expounding the mysteries of her spiritual illumination to Kinglake, as recounted by him in his book *Eothen*.

THREE

FIRST PIECES OF THE PUZZLE

I came away from Asolo with the conviction that the time was past for getting anything concrete from Freya about her Brethren. She had entered into her own mythic identity, and was lost to commonplace enquiry. There was no dialogue. Freya called the shots. She had certain fixed ideas she wanted to publicise and, to use one of her own metaphors, one was a receptacle, into which the message could be poured. But what exactly that message was remained opaque. Something, somewhere, must lurk beneath the uplifting rhetoric, to explain the reputation, but so far I had failed to focus on it. It was difficult to reconcile the gossipy, inquisitive, petted old woman, delivering her seemingly well-rehearsed anecdotes and surprising throwaway conversational initiatives, with the earnestness of her manner when she spoke of the spiritual dimensions of her wartime activities. It made me think of a medium; there was the same comforting spiritualist phraseology, the departed 'only moving into the next room' and still available to the bereaved.

Her appearance supported this. Her head concealed in an unbecoming cotton hood, only the sharp glance of her bright little eyes, peering out of a toothy, smiling, rosy face, suggested anything other than a comfortable old woman, as homely as a tea-cosy. Brooches, scarves, necklaces adorned her person. Rings glittered on her small, manicured hands as she expounded a particular point; and then were folded into her lap. Deferred to by the people about her, yet jollied along too, she reminded me of an elderly child kept in good humour and propelled through daily routines by somewhat exhausted attendants.

What was her origin, I wondered: some metamorphic oddity born out of a coincidence of time and opportunity, or, as some claimed, a poet whose imagination spanned extra dimensions of sensibility? This was a question which was increasingly to occupy me as I delved into her history. How had she obtained her undoubted ascendancy over other people's imaginations? Perhaps one should concentrate on what it was in them that made them so responsive to her particular message? It was here difficulty began. Much of it was because I was going back in time, peeling off the layers of experience accreted around the original personality. People were very vague about her antecedents. Some thought she was of German descent, others wondered if she was Jewish. I soon discovered that nearly everything that was known about Freya's early life was what she had published in her autobiographies, and that by the 1980s hardly anyone remained who recalled Freya before the age of forty.

When I started to check back, to look for her in other people's accounts of the period, and in the official records of the war, it was difficult to find any mention of her. Elizabeth Monroe had already warned me that much of the material relating to her wartime activities had gone to the shredder. The Public Record Office files had been extensively 'combed', and little trace of her remained. This I found to be true. Despite several interesting leads in the indices, the papers when called for often turned out to be non-existent. I found however Freya's own account of the inception and implementation of the Brotherhood scheme, *A Pamphlet in Defence of Propaganda*, a lengthy document written in a flowing, resolutely personal style, and published under her name in August 1944, on her retirement from the Ministry of Information. C. A. F. Dundas,[1] in June 1944, tersely noted on the file that much of it should be taken with a pinch of salt, 'as though interesting, it has not been the unqualified success suggested, though it has done very good work'.

Reading back into the files of the 1940s I realised that

although in Europe the British might seem beleaguered, they were still the dominant power in the Middle East, their position attested by the armed forces at their command. The daisy-chain innocence of Freya's account to me of her activities was more compatible with an artless debutante than a seasoned woman of the world, and produced feelings that were the reverse of what she perhaps intended. Visions of a large, rosy hot-air balloon troubled me, rising in stately solemnity over the fierce Arab lands, sustained by its own emissions and the gullibility of others. Where was the reality? Did it warrant all the shot and shell? I soon realised, as I continued my researches into Freya's personality, that (with one exception) everyone I spoke to on the subject of Freya, 'old friends' or mere acquaintances alike, shared two topics which they couldn't wait to bring to my notice. One was the sale in wartime on the black market in Teheran of a car she had brought out under the protection of Field-Marshal Lord Wavell's authority as Commander-in-Chief India; the second was her marriage with a member of the Colonial Service, Stewart Perowne, in October 1947, a union quietly dissolved after the statutory five years. The bewilderment here centred on the impossibility of advising, or even warning, her against an imprudent decision. She put up such a bland front of smiling incomprehension when tackled on the pitfalls of marriage to a homosexual that people gave up the attempt, and the better-minded resigned themselves to wishing her well. Many were convinced that she did not understand what homosexuality was.

This stonewalling tactic was used also in the matter of the car. The story leaked out through the go-between employed, the Armenian chauffeur of the Oriental Counsellor at the Teheran Legation by whom Freya was put up in April 1943 on her way back to Baghdad from New Delhi. When tackled by her host on the impropriety of her action and the discredit it brought on him, Freya smiled her quizzical little smile and changed the subject. Expostulation was wasted breath. The car was gone, driven off immediately the cash, £5000 – some said £7000, an enormous sum at that period – was handed over. All that remained was a scandal, muffled but persistent, whose reverberations were still sounding forty years later.[2]

What interested me in this tale was Freya's coolness in the face of what might be seen as very awkward explanations. Was it calculated effrontery, a bluffing of her way out of a tight corner? Or was it over-confidence, a belief in her own impregnability, not answerable to petty bureaucratic restrictions? Either way, it offered room for speculation.

The common denominator in both stories was the sense of bewilderment at Freya's intractability experienced by people who thought of themselves as her friends. I wondered what impelled her, who tended to be careful of the impression she made, to discount the feelings of people whose good opinion she normally cultivated.

Field-Marshal Lord Wavell's *laissez-passer* perhaps contributed to this.[3] The original typewritten note is preserved among his letters to her. Dated 3 March 1943, on notepaper headed 'Commander-in-Chief in India', it reads: 'I should be obliged if you could lend any assistance necessary to Miss F. Stark who is travelling from New Delhi to Baghdad,' and is signed by him.

'It would have been rather foolish, would it not,' Freya replied sweetly, when I expressed my surprise at the apparent ease with which she had evaded wartime restrictions on private travel in leaving India, 'to have a pass signed by the Commander-in-Chief and not use it? One young officer was inclined to be difficult, but I just showed him Wavell's *chit*, and that did it.'

It wasn't until much later that it occurred to me that the note might have applied to one specific request, the grant of an export licence from the Indian government for the car, something then virtually unobtainable under wartime restrictions. Was it spirited into Freya's keeping by some crony on Wavell's staff, to back up the impression that her journey had been officially sanctioned, and so to validate what was called a 'swan' in wartime parlance, paid for by HMG?

The black-market story, far more than the gossip about the marriage, was what aroused my curiosity about Freya. It seemed so odd in the context of the period, and the people with whom she associated. It was as if some faintly discreditable element in her personality had escaped her control, a cloven hoof peeping out from under the skirts of conventional behaviour. Was it that under the confident grand manner a more erratic personality existed, out of line with the artless simplicity of her early literary persona?

Other enquiries were prompted by those photographs of Professor Ker and Wavell, so prominently displayed in Freya's sitting-room, as if they hallmarked her own intrinsic worth. It was a disappointment to discover that neither of Wavell's biographers, John Connell and Ronald Lewin, mentioned her. No trace of her was found in his papers, Ronald Lewin told me. The friendship on which she so prided herself, and which caused such surmise in the wartime Middle East, apparently meant less to him than to her. Freya's solipsist view of life, I began to suspect, tended to magnify and distort the emotional content of what she wrote. Bernard Fergusson, Wavell's former ADC (later Lord Ballantrae, Chairman of the British Council), did tell me that 'Wavell thought the world of her', but was unable to be more explicit, his own acquaintance with Freya being of a fleeting, formal nature, and he only saw his old Chief in her company three times.[4]

Professor Ker was another surprise when I examined his papers in the archives of University College, London, where he had held the Chair of English Literature until he retired in 1922. Hypnotised by Freya's tender accounts in *Traveller's Prelude* of the influence exerted on her young womanhood by the dauntingly silent and erudite Professor, I did not expect to discover a correspondence with one of his godchildren, Olivia Horner, which far outstripped in bulk and intimacy anything in Freya's possession.

Ker had a large circle of young people, the offspring of the friends of his Glasgow boyhood and early academic years, godchildren to whom he wrote regularly, and whom he delighted to assemble about him on yearly holidays on the Isle of Arran. Their high spots were boat and picnic excursions with the Professor and his two spinster sisters and other members of his family, and the large Scottish high teas to which his young guests were treated on their return, wet and windblown, to the hotel. These were his 'April children', so called from the

annual month of meeting, and as they grew older they were
included in the theatre parties he arranged in London, and taken
on walking tours and climbs in the Alps. He saw *Peter Pan* on
eleven different occasions.

Of these young people none was a greater favourite than
Olivia Horner, the daughter of a London University colleague,
one of the family from Mells in Somerset to whose nursery
publications he contributed doggerel verse, and to whom in
later life he wrote on an almost daily basis. The bundles of this
correspondence are in the library of University College,
London, where they were deposited by her family on her death.
Freya, by contrast, five years younger than Olivia, came late
into his orbit, being adopted into his circle only in the last twelve
years of his life. 'My child,' he wrote to Olivia on 20 August
1920, while climbing with two Oxford colleagues in the Alps, 'I
have always known that you are more than anything to me . . .'
and continued the next day from the top of Rothorn (m. 3418)
to 'Dearest Olivia . . . sounds of water coming up from the
glens. It was cold grey mist when we left our hotel at 6.10 a.m.
But we walked up through it into sunny mist and then out into
the clear sky – The Real World! AMEN' and signed it WPK
with his characteristic little emblem of an Athenian owl.

Further research for others' personal reminiscences of Freya
yielded little. There are brief mentions in the diaries of Lord
Killearn (as Sir Miles Lampson, HM's Ambassador to Egypt,
in her Cairo wartime period). Peter Coats, Wavell's ADC in
Cairo and Household Comptroller in Delhi, has a pleasantly
affectionate account of her presence in the Wavell circle, and
of 'that piping laugh, never so prolonged as after one has said
something slightly malicious!'[5] Vita Sackville-West in 1937 told
Harold Nicolson that Freya was small and biscuit-coloured, and
not impressive in looks or manner.

Only Maurice Collis, in his Diaries of 1949–69, devotes any
considered account to her personality. In June 1953 he records
meeting 'the celebrated writer Freya Stark' at an Astor house
party at Cliveden '. . . stoutish, rather a bundle of a woman –
who possesses a marvellously bright eye . . . I felt immediate
strong sympathy – held her to be one of the leading stylists of

the day.' In November 1955 he lunched at Cliveden and met Freya again. 'I sat next to her and had an animated conversation, the best I have had for a long time . . . She told me she was done with travel books and was now going to devote herself to history or historical disquisitions on Asia Minor . . .'

It was not much to go on. I did better with iconography. There are plenty of likenesses of Freya. She was painted by her parents and their circle of artist friends, and she herself commissioned other portraits and drawings, as well as a sculptured head. She was often photographed, and lent herself readily to such attentions. A strange experience was to find her grinning cheerily out of the frame in an exhibition of photographs by the late Robert Mapplethorpe, best known as the recorder of the New York bath-house scene and of the male physique, at the National Portrait Gallery. Some of these likenesses are to be found among Murray's gallery of their authors, a cast of her head is in the RGS, and the National Portrait Gallery has Herbert Olivier's 1923 oil painting of herself as a young woman, which she donated in 1981. There was some controversy about the accompanying précis of her achievements and the picture was temporarily withdrawn from exhibition after queries from the public about the claim that she was the first European woman to enter Hadhramaut. It had been overlooked that Mrs Theodore Bent in the 1890s, Frau von Wissman, the wife of the German topographer, and Mrs Doreen Ingrams, a Gold Medallist of the RGS, had traversed the interior in the 1930s, before Freya appeared there in 1935.

PART TWO

THE EARLY JOURNEYS
1928–1935

FOUR

THE FIRST JOURNEY –
LEBANON AND SYRIA

'*Dieu adoucit le vent au brebis tondu*' – God tempers the wind to the shorn lamb – wrote Sterne at the beginning of his *Sentimental Journey*, a thought that sustained me in many discouraging moments of my exploration of Freya's history. And indeed, this is how things turned out. I was rescued from this first period of frustration and stagnation by a series of separate events, unanticipated windfalls falling into my lap through personal connections.

The first was the earliest independent sighting of Freya I obtained, from Dr Francis Edmunds, a distinguished educationalist, still, in his eighties, active in the Rudolf Steiner anthroposophical movement. As a man in his twenties he befriended Freya on her first appearance in Lebanon in 1927 when, a shy, unattached young woman of thirty-four, she arrived in Broumana with an introduction from the School of Oriental Studies at London University to the Syrian head of the Quaker Mission School, Dr Manassah and his English wife.

Francis Edmunds' recollection was of someone deeply thoughtful, very serious, rather lonely, a quiet figure with a history of illness and disfigurement. There were scars about one eyebrow and temple that were never explained; and it was generally assumed, in default of precise information, by the mystified mission staff, that Freya had come to Broumana to recuperate from a recent accident. Dr Edmunds' account filled out the impression I received from the photograph Freya published of herself at this period in Broumana. There is something sad and defenceless about the figure posed in the carefully adjusted finery of Arab male dress, trustful, yet with a watchful passivity that might engulf the unwary. Later, when I read her *Letters from Syria*, Freya's own jaunty account to her mother of her experiences came as rather a surprise. The dimness and shyness recollected by Dr Edmunds disappeared in her report of her doings.

Freya made little attempt to assimilate with the mission community, or to understand their aims. They in turn were puzzled by her presence. Dr Manassah, a medical man turned educationalist, was a charismatic figure in his period, and drew his pupils from a wide range of local religious and social backgrounds. His was the first co-educational school in Syria, an achievement of which he was proud, and which gave the school valuable connections among the more progressive elements of Syrian and Lebanese society. It was through these connections that Freya was enabled to make her first entry into Arab life.

She was not interested in education or in philanthropy. She preferred solitary explorations of the locality, something which excited comment in the school, at a loss to understand her interest in the local people's lives. Theirs was bound up in education; they lacked her curiosity or her romantic vision.

Sometimes she persuaded Francis Edmunds to accompany her on her walks, and with another of his colleagues they made expeditions together to Damascus, and went sightseeing. Edmunds at this time was discovering Anthroposophy, and Freya encouraged him to explain the Rudolf Steiner system to her, and to share his own ideas. She was always at her best in one-to-one relations with younger men, and Edmunds recalls the feeling of true friendship and sympathy these eager conversations and discussions evoked in him. Freya was very keen that he come to Italy during the summer vacation of 1928. They would read Dante together, she told him, among the scenes the poet himself had frequented, and in his native tongue. It was a tempting inducement to a man of Edmunds' elevated sensibility, but he declined. He had not wanted, he explained hesitantly to me, perhaps to arouse expectations which would not be fulfilled. It was with disappointment, he added, that many years later he found himself dismissed rather slightingly by Freya in her autobiography as an emotional philanderer attracted to younger and prettier girls. It seemed a betrayal of friendship.

Yet dismissed though he might later be, he figures quite extensively in Freya's letters of the period. The 'charming Mr Edmunds', in her account, was a target for sprightly attentions, an interesting young man who had been engaged on famine-relief work in Russia, and was now turning towards his true vocation as an educationalist. They corresponded after she had left Broumana, in the spring of 1928, with a friend Venetia Buddicom on a journey to the Syrian Hauran; she received a note at Asolo to say that the two of them had left 'a trail of surmises and not a little dust' as to their antecedents and purpose in undertaking such an adventure, which rather gratified her.

She wrote to him in September from Italy confiding certain unspecified problems to do with spiritual progression. She was interested in Rudolf Steiner's exercises in concentration, she wanted to get control of will and thought and feeling as a way to enhance her consciousness, and begged Edmunds' assistance in setting her on the right path.

I know I accept ideas more easily if they come from people I like. I mean that I know, quite independently of you or anyone else, that your way is the direction in which I want to go. If the fact of your being a friend makes it a little easier to follow, is there any harm? I suppose you mean that one should not take one's ideas ready-made from anyone? I think I would never do that, for on the whole I respect ideas more than people; but when it is connected with a person, it becomes more valid to me, and easier in that way. Even when I read a book, it is usually with the thought of someone who would enjoy it also.

Freya's problem seems to have been to do with having your cake and eating it. She agrees there has to be a spiritual goal.

'I have long felt that there is a Purpose for us, and that if one could know it, recognise it I mean, and be convinced, the whole of life would fall into a proper proportion, and would become independent of circumstances.' But the example of all the greatest teachers seemed to imply shutting oneself off from life, and Freya feared she could not bring herself to renounce 'this beautiful world: I love it all . . . and I love everything that is living on it, just because it is alive. I feel it is part of me too.' There must be a way, she pleaded, not of renouncing, but of accepting the world, and transmitting it to its greatest possibilities . . . a way of *interpreting* it all. She felt Edmunds could do this for her.

It was a tall order. Freya returned to Broumana in October 1929, for a short visit to her old landlady, before going on to Baghdad. She found Edmunds 'absorbed in a new and promising pupil; she was younger than I was, and much prettier, and a visible proof, I felt, of how difficult it is to keep to the abstract in this world.' The girl in question, Francis Edmunds explained to me, was Dr Manassah's daughter, a girl of fifteen or so, a simpler, more artless and more unawakened creature you could not imagine. It distressed him that Freya should slur the recollection of an innocent and charming child.

The next piece of luck I had was an impromptu meeting with the late Wilfrid Blunt, the biographer of Sir Sydney Cockerell. This was my second windfall. It led to the passing to me of a large cardboard box full of Cockerell's papers, which included not only all Freya's correspondence with him, but his own notes and associated memorabilia – Starkiana in Blunt's phrase – relating to their friendship.

Cockerell met Freya at the end of 1933 at the house of a friend of her mother's, Viva Jeyes. He was immediately invited by Freya to a sherry party to be given by her at a studio belonging to Dorothy Hawkesley, a mutual friend whose pencil sketch of Freya was to be the frontispiece to *The Valleys of the Assassins*, about to be published in May 1934. The correspondence began almost immediately, starting in January 1934 with a congratulatory letter from Freya on his knighthood.

Dear Mr Cockerell, I cannot call you by your proper title, because I don't know the names your initials stand for – but I *do* want to write all the same to say how nice it was to see your picture in the *Illustrated London News* the other day and to read of the recognition given to your work . . .[1]

The correspondence was eventually to run into hundreds of letters, postcards, little affectionate notes, detailing meetings in London, visits to Kew, walks in Bushey Park, attendances at theatres, exhibitions and publishers' parties, and at Freya's lectures. Cockerell was a recipient too of the long descriptive letters which served to fix the details of a scene while the impression was still vivid in her mind: they were a quarry from which much of her later travel writing was extracted.

Cockerell was by nature vigorous and positive. You might say he was meddlesome. It was a quality which Freya shared, but her first approaches to him, then a man of sixty-six and about to retire from the directorship of the Fitzwilliam Museum at Cambridge, have the same ingenuous and flattering humility that Cockerell as a young man displayed towards the objects of his own admiration. A belief in the power of the Individual to make himself over anew in response to his Ideal was perhaps the basis of the sympathy between Cockerell and Freya, but Cockerell as a youth had discovered Ruskin and Morris for himself, and deliberately abandoned Commerce, in the shape of the family coal business, to devote himself to Art; he was literary executor to William Morris, Wilfrid Scawen Blunt and Thomas Hardy. In Freya the imprint was more fugitive, something absorbed unconsciously in childhood from the Arts and Crafts and Simple Life atmosphere of her family life, but reactivated and reclaimed in response to Cockerell's interest in herself. Cockerell was a collector of people, as well as of books, manuscripts, fine bindings and recondite information. An inspired fund-raiser and promoter, he made himself useful to all his heroes; it was a genuine homage to talent. He was industrious and businesslike, and brought order to the management of the often confusing circumstances of their lives. Bundles of correspondence from writers – male and female – other than Freya are among his papers, filed and annotated just as carefully; the poet Charlotte Mew was among these, while a long and intimate correspondence with the Abbess of Stanbrook Abbey, an enclosed nunnery, was published under his supervision in his lifetime.

Ten years before his death he took to his bed after a fall, but he kept his mind alert in his old age by his interest in other people. His curiosity was insatiable, fed by the gossip of his innumerable visitors and correspondents. He admired talent, a quality that seems to have made tolerable to him several difficult temperaments, though he was uncompromising where the ethics of behaviour were in question. He did not lack moral courage and was prepared to speak up and to stand the consequence of a possible rupture. Having volunteered himself in 1937 as Freya's unpaid secretary and general factotum, he was used mercilessly by her to execute her commissions. A characteristic list of jobs to be done by him on return from a visit to Asolo reads:

3 July 1938 leaving Asolo – orders from Freya
(1) Post letters at Victoria – *Times* & *Literary Supplement*
(2) Take photographs to Albemarle Street
    1. for picture book
    2. for book
    3. large photographs
(3) Take films to Sinclair, 3 Whitehall
(4) Take photographs to *Illustrated London News*
(5) Parcel for Elinor Gardner, The Bothy, Barden Village, Liphook
(6) British Museum – about 2 coins – John Walker, Wadi Mai'fa

He was involved from the start with Freya's Arabian adventures in the winter of 1934–5 and of 1937–8. Shipwrecked himself in 1900 with Wilfrid Scawen Blunt on a pilgrim ship in the Red Sea, a certain glamour of the past hung over this Arabian association and perhaps enhanced his interest in Freya's exploits, though it was the difficulty that arose over her book

A Winter in Arabia on the Wakefield archaeological expedition of 1937–8, her second visit to Hadhramaut, that brought him into the most intimate involvement with her work. His tactful but firm handling of the problems that arose over Freya's treatment of her material and attitude to her companions cemented their intimacy and his visit soon after to Asolo in the summer of 1938 allowed him to meet Freya's mother Flora Stark, for whom he immediately developed a great liking.

Wilfrid Blunt, summoned to his bedside to be told he was to write the biography, received the accumulated mass of his papers from Cockerell himself, to make use of as he saw fit. It was a command rather than a suggestion; the book was to be a 'warts and all' account of his life, nothing was to be concealed.[2] Included in the material relating to Freya is an assortment of newspaper cuttings, postcards, photographs and some notes on Luristan, which she believed were destined for the Fitzwilliam Museum. There is also a small notebook of Cockerell's own, the pages divided into sections, each section comprising a year. Beginning with her date of birth, he inscribed in his small clear level script such facts about her as he acquired from her writings, from her conversation, from her friends, and her own written replies to questions he submitted. It provides a skeleton outline of her life up to July 1943, when the entries cease.

Not all the sections are filled. There are many blanks, and some bonuses. Slowly and patiently he documented the people associated with Freya's youth, filling in details of their careers and their dates. It was as if her life was a jigsaw. Sometimes he links the information to its source, often something in the bundles of Freya's correspondence, which totals over five hundred items, meticulously numbered in consecutive order.

Cockerell's admiration for Freya developed as much from the intrepid nature of her early adventures as from her literary talent. That came later. What impressed him was the boldness and optimism with which she flung herself into her experience, like a swimmer into the sea, confident that the wave would uphold her. Notably zestful in his own approach to life, it was this buoyancy in Freya that appealed.

*   *   *

Wilfrid Blunt opened the way for me into the beginnings of
Freya's fame in the 1930s. Cockerell's putting together for publication in 1942 of Freya's *Letters from Syria* (originally written
to her mother in 1928), and the consignment to him, after
Flora's death in 1942, of her own written memoirs, emboldened
him to seek out pre-war friends from the Italian Riviera and
Asolo and to record their comments. Their letters relating to
the Starks, neatly docketed with dates and relevant identifica-
tions, provided insights into the 1920s and allowed the hinterland of Freya's charted territory at last to come into view.

Freya in 1943, passing through London on her way to lecture
in America, contacted her old family friends of the 1920s, Minnie
Granville in London and Lucy Beach in California, who recorded
their impressions of her to each other after an interlude of
nearly six years. Several of these letters passed into Cockerell's
keeping and were filed away along with other miscellania relating
to the family. Freya's improved appearance and greater self-
confidence impressed both these old friends: '. . . a woman of
the world accustomed to attention . . . she looks so much happier – not a line on her face – Flora would be proud of her.'[3]
    The end of the Twenties was the period in Freya's life when
she was working out her own guidelines and recording them in
her journal, extracts from which appear in her autobiography.
A collapse into invalidism in 1923, and the frustrations inherent
in waiting for a declaration from men earmarked as possible
husbands but never coming up to scratch, were finally put to
one side. What Freya was escaping when she came to the East
at the end of 1927 was the stigma of the unmarried daughter
at home whom everybody is trying to marry off. Approaching
thirty-five, she opted at last for positive action and cast herself
on the world.

Freya's 'real' life as a traveller and acclaimed literary stylist
began in 1927, the one on the heels of the other, but its inception dates from 1923. At that period Freya was a young woman,
troubled by ill health and self-conscious about a slight facial
disfigurement, the result of an accident in childhood. She lived

with her mother Flora on a two-and-a-half-acre flower farm, L'Arma, bought for her by her father at the end of 1918, on the coast at La Mortola, on the Franco–Italian frontier. It was intended to give her an independence, but for some years, since the end of the 1914–18 war, she had aspired to a journalistic career rather than undertake the constant physical labour horticulture entailed.

W. P. Ker's death in 1923, and the removal of a concerned, but controlling influence, which had been important to her since her father emigrated to Canada in 1911, left Freya more free to develop her own initiatives than she had ever been before. Up till now she had depended on Ker's friendship, and the circle of her parents' friends dating from their youth as dilettante artists hanging about the studios and artists' colonies of the 1880s and 1890s: these supplied the sustaining interest and affection she needed. Even though she criticised and bullied her mother – a forceful, talented, energetic woman – she clung to her too, and was dependent on her for all sorts of services, as well as for protective devotion and loyalty.

In the late summer of 1923, however, Freya took an independent step. She had formed an acquaintance on the Riviera with a younger woman, Venetia Buddicom, whose parents owned the Villa Capella at Bordighera. The Buddicoms were well-to-do. The family's fortune derived from the railway boom of the 1840s, and was grafted on to an older stock of Shropshire landowners, parsons and academics. The railway engineer, Walter Buddicom, an associate of Sir Thomas Brassey, was Venetia's grandfather; examples of Buddicom engines are on display in both the British and French national railway museums. Their home was Penbedw, a 4000-acre estate near Mold in North Wales. Venetia, as eldest daughter, inherited this estate after the death of her father from a sudden heart attack in 1925. Her only brother had been killed in 1918, leaving no heir, while her younger sister, Marcia, was married to a member of the Arnold Foster clan.

As well as the Villa Capella the family owned a yacht at Bordighera, where Venetia and her mother spent a portion of each winter. Venetia's father was a clever, genial man, with a sense of family duty. Indeed his death occurred when Penbedw was filled with young men for the partridge shooting. Among them was a young naval officer, the brother of the local parson. He stayed on when the party broke up, to give support to the widow and daughter, and it was generally assumed that he would become Venetia's husband. But nothing came of it, and he married someone else.[4] Perhaps he was daunted by her possessions, and the fear of being taken for a fortune-hunter, or by something stubbornly self-contained and solitary in her nature. Whatever it was, she never married, and perhaps this disappointment, if disappointment indeed it was, made a bond with Freya, scarred by her own jilting in 1916.

The Italian Riviera at this time had a large community of foreign residents, distinct from the hotel visitors; these formed a local society of their own, graded by their status as property owners. Into this Flora Stark soon made her way and it was where Freya's first contacts with the East were made. She took Arabic lessons from a retired Anglican priest as a means of occupying her mind in a period of stagnation and indecision, while she pondered her future.

Freya's interest in the East had been aroused by the publicity surrounding T. E. Lawrence's exploits in World War I, and the glamour attached to the new desert kingdoms in the Arab lands. Up till now her ambitions had gone no further than seeking employment which would take her there. It was in this period she arranged to have herself baptised early one morning at the Presbyterian church at Bordighera, a move to facilitate her recommendation by some retired members of the Christian Missionary Society, found for her by her mother, as a teacher in their schools, or as a governess to a prominent Middle-Eastern family.

Such an idea would never have occurred to Venetia, who felt no need for money or independence, already having both. It set the tone for the relationship between the two young women. It was Venetia, bored, restless, who initiated in Freya the idea of exploration. In the late summer of 1923, she suggested to Freya that they join forces for a mule-trek to Andorra, starting from a rendezvous in Provence. From the onset, it was the younger one who was the banker. Freya contributed her share, but they travelled cheap – that was part of the adventure – and when they ran out of funds in the Pyrenees, it was Venetia who cashed the cheque.

The friendship thus begun in 1923 was cemented by visits from Venetia to the Dolomites in the spring of 1925, when Freya was convalescing there after an operation. In 1927 Freya visited Venetia at her home in North Wales for the first time. It was an ardent friendship on her part, though who in the beginning most impressed the other is hard to say. Freya with her aura of scholarly preoccupations and stance of independence might appear very congenial to a girl who had insisted on a university education – Venetia studied forestry at Bangor University – rather than the conventional debutante's London season, and who turned her back on the social preoccupations of her class. Venetia is recalled as forming friendships with what the family regarded as 'odd friends', picked up haphazardly. Freya was perhaps rather dazzled by the younger one's choice of herself as an intimate.

Penbedw was 'a lovely plain old house with its park and great trees all around it, on sloping land . . . The house itself is full of lovely things, rugs and panelling, old pewter and books, and delightful French pictures, china, silver, a perfect treasure house.'[5] Life there was very comfortable, if a little overpowering. 'The gardener fills the house with flowers, there is a huge log fire for me in the billiard room, my clothes are selected and laid out for me by the perfect maid . . .' The two rode and went hunting together; Freya was relieved not to disgrace herself by falling off. 'Venetia looked so nice: she rides like a centaur; all the people knew her, of course, and invited her, but she gets so bored with them . . .'[6] she told her mother. A few days later she elaborated. 'Venetia is very pleasant to be with, and glad to have me, I think. She is a lonely creature – and not as happy as I am, in spite of riches, and beauty, and everything – she would be so much happier with about a sixth of her income, poor thing.'

Later, in her autobiography, she wrote of Venetia at this period: 'I loved her quiet reserve, her feeling for style in all

things, and the beautiful carriage of her small head; she made
me feel that my gaiety and general curiosity were not very
dignified.' Freya admired Venetia for her self-assurance, and
the upper-class English manner which some might find arrogant.
It was so different from the Italian necessity to please in which
she had been brought up. Venetia offered another world to
explore, another identity to assume, and a rejection of all the
drabness and compromised status that her Italian life stood for
in Freya's mind.

The two decided to pool their resources. Aided by Freya's
Arabic studies, they would travel to the Middle East and make
exploratory journeys together to as yet undecided areas.
Venetia was due to stay with a cousin, Henry Lawrence (a
member of the Indian Civil Service and a future Governor of
Bombay), in India for the winter season of 1927–8, so they
would meet halfway in Lebanon, an easy sail from Venice, in
May 1928. Freya had an introduction to a mission school in
Broumana, in the hills above Beirut, and would spend four
months there polishing up her Arabic, while awaiting Venetia's
arrival from India, and making the necessary arrangements for
the adventure.

Freya's earliest contacts in Syria were Protestant missionary
teachers, installed in Ottoman territories since the 1840s. They
were a group rather despised by the people with whom she later
associated. Their modest, unassuming approach did nothing to
prepare her for what followed when she reached Iraq in 1930.
During that first winter in Lebanon, in 1927, at that period a
part of Syria and administered by France under its League of
Nations Mandate, she was introduced into the life of a small
summer hill station, Broumana, in the off-season. She learned
the routines of polite Christian Arab sociability from her landlady, a genteel Lebanese spinster, while the schoolteachers
sought about among their connections to find her a reliable local
muleteer, a Druze who was to convey the two young women
safely through the pitfalls of French military rule to British protection in Transjordan.

The people of the Metn, where Broumana lies, are muleteers
and drovers, and in the severe famine which followed on the

disruption of the grain market in Damascus after the Turkish defeat in 1918, they had gone inland with their trains of mules and donkeys to the Druze territories of the Syrian Hauran to bring wheat for the starving population of the coastal areas. In 1928 there was no lack of men willing to hire the services of themselves and their beasts for the kind of journey the two women had in mind.

Venetia joined Freya at Broumana in May 1928 from India. The two young women drove by taxi to Damascus, passing on the way their muleteer and his beasts, laden with their luggage, and trotting towards the city. Next day the party assembled on his instructions some way beyond the outskirts of the city, to avoid attracting the attention of the French authorities, and then they were off, losing themselves in the life of the countryside under the protection of their muleteer. The plan was to move southwards through the area of the old Roman frontier described by Gertrude Bell in *The Desert and the Sown* (1907) to the Transjordan border, and a return to more conventional touring under the auspices of a Mandated British administration.

Freya learnt her business as a traveller in the East in the course of this trip, and the lessons were to be the stock-in-trade of her travel expertise. The first was to arrange things quietly at local level, through local people and to avoid Authority at all costs. Officialdom was obstructive; you should never draw its attention to yourself. The second was the desirability of appearing among simple people as one not unlike themselves. No high-handed display or rejection of local manners and customs was advisable; it alienated rather than impressed the solid elements in the population, and evoked a cynical instinct to exploit among the baser sort. The utmost discretion in clothing and behaviour was essential for a woman, and the fullest advantage should be taken of Moslem protectiveness towards the female sex, and the privacy accorded it.

Long after Broumana and its sedate circle of teachers and missionaries had passed from her life, the unselfconscious sobriety of its relations with the local people remained with her. Under the slow patient guidance of their muleteer she assembled the modest gifts he deemed suitable to sweeten their passage through the rough country they were about to traverse. At the workaday end of the great vaulted area of the Damascus *souk* she bought the pocket-knives and combs, razors and mirrors, scissors, thread, needles and buttons, lengths of cambric for headcloths, sweets and toys to give children, a round box of the Damascus speciality of crystallised fruit for a Druze notable, recently released from political detention by the French authorities, to whom the school had given her a letter of introduction. It took all afternoon to achieve the purchases, and she chafed in the heat at the slowness of the negotiations over the expenditure of such trivial sums. But it was a lesson absorbed, an insight into another's sense of priorities, which many years later would be regurgitated thoughtfully to young men eager to travel off the beaten track.

This journey to the Hauran was the romantic sinking through the surface of a society which Freya sought as a traveller, the concentration of all her powers into covert observation. The humdrum necessities, for their muleteer, of avoiding a confrontation with an alien administration, of pursuing a traditional pattern of life in the face of autocratic interference, were veiled for her by the glow of Romance, which coloured all she saw with a delight which eventually she would distil into her individual literary style. At this period all was spontaneous and fresh, the eye catching and the spirit absorbing the transition from the mechanical routines of modern living to this older system handed down from generation to generation, old skills and knowledge of how to maintain the inner and outer defences of privacy and independence under the threat of foreign domination, and the rage and rapine of less fortunate neighbours.

In her ignorance, Freya had chosen to traverse a district under martial law following a series of armed attacks on the French military forces by the local people. Rebel Druzes, under threat of execution if caught, were sheltering in the traditional way among the shepherds and poor villages of the border country. Secure in the protection afforded them by their muleteer, the two women travelled on unmolested, in happy unconcern, oblivious of the consternation they were about to afford the French military administration.

The sense of being the chosen companion of so splendid a creature as Venetia may have gone a little to Freya's head. Her *Letters from Syria*, written in 1928 to record their journey through the Syrian Hauran, but only published in 1942, are rather a surprise. The tone is often very schoolgirlish. The ruses adopted by the two young women to evade questions from the French garrison officers who put them up for a night on their journey are crowed over with glee. Hiding the muleteer's gun in Freya's underclothes and her diary in his waist-band was an exciting game of wits. The two excused themselves early from dinner in the mess on the plea that they must retire to write letters to their mothers, and back in their own quarters were convulsed with laughter at their own cleverness as they recalled the expression of disappointment on their hosts' faces when they rose to go.

Freya, in Baghdad in 1942, when she received a copy of the book, edited in her absence by Cockerell, rather liked what she found of herself in the text. 'I feel it is more your child than mine,' she told Cockerell, 'and it seems to me that the person who wrote it fourteen years ago was very definite, ignorant, gay and rather nice! I feel I am in for a lot of trouble with Missionaries in general!'

Unlike her friend who was brought up to wealth and position, Freya in 1927 had no preconceived notions of what was due to her as an Englishwoman in the East. There was nothing in her background to instil this, so that though Venetia might later tell Sydney Cockerell that their 1928 trek through the Hauran 'was rather a grim little journey, really, especially for me, as I didn't know the language'[7] in Freya's recollection it was transmuted to the purest, most joyous Romance. How much this delight derived from the company of her friend, and how much from the actual experience, is impossible now to judge, but it set the scene for Freya's falling in love with the East, which ends the first volume of her autobiography.

Something of this first liberating rush of happiness and fulfilment remained with Freya all her life, buried under the accretions of worldliness and contrivance, but surfacing as she grew old in occasional successful exchanges with the young, to whom would be imparted in her slow distinctive voice the insights first obtained on the stony uplands of the Hauran, and among the debris of an earlier empire. Much of it had to do with establishing the right price for goods and services, and the mutual respect between the contracting parties that this engendered. Freya had a shrewd notion of the value of money, and drove a hard bargain. She reprobated gestures of spendthrift generosity as amateurish, and productive of disrespect rather than gratitude. A tip at the end of a trip for the muleteer was not automatically forthcoming; it depended on performance, and was graded accordingly. She had strict views on what constituted service, and kept people up to the mark, whatever the circumstances; it did not always make for happy relations with the people she employed.

FIVE

THE DECISIVE STEP –
IRAQ AND PERSIA

Following her trek with Venetia through the Syrian Hauran in
1928, Freya spent the winter of 1928–9 with her father in
Canada, where she experienced the life of a settler in British
Columbia. It enabled her to reach two definite conclusions. One
was that she was inalienably European, and the other that she
wanted to return to the Middle East and to develop a career
there, though how this was to be achieved she did not yet
know.

Armed with her new sense of purpose, on her return to
London from Canada she set about preparing for further ventures. The acceptance of an article on the Syrian journey in
September 1928 by *The Cornhill* gave her confidence and she
followed this up with another on her Canadian experience, which
was accepted in April 1929. This sent her to the British Museum
library in pursuit of more travel material; the idea of a future
career as a writer was taking shape.

It was the literary device of the Quest, which she was to
employ in all her subsequent writing. She told her father from
Asolo in May 1929:

I . . . have a good subject for the winter, if only it hasn't
been exhaustively done already, and that is to combine a sort
of history with travel notes to the fortresses of the Assassins,
who were the followers of the Old Man of the Mountains
and had a series of castles between Aleppo and the Persian

borders. I am very vague about it all, but am trying to find
out some more before going out. It seems to me rather
promising, although it may all have been done by some
thorough-going German already![1]

For a Briton in Asia to drop through the surface into native
life was to live almost always among the very poor. There were
few alternative means of entry, other than as doctor or teacher;
marriage was rare, and generally entailed ostracism by compatriots. Some element in Freya's personality responded to the
compartmentation of identities inherent in a double life; it had
the thrill of disguise without long-term commitment to the role,
but to achieve it required patience and finesse.

Freya's proclaimed intention in going to Baghdad in October
1929 was to immerse herself in local life. Broumana had been
too tame. What she wanted was to penetrate the world of the
Arabian Nights which she felt surrounded her, if only she could
slip inconspicuously into it. Had she stuck to this programme,
and kept quiet about it, she might have avoided a good deal of
mortification. Her error was to attempt to combine this with
social recognition by her fellow-countrymen.

Freya's indulgent view of herself on reading *Letters from Syria*
in 1942 was not shared by the British community in Baghdad
in 1929. This was a minefield of affrontable sensibilities, into
which she immediately blundered; the ignorance of their conventions that she displayed dismayed her compatriots and
aroused comment. Freya was close to her thirty-seventh birthday when she appeared there. The need to count the pennies
no doubt contributed to her difficulties when she arrived, but
over-confidence on her part did not help.

It had been planned with Venetia in England that Freya should
precede her to Baghdad, settle in and improve her Arabic, and
be joined by her friend the following spring. .Together they
would then make adventurous treks to as yet undecided areas,
on the model of their Syrian adventures in 1928. But Venetia
had a bad fall out hunting that winter and broke her neck. Her
recovery was very slow, and put future travel in doubt. She
had to live quietly and retreated to an isolated cottage, high on

the crest of the hill overlooking the Penbedw estate where she was eventually rehabilitated physically by the devoted attention of her nurse over a period of some years. The loss of Venetia's companionship and support at this early stage of her new life was to affect Freya's plans and to force her to follow her own initiatives alone. Her private income was roughly £320 a year, about £6 a week, from investment and the rent of her property at La Mortola, so her financial situation was one of chronic hard-upness, rather than real poverty. Venetia's loss was a blow, but not a total disaster, especially as she sent generous cheques to Baghdad at Christmas and Easter and was a responsive recipient of the long lively accounts which Freya used to record her impressions and adventures.

Arrived in Baghdad, Freya put up at the Zia Hotel at fifteen shillings a day, and immediately threw herself into her adventure with a search for somewhere cheaper to live. This she found while wandering about the immediate locality. It was a small mud house in a warren of narrow alleyways off the town's main thoroughfare, Rashidi Street. Her Arabic was sufficient to read the notice that it was empty, and on her own initiative she decided to take it. She negotiated a lease with the help of one of her Syrian introductions, a young member of the Baha'i sect employed in the Government Irrigation Department, and a few days later called at the Education Ministry, and left a note and her address for the British Adviser there, Lionel Smith, a friend of the Ker family, to whom she had an introduction.

Thus warned of her arrival, he called in the afternoon, while she was out, and was appalled at her choice of accommodation. Very soon a rescue operation was mounted by concerned compatriots, led by the wife of the legal Adviser to the government, Stefana Drower. She was a rarity in the local British community, an Arabist with a scholarly expertise in the country's differing religious sects, to whom Freya had been recommended by the School of Oriental Studies in London. Alerted by Lionel Smith, she took Freya under her wing and helped her to find a more acceptable district in which to live, in an Arab Christian household where she rented a large room and a terrace overlooking the Tigris. Unknown to Freya, her first lodging in the Amara

Quarter was in immediate proximity to a well-known community
of local prostitutes. A turn or two away from her own particular
alley, these women could be spied from Rashidi Street sitting
shamelessly on their doorsteps, awaiting custom. That such a
trade should exist in proximity to households of respectable folk
was a reflection of the realities of life in a slum, but was tolerated
with tacit disapproval by the neighbours. If Freya too chose to
overlook it, or was too ignorant to recognise what she saw,
no-one would enlighten her, or think it their duty to tell her.

It was not so with her compatriots. When it became known
that Freya was living in the native brothel quarter, in a fetid
and unhealthy slum, while attending classes in an American
mission girls' school to practise Arabic, a feeling of indignation,
particularly among the women, as well as disgust was generated, that an Englishwoman should so declass herself. The
rumour went around that she must be a Bolshevik agent, intent
on stirring up trouble. The British High Commissioner had ruled
that it was unsuitable for Englishwomen to enter buildings
where they were expected to remove their shoes in deference
to local religious practice, so the news that an Englishwoman
had 'gone native' aroused feelings of alarm and betrayal, as if
the whole mystique of the inviolability of British womanhood
had been placed in jeopardy.

Freya had embarked on her own Passage to India, and
immediately run aground on the prejudices of her compatriots,
but she edited out her initial social blunder when she wrote to
Venetia on 6 January 1930:

> My dear, you can't imagine what a place this is for taking an
> interest in other people's affairs, nor what a mutual shock
> my first contact with proper conventional civil servant society
> has caused. No-one else (respectable) appears ever to have
> settled in a shoemaker's home on the banks of the Tigris,
> nor has anyone succeeded in living in Baghdad on two rupees
> a day. One lady has asked me if I am not 'lowering the pres-
> tige of British womanhood' by sitting in school among the
> Iraqi girls . . . For a time, except for one or two people who
> were really nice all through, I felt rather like an outcast: the

men nearly all disapproved and looked on uneasily if their wives were nice to me – apparently expecting something explosive to happen every second. The East must have rather a distorting effect on people's perspectives. I feel that there was something to be said for the poor bull in the china shop, whose most innocent and natural movements all seemed to cause a crash.

To fit in, Freya learned in time, to conform to unwritten rules of behaviour, arcane mysteries passed on by word of mouth to the properly validated newcomer, was the basic requirement for acceptance by the ruling elite of her countrymen, and without that acceptance she would be hopelessly handicapped. Whatever idealistic lip-service might have been paid to the rights of subject people when the revolt against the Ottoman Turks was fanned in 1915, by the end of the 1920s the British were ensconced as the dominant power in Iraq, and they knew it. Techniques learned on the battlefield were applied to further administrative aims. A policy of active interference, strict enforcement of law and order, and the development of natural resources, undeterred by previous social structures, was imposed on the country, and a self-confident race of Britons installed themselves to make Iraq into a model Arab state.

The Royal Air Force, keen to establish its individual identity, was the visible token of Britain's domination rather than the army. It was a time of pioneering flights from the airfields in southern Iraq which prepared the way for future commercial air links with India and the Far East. It was also the time when the use of airpower for the control of irredentism and tribal raiding was put into effect by a home government anxious to effect economies in the running of the Empire. Bombing from the air of civilian settlements was used as a deterrent in Waziristan, in Kurdistan, on the Saudi borders, and in Hadhramaut throughout this final phase of self-confident colonial rule, and this is the political background against which Freya's career as a traveller and journalist developed. A network of CID surveillance, on the government of India system, extended over the whole area of British domination in the Middle East, and was discreetly operated by men seconded from the Indian army and police.

This was a society that preserved its identity by excluding rather than by gathering in the stranger. Much of the restrictive element in this attitude probably had to do with fear, a deep-seated but unpublicised uneasiness going back to the unrest of the early 1920s, when eleven of the political and Levy officers were murdered in the outlying districts by the local people, and the infiltration of Bolshevik professional agitators from Azerbaijan, and the harangues of religious zealots – Shi'a and Sunni – inflamed popular feeling against British military rule. There was an underlying awareness within the inner circle of the flimsiness of the structure of control should the great body of the governed unite one day to rise up against its rulers, like a horse determined to unseat its rider.

Looked at askance by her fellow-nationals, Freya's bold assertion of her individuality fell rather flat. It produced feelings of mortification and of rejection unsuspected by her new acquaintances, and in this perhaps were sown the seeds of her future overbearingly dismissive attitude to mere wives, and her distancing of herself from the preoccupations of the local resident community. As her only 'respectable' connections in British official society, Lionel Smith and Stefana Drower worked conscientiously to promote Freya's acceptability to their colleagues. Slowly, she made up the ground she had lost on arrival, when her association with the American missionaries, and her handful of introductions to worthy but unglamorous middle-class Iraqis, members of the Baha'i sect, did not commend her socially to her compatriots.

The British Adviserates regarded the missionaries with mixed feelings. While their scholarly contribution to Arabic studies was recognised, an attitude of patronising condescension for what was regarded as ineffectual meddling and dangerous political naivety had become habitual. The entry of America into World War I in 1917, and President Wilson's influence at the Geneva Peace Conference, had given impetus to Arab nationalist claims which saw in his Twelfth Point a far more concrete commitment to 'an absolutely unmolested opportunity of autonomous development' than anything envisaged by the British. It was referred to ironically in private as the Twelfth Commandment. Such dismissal of American political idealism filtered down to the men on the spot in the Middle East, where the educational activities of the missionaries, which had struck the spark of the Arab Revolt, were monitored with covert suspicion by the intelligence agencies.

In later life Freya made much of the narrowness and lack of vision of her compatriots abroad, and of the opportunities lost for consolidating loyalty in the host populations by the painful condescension of people imbued with notions of superiority, and easily satisfied by their own performance. Much of the imaginative fuel for her wartime Brotherhood of Freedom was supplied by this, and the conclusion of her final report on her creation is a ringing peroration and call for all men of good faith to work together in a common effort 'where the personal sense of inferiority, the frightful snobbishness of races, may vanish once and for all'. [2]

Her treks in 1927 and 1928 in Lebanon and Syria had the protective influence of the Protestant mission community behind them. Similarly in Persia in May 1930, when she set out alone from Iraq in quest of the Assassins' lairs, it was Baha'i introductions in Baghdad who put her in contact with a local landowner in Qasvin; he consigned her to the care of one of his tenants in the Alamut and held him responsible for her well-being. The tenant was a professional *charvadah* or carrier, who added Freya as one more bundle among the goods and passengers being carried on his mules from Qasvin to the scattered homesteads of the Alamut valley, in whose side valleys the remains of the Assassins' fortresses are concealed. Once through and out of the valley by way of the Salambar pass, a roadhead would be reached, and the descent to the Caspian coast could be achieved by car or lorry.

After her initial ten-day trek along this route Freya returned briefly to Baghdad from Persia at the end of May 1930, en route for the desert crossing by bus to Beirut and a ship back to Venice. She showed the notes of her journey to Lionel Smith before leaving, who pointed her in the direction of the Royal

Geographical Society by recommending her to its Secretary,
Arthur Hinks. She sailed for Europe on 18 June, sad to leave
the East, but very glad to find her father had sent her a cheque,
as her current account was £66 overdrawn, and the bank was
hinting that she should sell some securities.

She went out to Canada at the end of September to spend two
months with Robert Stark on his smallholding at Creston. It was
the last time she was to see him, for he died a year later, when
she was again in Persia, consolidating her emerging reputation as
a traveller. They dealt with family affairs, and decided how his
will was to be made. He was a man in his seventies now, and
weakened by a stroke in 1927. It was arranged that his entire
estate should pass to Freya; there was to be nothing for Flora or
for the four young children of Freya's younger sister Vera, left
motherless at her death in 1926.

In the New Year of 1931 Freya was back in London after a stop-
over on the way from Liverpool with Venetia at Penbedw. She
was following up the Assassins' history, and Venetia's Indian Civil
Service cousin, Sir Henry Lawrence, was being helpful at the
India Office. *The Cornhill* had published her account of her 1930
trek and she was receiving instruction in surveying from the
Royal Geographical Society's expert. She was to be supplied with
a case of surveying instruments for a second visit to the
Assassins' strongholds.

She sailed to Haifa from Brindisi in May 1931, having stopped
off in Rome to try unsuccessfully to get herself taken on as a correspondent of the *Oriente Moderno*, a specialist Italian publication
to which her father had given her a subscription. She reached
Baghdad in the middle of June, en route for Persia, where she
stayed at the Consulate in Hamadan for a month. Her acceptance
by the official British community was now complete.

'Marvellous what my one little Alamut trip last year seems to
have done,' she reported triumphantly to her mother from Hamadan in July 1931.[3] 'The Secretary of the RGS . . . has just sent
me a note of introduction to the First Secretary of our Legation,
saying that I am a serious student who avoids publicity and they
can *safely* give me any assistance.' Freya was very pleased with

this description, though she noted too that 'I feel I shall never be able to do what I really like again, as everyone has taken to a policy of Persuasion by Kindness, which is impossible to deal with. However, no-one makes objections to Alamut where I hope to return in a fortnight's time and thence find a Jungali (local guide) to take me across a bit of country where the Survey have put nothing but trees and a few question marks . . .'

Sir John Shuckburgh, another relative of Venetia's, and a deputy Under-Secretary of State at the Colonial Office, gave her a letter of recommendation to the British High Commissioner in Iraq, and this, delivered to Captain Vyvyan Holt, the Oriental Secretary, on her return to Baghdad, now produced the most gratifying results.

Vyvyan Holt, whom she had met on her earlier visit through Lionel Smith, now became more friendly. Previously, he had been cautious and tended to avoid her, despite her aptitude for putting people on the spot by the confiding friendliness of her response. He was a tall, lean, reserved bachelor, younger than Freya, seconded from India for political-intelligence duties after service on the North-west Frontier. Fluent in several Asiatic languages, a translator of Kurdish verse, he had been a friend of Gertrude Bell, whom he admired, and now, as Oriental Secretary, he held the same influential position that she had occupied in the early British administration of Mesopotamia. She had died there two years before Freya reached Iraq.

Freya was fascinated by Holt. His aloofness troubled her, and his occasional offhand helpfulness left her unsure of herself, uncertain as to its reason. He never married. He was absorbed in his work, discreet, reclusive, his sole relaxation polo. Detesting all forms of social activity, he kept away from the more racy elements of Anglo-Iraqi society formed around the Regent of Iraq's royal court.

In 1951, in the second volume of her autobiography, Freya wrote of three things that came into her life in this 1930s period in Baghdad. The third of these, she wrote mysteriously, was

a strange, unwanted falling into love, unprovoked and unexpected, inspired by the most conventional person who, for his part, hovered on the edge but never fell in, and yet held me with no active effort of his own so that for seven years I never felt quite free: then it all dropped, as a shutter might drop, and I awoke with an immense delight of liberation, though friendship and tenderness remained.

Freya's pursuit of the elusive Captain Holt is recorded in her letters to her mother. She never understood the nature of their relationship; her yearning sentimentality found no response in his dry teasing, which disconcerted and puzzled her. She was unused to this oblique English form of attention and her heavy-footed response provoked irritation in him, and impatient snubbing.

Holt, for all his refusal to be drawn into Freya's emotional dramas, was kind to her once her *bona fides* were established from London, and helpful in practical ways. It was he who told her on arrival in 1929 that if she wanted to explore the Assassins' castles it was Persian she needed, not Arabic, and who found her a teacher. He lent her his horses to exercise, and sometimes took her for a ride or walk.

He was a modest, reticent creature who disliked publicity, a practising Anglican whose reserves of courage and humour were to stand him and his fellow-captives in good stead during a harsh captivity in the Korean war of the 1950s. Her cocksure silliness on arrival in Iraq irritated him, while to Freya's need to impress he presented a challenge she found irresistible. It was more than just husband-seeking, something often discussed in her letters to Venetia, recuperating alone in Penbedw and forlornly regretting her single state and its stigma of failure. Why they themselves should prove unacceptable, when silly, commonplace women fell into matrimony with no trouble, was a small angry spot of doubt, a chink in their armour. Freya at least had her scars to fall back on, while Venetia's case was made worse by her good looks – she was a tall, leggy English blonde – and her fine possessions. Freya bemoaned her encroaching middle age. 'I am getting so plain which is *very* depressing: I always find it takes people about a month to overcome their first impression of my plainness,' she wrote to her mother from Hamadan on 18 July 1931. She was upset by Captain Holt's crossness and snubbiness on the eve of her departure on her second trip to Alamut and the Elburz.

> Captain Holt came the night before I left, very much on edge, and after a strained hour took his leave with me feeling thoroughly depressed. I am really so fond of him – it makes me unhappy to be able to do nothing and see him so very miserable . . . I feel if only I were a *little* prettier and younger it would make all the difference to him . . .

This note of uncomprehending distress runs all through her correspondence with her mother at this period. She was pitched into a society where bachelors were not a rarity; not boys just out from public school or university – though these filled the junior ranks of the big commercial companies – but marriageable men seasoned by exposure to succeeding invasions of the winter 'fishing fleet', the girls out from home after boarding school to join their parents and to find suitable partners among their fellow-exiles.

That bachelors only existed to be married was an unquestioned belief in the matriarchal society in which Freya had grown up. The glamour of position and power was fascinating to her and the notion of these quiet Englishmen unobtrusively pulling strings behind a façade of Arab institutions excited her ambition. It was an elite she immediately aspired to join, her most romantic imaginings made tangible and accessible. The difficulty was that, despite the example of Gertrude Bell, matrimony appeared the only acceptable avenue of approach for a woman, and none of these men seemed inclined towards it. That attention could be paid her for any other reason seems to have escaped her. By nature diffident, she had as yet to learn self-importance.

Freya's social verve deceived people and perhaps intimidated the cautious male. It implied a degree of sexual competence which did not exist. It was less the individual that attracted her than the depersonalised distillation of the various advantages that went with him. Something shrewd and calculating in her nature made sure that the society she sought was the best available. Freya was looking for recognition and acceptance of herself as an individual, not sexual adventure, from the men she was now meeting; she wanted to *belong*, not be an outcast, something difficult for her new acquaintances, with their coded acceptance of conventional sexual roles, to understand. Her emotional idealism was difficult to integrate with this cooler, more understated society in which she found herself. There was a general refusal to take anything too seriously which contributed to the appearance of effortless superiority which was the hallmark of the breed. It was a style that often led to feelings of inadequacy in those outside its charmed circle. Nothing in Freya's previous experience had prepared her for this, it was alien to all she had absorbed from her own upbringing.

It stung her into a determination to assert herself, to show herself the equal, if not the superior, of those she believed dismissed her for her lack of conventional status. This was a small, pricking discontent, a sense of alienation that expressed itself in a determined annexation of useful men. She would never, she claimed, do anything that would cause another woman a moment's distress. Since her affections were not engaged she could persuade herself no harm could result from her actions; what wives might feel when she monopolised their husbands' interest did not enter into it; she was preoccupied with the demonstration of her own power. It did not necessarily endear her to other women, though the more sophisticated were not taken in. Nor did it save her from embarrassing consequences, when more ardent or direct natures than her own were involved.

On her second journey to the Assassin stronghold in the Elburz Freya reached Qasvin from Hamadan on 2 August 1931, a bad time to travel in the summer heat, and was held up there for six days, awaiting her muleteer, Aziz. Eventually he sent his beasts with a servant, with whom Freya set off to seek the site of the castle of Lamiaser. She identified the castle but the valley bottoms were full of malarial mosquitoes, which the local inhabitants avoid by moving up to the higher pastures and cooler air until the heat of summer is over. Three days out from Qasvin she began to feel ill and by the end of the week, on her escort's advice, she made for the Alamut valley, where she lay ill with dysentery and malaria at Shutur Khan. There, she was attended by a young Persian doctor, summoned from a family property some hours' distance up the mountain. This was in a village high up on the flanks of the Elburz, set among fruit orchards and safe from the miasma of the irrigated valley. Freya was taken up there for a week, until the malaria abated, and she was fit to continue.

She was very frightened by this experience, and lying out at night in her sleeping-bag, alone and anxious, she thought she was going to die. The people of the valley were helpful and kind. The doctor reassured her as to the efficacy of his treatment by telling her that her dysentery and malaria were nothing out of the ordinary, and that he spent his life treating them. Once on her feet, Freya's appetite for adventure was soon restored and, reunited now with Aziz, she continued her trek, circling the peak of Takht-i-Suleiman, along the seaward face of the Elburz and so round the unmapped flank of the mountain to the vicinity of Teheran, taking compass bearings and height levels as best she could, and collecting names as they went along.

She did not feel up to attempting Takht-i-Suleiman, but camped beneath it, on a great shoulder of mountain they were slowly traversing. She was up in bare high country now, populated, except in the occasional villages, largely by shepherds living in rocky shelters among their flocks and frequented only by sportsmen hunting ibex and sable. This second stage of her journey lasted nineteen days, ending on 10 September when, threading their way down through the foothills, the party hit the main road being built by the new Shah, Reza Pahlevi, into Mazanderan from Teheran. Freya and Aziz completed the last twenty-four miles to Teheran in a taxi, leaving the retainer to trudge on with the mules another day and night into the city.

Delivered safely to the British Legation in Teheran, Freya handed her notes and measurements to the Military Attaché who sent them to the War Office, which in turn sent them on to the Survey of India, the intelligence-gathering arm of the government of India. This information, and what she acquired next in Luristan, was collated and drawn into the map of north-west Persia by the RAF mapmakers, and published by RAF headquarters in Iraq in 1932. It was the scientific basis of her reputation as a traveller; she had filled in, albeit scrappily, for her aneroid did not measure above 10,000 feet, a small area of north-west Persia, hitherto unsurveyed.

She did not linger in Teheran, although the news of her father's death in Canada had awaited her there. The chance of a letter to a tribal contact in Luristan from a local Jewish dealer in antiquities tempted her. Luristan was the source of smuggled bronze figurines and horse furniture that commanded high prices on the international antiquities market. It was a traffic the central government in Teheran was anxious to suppress, in line with the new ruler Reza Shah Pahlevi's policy of bringing the semi-autonomous tribal areas with their feudal rulers under his authority. A road was being pushed through Luristan, as in Mazanderan, but entry into the territory was not encouraged, the Lurs having a bad reputation for thieving and murder.

Two weeks after reaching Teheran, Freya was on her way to Hamadan, where the British Consul, Christopher Summerhayes, was helpful in finding her a muleteer prepared to convey her across country from Nihavend through the hill land of north-west Luristan to the small town of Harsin, where there was a motor road connecting to Kermanshah, and the railway back to Baghdad. She planned to evade the police patrols active throughout the district, and to reach the unknown area from where the bronzes came. Some of these she had already bought on commission for Lionel Smith from the dealer in Teheran, and now she hoped to find something for herself.

In the event, within two days, she was reported to and detained by the government authorities, and eventually escorted out of the country to the Iraq border by a patrol of mounted police, on instructions from Teheran. She did not find the grave goods she had hoped for, they came from a more remote area, but she was able to buy some bracelets and beads, spearheads and pieces of broken pottery for a few shillings. Government spies had been active in tracing those engaged in selling antiquities, and the people were shy, unwilling to compromise themselves with a stranger.

What she was able to do in the fortnight she spent in the Lur country was to take bearings surreptitiously, make notes and take photographs of what she saw on her leisurely progress under escort towards the frontier. The party was received with wondering curiosity by the people at whose poor encampments they stopped for the night, and sitting round the tent fire Freya could listen to the gossip and news exchanged by the people, and get the feel, so she told me many years later, of what they thought of their existing situation. The language of the Lurs was incomprehensible to her, but the muleteer spoke Persian, as did the headmen and government officials she encountered, while many of the Lurs themselves had worked as stevedores in Iraq, and had a smattering of Arabic. Freya's Persian, after several weeks' dependence on it as the only medium of communication, was now enough to follow the thread of a conversation, and to manage the simple question and answer necessary to elicit names of people and places from her companions and to glean some insight into the workings of the new administration.

SIX

MAKING HER NAME

Freya spent the winter of 1931–2 in Baghdad as a freelance journalist writing up her second visit to the Elburz mountains and her venture into Luristan. Her father's death did not necessitate any change of plan. She knew the provisions of his will, there was no anxiety on that score, and Canada could now wait. 'It felt very homelike to be back there [in Baghdad] again,' she wrote;[1] for she was now no longer an outcast, and everyone was being nice to her. ADCs waited on her with invitations to dine with Sherifian royalties; the Military Attaché in Teheran wrote to say her map had been sent to the War Office 'and that they rarely get such good and thorough work'; she was taken to call on the widowed Iraqi Queen ('who has cut her hair and wears short sleeves'). Rescued from 'going native' and with the right introductions, from the official viewpoint she had arrived. She told her mother:

I feel I have not wasted the summer [of 1931] and I have got into Luristan where none of the archaeologists could go and no European woman has ever been; and have mapped out a country so that the Government find it useful – and all on my own, with no pulling of strings or special facilities. And it is nice now to feel that the men who *do* things think of me as one of themselves in a way . . .

Financial troubles were looming, the worldwide Depression was affecting her income, and she told Venetia this looked like being her last winter in the East, her dividends having been reduced by more than half. At New Year 1932,[2] she was offered a job by the editor of the *Baghdad Times* at £20 a month and though she disliked the idea of having to write to order, the groggy state of her finances, she wrote, made it imperative that she accept it. The job consisted of writing up the Reuters news agency telegrams on which the paper relied for its foreign news, and she began work in February with the intention of staying on through the summer and returning home in the spring of 1933. She supplemented her salary by occasional articles, light thumbnail sketches of places and people she visited or encountered. Out of this came her first book, *Baghdad Sketches*, a garish little production, bound in brilliant yellow, of five hundred copies locally printed at her expense, from whose sale she eventually netted £55. Its novelty for the British community was that it dared, in an entertaining way, to poke a little quiet fun at the official life, and to write sympathetically of local life. This was considered rather subversive and perhaps lacking in taste by the more hidebound members of the British community but was acclaimed by freer spirits, who began to find in little Miss Stark an interesting personality.

British officialdom was very cautious in its dealings with the volatile Shi'a element in the Iraqi population, whose religious teachers and holy men had been prominent in the 1920 disorders. Especial care was necessary at the time of the Mohurram processions, when the Shi'a Moslems paraded through the streets in a ritualised re-enactment of the central tragedy of their faith, a passion play of the martyrdom of the Prophet Mohammed's descendants at the hands of their Sunni Moslem enemies. Then religious frenzy exacerbated popular feelings against both the ruling Sunni faction and its foreign Advisers. Rather than risk trouble, the High Commissioner preferred to discourage his nationals from frequenting native gatherings and religious occasions except in well-policed circumstances. To do so was to be odd and to show bad form. It was a negative policy general throughout the East that contributed a good deal to the triviality of expatriate life in the final phases of imperial rule.

Freya challenged this tacit conspiracy to avoid confrontation. Throughout this period in Baghdad she was busy placing articles and photographs in London. She was not uniformly successful: the *Spectator* turned down some, but the *Illustrated London News* took others, as did the Royal Geographical Society's *Journal*, the *Contemporary Review*, and *The Cornhill*. Freya pursued such openings assiduously, assembling and where necessary recycling material to supply her London market, ignoring the conventions of her fellow-countrymen. The more charitable of these attributed this rashness to ignorance, for it was obvious that whatever were her antecedents they contained no experience of the perils and problems of ruling subject races. Her irresponsibility, they felt, arose from a lack of awareness, and could be corrected. Others decided she was 'on the make' and her motive was self-promotion, fuelled by a foolish disregard of the possible effect of her activities on the community. Appreciators and detractors of Freya thus polarised early, an aspect of her career that remained constant and provided the basis of her eventual cult.

Freya's skill in using a camera surreptitiously in situations of potential danger irritated the CID. Under cover of an *abba*, the loose enveloping black cloak worn by Moslem townswomen, Freya could merge unnoticed among the groups of her Iraqi women neighbours watching from their screened rooftops overlooking the streets. As the emotionally charged processions of Shi'as, with their squads of flagellants and bloodstained mourners wound through the alleyways of the city, Freya managed to get a series of sixty photographs depicting the incidents of the passion play for the *Illustrated London News*. Some years previously, she wrote home exultantly, an American consul had been torn to pieces by an excited mob in Teheran for doing just this. Such advertised exploits did not impress Vyvyan Holt. He remained disappointingly unenthusiastic; this made his subjugation all the more necessary.

In May 1932, however, Freya got a real journalistic break, and it came through Captain Holt. It could be said that her future as a Middle East expert owed its kick-off to him. This was the year in which, under the second Anglo-Iraq Treaty of

1930, the League of Nations' Mandate to Britain expired, and Iraq was admitted to the League of Nations as a sovereign state. It was a year of unrest and nervous tension among the racial and religious minorities incorporated within the artificial boundaries of the Kingdom. The Kurds, whose nation straddled mountainous northern Iraq and Iran and eastern Turkey, once more sought independence through rebellion, while the Assyrian Christians, favoured by the British as a useful balance to the predominantly Moslem Arab element, and formed into military Levies officered by Britons, now threatened mutiny. They, and other religious communities, feared for their safety under an Arab government; their fears were justified, as large numbers of Assyrians were massacred by the Iraqi army in the following year. The steps taken to contain these threats to the stability of the Kingdom by troops brought in from India leaked out through the new foreign diplomatic missions, and excited newspaper interest abroad.

The uprising in Kurdistan began at the end of 1931 but news of it was officially suppressed, and such information as filtered out of the area was meagre. But the capture of two RAF airmen shot down on a bombing mission by the Kurds, whose release was discreetly negotiated on the spot by the Kurdish-speaking Captain Holt, attracted Freya's interest. To Holt's fury, she picked up the story from gossip among the official community's womenfolk, and suggested she go up independently to the north of the country, to see for herself what was happening. Her editor on the *Baghdad Times*, a hard-bitten Scot, was too experienced a man to risk his own position with the authorities by such a venture. The official policy was to discourage journalistic initiative, and care was taken to see that nothing slipped out through the Baghdad paper's link with the London *Times*. Freya got nowhere when she tackled Ludlow Hewitt, the Air Vice-Marshal in charge of operations.

It was the ingenious Captain Holt who came up with a compromise solution. Of course Freya couldn't go up to the war zone – that was a monstrous suggestion, but it *might* be possible to have the campaign explained to her, and maps of the terrain and photographs found for her by the RAF Information

Directorate, so that she could put together an article for *The Times*, clamouring in London for news, and drawing attention to a rather awkwardly managed campaign at a time when government policy in the Middle East was being questioned in Parliament.

Things now became wonderfully simple for Freya. The air force fell in with Holt's suggestion, and supplied her with photographs and maps, and the Air Vice-Marshal himself provided titbits of local colour for the story. Two articles appeared under her name in *The Times*, and a correspondence ensued in its letter columns. Freya's name was brought before an influential public, the British handling of the affair, despite what Freya might say in private to her mother, received a good report, and the *Baghdad Times* kept its nose clean.

It was all rather cosy. Captain Holt with oriental *finesse* saw to it that there was something in it for everyone, and Freya was cock-a-hoop at her success. 'I *am* pleased about *The Times*,' she wrote to her mother on 30 June. 'The style is not all mine, but has had assistance from various official quarters. It is rather fun to be the first female war correspondent for that paper. What a lot of different things I have done since July last: one map for the War Office, penetration of Luristan, delivered a lecture, taken to journalism, and been Special War Correspondent. What next I wonder?'[3]

Purists might say she had sacrificed integrity for personal advantage, but I doubt if she even thought in such terms. Freya wasn't interested in ethics or in journalism, she was interested in earning money and 'getting on'. And if she thought at all about Captain Holt's role in the matter, she probably saw it privately as a personal tribute to herself, providing a useful step up the ladder of Fame.

A friend of Viva Jeyes, Flora's friend from the first years of her marriage, who had met the Starks on the Riviera, arrived in the summer of 1932 to take up an appointment in the Baghdad courts as a judge. Eric Maxwell came without his family, who had no desire to submit themselves to the discomforts of the Baghdad summer, but bought himself a car, with a view to

extensive touring. Unconventional though it might be, Freya
was quite happy to go off with him for a week to visit the
Chaldean Bishopric at Senna and to see something of Kurdistan.
It was heaven to get up into mountain air after the stifling heat
of Baghdad. But what started so gaily ended miserably. The
car kept breaking down, Freya lost her camera, Senna was
disappointing, Kurdish dress banned by central government, so
that the ethnic identity was lost. Worse still, not only did her
companion ignore her travel expertise, so that none of her plans
to sneak across the Iraq frontier into forbidden west Kurdistan
materialised, but he also made amorous overtures to her.

The trip, instead of being a carefree jaunt at someone else's
expense, became a dispiriting occasion for irritation, snap-
pishness, and the sense of being harassed by a nice, unobjec-
tionable man who couldn't see what Freya was upset about.
Even learning to drive his car was no compensation for such
an ordeal. She confided to Venetia:

I have been dreadfully harassed by an old friend who, in spite
of wife and family (whom he has fallen out with), went off his
head and wanted me to care about him – and I find in myself
a host of old-fashioned ideas on morals that I had hardly
suspected. He says in fifteen years' time I shall be horrid
and soured for want of a husband. Do you think this is so,
dear Venetia? Shall we be two sour old maids together? What
shocked me as a matter of fact was not the fact of his being
married so much as the want of restraint – which seems to
me to distinguish love from lust. True love can wait and
master itself and live even on a shadow: or that is what I
believe. And I feel I could get no happiness in a relation which
was not tranquil and clear as well as passionate . . .[4]

To her mother she was more explicit.

Eric came three times and asked to be forgiven, and I did so
but refused to go out riding or driving with him. I think it is
better to see him as little as I can. It is all so painful . . . He
evidently *cannot bear* not to have all he wants. Even if there

were no other obstacles I could not respect such a man for long. I feel I don't want to go anywhere or see anyone this winter, just sit quiet and do Russian grammar after so horrid an experience. I feel absolutely *defiled*, not because Eric is a married man, but because it is not love, just a sort of delirium that has seized him.[5]

Like some affronted goddess of mythology, Freya punished her tormentor cruelly for his presumption, and for the emotional stress he caused her. No attempt was made to mask the pointed quality of her refusal to associate with him; she turned down invitations, and ostentatiously avoided him in company. In a small society such as Baghdad's senior official community, this behaviour was painfully discriminating, and hard on the victim. In the end his wife took pity on him, and came out that winter to give him countenance.[6]

After such an experience, Freya's second entry to Luristan in September 1932 was the kind of romantic escapade only too likely to appeal to her. She wrote mysteriously to her mother of secrecy and risk, and jumped at the prospect. 'Most exciting thing has happened. I am on the track of hidden treasure. Don't please mention to *anyone* for a few months.'[7] The trip was set up in the intelligence community, which supplied her with a guide and a story of an exiled Lurish chieftain's treasure hidden in a cave somewhere in the hill ranges divided from Luristan proper by the Saidmarreh river. The attempt ended in anticlimax. Freya crossed the frontier into Persia bundled up on a donkey, clad in a flowery Arab dress and with an *abba* pinned close under her chin, with her guide and two other Lurs returning to their homeland after working as stevedores about the Baghdad quaysides added to her party. As their own papers were in order they sensibly insisted on crossing at a recognised frontier post. After a week travelling through the scantily populated foothills to her guide's tribal homeland, encamped at night by the fires of Lurs wandering with their flocks, Freya and her companion were detained by a mounted police patrol and taken to headquarters at Pusht-i-Kuh, the provincial capital, to await instructions from Teheran. It was all very friendly and unthreat-

ening, but Freya was questioned about antiquities by the Chief
of Police. The appearance of guileless eccentricity and amateur-
ishness she projected disarmed but did not deflect the Persian
authorities. After four days sitting about the dusty little town
awaiting instructions from Teheran, she was escorted courteously to the nearest border post by a mounted sergeant and
three policemen, and put over the frontier to Iraq. It was a
pleasant four-day ride across lovely country, but in the opposite
direction to that in which she had planned to go. However, she
told Venetia and Flora, she had brought back enough material
to map two unsurveyed valleys and she hoped she had 'got
some interesting information though nothing to what so easily
might have been – and me on the edge of it all . . .'

Freya's small, stained notebook recording this journey is
among Sir Sydney Cockerell's papers, not in the Fitzwilliam
Museum alongside C. M. Doughty's manuscript of *Arabia
Deserta*, which she believed was to be its destination when
she gave it to Cockerell. It is a sketchy, smudged, pencilled
aide-mémoire rather than a detailed record. That was compiled
on her return to Baghdad when her patrons showed her a route
report and asked her to do something similar.

It has been suggested in this generation that Freya was the
first 'modern' traveller, a forerunner of the hippies wandering
in Whitmanesque freedom across the landscapes of Asia. Some
admirers have linked her to the American tradition of the mystical fusion with Nature of Thoreau and Kerouac, rather than to
the activities of Kipling's Kim, whose author harnessed *his*
talents to the government of India's Intelligence Department.

The truth of Freya's inner life probably lies somewhere
between these two extremes. 'If I could choose a reincarnation,'
she wrote in 1950, 'I should be a surveyor; even with an elemen-
tary knowledge, a new feeling for *form* in country, the climax
of the watershed, the intricacies of contours that determine the
meandering of streams, the tilt and exposure of slopes that
mean woodlands or erosions, gave and still give me unspeakable
delight . . .'

The actuality of Freya's experience was that in the 1930s

she was a late entry into a game already in the process of being superseded by modern technology, first by aerial survey and photographic reconnaissance, pioneered in World War I, now by electronic devices. She came in under the cloak of the Royal Geographical Society's scientific interests. They taught her the elements of surveying, but her real use was as a humble intelligence gatherer travelling and observing at a low level, and picking up gossip and news where it was difficult for an official to penetrate.

The men who befriended and made use of Freya in the 1930s were members of the intelligence community. The appreciation of her talents by her patron in the Middle East Department of the Ministry of Information in 1939, Sir Kinahan Cornwallis, dates from this period. The use made in North Africa by the French colonial theorist, General Lyautey, in the early 1900s of Isabella Eberhardt, a young Russian mystic and convert to Islam, may have coloured their imaginations, but Eberhardt went 'native' to an extent Freya never considered. 'Squalid' was her comment on the Russian's brief life. Gertrude Bell was a more likely model.

The Russian Revolution of 1917 had introduced a new element into the politics of the Middle East. As the oil industry in Persia and Iraq expanded, dependent for labour on wild tribesmen responsive only to their tribal chieftains, an obsessive fear of Communist infiltration and Bolshevik sedition dominated the British intelligence community. For men like Holt, discreetly putting together their networks of informants, through whom local feelings could be monitored, Freya presented a problem. The keeping of the tribes pacified and co-operative was the major preoccupation of the World War I political officers in the outlying districts, and this was imprinted on the minds of their successors in the Thirties. Gertrude Bell had set a precedent among influential Arabs for the intrusion in political matters of a woman, and there was a possibility that Freya might be credited with greater importance by her Baha'i contacts than she actually enjoyed. How to neutralise without scandal a woman with important metropolitan connections was a task to which Holt applied a subtle and discriminating intelligence.

Once, against his recommendation, she had accepted the job on the *Baghdad Times*, the ensuing contests between Holt and herself were less the joustings of courtly love, which is what she would have liked them to be, than a game of wits, Holt intent on controlling Freya's initiatives, Freya pursuing her journalistic career in defiance of official caution, while cultivating her social connections to ensure indulgence of her adventurous spirit. Circumventing Captain Holt added spice to the game.

Army officers like Holt seconded for political duties in Mesopotamia in 1918 were trained in the Indian government's frontier tradition where subsidies to client states were a regular item on its budget, and the playing off of one tribe against another was an accepted form of political intrigue. It rarely trusted natives to undertake such quasi-diplomacy; for this true-blue Britons were preferred. At a lower level, as early as 1844 the Geographical Survey of India had set up a special school at Dehra Dun to train native intelligence agents in surveying. These men, coded as 'pundits', were humble local employees of the Survey, who travelled anonymously through the borders of the sub-continent, avoiding officials and persons of consequence in the areas they passed through. Supplied with cleverly disguised surveying instruments, with a command of local languages, their work was almost entirely confined to the collection of topographical and ancillary ethnographic data. It was the reality behind the adventures of Kipling's Kim and his associates.

It was a well-entrenched policy of racial discrimination in which ideological sympathy had little part. Freya was sensitive about her status as an oddity in official eyes, and strove with all her might to be accepted as one of themselves by the people who ran the Empire. Being a pundit was not enough, once she recognised the subordinate nature of the role. She began to aspire to influence policy. It fretted her that she was not taken seriously and that her views were listened to blandly by people whom she met socially, while officially she was passed over. She hated the feeling that there were secrets to which she was not privy. It irritated her nerves and undermined her self-control, driving her into gestures of self-assertion frequently misconstrued by her associates.

Freya *knew* she had something to contribute, it was an intuition confided to her journal in 1929, that grew in the privacy of her own mind, and was fuelled by ambition as the tensions of pre-war diplomacy culminated in the state of war. Any personal loyalty was subsumed in a higher loyalty to her Ideal, a ragbag of borrowings and wishful thinking in which platonic symposiums, Christian brotherhoods, secret societies, the Empire and educational elites all had a part. Most importantly, this idealistic stance gave her an identity, and a cause to champion.

In her writing the deft concealment of the practical under the poetic increased as she aged, the mystical element gaining an increasing ascendancy over the factual. Her compromises to achieve recognition are what made her personality elusive and interesting. There was something in Freya's nature that made her reluctant to abandon the familiar, however unsatisfactory it might be; but the relentless drive of the talented adventurer pushed her irresistibly up the ladder. Her literary gift, never particularly valued by herself, was one of the rungs.

To go against Nature produces stress. One cannot help wondering how many of the ailments that accompanied Freya's adventures were psychosomatic in origin. The achievement of her programme of action brought tensions resolved in physical collapses and hospital. She suffered gastro-intestinal disorders, developed ulcers, her heart raced, her blood pressure sank. The solitary journeys she undertook were prefaced by feelings of depression and futility on the eve of departure, inner quailings of the spirit soon dissipated by the interest of the journey. Like Hans Andersen's Little Mermaid, she metamorphosed her singularity by forcing herself into another mould to entertain her Prince, but she walked on knives to do so.

Like the hero of some Edwardian romance, Captain Holt surfaces at intervals in Freya's correspondence, the subject of anxious consultation with her mother. Was he Freya's Prince, the secret prototype of the men of action whom she admired, whose friendship she valued, and whose mysterious reticences she never fathomed? The dandiacal self-control and impenetrable good manners of this caste of club-land heroes put up a barrier to intimacy which, for all her efforts, Freya could never get round.

Freya worked hard on Vyvyan Holt. She did all the things her compatriots did, attended race meetings and watched polo matches, even took up golf, in some fit of pique at his neglect. He was a Russian specialist, and spoke the language; this led her to follow suit, using the same White Russian teacher. She tracked him to Geneva, when he was an observer at the League of Nations Committee on Kurdistan, appearing with a suitable chaperone, a neighbour, Minnie Granville, for a week's stop-over from La Mortola en route to London. Yet it was all to no avail; some facet of his personality eluded her, and this left her defeated and depressed.

The tantalising shadow-boxing of such a relationship was to be repeated again in wartime Aden with Stewart Perowne, a blind-man's-buff in which Freya always appears the dupe. She kept her feelings to herself, her pride adjusted to a code of manners in which sentimental weakness on her part would have appeared ridiculous and out of place. The sado-masochistic element of this convention in the goldfish bowl of local society will be familiar to any student of the light romantic novel at the turn of the century.

In 1951, in her second volume of autobiography, Freya devoted quite a bit of space to the anonymous object of her infatuation, in which all the indications point to Holt. His reappearance in 1953, freed by the Russians at the end of the Korean war after having been given up for dead, was perhaps a little embarrassing, for he now disappears from the story. His health permanently damaged by captivity, he died in 1960.

SEVEN

HADHRAMAUT

Freya finished her job with the *Baghdad Times* and left Iraq in March 1933, touring through Syria and Transjordan unaware of the change in fortune that was about to overtake her. She reached Asolo at the end of April. It was Flora and Herbert Young, Robert Stark's old art-school chum, who broke the news to her that the Royal Geographical Society was about to award her the Back Memorial Prize for her journeys in Luristan.

On Freya, the RGS's recognition had the impact of a miracle. At last! It was as if the benevolent spirit of W. P. Ker was presiding over her destiny, for it was through his friend, Lionel Smith, that *Baghdad Sketches* had come to the Society's notice and received a favourable review in its *Journal*. From this, and her articles in the *Journal*, arose the decision to make her the grant.

It was a decision that shaped her destiny, for it made her a Traveller. Like an actor 'resting', she was in search of a part, and now she had found one. Before she had any considerable literary experience, she was accepted into the mysterious free-masonry of adventurous enterprise, and had its identity conferred upon her. It was what she needed. Freya that winter lectured to the Royal Central Asian, and in 1934, to the Royal Asiatic, Societies. The Back Memorial Prize was handed her by Admiral Sir William Goodenough, the out-going President of the Royal Geographical Society[1] in June 1933 while George Lloyd, a former colleague of Kinahan Cornwallis in World War

I and a future Colonial Secretary, presented her with the Royal
Asiatic's Burton Memorial Medal in October 1934, the fourth
person and first woman to receive it. One upshot of the prize
was her first proper book, *The Valleys of the Assassins*, published by John Murray in May 1934 and dedicated 'in loving
memory' to W. P. Ker.

In 1928 she had placed her article about her trek with Venetia
Buddicom through the Druze country in *The Cornhill* magazine,
which was owned by the firm of John Murray, and edited by
Dr Leonard Huxley, the father of Aldous, Andrew and Julian
Huxley. In 1929 she had placed another, written while on a visit
to her father in Canada, but it was painfully slow progress,
despite a previous introduction to Dr Huxley from Ker.

Dr Huxley's assistant on *The Cornhill* at this period was John
Grey Murray, a nephew of Sir John Murray, the head of the
firm, taken into the business to work his way up. It was his
task to assist Dr Huxley, and to clear his desk after his death
in 1933. Among the papers awaiting decision was some material
on travels in Persia from the Miss Stark who was about to
receive the Back Memorial from the RGS. She seemed worthy
of further attention. Expanded, her material could make a book.
The next time she was in London, young Mr Murray wrote,
perhaps she would call at 50 Albemarle Street? He would be
very willing to read manuscripts and advise about publication.

The relationship between a publisher and a successful author
is delicate, and each owes much to the other. The start of the
friendship between Freya and the Murray family is dateable
from a letter of 8 May 1933, when, on request, she sent Jock
Murray a copy of the original *Baghdad Sketches*, and a rough
map of her journeys in Mazanderan and Luristan. When they
met her appearance surprised him. Jock Murray was then
twenty-two, Freya a woman of forty. She was small, shy, English, yet oddly foreign; she had an engaging sense of fun, and
an unpretentious manner.

There was a lot of rewriting to be done before her work
passed the critical eye of her publisher.[2] Jock Murray as editor
steered the book through publication, selected her photographs
and arranged her publicity. It was advertised as travels in

unexplored Persia and was an immediate success, reprinted three times in the first six months of its existence, and is still in print in paperback, a recognised classic of adventurous travel.

By the time the book appeared Freya was in Italy, preparing for a follow-up adventure. She had elected to attempt southern Arabia, and set her sights on a journey northwards through the Yemen, an independent Arab kingdom on the Red Sea, with a view to tracing the route described in the ancient geographers, by which frankincense and myrrh, valuable commodities in the classical world, were carried northwards from Hadhramaut to Petra and the Mediterranean. The emporium of this trade, ancient Sabota, still unidentified, was believed to be Shabwa, in the western half of the Aden Protectorate, and as yet unentered by Europeans. By collating an early Arab map with the modern one, and meticulously filling in place names, Freya compiled a map of her own with more than five hundred names on it, and was confident she would trace the frankincense route of antiquity: 'and if I *do* succeed, it will lift the veil off quite a big little corner of historical geography,' she told Venetia.

The immediate literary and financial success of the *Assassins* book, and the encouragement of the geographical societies, put pressure on Freya to continue her adventures. It was what was expected of her, and however much she might have preferred to rest on her laurels, and enjoy her success, the need to consolidate her new identity forced her on. It was exciting and pleasurable to be a celebrity, and all sorts of distinguished people were ready to be helpful, and to put their knowledge and connections at her disposal. She did her homework in the British Museum, read up the ancient geographers, took copious notes, consulted scholars, looked up local botany, and generally prepared herself, so her mother wrote to Sydney Cockerell immediately after she sailed, better than she had ever done before. 'She worked hard to the very last minute . . . she plans a preliminary stay at Aden, from whence she can study conditions and possibilities better than from here . . .'[3]

Freya's apparent reliance on chance and on-the-spot decisions was underpinned by extensive preliminary activity.

She collected letters of introduction assiduously. Mary Sanders, the daughter of the painter Herbert Olivier and his wife Margaret, friends and contemporaries of her parents' youth, and now her neighbours at La Mortola, was married to an air-force officer previously stationed in Aden; she recommended Freya to the then Group Captain Portal – he was senior airman – and to a French trader, Antonin Besse – resident in Aden.[4] More importantly Lady Allenby wrote to Besse on her behalf, while a complicated series of connections arrived at through her mother opened the door for her with the Aden government.

At the beginning of the 1930s Lord Iveagh, the head of the Guinness family, had settled in Asolo. Here Freya and her mother Flora were now living, since 1926 sharing the house of their old family friend, Herbert Young, a fellow-student in the 1870s of her father, Robert Stark, at the Kensington School of Art and Design. Lady Iveagh in Asolo took an interest in Flora Stark's craft-work schemes for the welfare, training and employment of the young girls of the community and, when approached, was helpful about Freya's plans. Through her sister, Lady Halifax, whose husband was now Colonial Secretary, a way into Hadhramaut opened for Freya.

Hadhramaut was then part of the hinterland of the Aden Colony and a British Protectorate. It is the long coastal strip of south-western Arabia which faces the Indian Ocean between Bir Ali and the country of the Mahra, adjacent to Oman. Inland a rolling stony expanse of bare upland rises in steps to a plateau cut by the wide expanse of the Wadi Hadhramaut, to the north of which lies the southern edge of the great desert of southern Arabia, the Empty Quarter.

It was a land torn by tribal feuding, divided between two reigning dynasties, the Qu'aiti and Kathiri Sultanates, of whom the former ruled the seaboard and border abutting on the tribal states of the then western Aden Protectorate, while the latter held an enclave in the north and east, adjacent to the Mahra, with a string of towns hidden in the seclusion of the wide cultivated floors of the wadis, canyons where date gardens flourished, and where the tail of the monsoon rains and irrigation made farming possible.

Freya arrived in the Aden Colony at a period of change, when the supercession by the Royal Air Force of the military garrison, as in Iraq, was to herald a forward policy and an expansion of British peace-keeping into the independent Treaty Sultanates of the Protectorate. Strenuous efforts were to be made to effect durable truces among the tribes, apt to feud and to exact tolls on the transit of goods in the name of their own immemorial rights. These probably dated back to antiquity, when the incense cultivation and its harvesting and dispatch northwards was a monopoly in the hands of the inhabitants, and fiercely guarded against takeover by foreign traders.

Freya's arrival in the Aden Colony was well heralded. The Colonial Office was aware that the Nizam of Hyderabad, one of India's leading princes, recruited his personal bodyguard from Arabs of the Qu'aiti Sultanate. Lord Halifax's recommendation was sent to Sir Akbar Hydari, the Nizam's Prime Minister, with the request he write to the Sultan of Mukalla asking for introductions for Freya and assistance on her journey. The plan was to reach Shabwa and then proceed to the Yemen frontier, there to await permission to enter and proceed north. Six letters, decorated with crimson coats of arms, reached Freya in Asolo before she set out. 'They say that I am a lady of the Aristocracy and must be given two servants and two sepoys; this will have to be toned down to be useful: I shall take up poverty as a religious principle; there is nothing like making a virtue of necessity,' she told Venetia on 2 September.[5]

Freya arrived in Aden on 19 December 1934 and immediately deployed her letter of introduction to Antonin Besse. She could not have done better; she was at once adopted into the paternalistic ambience of his expansive personality, and had all the help he could offer placed at her disposal. She was tremendously impressed. It was a greater stroke of luck than she had imagined, for Monsieur Besse, a Provençal Frenchman of energy and individuality, was more than a mere trader, he was a merchant in the style of Conradian fiction, and his commercial empire extended over the whole area of the Red Sea, the Horn of Africa, and the southern shores of Arabia.

His warehouses, so Freya reported, were stacked with

commodities awaiting world-wide export, the recital of whose origins was enough to inflame the dullest imagination. Hides of all kinds – goatskins, sheepskins, leopard, gazelle, antelope, cheetah – were brought into Aden from Ethiopia, Eritrea, the several Somalilands, along with snake and lizard skins, and even the occasional otter. The best of the coffee crop from Yemen, and that of Ethiopia; frankincense from Hadhramaut and Somaliland, myrrh from Somaliland, beeswax from Ethiopia, the Sudan and Yemen; aromatic gums from Kordofan, opopanax, gum Arabic, methi, used in the production of perfumes and sweets, ambergris, civet, mother-of-pearl for button manufacture, dom-nuts; the network of native agencies and upcountry collection points operated by the firm of A. Besse is staggering.[6]

Parallel to these activities, Besse imported and distributed textiles, machinery, cars, tyres, radios, electrical goods, cigarettes, pharmaceuticals, air-conditioning, dyes and, most important of all, he held the agency for Shell petroleum products in the area, and the monopoly distribution of paraffin for lamps and primus stoves, the essential sources of light and cooking heat in the primitive economies he serviced.

Antonin Besse was a bigger fish than any that had hitherto swum into Freya's net. His situation in the British colony was anomalous; it was a convenient centre for his firm's headquarters, but he made no attempt to adapt to official expectations. He lived with his second wife, the Anglo-Scottish mother of his younger children, in the commercial district, Crater, well away from the British residential area at Steamer Point, in a house built by himself over godowns and storehouses, with offices on the first floor, sheltered by deep verandahs to keep out the glare of the sun refracted from its barren surroundings. Above, a commodious double-storeyed penthouse was the family residence.

He did not belong to the Union Club, the gathering ground of the British community, and drank only water, bottled in Egypt and shipped to him from Suez. He did not smoke, nor did he encourage his European employees to do so. This did not endear him to the luminaries of the Union Club bar, and Besse throughout his fifty years in Aden was the subject of a good deal of spiteful gossip, and of pinpricking surveillance of his trade practices by government agencies.

Freya's imagination was readily inflamed by such a personality. Power impressed her, and the sight of her host conducting his world-wide business, accessible at his desk to callers, yet quiet, definite and rapid in his decisions, had its effect on her. She was gratified to be admitted to the domestic intimacy of such an extraordinary man.

And it was useful. Besse took charge of her adventure, put her up in a flat, found her a teacher to polish up her Arabic, gave her a desk to work at in his office, a car to ride about in, and the benefit of his experience, as well as that of his dhow captains and suppliers. He took her scrambling among the volcanic rocks of the crater, and to swim in the bays off the small empty beaches of the shark-infested coastline. These were the standard offerings of Besse hospitality, along with excellent cooking, Wagner on the gramophone, earnest philosophic discussion and the reading aloud of favourite books after dinner. Evelyn Waugh has a charming account of Besse at this period in *When the Going was Good*[7] which entertained and pleased the original. Waugh's only inaccuracies are Besse's dress after bathing. He never wore crêpe de Chine shirts – his tastes were simple and modest – only Aertex cotton, and he would not wear, or allow his staff to wear, socks with shorts, no doubt on aesthetic grounds. His mercerised cotton stockings were specially made for him in India.

Aged fifty-seven when Freya arrived in Aden, he was a short, stocky man of driving energy; his was a testing nature with an obsessive attention to detail. He could be cruel, ruthlessly dismissive of anyone who failed to measure up to his expectations. Already a three-times millionaire, he had made, lost and recovered two fortunes since he arrived in the colony in 1899 as a junior employee in a trading firm, with no resources other than his energy and intelligence. To circumspect Britons Besse was an unscrupulous adventurer, and something of a mystery man; in Freya's eyes this made him even more interesting. His elder daughter, Meryem, kept house for him in the absence of Hilda Besse and the younger children in France, and was friendly and welcoming to her.

Freya's accounts of her reception imply an immediate intimacy, special to herself, but she was always prone to attribute what was general to the particular in her account of people's response to herself; and perhaps she was deceived over her host's attentions to one who came with such impressive credentials. Many others besides Freya had occasion to be grateful for the intellectual breadth that characterised the Besse household, a commodity rare in the outposts of any empire.

Freya remained in Aden for three weeks, put up by the Besses except for the last three days of her stay when she moved to the Residency, to be briefed on her journey by Colonel Maurice Lake, of the Political Secretariat. This was to do with the procedure to be followed when she reached the borders of Yemen. There was to be no question of slipping unperceived into the country.

Meanwhile Sir Bernard Reilly, the Resident – like Colonel Lake, a long-established Indian Political appointment – was writing to the Imam of Yemen's *wazir*, or Prime Minister, on her behalf. Freya's credentials, with Lord Halifax behind her, ensured some effort being made for her by the Secretariat. Besse told her mischievously that they were all rather relieved to find her an ordinary human being, as they had so many letters announcing her arrival they feared she might come demanding trains of camels, and be a dreadful nuisance.

It was perhaps with relief that they saw her taken under Besse's wing; it saved a good deal of trouble. She left Aden on the night of 13 January 1935 in one of his steamships, bound for Bir Ali and Mukalla, where her journey inland would begin. It was all wonderful. She had slipped through the obstructive mesh of tepid official assistance, and was entering Arabia in the most romantic circumstances, an independent traveller carried forward on a network of indigenous contacts. Besse's agent met her at Mukalla, she was housed in the Sultan's guest-house, a beduin escort was provided for her six days' donkey ride over the rolling upland country – the Jōl – of the plateau, to the high, sparsely populated Du'an, with little towns hidden in the clefts of its great wadis. It was an experience on a par with the first enchantment of her journey in the Hauran in 1928. She revelled in the strangeness of her surroundings, the beauty of moonlight flooding the empty, mysterious countryside, the quiet, subdued awakenings in the cold grey morning light before the sun came over the horizon.

No-one was better equipped than Freya to respond to such an adventure. The very fluidity of her personality, her capacity to lose herself in an experience, was her passport. Imaginative sympathy coloured every perception, and endowed each incident with significance, and her companions with delightful interest. It was the heightening of her powers of observation and awareness that, distilled into prose, made her a writer; a celebration of life, affectionate and disarming.

Freya's progress through this wild country was very different from poor Doughty's travels in Arabia Deserta when, friendless, despised, unspoken for, an Unbeliever in a fiercely xenophobic society, he struggled across the stony steppe-lands of northern Arabia at risk of life. Freya's journey to the Wadi Hadhramaut and its hidden cities was organised for her by Besse, a man far more familiar with the intricacies of its local politics and the resources of its inhabitants than the British officials hundreds of miles away in Aden. Primitive and rough though it might seem to people at home, she was travelling as a person of importance, the Nizam's recommendation to the local Sultan ensuring her hospitality and safe conduct along the route, while the power and commercial influence of Besse, and the distant threat of the Aden government, guaranteed her a welcome among the wealthy Hadhrami merchants of the interior.

She reached Masna'a in the Du'an on 27 January, and was hospitably received by its Governor. There was an RAF emergency landing ground on the plateau, marked by whitewashed stone cairns, but the agricultural population lived down below in the wadi, on the cultivated valley floor.

Too late, eating supper in the harem, she learned one of the children had measles. There was no doctor, she had entered a medieval world, and one had to get on as best as possible. Feeling increasingly ill, she visited, photographed, observed, endured, succumbed: developed measles with three days of high fever, and was looked after kindly by the ladies of the harem. On 7 February she felt strong enough to ride on to Hajarein, where a car had been sent to meet her, and bring her to the comfort and seclusion of Seiyun in the Wadi Hadhramaut, part of the Kathiri Sultanate, partially linked by an unfinished motor road to the coast.

Here the al Kaf family, wealthy Hadhrami merchants who owned hotels and businesses in Java and Singapore, looked after her. A powerful clan, progressive by inclination, they were the apostles of modernity in their native land, and responsible for the unexpected amenities of the interior. Among these was a dispensary, staffed by an Afghan chemist trained in Aden, at Tarim, a neighbouring town, to which Freya was driven in an al Kaf car. There were eighty of these vehicles in the wadi.

Every luxury of modern life was provided by these wealthy cosmopolitan businessmen both for themselves and in their guest-houses, where the RAF air-crews flying in on training exercises put up, visible reminders of the distant Aden authority which sustained the al Kaf efforts to ameliorate the quality of local life. Far from being a primitive wilderness, the Wadi Hadhramaut had electricity, cool, clean guest-houses, with modern sanitation, swimming pools, gardens, a postal service and even a telephone network linking the towns of the valley floor. Freya regretted the new concrete villas, with their casino-like opulence of electric light and coloured glass, but she was glad enough of the amenities. The ancient unhygienic past lay all around, accessible to anyone who ventured into it, and Freya did not hesitate. The fantastic appearance of the women – their plaited hair, extraordinary make-up, brilliant silks and embroideries – their trailing outer garments and tall, witch-like straw hats – was too extraordinary a spectacle to pass up.

Shut away in the top terraces of the multi-storeyed buildings, their façades ornamented with whitewashed trims like wedding cakes, the harems had all the glamour of the exotic, and the homeliness of feminine preoccupation with dress, adornment, sexuality and children. Outside was the masculine world of politics, commerce and religious obligation; inside a hothouse of energies and inclinations destined for only one use, a monoculture of sensuality, whose only spiritual relief was religion, or ardent lesbian passions.

In such a society, Freya was a source of intense interest and bewildered curiosity. The only other European women they had seen were Mrs Theodore Bent in the 1890s and Doreen Ingrams, a tall, handsome, blonde woman, the wife of their Political Officer, who had recently returned to Aden after completing with him the first of the lengthy series of explorations of the territory which were to gain for them the Founder's Gold Medal of the Royal Geographical Society. Freya in her breeches and hat was a sort of raree-show, followed by crowds wherever she went, but that in itself suited her, and liberated her from the self-consciousness of her ordinary life. Accepted as some sort of a freak, an asexual solitary who by no stretch of the imagination could be considered a real woman, she moved between the male and female societies unimpeded, an eccentric apparition whose singularity absolved her from conformity with their own conventions.

Perhaps she overdid things. She visited, talked, filmed, explored the environs of the different towns. She still felt ill, and fluctuated between a sense of increased well-being and lassitude. She was dosing herself with emetine for dysentery, and anxious about the increasing heat and the prospect of a waterless journey to Shabwa. This was estimated by the local people to be three days away from Shibam. It was unlikely to be accomplished by Freya in that time. Her own accounts show she rarely achieved the schedules her guides considered as standard when calculating a journey.

Freya's adventure ended at Shibam; she never got to Shabwa. Her ambition to make her name as an explorer was thus denied the kudos of being the first European traveller to reach the fabled city. The elaborate arrangements to enter Yemen came to nothing too. She made a car drive from Seiyun to Shibam and a preliminary trip into the adjacent Wadi 'Amd to visit Hureidha, the jumping-off point for the next stage of her journey northwards, a small ancient town which was to feature in later exploits. This was to make certain her beduin camel men, who were to guide her to Shabwa and on to the Yemen border, were warned and waiting for her. A cursory look around the environs led to the confident report that she had discovered the site of the classically identified town of Andal, among the stones and traces of mortar on the far side of the wadi. She was later shown to have been mistaken. What she had seen was the remains of an ancient irrigation system.[8]

That was on 25 February. In Shibam, she had the use of

a charming little bungalow which is always lent to the RAF . . . with a lovely view. It is delightful, the valley open all round it and the skyscrapers of Shibam to the northwest: a little pool of water, pomegranates and palms. What one likes here about the green and growing things is that they are *clean*: I can't tell you what a strain it is always to be bothering about the dirtiness of objects: I almost wish I knew nothing about microbes and put it all down to God as they do . . .[9]

Installed in this haven, she began to feel increasingly ill. Shivers and 'peculiar and unpleasant pains' began. She feared malaria and, on top of the emetine she was already taking, she now added heavy doses of atebrin prior to driving to Hureidha. It is perhaps not surprising that her heart began to behave oddly, and that feelings of faintness and distress overcame her, aggravated by the demands of sociability in Hureidha. Back in the RAF bungalow she collapsed completely, her heart jolting and thumping in a frightening way.

On 9 March Freya wrote despairingly to Venetia Buddicom:

I have been very ill but am better now – heart went and for three nights was on edge of stopping. In what I thought my last moment I wrote to Aden and don't know what if anything they will do about it . . . You can imagine my sorrow at this illness, my Bedouin and all waiting ready. And now a last dramatic touch has added itself to my bitterness – a horrid stunting German who has already written a *cheap* book about this country, is here again, making for *Shabwa*! . . . I know it is vulgar to want just to *be the first*, but yet it is bitter when one has come so far, and but for this illness I would have been there five days ago . . . as a matter of fact, I had given up all hope, and would not have lived but for the Afghan chemist. Anyway, Shabwa or no Shabwa, I am glad to think I may yet be seeing you again . . .[10]

The Afghan chemist was sent for from Tarim. It was an anxious time until he arrived and diagnosed angina, and injected her accordingly; after four days the heart became more normal and Freya was able to move about, write letters, and read Nietzsche's *Zarathustra* borrowed from Anton Besse.[11] Messages had been sent to Aden asking for a doctor to come up with the next RAF flight, expected early in March. This arrived on the fourteenth, bringing a doctor who told her the heart muscle was strained and any further travel was out of the question if she wished to live. On 15 March she was flown to Aden, strapped into a stretcher in one of the bomber planes, and put into the government hospital.

Her misadventure attracted publicity, and was reported in the English papers, where her mother picked it up. There was a lot of fuss, as the Air Ministry had to authorise the mission before its aeroplanes could be used for the rescue. Lord Halifax telegraphed for news; Freya was described in the press as 'one of our most daring young explorers', an accolade made more bitter by the knowledge that while she lay languid and exhausted at Shibam, a young German, Hans Helfritz, had made it on his own to Shabwa.

Freya's lack of caution when treating herself for real or imagined illness was later to arouse comment on her second visit to Hadhramaut with the Wakefield expedition. The English doctors in Aden now told her there was nothing really wrong with her except absolute exhaustion, due to the measles and the fact 'that I was unable to diagnose the symptoms that followed them and did all the wrong things'.[12] There was nothing the matter with the heart; all she needed was rest and nursing.

The fiasco of Freya's journey to Shabwa in 1935 gains in perspective when seen as one of several attempts in the 1930s to reach the site of ancient Sabota. That of H. St John Philby, the foremost Arabian traveller of his day, was the most successful and the most scientifically rewarding. In 1936 he came down from the north to Shabwa through unsurveyed territory whose acceptance of Saudi Arabia's, the Yemen's, or the Aden Protectorate's authority was loosely dependent on current political events.

Shabwa lies roughly halfway down the Arabian peninsula between the Mediterranean Sea and the Indian Ocean, and was incidental to Philby's more ambitious plan to pioneer a motor route from north to south of the peninsula. This he accomplished over a period of some nine months in the course of which he surveyed tens of thousands of square miles.

The sparse local population of Shabwa maintained a pastoral lifestyle supplemented by earnings from salt mines whose product they traded north to Asir, and south to Hadhramaut. The rapacity and fierce dislike of intrusion of these descendants of the pre-Islamic people who operated the caravan routes of antiquity made any attempt to enter their territory risky. A hail of stones from the women, and shots from the men, was the experience of the few strangers who had got in sight of the place.

The leisurely approach of Philby's party, hunting and collecting natural-history specimens, and detouring to survey along its route southwards from Najran, had been heralded by beduin encountered on the way. The news lost nothing in the telling. Coming under the protection of Ibn Saud, now the dominant ruler in central Arabia, Philby with his two cars and his escort of twenty armed camel men in their distinctive Nejdi dress and trappings received a civil welcome from the inhabitants of the mud village straggling along its low, stony ridge. He spent three days exploring the ruin field, measuring and photographing the remnants of the stone-cut walls and buildings, the rumour of whose splendours had travelled in antiquity to distant Rome along with the spices and gold of the caravan trade. 'Of all Sheba's daughters,' he wrote, 'Shabwa was the shabbiest, like a harlot in her old age, poor and vicious and mean; the passing years had ravaged her youthful charm, the beauty of her prime had perished utterly as if it had never been.'[13]

In what Philby robustly presented as a personal piece of scientific exploration, funded by himself, and with no other aim than the extension of knowledge, others saw a sinister poaching on private preserves. The area was acquiring a topical interest as American pressure to open Arabia to oil exploration increased. Indeed, what Freya projected in 1935 as a romantic quest on her part to visit a lost city in the desert – a sort of updating of Lady Hester Stanhope's visit to Palmyra in 1820 – may well have received its original impetus from conversation in London with Sir Percy Cox, the new President of the Royal Geographical Society, while discussing what would constitute a notable journey. In his view, the south-western fringe of the Empty Quarter was the last unexplored area of the Arabian peninsula. This was the stone from which the spark of Freya's ambition to make her name as an explorer was struck. Nearly twenty years previously Cox had sent Philby from newly conquered Mesopotamia in the winter of 1917–18 on the first of his desert journeys across Arabia. Its object was to visit Ibn Saud, then a young tribal sheikh engaged in winning back his family's ancestral position in central Arabia by the might of his sword and the ferocity of his Wahabi followers. In 1934, unknown to Cox in London, Philby was already actively engaged in planning his north to south journey down the Arabian peninsula, under the patronage of Ibn Saud.

Philby, in 1936, reached Shabwa unaware that he had been preceded there by the German Hans Helfritz. By coincidence, a review of Freya's *Southern Gates of Arabia*, the account of her own abortive venture in 1935, was in a batch of back issues of *The Times* which Philby received before leaving Najran for Shabwa and the south. The reviewer had written, 'Miss Stark's objective was the ancient city of Shabwa, whose sixty temples the eye of an infidel has never yet beheld.' This turned out to be an adaptation of the last sentence in Chapter 25 of Freya's book: 'the ancient city with its sixty temples still awaits the traveller.' It was not until he reached Seiyun in the wadi, and was shown a presentation copy of the German's book[14] sent by the author to a local merchant, that Philby realised that the reviewer had been mistaken.

He himself, he wrote in *Sheba's Daughters*, did not read Freya's *Southern Gates of Arabia* until he had returned to Mecca.

It seemed strange to me that one who had heard so much of the local gossip should not have heard the tale of Hans Helfritz and his successful visit to Shabwa during the days when she herself lay seriously ill at Shibam . . . She knew of course that Helfritz was in Hadhramaut at the time, planning a visit to the same objective as herself . . . And she lets us see how strongly prejudiced she was against the man, whom she even refrains from naming in connection with this project . . .[15]

Philby found this rather shocking. He himself took his demotion from being the first in Shabwa with good-humoured philosophy, as Norman Stone Pearn records in his *Quest for Sheba* published in 1937. Pearn was a young Englishman, a romantic traveller like Freya, attempting Shabwa a year later from the south. With little Arabic and only a sketchy understanding of the country, he reached the inner recesses of the Wadi Hadhramaut then struck out for Shabwa with a party of two tribesmen, his servant and three camels. A day later he was abandoned by his people while lingering to take photographs, and was fortunate to be able to attach himself the next day to a party of woodcutters and to trudge back in their company to safety, and an eventual departure from Hadhramaut.

By the time I had picked my way through the timetables and accounts of the four attempts on Shabwa between 1934 and 1936, I began to wonder why anybody had bothered about such an unrewarding place and people. Philby, completely professional and intensely pragmatic, wrote off his disappointment in the context of his much larger and more important undertaking. Helfritz succeeded at his third attempt on Shabwa, to record in a series of excellent photographs what remained of the walls of ancient Sabota, before being driven off the site by its surly inhabitants. Philby, after a conscientious survey of the ruin field, concluded it was unlikely that even six, let alone sixty, major buildings had ever crowded into its walled circumference and suggested the district, rather than the site, might have contained the fabled temples; without scientific excavation the truth of Pliny's account will never be known.

In spite of her statement in her book that 'the ancient city . . . still awaits the traveller', Freya undoubtedly did know that Helfritz had got to Shabwa, as a published letter to Jock Murray dated 31 March 1936 proves.[16] Philby had an indulgent kindliness towards women travellers, and made no further comment.

Freya left Aden on 9 April 1935 on a wave of sympathetic friendliness. Everyone was very kind about her misadventure. Her old RAF acquaintance from Baghdad, Sir Edgar Ludlow Hewitt, out in Aden on a tour of inspection, waived the costs of the rescue mission. Only Colonel Lake was doubtful – in the pleasantest possible way – when he visited her in hospital, about the possibility of her being granted further permission to explore, and this depressed her and brought home a sense of failure. 'I suppose I have dished women's chance of going alone for at least half a generation,' she told her mother on 3 April. 'This is the really sad part about it all – and I can hardly bear to think of it.'[17]

But there were consolations. The year 1935 was momentous for Freya; it marked the transition from the private individual to the public personality. From the moment Freya was carried on a stretcher aboard the SS *Orontes* in Aden, under the fascinated gaze of the liner's passengers and crew, she was a celebrity. Put straight into the ship's hospital, and only carried up on deck each afternoon in the full flurry of invalidism, she was looked after by Meryem Besse, who accompanied her to Asolo.

Thanks to a letter from the archaeologist Leonard Woolley's wife to Cockerell, Freya's narrow escape from death in Hadhramaut was now an accepted part of her legend among her London friends. It added a heroic dimension to her exploit. Katharine Woolley had seen her in Aden hospital and wrote she looked rather well.

. . . Only her face was thin and she was in great spirits and we had a very good gossip. You will probably have heard what happened to her. After measles her heart gave out and she treated herself for malaria. Her life was saved by an Afghan chemist who saw it was heart and gave her the right injection. She had a bad fly back in the plane with a pulse 25 to the minute but she's being well looked after with English doctors, matron and nurses and lots of friends. Of course she is very disappointed for she was just on the edge of her adventure and there were no difficulties.[18]

What was said in Hadhramaut was not heard until the accounts by Norman Pearn and by Philby of their respective visits were published in 1937 and 1939. They reported that the general view among the Hadhramis was that she had not listened to advice about the measles, and had insisted on washing – with scented soap too! – and this had occasioned the collapse. Philby also noted that the rivalry to be the first to reach Shabwa between Freya and the young German had provided, within the bounds of politeness, welcome entertainment for the people of the wadi. In view of the nature of Shabwa and its inhabitants, this no doubt appealed to the sardonic strain in Arab humour.

PART THREE

ASSERTIONS OF IDENTITY
1936–1938

EIGHT

ANTONIN BESSE AND
VENETIA BUDDICOM

Perhaps Freya's most important acquisition in 1935, apart from publicity from her Hadhramaut experiences, was her acquaintance, rapidly developing into admiring friendship, with Antonin Besse. Resistant as a boy to formal education, Besse had formed himself as a young man in the rough and tumble of Red Sea trading in the 1890s by the unfettered use of a keen and intelligent mind, backed by a wide programme of reading. This element of self-education was something shared with Freya. It may account for the eclecticism of their views, and a tendency to uncritical admiration of what they believed were superior minds. In Besse this developed a personality of considerable forcefulness and imaginative subtlety, whose creative flair was expressed through the medium of his trading empire. He admired energy, enterprise and independence, qualities in which he himself excelled. Perhaps he recognised them in Freya's strange little person, though he may have been influenced by the combination of her powerful metropolitan connections – outgunning provincial Aden – and her eager falling-in with his views. He was human and liked to be loved. His benefactions, always anonymous, and always practical, were spread through all the elements of the cosmopolitan Aden community. On news of his death in 1951 reaching the colony, offices and shops closed spontaneously.

An ardent supporter in his youth of the Dreyfus cause, his intractable temperament did not adjust easily to the constraints imposed on its activities by bureaucratic officialdom. In the hard years of his young manhood the writings of Frederick Nietzsche were read and reread, a powerful stimulus to his own formation, and productive of an outsize personality daunting to weaker natures. A labour of love, spread over many years, was the translation into French of Kipling's poem 'If'.

The turnover of his European employees was often rapid. Not all the young men found for him by his London office and the Universities Appointments Board were prepared for the patriarchal style of their employer's organisation. Besse could be scathing about their social pretentiousness and general use-lessness.

It was not his nature to mix other people's designs with his own interests; nor did he lend himself to commercial initiatives for political ends. This may account for the somewhat priggish suspicion with which his activities were regarded by the Political Secretariats of the British possessions in the area. It was entirely in keeping with his personality that he should trump his detractors' spite, shortly before his death, by the anonymous gift of one and a half million pounds to found St Antony's College, Oxford, opened in October 1950 and now a centre for Middle East studies. He hoped it would inculcate in its students the virtues he believed essential for the formation of a superior person. These he defined as 'Public Spirit, Sense of Justice, Ability to state facts precisely, Ability to follow out what he believes to be the right course in the face of Discomforts, Hardships, Danger, Mockery, Boredom, Scepticism, Impulses of the moment . . .' An attempt by fundraisers to extract a further £250,000 from him produced fiery indignation and a refusal.

How much commercial rivalry, how much humanitarian conviction contributed to Besse's antipathy to Italian colonial methods in the Horn of Africa and to his supply of arms to local irredentists cannot be estimated. Mussolini's policy of colonial settlement by Italian nationals did not favour interlopers. Whatever the cause, by the time Freya reached Aden towards the end of December 1934, nothing was too bad to be believed about the Italians in the Besse household, nor of the iniquitous oppression and brutality of Fascist-style colonisation.

Freya absorbed uncritically all she heard, and lost no time in ramming home the stories to her mother in Asolo. Besse's influence was very much in the ascendant when Freya returned there from Aden in May 1935. Venetia now became the recipient of her confidences. It was to her Freya recommended the reading of Nietzsche's *Zarathustra* which had been her support during her illness in Hadhramaut. 'Not a book for the weak and sentimental but a great book,' she wrote from Shibam in a postscript to a letter in February 1935. 'I have been fortifying myself with it in moments of weakness. I have come to the conclusion that I am poor in courage really – all I have is a certain obstinacy, but not that serene cheerfulness which one should have to face death if it comes.'

The Nietzschean injunctions to be strong, to be hard and so forth, which so impressed her in Aden, did not obtain the same sympathy from her in Mussolini's Italy, when, transformed into uplifting patriotic slogans, they appeared on walls and buildings to exhort and prepare the nation for the impending conquest of Abyssinia. It was not long before Freya's denigration of Italian patriotic fervour and her accounts of atrocious behaviour in Abyssinia caused difficulties.

Freya's excitement over Besse had a distorting effect on her judgment. No story was too sensational to repeat. This gave rise to gossip, whose expanding ripples eventually reached the Fascist provincial authorities in Treviso, from whom a warning was indirectly conveyed to Flora. It was an ominous indication of future trends, disturbing for foreigners dependent on the toleration of the host country, and Flora exerted herself to obtain a written denial in Italian from Freya of the remarks and actions – in which photographing Fascist slogans and inscriptions figured – which were attributed to her.

Throughout this period Freya's enfeebled health, and the need for a quiet life, play a considerable part in her correspondence. Despite repeated assurances from the various doctors in Aden, Italy and England whom she consulted that her constitution was sound and there was nothing wrong with her heart, the status of invalid was firmly established in her own mind, and enforced with plaintive fortitude on those surrounding her.

Much of it probably had to do with the Hadhramaut fiasco, and anxiety about her future. There was a book, *The Southern Gates of Arabia*, to produce for Murrays – Jock Murray had already been to Asolo to talk about it – photographs to sort through for another book, *Seen in the Hadhramaut*, and a lecture to prepare for the RGS on 16 December 1935, as well as occasional journalism and BBC talks.

An invitation from the Besses to stay with them on their estate in Provence came as a welcome escape from Asolo and from playing second fiddle to her mother. She expressed this to Venetia on 9 July, while awaiting the arrival of Antonin Besse by car to fetch her.

> I think the saddest thing is when on the really deep subjects one is at variance with one's own people. Mama and I have really been on opposite sides, first in the war when she was swayed by her sympathy for my brother-in-law in favour of all the Italian *imboscati* and anti-war egoists of that time: and now she is really at heart with the Italians, or at least not against them . . .[1]

Freya was switching her emotional dependency at this period towards Venetia. She writes of the two joining forces and retiring together, of spending their lives between Penbedw and Asolo, as if failure to impress Flora with her new discoveries had set in motion a process of wounded affront, to be compensated by alternative reinforcement. Many years later, speaking of the Stark mother and daughter, Mme Hilda Besse recalled how surprised she had been by the intimacy, affection and frankness of the letters to her mother published by Freya in her old age. It had not been the impression in 1935 and 1936; the daughter, she said, was frequently at odds with her mother, who was the larger personality. This was an observation confirmed by the late Gerald de Gaury, who visited and stayed with the family both at La Mortola and in Asolo in the 1930s. The superficial manner between mother and daughter might be 'very lovey-dovey', in his recollection, but there was no question of who was the dominant personality. That was Flora. He

recalled Flora's eagerness to be helpful as a notable characteristic. 'She was the kind of woman,' he said, 'who if there was
a dish or pudding you particularly liked, always took care to see
it was served next time you visited . . . I still have a recipe for
painting in tempera,' he added, 'which she gave me when I
expressed an interest in that technique. She looked it out and
copied it for me before I left . . .'[2]

All in all, Freya's return home was not a great success. Balked
of an audience at the Villa Freia, she concentrated on Venetia,
urging her to meet the Besses when they were in London in
June. The meeting was duly recorded in the correspondence of
the two women, and pleasure and satisfaction at the connection
was expressed.[3] On that front all was smiles and Freya eagerly
awaited the arrival of Monsieur Besse by car in July to carry
her off to his family house on the French Riviera coast. They
set off together on what appears to have been a magical journey,
dropping Flora off en route to be with her Italian grandchildren,
and crossing the western Alps at Barcelonette and so down to
the coast through the wooded hills of the Côte des Maures. It
was a long drive. Freya, writing in 1953[4] after Besse's death,
recalled it as an enchantment. Exposed to the full force of her
host's virile charm, she finished the journey *tête-à-tête* with him,
and was welcomed into the patriarchal hospitality of Le Paradou
by Hilda Besse. She was to rest and convalesce with the family,
and in the privacy and quiet of the estate, settle to work on
her book.

On 22 July 1935 Freya wrote mysteriously from Le Paradou
to Venetia of a 'shattering crisis' she had just undergone, about
which she could not write but would tell Venetia in person. Five
days later she was shrugging off her previous mood with 'My
dearest Venetia, What *can* I have written to you? The crisis
was not financial and I am sailing into more peaceful waters; it
was just one of those Decisions which are apt to appear like
sudden dragons in one's path – and when the time comes, there
you are with the necessity for choice upon you, and nothing to
substitute it.'

Something had been said, or occurred, between Besse and

herself that agitated and alarmed her. Any transition from
flattering attention to direct sexual overture was likely to throw
her, and this seems to have been what happened with Besse.
It was an intrusion of reality into the reveries in which she was
apt to trace amorous designs in any sympathetic approach. That
Besse must be in love with her was a heady thought. Freya
consulted her mother, who counselled common sense and discretion, and a tacit ignoring of the incident. She retreated to
the protection of Hilda Besse and the family's company, and
the needs of her book. Besse's overture had taken her by
surprise, but she avoided further dangerous *tête-à-têtes*, and no
other incident is recorded in a stay extending over six weeks.

Besse was no fool where women were concerned, and, unlike
Eric Maxwell in Baghdad, knew better than to persist. In Aden
in the British community he had the reputation of being something of a stage Frenchman, apt to make overtures to any available woman, for the honour of France, so to speak. Privately
he liked to test people, to bustle them up into a corner, and
see how they got out of it. Some cynical curiosity was perhaps
satisfied, some boredom assuaged by these games. Though to
the unsophisticated he might appear a threat, to any woman
with an ounce of experience his opportunism was more of a joke.
He liked to dismiss sexual infidelity as something essentially
unimportant in the relations of men and women; it was a talking
point as much as anything.

Freya, anxious not to lose a useful connection, kept up the
pretence that nothing had occurred, and consolidated her position with Hilda Besse. Whether Hilda Besse observed anything
of this by-play one does not know. She was an intelligent woman
with a good understanding of her husband. As a widow, she
spoke of him with admiration and regret, and of Freya with
kindly sympathy. Freya liked the Besses, and liked what they
provided. Hilda Besse, she told Venetia, was pure gold, and
Besse was a very lucky man. She was happy at Le Paradou,
the weather was cooler, and she could work hard; the chapters
were coming along. But by the end of August she felt it wiser
to return to Asolo. 'I don't want to be caught there by any sort
of war – and so you *may* get an SOS and me arriving after any

time . . . I have now got to Chapter IX, but feel tired and *shock*; it is horrid to have no sort of elasticity to draw on and writing is a gruelling business . . .'

On 9 September she wrote from Asolo to her friend. 'My dearest Venetia, May I spend October with you, more or less? I have to be in London in November – and there is nothing to keep me here, and every reason to get away before I talk too indiscreetly.' She was reading, she added, T. E. Lawrence's *Seven Pillars of Wisdom*, a copy of which Venetia had sent her at Le Paradou, and signed herself 'Your own Freya'.

On 7 October there was a postcard from Alsace-Lorraine, where she was stopping off en route to England with the Schlumbergers, whom she had met at Le Paradou. Their son was an archaeologist in Syria, and this was a useful introduction for Freya. The postcard read, 'Venetia, I have had a touch of heart again from too hard work – so annoying – but will get right at Penbedw . . . Yours Freya.'

Freya stayed with Venetia at Penbedw until 10 November, when she went up to London and a round of visits prior to her lecture at the Royal Geographical Society. This was on 16 December 1935. Her nourishment supplemented by Venetia's housekeeper with egg-nogs (two eggs beaten up in a glass of port) three times a day, and treated as an important invalid, Freya soon recovered form and had produced a total of twenty-two chapters by the time she left for London. There Rhuvon Guest, the elderly scholar and Arabist who had helped her with her original researches into Hadhramaut history, corrected her manuscript. There was quite a lot to do.

Freya's lecture was a resounding success, her slide show novel and impressive. She dined before the lecture with the President, Sir Percy Cox, and twenty-five distinguished gentlemen. Sir William Goodenough wrote later to say that no woman since Gertrude Bell had been given such a reception – the lecture room was packed. It was a wonderful triumph. Colonel Lake was in the audience, and spoke after Freya, 'and said nice things'. Feted everywhere and emboldened by success, she attempted to extract higher royalties from Murrays for the new book – fifteen per cent on the first 3000 rising to seventeen and a half per cent for the second, and twenty per cent for the third. She also received an advance of £150, which was immediately invested.

By the New Year 1936 she was back in Penbedw, having cancelled all her engagements, and committed herself to three months' rest. 'Venetia has put her foot down,' she told her mother.[5] 'The doctor spoke seriously to her and told her I *must* have three months' absolute rest and nursing.' General exhaustion was diagnosed, hardly surprising in view of the demands she was making on herself, parties in London, twenty-five pages of lecture to learn by heart, 170 Christmas cards to send off, 'along with twenty parcels and I don't know how many letters'.

Freya's talent for public relations was now fully engaged, her enormous correspondence a feature established for the rest of her life. Every day notes, letters, cards, flew from her pen, charming, affectionate little communications in which a touching gratitude for hospitality received flattered the recipient, from the heroine of such original adventures. It added a wistful dimension to her personality which stimulated the chivalry of men brought up in the Victorian tradition of respect for womanhood.

Jock Murray came up to Penbedw to discuss her book with her. *The Southern Gates of Arabia* was completed by February 1936. Freya dealt with proofs, captions, references, bibliography, and all the tedious follow-up that accompanies the acceptance of a manuscript. Bulletins as to her health went out to her correspondents, and were passed about among her friends; Freya's undiagnosed ill health provided an excuse for remaining where she was. She wrote from Penbedw in March 1936:

My dear Jock, I waited before sending this to see the doctor, who has just been with the results of the Liverpool people's researches. [Sir William Goodenough had suggested she consult a specialist in tropical diseases there.] It seems to be chiefly anaemia, and absolutely nothing organic, except the effects of sheer exhaustion . . . they say it means a quiet life for the rest of this year and alas no Shabwa in the autumn. Let us hope no-one will think of going till after 1937.

The Southern Gates of Arabia was to be published at the end of May 1936. Freya stayed on at Penbedw until early May when she moved to London to be on hand for the launch of her book, confidently predicted a success by Jock Murray. Unlike last time with the *Assassins*, when she was at home in Asolo preparing for her Hadhramaut venture, Freya wanted to be on hand for all the fun. Now she was installed for a month in Sister Agnes' fashionable nursing home in Beaumont Street, arranged for her by Venetia's doctor, with visits from a heart specialist an additional reassurance. Here she was able to go shopping, and to take walks in the park. 'Dear Sir Sydney,' she wrote to Cockerell, 'I am in this nursing home for a month, but not too ill to see friends or even to walk about in the Park at a very slow rate – so if you are in London please come and talk to me. They have found the trouble at last – not heart at all: but the heart is a little tired at doing other people's work for over a year.'

Where the truth of Freya's ill health lies will never be known, but immersed as I was over several years in her history the feeling grew in me that she unconsciously produced symptoms – along with nostalgic regret and other tender feelings – to generate indulgent pity in her friends and secure their attention.

It was as if this was the only means she had of signalling distress, a return to the blissful period after her accident in childhood in Piedmont. Then her disfigurement and pain concentrated her mother's attention entirely on herself and she experienced for the first time the warmth and well-being of loving something outside herself. Release into gratitude and love, triggered by the comforting kindness of another's concern for the sufferer, is something many women experience for their attendants in childbirth. In Freya this sense became an appetite that had to be fed, so that when real relationships failed, other objects of affection had to be generated.

She was a master of pathos and of self-suggestion, but the fact remains that her constitution was sturdy, her heart strong, and she has outlived all her contemporaries and many of her younger friends. Her appetite and mobility have remained, only the faculties have decayed.

It had been planned before Freya left Penbedw that Venetia should come to London to share in the fun of the launch of Freya's book. The Besses always came to England in June, and Freya in the Beaumont Street nursing home eagerly awaited both Venetia and Anton Besse's arrival. On 31 May she was badgering Jock Murray for a copy of the *Southern Gates*, so as to have it at hand for the visit she expected on Besse's arrival on 10 June. She waited in for him that evening, but was disappointed. Instead, he took Venetia out to dinner, and then called the next day, with his daughter Meryem, at Beaumont Street, to tell Freya about his evening, mentioning too that Venetia would be going to hear *Tristan and Isolde* at the Opera that night.

Besse's capacity to strike like a snake when disappointed in an individual was well known to his staff. At first Freya had only enjoyed his generosity; now she was to experience a different side of his nature. His visit on 11 June, chaperoned by his daughter, was conducted with a formal politeness that served notice of the withdrawal of intimacy and prevented any sort of scene. It was guaranteed to cause maximum discomfort in Freya, which is what he probably intended. He took the ground from under her feet by telling her about his evening with Venetia, while doing nothing to reassure her as to his relations with her friend.

Freya felt very threatened. The sense of being shut out of a relationship was something she could not bear, it activated feelings of insecurity rooted in the events of her girlhood. With unerring malicious precision, Besse injected his dart, and left Freya a prey to every sort of disagreeable emotion, among which jealousy loomed large. Her emotional storm, however, was reserved for Venetia, and not directed at Besse. If he had intended to cause trouble, he succeeded. She wrote to Venetia, 'I waited for him all that evening while you were dining together, and I heard of it only the next day *from him.* I asked you later hoping it was a mistake; a word from you beforehand would have saved that last humiliation of feeling that things were not being told . . .'[6]

She left next day for a round of country-house visits, and to sit for her portrait to Lord Methuen at his house in Wiltshire.[7] Venetia did not come to the station to see her off. She cut short her stay in London and returned to Penbedw cross and upset by the drama. Things were not improved by Besse's pursuit of her there, when he arrived with the intention of making some sort of declaration, and was repulsed with difficulty. The annoyance occasioned by the theatricality of this behaviour possibly strengthened Venetia's decision to distance herself from Freya and her concerns. By nature reserved and private, such a drama was the last thing she needed.

After this first upset, Freya patched things up by letter. Excuses and self-justifications were interspersed with gossipy accounts of her activities and the interesting people she was meeting. She apologised for suspecting Venetia of duplicity. 'You must not think I minded your *going*; it was *not being told* that I minded, but this is all a fuss and the only abiding sorrow is due to my own mistake . . .'

This was rather Freya's way. Possessively jealous if she suspected an intruder was poaching on her preserves, she still did not like losing a friendship, and would take pains to knit up the skeins unravelled by her intemperance. Yet several intimacies were lost in this way. Not everyone could dismiss as easily as she did the stress of these episodes. This appears to be what happened with Venetia. Although she was generous to people she was fond of, and Freya had spent months at a time in her house, and was helped with hospital and other bills, perhaps she felt she had done enough. In later life she never discussed her association with Freya. One of her few recorded utterances on the subject was that if there was only one animal to ride, Freya was always on it.

The revengeful spite with which Freya later wrote of this episode during Venetia's lifetime supports the idea that she was the one who was dropped. As her own fame increased, she apparently felt no compunction at leaving her friend behind.

They still met occasionally in London, and a somewhat stilted correspondence was maintained spasmodically into the war years. But for Freya the enchantment was ended, and she was cold and aloof, fixed in her belief that she was the injured party. Nothing remained of the former confiding intimacy and warmth. Umbrage predominated.

Venetia's physique and health, patiently restored over a period of years by careful nursing, never allowed her to ride again, but she was able to run her estate with its fifteen tenanted farms, and raise sheep in partnership with her sister's godson. In 1961 she had a stroke which left her capacity for speech impaired, though her mind remained clear. She had to relearn the skills of walking, and of writing. Two years or so before her death in 1969, Freya reappeared at Penbedw for an overnight stay, the first visit for many years, possibly to retrieve her letters. The big late-Georgian mansion, remodelled in 1906, and its lavish conservatory, had now disappeared. Used as a Red Cross convalescent home in World War II, it had stood empty for five years, its panelled fitments auctioned off prior to its demolition in 1958. Venetia since 1953 had lived in an estate house at the back of the old Hall site.

This visit, unmentioned in Freya's published writings, is recorded in the Penbedw visitors' book.

In 1953, writing the third volume of her autobiography *The Coast of Incense*, Freya devotes a couple of paragraphs to the ending of a friendship which for thirteen years had been so important in her life. In an airy evocation of a lifetime of romantic involvements, the reference to the treachery of a woman friend is so specific that no-one knowing the past association with Venetia could have failed to grasp the allusion. Freya's story was that her friend poached an admirer from her and, though uninterested herself, refused to give him up. 'She rejected my appeal, and my whole world drowned. So much so that for many years I never trusted a woman again in any intimate matter . . . I still think that the general rule of women is the jungle rule, only to be mitigated, and that imperfectly, by advancing years, hopeless plainness, or the total elimination of men.'

The *Letters*, published more than twenty years later, when both Besse and Venetia were dead, tell a fuller story. Most mystifying are the references to Besse himself. 'AB and Meryem came this morning,' she wrote to Venetia in her emotion-charged letter of 12 June already quoted, '. . . I did not see him alone so that, even if I had felt able to face it, I could not put an end to things: and I have decided to wait. If you do not have him in Wales . . . I will go to Paradou, break it there more gently and so perhaps keep a friendship though all else must go.'

On 5 July she wrote again to Venetia.

. . . I do seem to have given and must rectify an unjust impression if I suggested he was ever morally fickle to Hilda. He gives little importance to the physical side of love, and I think he is right *so long* as the spiritual position is very rigidly kept in order; this he has never failed in with her, as far as I know . . . and if he had gone on caring for me, he would have been able to tell her as he promised – or I would. I don't think I have ever caused any woman a moment of real unhappiness – at least I would do anything to avoid that – but feeling as we did I think it was possible to make of our love a beautiful, creative and enduring thing for all three.

He is angry now with me for having withdrawn myself, and does not realise that, since he has swerved away from me in spirit, I *cannot* continue more than a true friendship but no love. The physical is unimportant, I do agree, but only on the condition that the spirit is *everything* and then there can be no compromise: if it is damaged the whole thing must stop at whatever price of pain, otherwise it becomes mere disorder and license. . . . Given a chance and a long time . . . a very tender friendship may return, but I know I must not compromise now, and if just friendship is not enough for him from me then everything must stop.

Freya's projection of herself as a woman of experience is not substantiated by any evidence. She was a nimble performer on several stages, a *comédienne* rather than an *allumeuse*, but a

cautious swimmer when it came to love. Besse was not the
first, nor would he be the last, of Freya's romances involving
prominent men. She liked, with women friends, to discuss marriage in a way that rather surprised her listeners. There was an
affectation of knowingness probably picked up from the harems,
where talk was much freer than anything likely to be experienced at that period in polite English society, though the garru-
lous preoccupations of Italian matchmaking in her youth – and
the talking up of possible options – may have contributed.

She was clearly more interested in sexuality in the abstract
than in performance, *amitié amoureuse* rather than the *coup
de foudre*. Death ended so many tender chapters in Freya's
reminiscences that in old age this cohort of phantom lovers had
become an accepted part of her legend, and enabled her to
pronounce with majestic authority on the conduct of younger
friends. The rebuttal by one god-daughter of her godmother's
qualifications to pass judgment in affairs of the heart produced
an angry reversal of favour.

More than half the first edition of *The Southern Gates of Arabia*
was sold before publication, and the book was recommended
by both the Book Guild and the Book Society. The reviews
were ecstatic. Sir John Murray told her 'it was nice to publish
a great book', while Sir Sydney Cockerell wrote that it would
rank not below but next to Doughty's *Travels in Arabia Deserta*
as a classic of travel literature. *The Southern Gates* was the
book which really established her reputation as a travel writer
and gained her a devoted following of admirers, enchanted by
her easy style and her fascinating insights into others' lives.

Freya, enjoying London in the early summer of 1936, busied
herself catching up with ideas being canvassed by new political
alignments. She was looking for an opening; the difficulty was
to find people prepared to take her seriously. Her knowledge
of England was very superficial. Her upbringing was cosmopolitan and she had lived abroad since a brief period in wartime
London in 1916–17. By 1935 the economy was picking up in
England, and Freya came fresh to a country where the leisured
classes still regarded politics – and imperial politics in particular

– as an hereditary occupation, which they alone were fit to direct.

She wrote to Venetia from Beaumont Street in May:

> Lady Iveagh came yesterday and said that if we *had* gone to war, the country would have jibbed. I don't really believe this (especially if one had manoeuvred the Italians into attacking) but I do feel this pacifist attitude is doing fearful harm . . . It is this wretched intelligentsia we suffer from; people who deal with disembodied ideas and have never in their life actually seen an action and its consequences side by side. I hope I may some day have a little influence in the world, some young people to feel that things are worth living and dying for, not just talking about . . . [8]

Freya as a child was deeply impressed by Charles Kingsley's *The Heroes* and the imprint remained. In summer 1936 the 'new imperialism' was being talked about in the anti-appeasement lobby forming around Churchill and his following of younger and more pugnacious Conservatives. Freya by now was a newspaper celebrity, her book reviewed in all the leading dailies and journals, her achievements praised and her presence solicited at a variety of social engagements.

She herself, though suitably overcome by the unexpectedness of it all, was beginning to feel she indeed had something to offer.

> The point is I feel that in this welter of matter-of-fact muddles the minds of people are craving for something brave and romantic; cleverness is going out of fashion, and the more fundamental values are coming back; and the voices of those who well or ill do stand for simpler and deeper things are coming to be listened to. This pleases me more than the personal success of the book. [9]

From the nursing home in Beaumont Street she wrote privately to Lord Halifax, giving him her thoughts on British relations with the Middle East. Nothing came of it. It was tantalising to be in proximity to the decision-making process, and yet be unable to influence it. It made her impatient, and gnawed at her self-esteem.

Freya's recommendations to Lord Halifax had all to do with appearances. Europeans, she said, were looked upon everywhere as people entirely bent on their own interests and out to exploit the native everywhere; there was no particular bitterness in this view, it was just taken as a matter of course. It would be far-sighted, from the point of view of Britain's position in Asia, to make a definite stand on Abyssinia, and not, by negotiating with Italy, allow the idea to take hold that Britain was just another European profiteer. Freya felt that by showing ourselves as different from the other colonial nations great advantages would accrue. 'This seems to me such an important gain from the point of view of the future, such a great step in our Imperial history that I have ventured to trouble you with this letter at this time . . . I am still rather ill,' she concluded, 'and spending a quiet country summer; not fit for serious travelling till next year I fear.'

'Giving a lead', '*Doing* something, not just talking', were cant phrases of the period, echoed in all Freya's pronouncements at this time. *Action* was the great thing, against the dictators, against complacent politicians, against social misery and deprivation. There were many options to choose from. Freya chose imperial politics, and the subtle allure of power and prestige which surrounded its practitioners.

From the moment her literary success was assured she committed herself to becoming an authority on Middle-Eastern affairs. It was an area she felt she could make her own. She promoted herself through journalism, lectures, radio talks and country-house weekends where politics were the common interest of the people assembled. It was a gamble, but she deployed her assets shrewdly. In February 1936 she put pressure on Jock Murray to reissue *Baghdad Sketches* under the firm's imprint. She was receiving tempting offers from other publishers, she told him. 'I can't remember if the House of Murray really had made up its mind about them – so am waiting to reply till I hear from you; I have an idea you said you *did* think of publishing them?' An expanded *Baghdad Sketches* was published by Murrays in 1937.

Before setting off in February that year for a four months' tour in the Middle East to work up extra material for its reissue, Freya noted 'with sorrow' that on studying the proposed agreement she found Murrays were offering less than for *The Southern Gates of Arabia*. 'You will have to give me the same royalty as *The Southern Gates*,' she wrote to Jock Murray, 'and you needn't give me any advance royalties . . . I hope this isn't going to ruin you – and if it is I will have to put up with what you suggest: but I will always remind you that the nice man I met at dinner and whose name I can't remember offered me more, and I'm sure this will give you pain. Yours ever affectionately, Freya.'[10]

Freya's long ascendancy over her publisher had begun.

NINE

HADHRAMAUT AGAIN

Freya first met the archaeologist and prehistorian Gertrude Caton Thompson at Sydney Cockerell's house in Cambridge in November 1934, prior to her departure to Aden. Freya at this time was gathering all the information she could about her proposed objective in Hadhramaut (which she had christened the Incense Route of Antiquity), and Miss Caton Thompson was helpful.

It is July 1936 before a first mention of the archaeologist's name appears in the index of Freya's correspondence. She was introduced to Lady Rhondda, owner and editor of *Time and Tide*, and her friend Miss Bosanquet over lunch in Miss Caton Thompson's large flat at Albert Hall Mansions in Kensington. By autumn some sort of intimacy was developing, based on a mutual interest in south-west Arabia and a shared distaste for Italian methods of colonisation. It is charted in the archaeologist's diary and Freya's letters: by quiet luncheons and dinners together to talk over the prospect of joining forces for an expedition to Hadhramaut in the winter of 1937–8.

Gertrude Caton Thompson was born in 1888, and was therefore five years older than Freya. Caton, as she was known to her intimates, was a prehistorian and archaeologist whose interest in her subject had been aroused in 1915 while visiting friends in Menton. A key site in palaeolithic prehistory, the Rochers Rouges was being excavated by the Canon de Villeneuve, with whom she formed an acquaintance. In 1921 she set to work in London to study her subject seriously, attending classes at University College, reading at the Royal Institution, studying museum collections, and taking lessons in Arabic at the University's School of Oriental Studies, and in surveying at the School of Mines.

So far her approach was not dissimilar to Freya's in the same period, but there the likeness ends. She had a more solid mind than Freya and her background too was different. She belonged to the same well-to-do world as Venetia Buddicom, and began where Freya left off. The editorial review in *Antiquity* by Professor Glyn Daniel of *Mixed Memoirs*, the retrospective of her personal and professional life, published in her ninety-fifth year, describes

> the elegant, beautiful Edwardian upper-class young woman in her pre-archaeological days living in Maidenhead Thicket, being taught to play the fiddle by the brother of Stanley Spencer, riding to hounds with the Queen's staghounds and the Garth Foxhounds, fittings at Bradleys, balls at Cliveden, Taplow Court and Bisham Abbey, constant ill-health, wintering in St Moritz (and crewing on the Cresta runs) and travelling in the Mediterranean and Egypt – Shepheards in Cairo, the Winter Palace at Luxor, the Savoy at Aswan, the Villa Politi at Syracuse . . .

Her personality emerges clearly from the detailed diary she kept from the age of eleven, assured, practical, uncompromising, fearless; fastidious to an Edwardian degree, forceful, devoted to friends and field-work. She did not suffer fools gladly. Caton became friendly with Sydney Cockerell in Cambridge while spending 1923 as a Research Fellow at Newnham College. This was a year devoted to improving her understanding of geology and physiography before returning to Egypt in 1924, to rejoin Flinders Petrie's dig, and begin her career as a prehistorian. Her field training had begun under him in the winter of 1921–2 at Abydos in Upper Egypt and, under the notoriously austere management of his camps, she learned to rough it on the sites she worked on, and to set up and provision camps of her own in the desert. Her nerve remained unshaken by the many dramatic episodes – floods, cyclones, predators, human and animal – of her field career. She carried a pistol and knew how to use it.

She was forty-six in 1934 when she and Freya met; a tall, beautifully turned-out creature with a cool, assured manner and a well-established record in the prehistoric archaeology of Africa and Malta. Five years previously, in 1929, in Rhodesia, she had outraged local settler opinion by confirming a previous attribution of the mysterious stone ruins of Zimbabwe and associated sites to an indigenous African population,[1] when she was sent by the Council of the British Association for the Advancement of Science to renew investigations into the history of these ruins. The notion that an indigenous culture capable of producing such memorials had ever existed cut right across the accepted views of the white man's civilising role in Africa; to challenge this *in situ* was an act of some bravery.

The British Association meeting at Pretoria was stormy; Caton's opting for the medieval attribution was uncompromising and indicative of her personality.

I have tried to eliminate all theory and vague generalities incapable of proof . . . It is inconceivable to me now I have studied the ruins how a theory of Semitic or civilised origin could ever have been foisted on an uncritical world. Every detail in the haphazard building appears to me to be typical African Bantu. It is also inconceivable to me how a theory of antiquity in the sense of Oriental archaeology could ever have been formulated by observant people. Instead of a degenerate offshoot of a higher Oriental civilisation, you have here a native civilisation . . . showing national organisation of a high kind, originality and amazing industry.

Professor Frobenius, President of the Frankfurt Research Institute of Cultural Morphology, who also attended the meeting and spoke against Caton's interpretation, believed the age and origin of the Rhodesian ruins was linked to a great intertwined prehistoric civilisation, which he named Erythràa, of 7000 to

5000 years ago, which dominated Egypt, Crete and the Near East, Mesopotamia, Arabia and East Africa from the shores of the Red Sea.

The attractions of this cloudy, imaginative – one might say Jungian – approach to prehistory, compared to the meticulous unfolding of dateable scientific evidence – metal analysis, bead sequences, pottery shards, porcelain and glass fragments and so on – in which modern archaeology excels, may explain some of the trouble that subsequently arose between Freya and Miss Caton Thompson and the bitterness that later shadowed their relations.

Freya in 1936 was on the full tide of her success as a historical geographer. Her Appendix to *The Southern Gates of Arabia*, the fruits of her 120 pages of notes, and Rhuvon Guest's corrections,[2] displayed a scholarly familiarity with the literature of the area, while the award of the Mungo Park Medal from the Scottish Royal Geographical Society in Edinburgh (where she lectured to an audience of 1600 people) underlined her status as an explorer. It was this perhaps that led Miss Caton Thompson to suggest they join forces on a venture which would allow further investigation of possible contacts between south-west Arabia and Zimbabwe via ports on the East African coast.

There was in Caton a certain debunking relish, not uncommon among blue-stocking women of that period, for whom the right to an education had been not so much a material struggle as a repudiation of the conventional expectations of their family. Often conscious of their singularity, they tended to adopt a dauntingly high standard of professional competence in their work. It may account for the brusqueness of Caton's dismissal of anything she considered ill-founded, and the steam-roller efficiency with which she demolished amateur interpretations.

The expedition to Hadhramaut was something of a comedy of errors. The coming together of Freya and Caton was more a means of each obtaining something that might otherwise be difficult than an expression of true sympathy. For the archaeologist, it was the entry into Hadhramaut, until now inaccessible to scientific study, which Freya's influential contacts in London and Aden might obtain, while for Freya the association with the distinguished archaeologist would be an earnest of the seriousness of her own pretensions as an explorer, somewhat dented by the fiasco at Shabwa. Freya had little interest in prehistory; while Caton, perhaps unwisely, took at face value the publicity and awards bestowed on Freya for her recent travels. The ability to rough it on site was part of the package.

There was a third element, too, in the successful launch of the plan. This was the prestige of the Royal Geographical Society, and the effect of its interest in the scheme on an ambitious colonial official with a bent towards exploration. Harold Ingrams with his wife Doreen were subsequently to receive the Society's Founder's Gold Medal for their exploration and survey of the wadi systems of the Eastern Aden Protectorate in 1934. Doreen Ingrams, in 1940, was the fourth woman to have received the Gold Medal, the fifth being Freya.[3] The first was Lady Franklin in 1860, for her continuing support of Arctic exploration, and the second Mary Somerville, in 1869, a Victorian mathematician and cartographer who never travelled and for whom Somerville College in Oxford is named. Gertrude Bell was the third, being awarded the Medal in 1918 for her penetration of Arabia Deserta, and archaeological surveys in Syria, Mesopotamia and Turkey.

In October 1937 Ingrams, appointed Resident Adviser in Hadhramaut to the Sultans of Mukalla, on the coast, and Seiyun, in the Great Wadi, with his wife took up residence at the port of Mukalla to initiate and sustain the intricate network of tribal truces by which endemic warfare in the interior was suspended during this period.

Prior to this, on 24 December 1936 Freya had written to Ingrams from London congratulating him on his appointment and soliciting the reservation of any permit to dig in his new territory for herself and Miss Caton Thompson. She astutely played on the RGS's interest in the proposed venture, and on her companion's distinction in scientific circles, as a member of the Councils of both the Royal Anthropological and Royal Geographical Societies.

I think we would do you credit and start your administration
with the discovery of whatever there may be to discover in
the way of archaeology . . . It would not be easy to find
anyone so well qualified or with such a reputation as Miss C.
Thompson, and the new President of the RGS has been smiling on our proposed collaboration very kindly. It would be
lovely if this could be brought off and if you and Doreen were
there to share in it all . . .

A few weeks later she was telling her mother of a wonderful
coup she had achieved. Staying with the Misses Ker, WPK's
sisters in Scotland, for her lecture to the Scottish RGS, she
had told his brother Charles Ker about her proposed venture
with her distinguished new friend, and of their need for financial
backing for the scheme. He suggested she approach Lord
Wakefield, a philanthropic millionaire who had already subscribed to Amy Johnson's flight to Australia. Charles Ker, who
knew him, volunteered to write to him and guarantee Freya
was not bogus. An appointment was made at Lord Wakefield's
London office, and Freya emerged half an hour later with a
cheque for £1500 in her handbag, a sum she had estimated as
sufficient to cover the whole cost of the venture. Lord Wakefield's explanation to Ker of his generosity was that 'she didn't
look like an explorer'. His gift enabled Caton to add a geologist,
Elinor Gardner, a partner in previous digs in Egypt and Libya,
to the team. Elinor – Elli Nur to the Hadhramis – was by all
accounts the nicest of the women, pleasant and unselfish,
whereas Caton and Freya, she explained subsequently to
Sydney Cockerell, 'had unforgiving natures' and did not let up
on each other easily.
    The thing got off to a bad start. Once her lecture to the Royal
Scottish Geographical Society was over, Freya went back to
Asolo in January 1937, leaving the planning of the expedition in
Caton's hands. From Italy she sailed to Alexandria en route for
Baghdad in February, and a leisurely tour around Iraq, Kuwait,
Syria and Lebanon, revisiting her old haunts and putting up with
friends, while she gathered additional material for the reissue
of *Baghdad Sketches*. By July she was back in Asolo, writing,

and at the beginning of September flew to London for a brief consultation with her partners in the expedition.

There is an ominous note in a letter to Flora on 11 September 1937 from the Overseas Club in London.

Dearest B [one of Freya's pet names for her mother], All the expedition stuff is more or less bought. We have . . . tents, chairs, a table, bedding – and an immense and rather dreary food list. The dietician looked Gertrude's list over and said it was sufficient for the 'very poor in a hot climate: for those who have nothing to do' or something to that effect; and she has added numbers of vitamins. Your Freya.

Freya had no experience of expedition work, and took only a cursory interest in the putting together of a six-months' field trip, and the assembling and packing of its stores and scientific equipment. She saw all that as Caton's province. Her contribution had been the raising of sufficient funds – Lord Wakefield's £1500 far outstripped the £400 contributed through Caton's sources – and the use of her own connections in the Colonial Office to enable the project to get under way.

At the beginning of October 1937 she flew to Cairo, and drove to Alexandria to stay with the Jennings-Bramleys at Burg el Arab, close to the Libyan frontier. Here she found her hosts in an excited turmoil with rumours of war multiplying every day. On 12 October she wrote to Jock Murray:

We are in all the familiar detective-story atmosphere of the Near East . . . and rumours and counter-rumours from the barbed wire of the frontier. I have never really doubted for the last few years that Italy means war, and feel more and more convinced . . .

A week later she continued:

Every prospect of a fine good battle quite close as soon as the fireworks start, and I am awfully sorry to think of missing it. Whiffy (Colonel Jennings-Bramley) is great at strategy, and has been showing me exactly where it will be. I think I would stay here if one could in the least tell when it will start, but it may be delayed a good deal. I am convinced it will come; the news from Abyssinia seems to get worse (from their side) and I feel sure they will prefer to say they lost it in a general war rather than quietly on their own as would happen otherwise . . .[4]

Freya's utterances on the local scene at this period have a dated flavour. In part it is to do with the phraseology. Her sensitive ear picked up the verbal nuances of the people with whom she associated very quickly, and it comes to one now with a husky, tinny reverberation, like an old wind-up gramophone producing whispered gaiety from piles of dusty seventy-eights. War is fun, the navy is simply longing for a scrap, 'everyone is devoted to Whiffy, who is the little uncrowned king of all the local beduin'. The self-assured silliness of the tone has the authentic period touch. But in the same batch of letters come glimpses of the other Freya, the one who spoke to lovers of poetry, and of the written word.

A few nights ago, lovely moonlight with white clouds scattered here and there, we heard high sweet voices in the sky as we sat outside at dinner. Those were the cranes flying south. One could not see them, but just heard those lovely voices calling to each other in the moonlight spaces, flying over the desert.

As I read this I was translated back in a flash to early 1947 and a gaunt old pre-Mutiny bungalow on the Indian North-west Frontier. Amazed by the sounds high in the air about us, we ran down in the moonlight on to the grassy unkept lawns and stood peering up into the starry sky, mystified and impressed. Now, as I write, I wonder if this was the music of that unearthly choir of whom Cavafy wrote, the signal of another loss. Much of Freya's gift lay in her power to evoke a sense of spaciousness that was once familiar to her countrymen and is now gone.

The Wakefield expedition, however, was not concerned with

ephemeral intuitions. It was scientifically based, and meticulously fulfilled its professed function, which was by means of excavation to examine possible links between the Sabaean culture of southern Arabia, with its traces of Mediterranean and Mesopotamian influence, and the Zimbabwe ruins of Rhodesia. Gertrude Caton Thompson having in 1929 already come out strongly against such a theory, now, in the winter of 1937–8, hoped to confirm or overturn her own view on the spot. An experienced field archaeologist, in Elinor Gardner she had a trusted companion and friend of many years' standing, as well as a geologist familiar with her methods of work. Indeed, the whole irony of the episode lies in the circumstance that the two scientists, disciplined and methodical in their approach to the matter in hand, exemplified in themselves much of what was popularly believed of Freya by her readers in England. Used to roughing it on remote sites, and to arduous days spent combing the shores of dried-up lakes for traces of prehistoric settlement, they were intrepid and self-contained, absorbed in their work, and indifferent to temporary discomfort.

It was a far cry from harem gossip, and that deliberate abandonment to the triviality of the moment by which Freya obtained her unfettered insight into the manners and customs of the people about her. Freya believed that one was liked 'in just the measure in which one can elicit from people their secret loves, the things they rarely speak of'.[5] This was a precept she followed with everyone whatever their race. It acted as an open sesame with simple people – who were those she preferred – unused to such a flattering concentration of interest on themselves, but it fell more flatly with the sophisticated, who were not always convinced of the genuineness of her approach. The scientist's manner with people was different. Caton was aloof but courteous, and sympathetic to her host's, the Mansab's, interest in Himyaritic remains. She left him eleven inscriptions, when the dig ended, to add to his collection, while Freya engaged in a rather dubious financial speculation over some early Arabic manuscripts.

On 13 January 1939 she wrote from London to Doreen Ingrams:

Just posted you a length of green and pink velvet ribbon for the old Mansab of Meshed to replace his filthy old sash. I promised it and feel ashamed not to have attended to it before.

There is another question . . . Sultan Ali Ibn Salah lent me a MS of AD 1600 [Yemen history]. I thought it might be rare and when he seemed to be rather peculiar in his politics I thought I had better secure the MS and brought it to the British Museum. I sent him a cheque for £16 telling him that if he did not wish to sell he could send it back and I would return the book. He now writes rather obscurely and I cannot make out if he wishes the transaction to remain or not! Anyway he has not sent back the £16 . . . awful shame to burden you with more chores, but I know you will understand . . . The book is unique but no-one seems very enthusiastic to buy it: the BM have photographed specimen pages. Anyway, I am quite ready to send it back if the Sultan wants it, only think it sound policy to get back the £16 first!!

The scientists and their gear sailed from England on a P & O liner in October 1937, and it was arranged for Freya to join them when the ship reached Egypt. She spent the last few days in the hospital in Alexandria, resting after cholera and typhoid injections. Her rendezvous with the main party nearly misfired. Instead of Port Said, as arranged, she went to Suez, and only reached Port Said after a hectic overnight taxi drive in time for the boat's departure the next morning.

The stress her companions experienced at her cutting things so fine was not improved by a rough passage down the Red Sea in a second-class cabin with portholes closed in the heat. By the time the party reached Aden doubts about Freya's reliability as a conductor were forming in her companions' minds. Perhaps she too experienced reservations as they approached their destination, and wondered if she had been wise in hitching her wagon to such an untwinkling star. Freya's interpretation of her job relied a good deal on her ability to charm people into doing things for her, rather than forward planning.

There was an official oil-exploration party on board, with whom Freya soon chummed up; this got her party landed for free at Aden in the Resident's launch, which came out to meet the oil men. It was an alarming experience, as the launch was badly bumped by another craft. Once on shore, more aggravation. The hotel was full, no rooms having been reserved by Freya, who had counted on Anton Besse being there to look after them, but he was away in Abyssinia, and would not be back for two weeks. Worse still, Ramadan, the Moslem month of fasting, was impending, when all normal activities would slow up or cease, while the nights were devoted to feasting and sociability.

All in all, it was a bad start, with Freya's inefficiency prominent in her companions' minds. Put to it, her instinct for self-preservation galvanised her into action. The oil party, with its two American geologists, had been met on board by

a nice-looking enthusiastic young man who had been reading *Baghdad Sketches* (the old one) and welcomed me *most* cordially. His name is Perowne and he is political here, and keen to dig and ready to give all help and encouragement – so pleasant, and he quoted Milton and Tennyson before we got off the boat into the Residency launch, in which he took us regardless of the Oil party he was supposed to be attending to . . .[6]

Immediately charmed, Freya lost no time in cashing in on his offers of help.

Harold Ingrams, who was to be responsible for the party in Hadhramaut, was fortunately in Aden on business that day and stayed to lunch and talk with the party, while the tedious business of waiting for rooms to be found for them ran its course. The scientists found him touchy and overbearing about their plans, over-anxious in their view about his fragile arrangements with the tribes of the interior. By evening accommodation was at last arranged, but meanwhile it was discovered that a portion of the seventy-one pieces of baggage belonging to the expedition had not been unloaded, and some of the personal

luggage, and all the instruments, were now on their way to
Singapore only to be intercepted after much urgent telegraphy
by the shipping agents. The loss of their luggage earned the
party the title of the Foolish Virgins, or FVs for short, among
the lighter-hearted members of the resident community.[7]

Freya was on the defensive with her companions within a
few days. She told her mother:

> I find I get through much more with far less exertion than
> my own party. It is far more useful in this climate to sit quiet
> and make other people do things. A little chat about their
> family affairs does more to get willing and efficient helpers
> than all the ordering about in the world; I think Elinor Gardner
> still considers it a waste of time, being used only to Egyptians
> who can be browbeaten . . . It is a great mistake to look as
> if you can do anything for yourself if you *want* people to put
> themselves out for you.[8]

The expedition sounds just the sort of party one would be
glad to miss. It soon split into two camps, with Freya and
Caton at opposite poles, and Elinor Gardner floating somewhat
ineffectually in between. Caton found the sheer inefficiency of
Freya's failing to take into account the operation of Ramadan
on their schedules hard to take, and Freya, rather than conciliate, soon mounted her own high horse, and was scathing
about Gertrude's rigidity of outlook, and lack of human
understanding.

Things were a little redeemed on arrival in Mukalla, in one
of Besse's commercial bi-weekly air flights, on 7 November.
Freya had been secretly nervous lest her previous accounts of
the possibilities of the Hadhramaut terrain should be unfulfilled,
but fortunately the environs of Mukalla are littered with palaeolithic flints, and this assuaged Caton's parallel misgivings. The
depleted and repacked stores and a cook, a Yemeni youth of
twenty, had been dispatched ahead on one of the Besse
steamers on 4 November, but once arrived at their point of
departure inland more delays supervened. 'Ramadan spread a
canopy of procrastination over everything,' Freya wrote. Her

previous journey had been entirely organised by Besse, and she now found herself having to manage everything on her own, and at considerably greater cost. The party was put up for five days by the Ingrams, who already had the oil party's geologists to look after, and slept on the roof in midnight temperatures of 85–7 degrees; Doreen Ingrams recalls that the FVs demanded a good deal of attention. Eventually the party was packed into a lorry with its gear and various hangers-on and was on its way inland over the Jōl to Tarim on 13 November.

Freya's lively and entertaining accounts of the tribulations she endured at the hands of the two scientists gained her a good deal of sympathy in the Aden community, when she flew there in mid-December to spend a week in hospital to recover from quinsy before rejoining her party on Boxing Day. All three women had by now been ill with septic throats, fevers, influenza, the usual accompaniments of a Middle East dig, starting with Elinor Gardner succumbing on 25 November, followed a week later by Caton, who ran a temperature of 103 degrees. Freya stuck it out – they were being put up in Shibam in a house found by Freya through the Besse agent, as no prior arrangement had been made for their reception – until Ramadan ended on 3 December. Despite a sore throat she was determined to capture on film, both movie and still, the celebrations at the end of the month's fast, when everyone receives new clothes, and a three-day holiday of feasting and dancing is held to mark the end of the fast.

By the ninth she had collapsed into exhaustion, hypochondria and hysteria, and demanded attention from her companions. She experienced fainting fits and believed herself dying.[9] With Ingrams' help she was flown to Aden from Seiyun in the Besse plane. Left to themselves, the two scientists removed themselves from Shibam, which even St John Philby, the most spartan of travellers, described as the only urban area in Hadhramaut to offend blatantly against all principles of public health, cleanliness and decency.[10] They took refuge in the hospitality of the al Kaf family, and the garden suburb luxury of their guest-house at Seiyun, until 20 December, when they were driven by the al Kafs to Hureidha, their ultimate destination, ninety-two kilometres away in the Wadi 'Amd.

When Freya returned from Aden to Hureidha, the scientists had negotiated for and were installed in a house on the outskirts of the little town, overlooking on one side the settlement of about 2000 inhabitants, on the other the sand river of the Wadi 'Amd, over a mile wide.

The two women were welcomed by the Mansab or head of the local Seyyids, the spiritual and temporal head of the community, with all civility, so that by 24 December an excavation site had been chosen, and a team of six men and four basket boys selected and employed. Work now began on the excavation of the Moon temple, the first archaeological excavation to be recorded scientifically in Hadhramaut. Nearly two months of the expedition's time had elapsed since their arrival in the country.

On the face of it, in Caton's terse account of the expedition, derived from her diary, its work was accomplished more expeditiously without Freya than with her.[11] In any case, within a day of Freya's arrival in Hureidha, she retired to her room where she remained on and off in bed until 30 January, receiving the visits of the citizenry, and listening to the local gossip. There was again an alarm about illness, with messages sent to Seiyun asking for a doctor, and with Ingrams himself arriving and advising Aden hospital once more. On 27 January a plane duly arrived, on charter for the oil survey, one of whose American geologists, Pike, had been signalled by Ingrams. It came with a view to carrying Freya off to Aden, but she by now felt sufficiently restored to refuse the offer, to the extreme irritation of the pilot and of Pike, for whom the unmade-up landing ground of the wadi floor offered considerable risk. Three planes had recently crashed on similar landings.

This incident aroused gossip and criticism in Aden, and led to the circulation of a ribald little ditty by the RAF Information Officer which commenced 'Evacuate, evacuate, A maiden most immaculate', and went on through several stanzas which one hopes were never seen by Freya herself, or by her companions.

*   *   *

Among the Starkiana collected by Cockerell is his note of a conversation with Elinor Gardner in July 1938 regarding the Wakefield expedition. This took place at Miss Gardner's home in Surrey, when he was delivering film to her on his return from visiting Freya in Asolo. She remarked on Freya's reckless impetuosity in treating her own illnesses: 'She simply went through the medical dictionary, discovering now this, now that, symptom . . .' Freya appeared able to believe anything she wanted to believe, she added, and that though she herself would always be prepared to accompany Caton on another expedition, nothing would induce her to travel with Freya again.

Freya's panicky fainting fits, her conviction that she was dying, now from heart failure, now from suppressed double pneumonia, now from malaria, seemed extraordinary and exaggerated to the two scientists. They themselves had also suffered from quinsies, fevers, chest irritations, the familiar accompaniments of tomb excavation among the ancient germs of the East. These they treated from the expedition's medical chest without recourse to outside assistance. They noticed that Freya ate all her meals, while a constant stream of visitors admitted to her room entertained her with chatter and local gossip. Caton in particular had no time for the hysterical element in Freya's personality, and was unsympathetic to her demands for attention, and the way this ate into the expedition's schedule. Her concept of what was owed Lord Wakefield for his support was rather more rigorous than Freya's, and the justification of the expedition's presence in Hadhramaut by a useful contribution to science kept the two scientists, despite illness, to a strict schedule and eventually to the publication in 1944 of a comprehensive report on their findings.[12]

Freya's strategy of accessibility to the people of the wadi was not taken seriously. They couldn't see the point of it, it interfered with the *real* work. 'Freya is collecting Dresses!'[13] Elinor Gardner exclaimed in a letter home. Much of the rancour which Freya later consistently expressed towards academic women arose now. She was hypersensitive to any hint of not being taken at her own estimate. To be dismissed as some sort of mountebank was an affront whose effect was to fuel the mordant humour and spitefulness which made her such a tricky proposition once it was aroused. 'Stewart has got a new strong-box with a self-locking device,' she told Jock Murray from Aden in 1940. 'We call it the Caton Thompson . . .'

As early as 28 November, Freya had told her mother that while lying in bed thinking over her troubles with her companions, and the pedantry of the 'academic' approach, it had suddenly come to her that an amusing book could be made out of the situation. It was a wonderful solution to a problem which had been already exercising her mind, how to produce another book on Hadhramaut without going over familiar ground. What she had needed was a new angle, and now she had got it.

From then on, as is the way with writers, the theme developed almost of itself. Freya was later to defend her work as less an account of Hureidha itself than 'a picture of *methods of meeting* between East and West. It is not a point of literature at all, but is something far nearer to my heart, and on which I have a thing I *wish* to say. Anything that goes counter to this primary object of my book, I will not entertain for one moment.'[14]

The antipathy that developed between Caton and Freya arose from temperamental incompatibility. Freya elevated this difference to the loftier plane of Statesmanship, though to Jock Murray and Cockerell it appeared more like spitefulness.[15] Given Freya's hypersensitivity it is perhaps no surprise that Caton's icy self-sufficiency and unbending dismissal of her activities as trivial should produce a burning indignation, or that her wounded feelings should find expression in gestures of defiant independence.

The dig was scheduled to end in March, and packing up began on the third. A temple and cave-tombs had been excavated and seals found, later dated to Achaemenian times. The archaeologist's conclusion was that the temple and tombs belong to the middle fifth and fourth centuries BC, the first intimation in Hadhramaut of such an early date. No evidence of cultural contact between Arabia and the African continent was established, though she accepted that the slave trade from Africa and the presence of Arabs on the African coast probably had an age-old history before the Roman period. A detailed survey of ancient flood control of the wadi, and the extent of land under seasonal irrigation, considerably more extensive than in the present day, was prepared by Elinor Gardner.

The expedition's gear and personnel were to be driven by way of Tarim out of the wadi and so down to the coast and a boat to Aden. There had been trouble in the wadi, tribesmen holding up goods and travellers on the road, and a renewal of feuding threatened Ingrams' tenuous peace-making strategy. RAF bombing, with a small loss of life, had put a stop to this unruliness,[16] and the road was now open. Freya, smouldering under the affronts she had suffered from Caton's indifference, had meanwhile been evolving a plan to ride down to the coast by a different route, following a portion of the ancient camel track from the head of the Wadi 'Amd through the network of valleys leading from the uplands to the sea, via the Wadi Maifa'a. This was a route partially travelled by Doreen Ingrams in the previous winter over country mapped by von Wissman and van der Meulen in 1931.

Freya sprang this scheme on her companions on the eve of the party's departure, and suggested they – or Elinor – might like to accompany her. Her three camels were ordered for next day and her plan made. How serious her invitation was one will never know, but it was bold to attempt to poach Caton's friend from under her nose, and guaranteed to annoy. It failed in its first object, as also did a request that the two women wait for Freya on the coast, until she emerged safely from the interior in the vicinity of Husn al Gharb, which she was anxious to establish as the entrepôt port for the ancient incense traffic. The scientists had other engagements to fulfil, Caton replied, and could not afford the time.

It was a bruising encounter, and could be seen as a calling of Freya's bluff, which forced a decision on her. She left next day, 4 March, on her own, in all the hustle and bustle of the lorry's arrival, only Elinor paying her any attention. She took with her Qasim, the servant, and was seen off by the Mansab's son. She set off on his father's pony, lent as a mark of distinction, until the camel party was reached, when she continued on her way reclining under a sunshade on an orange quilt spread over a baggage animal's load.

She had embarked on a three-weeks' journey of some 120 miles, travelling in part through unvisited country. The adventure followed a familiar pattern. Physically exhausted, emotionally overwrought, two days later and some twenty-five miles from Hureidha, she felt feverish and, worn out by the demands of local hospitality, ill. She retreated to the little town of 'Amd, from where messages were sent to Ingrams to order a car to fetch her away. By the time it arrived she had recovered her spirits and was on her way to Azzan, which she reached on 18 March, travelling in defiance of her party's tacit agreement with Harold Ingrams to cause him no trouble by venturing into unpacified areas. The local Sultans, mindful of possible retribution if anything went wrong, insisted she wait until a proper caravan was formed, so that members of the family themselves with their armed guards could escort her to the coast.

Travelling by night in a party of twenty-seven camels, mostly carrying tobacco, they reached the coast and got an unfriendly reception from the local people, but all was safely resolved, and a passage on a dhow found for her. By 28 March she was writing from Aden, from the hospital, that all was well and she safely arrived, but suffering from dengue fever, which would detain her a week. On 6 April she was on board the *Orontes* and sailing up the Red Sea, en route for Piraeus and a meeting with her mother. Her adventure was over, leaving the customary reverberations of scandal in the resident British community.

Freya's journey down the Wadi Maifa'a was her last direct contribution to geographical science, and her last independent journey. In future she moved around the Middle East as a government servant, with all the backing that went with the job; not until 1952 did her private wanderings begin again. Her escapade, as it was seen in Aden, slipping off from the authorised expedition route to make a risky journey through difficult country, raised tempers as well as eyebrows in official circles. Freya in hospital received a visit from Colonel Lake and a penny lecture, mitigated by relief at her safe arrival.

She did not care. She had fulfilled her ambition, at least in part, and travelled the ancient road in the romantic circumstances of an armed caravan, and in conditions similar to those of antiquity, when the trade route north to the Mediterranean began on the Hadhramaut coast. The restrained scale of the Hureidha dig had disappointed her; she had perhaps anticipated something more showy, on the lines of Palmyra and Petra, and palaeoliths, fossilised skulls and lost irrigation systems never gripped her imagination. Nor did she think they would grip Lord Wakefield's. The incense route was a more attractive proposition, and she had photographs of hill forts, Himyaritic proto-Arabic rock engravings, cisterns and rock-cut cliff stairways to prove it, as well as her own lively account of the adventure.

The two scientists passed through Aden before Freya on their way home. They arrived by boat on 12 March and left in one of the Besse steamers on the sixteenth. They had run into Harold Ingrams at Tarim, on their way out of the wadi. He was incensed at Freya's action, and at lunch in the Residency with Sir Bernard Reilly, Colonel Lake told them that after the earlier aeroplane incident at Hureidha, Ingrams had requested her recall to Aden, but this was not adopted because of the expedition's support from the Royal Geographical Society, with whom difficulties might arise.

The scientists also met the Besses for the first time. He reminded Caton of Cecil Rhodes, compact, purposeful, far-seeing and ambitious for his ideals. She was struck by his extreme dislike of Freya which, so he indicated, was shared by many in Aden. 'She uses people,' he said, 'and returns no gratitude,' and had they met earlier, he would have taken the liberty of warning the scientists.[17] The Besses were welcoming and hospitable, and the two women dined with them, and were put aboard the *El Hak* by their host and hostess. It seems to have been a satisfactory encounter. The journey to Suez was a good deal more comfortable, and indeed luxurious, than the previous one, and the food excellent.

TEN

A LONDON WINTER

Freya's instinct was always to conceal damage, to deflect observation from hurt. However much she might make fun of her companions on the Wakefield expedition, the fiasco of her relations with Caton was a bitter pill. She had been proud of her intimacy with the archaeologist; it was a feather in her cap, a consolation prize for the rupture with Venetia Buddicom. But Caton was accustomed to admiration, and had a large circle of friends. She had no need or time for the self-dramatising element in Freya's personality, nor for her readiness to jump on other people's bandwagons. Freya's pretensions as a historical geographer are put down with ruthless finality in a few sentences at the end of Caton's report for the Society of Antiquaries,[1] on the Wakefield expedition and its findings.

From now on Freya's intimates tended to be drawn from the social and political rather than the intellectual world. Her preferred associates were wealthy, with important connections or influential family backgrounds, preferably rather grand. She had little time for the humble and the obscure except as ministrants to her own comfort and needs, on whom her bland affability and easy manner usually produced a gratified willingness to be made use of.

Freya had served notice of her feelings about Caton to Sydney Cockerell as soon as she reached Aden. 'I fear I did not get on with Gertrude Caton Thompson; she has a pedagogic mind not suited to the carelessness of Arabia and wanted to run us on Anglo-Egyptian lines, an effort I was determined to resist: she was very unkind, and I did not wait for seventy times seven slaps before slapping back!'[2]

Henceforward Freya was determinedly *feminine*, a man's woman paying lip-service to masculine superiority and identifying with the dominant sex, a reversal of her earlier stance of competitor. Caton's snubbing of her aspirations as a historical geographer had a damaging effect; it wound up Freya's need to justify herself in her own as well as everyone else's eyes, and pushed her into insistence on her own unique understanding of Middle-Eastern people. In periods of intensified excitement when her independence was threatened, or her suggestions ignored, normal behaviour went by the board. Everything had to be subsumed to this need. It was a primitive energy as dangerous to the unalerted bystander as any swarm of bees, a mysterious dimension to a personality more commonly associated with delicate perceptions and an elegant literary style.

Freya was now something of a celebrity. Her adventurous ride from Hureidha to the coast, after the break-up of the Wakefield expedition, had been well publicised. Much in demand for broadcasts, lectures and journalism, when first Austria, then Sudetenland were annexed by Germany, and public opinion divided sharply on the issue of appeasement or action against the dictators, she came out strongly against appeasement and pressed her views on any politician who could be got to listen.

The war scare of September 1938 sent Freya away from Asolo, travelling hurriedly in trains packed with people anxiously seeking safety on their home ground or in Switzerland. She stopped off in Paris on 28 September – 'just in time to rush out and get adorable hat – yellow, pink and dark-red ostrich feathers, very 1890!' – and to order clothes for her London winter. On arrival in London she put up with the Herbert Oliviers on Campden Hill, in preparation for the Wakefield expedition lectures at the Royal Geographical Society in November. Here Margaret Olivier ministered to another of Freya's collapses into invalidism. 'The blood pressure has gone bang down,' she told her mother on 13 October. 'Nobody could help as Margaret does. She really is an angel of goodness – tells her guests to leave early, keeps me in bed for breakfast, and spares me in every way. I had no idea one could be so cared for when staying in anyone's house . . .'

Her mother's old friend, Viva Jeyes, had died of cancer at the age of sixty-seven the previous year. Before her death in 1937 Viva wrote her will, leaving Flora and Freya £500 each in token of long friendship and affection, but the silver and the jewellery which Flora expected to be Freya's were not mentioned. Flora, so the story goes, descended like a tigress on the executors, and apparently 'shook out of them' the pearls, the diamond rings, brooches and other trinkets that then became part of Freya's presentation of herself as a successful woman of the world. This episode gave rise in the Olivier family's collective memory to the view that Freya's well-known force of character was but a candle-flame compared with the blowtorch of her mother's personality.

On 10 November 1938, at a dinner given her by the Goodenoughs at the Hyde Park Hotel, Freya appeared dressed to the nines. She reported to her mother:

The evening was really great fun. My dress (from Paris) quite lovely, but almost *too* bridal: yards and yards of tulle, and silver and gold shining through, the diamond brooch in my hair! There were twenty-five people – Huxleys, Balfours, Lady Allenby, Jock, Sydney Cockerell, Mr Hinks (of the RGS), and Violet Leconfield whom I know, Dean of Westminster and his wife, Editor of *The Times* and wife, Admiral Little, three other Goodenoughs, Lady Stanley of Alderley (charming), Viscount Gort, and a few others I didn't know.

Freya was now well into the swing of a London winter. *Seen in the Hadhramaut*, a collection of her photographs, was published on 28 November, the day of her lecture to the RGS, to which 800 people came. She had not been in contact with her expedition companions since her arrival in England, but showed herself at Caton's lecture at the RGS earlier in the month, though not at the Society's tea-party afterwards, so as to avoid an encounter. Cockerell tactfully decided to attend the lecture independently.

Freya now had the use of the archaeologist Leonard Woolley's house and staff in Chelsea, while he and his wife went to India for the winter. She remained there until the end of January 1939, prior to returning to Asolo in February to work on her fourth book *A Winter in Arabia*, her account of the Wakefield expedition. From Chelsea she set off for grand country-house weekends, or entertained her friends and new acquaintances to small luncheon and dinner parties, or more economic sherry parties, where she pressed her claim for recognition as an expert on Arab affairs; she was determined to be more than just an interesting novelty. Invited to speak at Chatham House, she also appeared on fledgling television and spoke on the radio.

It galled her that Society was glad to hail her as a Traveller, but failed to take seriously her political views. Her frustration found expression in the New Year of 1939 in an outburst of grief which prostrated her for two days over the death of a pet lizard she had brought back with her from Hadhramaut. Named Himyar in token of his provenance, he was a scaly-tailed creature with blue gills and a crest, like a small dragon, about eighteen inches in length. His appearance, nestling around her neck for warmth, or peeping from under her jacket, was guaranteed to cause emotion in the unprepared. Freya carried him around with her on her visits, where extra hot water bottles had to be provided for him, but the northern winter, and perhaps an unsuitable diet – she fed him violets and nasturtiums and other poetical offerings – were too alien to him, and he simply faded away. Freya wrote pathetically to Asolo: 'My poor little Himyar is dead . . . and even now I can't think or speak of him without crying. It is absurd for so tiny a creature – but I think he and I were alike in lots of ways, both rather small and lonely in our hearts and he was a gallant little fellow . . .' Her distress elicited a sympathetic note of condolence from Sydney Cockerell. Freya during this period was like a child at a birthday party, for whom the glitter of the occasion and the attention showered on her produce a crescendo of excitement only too likely to end in tears.

In December 1938 Freya was invited by the Iveaghs to attend their daughter Patricia's marriage at Elveden, their house in Suffolk; she was one of thirty-five house-guests gathered for a grand country wedding. The bridegroom was Alan Lennox-Boyd, the only one of four Lennox-Boyd brothers to survive the impending war.

Another brother was Donald, a soldier, a captain in the Scots Greys, a friend of Stewart Perowne's, and unmarried. A few weeks later, 26 January 1939, just prior to Freya's forty-sixth birthday, she reported home:

> I had such fun last night – Patsy's (the bride's) brother-in-law, a charming young man, gave me a party with the Christopher Sykeses [first met in 1933], to see the pantomime in Covent Garden. I don't think I have ever enjoyed a show more – we had the Duke of Bedford's box, and a supper with champagne in the room behind it, and ended up with beer and vodka at the Savoy at 1 a.m.

Perowne at this period was thirty-seven and Lennox-Boyd thirty-two. Freya was forty-six. The Iveagh connection was a reassuring confirmation of Freya's Italian background to a socially ambitious man like Perowne and this, coupled with her increasing celebrity, encouraged him rather to take her up. Ideas and schemes for further adventures were talked over gaily among their associates. As always in her relations with men, the conventions of Freya's upbringing ruled. Her playing of the feminine card[3] and her love of dress added piquancy to her identity as a dauntless traveller, and inspired feelings of protective admiration among chivalrous old buffers such as Cockerell and 'Barge' Goodenough, and a more condescending appreciation among epicene younger ones. Freya herself accepted everyone's attention with undiscriminating delight, and a satisfaction untouched by doubt of any kind.

She was very quick to adjust to the people with whom she associated. Her confident parade of archaeological know-how was one of the things that had irritated Caton in Hadhramaut.

She never doubted her fitness to arrange others' lives for them, and prided herself on her ability to get rapidly to the bottom of a personality. Much of her reputation as a clever woman came from this. Having had the accolade of Traveller bestowed on her in 1933, Travel became her big thing, a talking-point to which metaphysical subtleties were soon added. It was a character-forming experience which enabled the genuine article to be distinguished from the accidental or the superficial. The ability to make a quick decision – upon which safety might depend – came into this, and was the facet of personality that set people like herself apart from the conventional stay-at-homes. It struck me on reading 'In Defence of Travel', a paper delivered at a book exhibition in autumn 1935,[4] that it hadn't taken long for Freya to believe her own publicity, however lighthearted and unpretentious her presentation might seem.

Freya's conviction that she had been put into the world for a purpose was obscured at first by the modesty of her appearance when she entered public life. People often came up with the description 'governessy' when seeking to recall first impressions at this early period. It was only with financial success that she began to spend money on herself, dresses from Schiaparelli, hats by Suzy, shoes from Pinet. In the 1930s she was faced with an elite of supremely self-assured and highly trained people, very conscious of their own superiority. To vanquish the feeling of inferiority induced by the dismissal of anything outside the range of their own imaginative understanding, Freya learned to assert her individuality by an increasing flamboyance of style. This in turn deflected attention from the sense of mission already colouring her ideas at the time of the Munich crisis.

This shift in direction surfaced in the difficulties with Murrays over *A Winter in Arabia*. Her pillorying of her companions' attitude towards the local people was a necessary step, she claimed, in alerting her countrymen to the dangers of such insensitive behaviour. If the Empire and its beneficial rule were to fail, future generations would see in the overbearing manners of her compatriots a contributory cause. She was adamant about

this, she told Cockerell. The book was to be the vehicle, and
she the medium through whom the benefits of enlightened
behaviour would be transmitted. What less exalted minds might
see as wounded feelings, Freya claimed as far-sighted patriotism and the need to demonstrate how greater loyalty to the
Empire could be obtained by more conciliatory manners on the
part of its representatives. The buttering-up of people for private ends was translated into a moralistic stance, and the odd
thing is that Freya seemed genuinely unable to distinguish
between the cosmetic and the pragmatic in the exercise, or to
recognise the mechanism whereby such grandiose interpretations were assigned to private expediencies, and proclaimed
as public need.

Cockerell did eventually persuade Freya to descend some
way off this excessively high horse, and the pointed malice of
her attack on Gertrude Caton Thompson – Freya suggested
calling the book *Newnham in Arabia* – was toned down by him
before its eventual publication in 1940. He was in a difficult
position. He had brought the two women together, but Caton's
was the longer friendship. His notebook records his letters to
her as well as to Freya, and shows that though he might cajole
Freya into a more reasonable frame of mind, it did not prevent
him from coming out in support of Caton at the Royal Geographical,[5] by making sure Admiral Goodenough was made aware of
her side of the story.

Freya was far from pleased when Wilfrid Blunt, Cockerell's
personally appointed biographer – without identifying the recipient – used a letter from Cockerell to herself in his biography
as an example of his subject's capacity for objectivity in his
response to calls on his judgment. It was a long, tactful letter,
remonstrating at Freya's attitude to her companion and pointing
out the damage she was doing to her own reputation by such
a display of ill feeling. It had taken Freya three weeks before
she came to terms with Cockerell's reproof and accepted his
editing out of the offensive material. She had not welcomed
Blunt's decision to use the letter, but the copyright was not
hers. Next time they met at a party in London, she cut Blunt
dead.

Freya, somewhat reluctantly, left London for Asolo on 22 February 1939. She was preparing a leisurely tour around the Crusader castles of the Syrian coastal area, once her book was finished. On departure, she wrote rather mysteriously from the train to Cockerell:

> My London winter is over, and, as for Cinderella, the clock has struck twelve . . . For the first time in my life I have had a swim in the Social World, and begun to find my feet among its reefs and pleasant places, and found that it is a good world too if one can bear in mind to live there *sans peur et sans reproche* – fear of other people or reproach from oneself – the truth in others comes out, whether in society or desert: there is no particularly adapted locality for it apart from one's own heart. My last weekend was with Jock to whom I talked about the folly of wasting *too* much time on work!

Meanwhile schemes for more adventures were being spun. There was a plan for the autumn: Perowne and Donald Lennox-Boyd were to ride south from Gaza to the Indian Ocean to trace the incense route in reverse; and a suggestion that Freya might join them on the trip was discussed. So fluid was the political situation that the options were very open; it was a kind of vicarious camaraderie not necessarily to be taken seriously. The idea of travelling in company 'with the Son of a Bishop!' rather tickled her, she wrote coyly to her friends; the adventure was to begin in October 1939.[6]

When she left Asolo in March for her tour in Syria, her mother was on a visit to her friends the Beaches in America – they had sent Flora a ticket – and Freya had packed up the household silver and other valuables and given them into the safe keeping of Italian friends. Her book was still not completed, but she was sending it to London in sections. 'You shall see and criticise before long,' she told Cockerell. She ended on a sour note. 'Jock has gone and got himself engaged to be married . . . It is a dangerous thing to be a sentimentalist in this world: it spoils the perceptions of real sentiments.'

There was another blow a few weeks later. She returned to Hama in mid-April from her horseback tour around the castles of the old Latin kingdom of Outremer to find a letter from Donald Lennox-Boyd awaiting her, and another from Perowne, telling her that Lennox-Boyd had been killed on 5 April in Germany.

Freya's acquaintance with Lennox-Boyd developed over a period of barely two months, from the period of the wedding party at Elveden in December, to the last week of February 1939 when Freya left London for Asolo. His death was mysterious, killed in a German garrison town in undisclosed circumstances, his body, so a story circulated in the London clubs, handed over apologetically by the German police in a packing case at the frontier to his brother and Chips Channon (married to another Guinness daughter) and brought back for a private funeral in Bournemouth on Saturday, 15 April, attended only by one brother.[7] There was no inquest.

After this Donald Lennox-Boyd disappears from the public record, only to surface after many years in Freya's account of her life. A strange fate awaited him. He joined the increasing company of men who she claimed had admired her, and whom she could have married had not death intervened. In the third volume of her autobiography, published in 1953, he is the 'young man killed in cold blood by the Germans in Stuttgart' on the day she was attending the Good Friday mass in the Templar church at Safita. 'Before he went to Germany, in a letter full of hope and foreboding, he asked me to marry him: I found this letter on my return to Aleppo, and another from a friend, written later, to tell me of his death.'

Her *Letters* of this period add little to the facts. She wrote emotionally to Cockerell from Aleppo telling him of the great shock and sorrow she had experienced:

Dearest Sydney – very dearest friend – I write to you in such grief, as one turns to a safe beloved haven. You have probably seen that Donald Lennox-Boyd is dead, who was to have travelled with us in Arabia: he went on some mission to Berlin and is dead. I have not heard how – in some grim way. Some day I may show you the letter he wrote to me in Hama . . .

To Jock Murray she wrote on 19 April:

> I don't think in this whole world there was a truer, more chivalrous, more absolutely pure and gallant soul – he and I were very true friends and I have his last letter, waiting at Hama for me, by me now, so full of all the future he will never see. Among my friends, he is the first victim of this war.

There is a footnote to the printed text. 'Donald Lennox-Boyd, brother of Alan, proposed marriage to F.S. in this letter.'[8] Cockerell, on her letter from Aleppo giving him the news, has written tidily into the text above Lennox-Boyd's name, 'shot as a spy'. There is no other comment.

Later she was to write to Cockerell from Simla on 6 May 1943:

> I do regret now not being married: but not the marriages of those days I wrote to you about. The man with whom I would have been happy, and who cared, was killed by the Germans in April 1939. Now I feel lonely, but I know it does not matter much. Also I have so much love for which to be grateful or humble. In that I am spoiled above most people and at least I do value it at its worth. Your ever loving Freya.[9]

'I think of Donald and weep and weep – I can't write more today,' she told Jock Murray at the end of a rather cold and snubbing letter about his engagement. This was a piece of news that evidently rankled, though in Hama on 29 March she had mastered her spleen sufficiently to send him blessings and good wishes on his marriage before setting off on her riding tour.

But his defection was felt. Freya was entering middle age, and the gay young friends of her late blossoming were being drawn inevitably into considerations of their own positions as war drew closer. She hated the sense of being put aside, of taking second place. Perhaps her depression contributed to the collapse she experienced at Antioch where, finding the hotel filled with noisy young people, she took refuge in the hospital run by French nuns. It was clean, up-to-date and quiet, and she lay for two days being poulticed for a sore throat, drinking *tisanes*, and reading about the first Crusade in the chronicles of Villehardouin and de Joinville. 'It is always a surprise that a physical effect follows a mental shock – but it always does, and this time took the shape of a throat and coughs,' she told her mother. Reading, with the hills and walls of Antioch in view, 'of those single-hearted, full-souled people, I felt somehow very close to Donald who was so much more like a Crusader than anyone I knew.'

In 1984 I received, through Pamela Hore-Ruthven, a communication from Alan Lennox-Boyd, the late Lord Boyd of Merton, Donald's sole surviving brother. Donald and Freya were certainly friendly, was the message, but in the family's view, any question of marriage on Donald's part was unlikely. Like so many of Freya's proclaimed sentimental attachments, it seems she persuaded herself there was more in the relationship than really existed.

Perhaps it was the knock-on effect of her distress that persuaded her to the risky experiment of taking on a handsome young Nosairi guide whom she had picked up on her ride, as a permanent servant, with a view to taking him back to Asolo with her. The Nosairis are a minor Islamic sect believed to be a survival of pagan tree-worshippers, but Freya saw Isa (or Jesus) in terms of her Crusader imaginings, and was seduced by his green eyes and handsome looks, as well as by his devotion to her well-being. More difficult even than her lizard to introduce as a pet into Asolo, she nevertheless decided to employ him. This experiment was ill-fated. In January 1940, against Perowne's advice, but through the good offices of Lord Halifax, Freya eventually obtained a visa for Isa to join her in Aden, at a cost of £26 to herself. He accompanied her to Yemen, but he did not adapt satisfactorily to conditions in Aden and proved more trouble than Freya felt he was worth. He was difficult to train as a lady's maid, was quarrelsome and temperamental. By

April he was asking to return to Syria. Freya jibbed at paying
his return fare, so he commissioned a public letter-writer to
petition the Governor asking for repatriation at government
expense.

On 9 June 1940 Freya replied to a note from the Civil Secretary, Aden.

> It is quite inaccurate that my servant Isa Abbas came here
> at Government expense . . . He is a very unsatisfactory ser-
> vant and has been warned that the police will interfere if he
> is again disorderly or quarrelsome, so I should be delighted
> if he went. At the same time, as he is a perfectly able-bodied
> youth, I have no wish to pay for another very expensive
> passage, when he can quite well find some work to do.[10]

A few days later she writes she has sacked Isa, and he disappears from the story. Whether he ever made it back to Syria
one does not know.

PART FOUR

FREYA'S BROTHERHOOD
1939–1941

ELEVEN

FREYA'S WAR

Freya's wartime career was the logical continuation of her activities in the 1930s, leading on from low-level topographical survey to the manipulation of Arab opinion through clandestine political agencies. In the dark period of Britain's reverses between 1940 and 1943 she argued convincingly for a tolerant response to the nascent threat of nationalism among the local Middle East populations, vassal states occupied militarily and firmly held to their treaty obligations with Britain. The stirrings of nationalist sentiment among young Arabs should not be reprobated, but taken over as a propaganda initiative – a big brother helping a younger brother was a favourite analogy – and so contained. It was foolish, in her view, to cast oneself as an adversary, when by paying discreet lip-service it would be possible to lay the foundations of post-war influence through sympathetic educational and cultural institutions.

The flimsy Western political scaffolding erected in 1920 on the former Ottoman territories and held in place by the Adviserate system of 'indirect' rule was a house of cards she had no wish to see pulled down. Mental agility and fertility of invention was what advanced her as a propagandist. Her patriotism and her stance of adamant refusal to acknowledge the possibility of defeat was an asset her senior colleagues were glad to acknowledge, and at war's end to reward, when her actual usefulness in the field was over.

There was so much gossip attached to Freya's goings-on in

middle life when she was an employee of the wartime Ministry
of Information that it was hard in the 1980s, when I began
seriously to explore her life, to disentangle fact from fiction.
Freya's preoccupations in the war period mirrored those of her
associates in the closed circle of Middle East political intelligence and counter-propaganda. It was an exciting, glamorous,
superficial world she evoked in her memoirs, the sense of being
a part of the shifting panorama of world conflict supplying the
artistic chiaroscuro to what was essentially a covert association
with the events occupying the centre stage.

This was one area which offered me some firmness of footing.
Here at least I was on documented ground, and I decided to
concentrate on unravelling what came first to hand – the mysti-
fication surrounding her activities in Cairo and Baghdad; this
might supply me with the connecting link between the popular
travel writer of the Thirties and the acclaimed expert on Arab
affairs of the post-war years. What *were* Freya's tea-parties all
about? How did they come into being? The Public Records
Office did at least supply some facts about the Brotherhood
scheme, and insights into its scope, but it got me no further in
elucidating the mysteries of Freya's origins, and what formed
her. That had to wait.

The aspect of Freya's personality most difficult for her colleagues to contend with was her ability to justify herself, not
only in others' eyes, but in her own as well. Here it fostered
convictions difficult to dispel. Her rapidity of mind induced distrust and in the more experienced of her associates wariness.
In her own view this was mere irritating masculine prejudice.

Like a cuttle-fish, she emitted ink when challenged or disturbed, within whose dusky clouds she could manoeuvre
unseen. This led to disagreements with colleagues in which
Freya did not hesitate to invoke higher authority to support her
case. Out of this arose a feeling among many who had dealings
with her at this period that she was a dangerous enemy whom
it was unwise to cross, 'as she had friends in high places' and
could make things very awkward for the unwary.[1] The fuss
these upsets engendered eventually detracted from her value

in practical terms; it was generally felt, when the future of her Brotherhood was reviewed early in 1944 by the Foreign Office, that it had not developed into a viable proposition capable of sustaining itself without clandestine support. It was too much the projection of one person's personality to function independently, relying as it did entirely on word-of-mouth propaganda and personal influence.

The Brotherhood survived after the war in Egypt until 1952, though the Iraqi government closed it down as soon as British military occupation was ended, and in Palestine the scheme never got off the ground, being considered too double-edged for safety by the British High Commission. Freya's departure from the Middle East in 1943 was final, though she did not sign off from the Ministry of Information until her return in the summer of 1944 from her lecture tour in America. This enabled her to write *East is West*, a book commissioned by an American publisher at the suggestion of the head of the Oriental Institute in Chicago; the parallel English edition was published by John Murray in 1945. It aimed to show America that the Arab world was an entity whose voice it would be unwise to ignore, and it licensed her to bombard former senior associates with extracts on which she sought informed comment. It gave a bland and heart-warming interpretation of Arab relations with Britain in wartime which was immediately popular with British readers; it flattered their own self-esteem. Disillusion with its viewpoint was yet to come, as the British position in the East crumbled irretrievably, and the old paternalistic relationship which Freya so admired was rejected by the very elements in the local populations she had claimed to capture through the Brotherhood.

Up to the Munich crisis of 1938 Freya's personal fame was largely localised in her circle of friends in Italy and England, and in the communities of her fellow-countrymen in the Middle East on whom she had impinged in the course of her early travels. But as the political tensions in Europe intensified, and the Italian war of conquest in Abyssinia polarised opinion in Britain on the matter of sanctions against the Fascist dictatorships, Freya's own ambitions expanded. She was no longer content to be a best-selling travel writer and journalist, appealing to a cultivated middlebrow readership, she wanted to exert influence on her country's attitudes by guiding the politicians to awareness of the threat to Britain's interests of Mussolini's expansionist policy in Africa. She was insistent on the need to stamp on Italian pretensions at once; she didn't exactly hear voices but she did want to play a role in the events impending.

Her appetite for political life was whetted by her proximity in Asolo to the families of wealthy fellow-countrymen such as the head of the Guinness clan, Lord Iveagh, a resident there since 1931. Lady Iveagh was a sister of Lady Halifax, wife of the former Viceroy of India, now at the Colonial Office, and shortly to become Britain's Foreign Minister in the Chamberlain government of 1938. Through Lady Iveagh, Lord Halifax had been persuaded to take an interest in Freya's first journey to Hadhramaut in 1935, which greatly facilitated her entry to that British Protectorate. This gave her the material for her successful second book, *The Southern Gates of Arabia* and, in turn, a new identity as an authority on southern Arabia.

Freya, at the time of the Munich crisis of 1938, taking her cue from the Iveaghs' movements, went to London to lobby her usefulness for government work in the event of war. When war became imminent in 1939, she again travelled to London from Asolo at the end of August, so as to be at hand should her services be required.

Nothing concrete awaited her, but she was passed by the Foreign Office's Middle East Department to the newly formed Ministry of Information, whose Middle East Propaganda Section was temporarily housed in the Foreign Office itself, under the direction of Professor Rushbrook Williams. Freya was taken on by this organisation as an expert on South Arabia, at a salary of £600 p.a. She took up her duties on 4 September 1939, one of a small group of people sharing a knowledge of Arabic and a familiarity with the Middle East. She sat at a table with Sir Kinahan Cornwallis, a retired Iraq government official and former member of the Sudan Political Service, an acquaintance from the period of Freya's arrival in Baghdad ten years previously, where since 1921 Cornwallis had been Adviser to the Iraq Ministry of the Interior. Prior to that appointment, he was Director of the Arab Bureau in Cairo, in succession to Dr Hogarth, its wartime chief. This was the organisation that financed and set in motion in 1916 the pan-Arab revolt, led by the Hashemite ruling family of the Hejaz, against their Ottoman overlords, in which T. E. Lawrence, Sir Ronald Storrs, Cornwallis and Major Gilbert Clayton played a part.

Less than a fortnight after she joined, the department was reorganised, and to Freya's disappointment she was not retained in London. A request, however, had come from Aden, where Stewart Perowne, the recent friend acquired on her second visit to Hadhramaut in 1937–8, was now installed as Government Information Officer. He asked for her services as his assistant on the programme of Arabic news broadcasts he was instituting to counter Axis propaganda, beamed to the Red Sea area from the neutral Italian colonial possessions in the Horn of Africa.

Freya's friendship with Stewart Perowne, a political officer in the Aden Secretariat, dated from her second visit to Aden with the Wakefield archaeological expedition, when he had enthusiastically welcomed the celebrated author and made himself generally useful to her. They corresponded after her departure, and the acquaintance developed further in London during the winter of 1938–9, when he was seconded for a year to the BBC to be instructed in the running of a radio news service in the event of war. An entertaining, erudite, snobbish and ambitious man, he was tailor-made to attract her attention, both as an Arabist and a lively conversationalist. Having begun his career in the Palestine educational service on coming down from Oxford, he had a background of intimate experience of Arab life, which made him not only a congenial but also a useful friend for Freya to cultivate.

On Cornwallis's advice, Freya took up Perowne's offer. Nothing else had presented itself and, on the principle of a bird in the hand, Freya began her preparations for her departure to Aden. This entailed a detour through Asolo to pick up her wardrobe and say goodbye to her mother. In the first week of October she left London and began a leisurely train journey via Venice to Turkey and on to Cairo, carrying in her luggage the first batch of newsfilm to be sent by the Ministry of Information to the Middle East.

She broke her journey to look up connections in the various British missions en route. Calling on the British Ambassador in Ankara, she was briefly introduced to the newly appointed Middle East Army Commander, Lieutenant-General Wavell, there with the French General Gamelin to initial an Anglo-French military agreement with the Turks.

When Freya travelled to Cairo, it was as an employee of the Ministry of Information, as indeed she remained until 1944 when she resigned to write *East is West*. The Ministry was an offshoot of the Foreign Office, from which it took its policy directives. On her reappearance in the wartime Middle East Freya experienced what she described as a sort of prodigal's return, received with open arms 'and everyone so welcoming and kind'. By now her reputation as a pundit on Middle-Eastern affairs was considerable. Her influential friends in London, her literary success and travel adventures had made her a local celebrity.

She arrived in Cairo on the last day of October 1939, and had several days to wait before a passage could be arranged on a small coasting steamer to Aden. She did not waste her opportunities, but embarked on a round of 'social giddiness, lunching and dining every day . . .' she told Sir Sydney Cockerell on 2 November. 'I could stay here for the duration,' she continued, 'as they asked to have me, but it would not be very fair to drop Aden now, and I rather think my work there may be more useful.'[2]

Freya on the spot was a better proposition to men casting around for instruments than Freya in Italy or in an office in London. She told her mother:

I seem to have lots of friends all congregated in Cairo, and they wrote to ask me to work here, but the letter never reached. Do you realise that it is almost *unique* at present to have been asked for by *three* Government departments? My nice gay little Colonel in Jerusalem . . . confided that he would give almost anything to have such a thing done for him and walk in as a Lion . . .

General Wavell's appointment to Cairo in July 1939, with a staff of six planners and an ADC to set up Middle East Command headquarters, had soon caused ripples of anxiety to reach the Foreign Office from the Embassy there. As long as Italy remained neutral, Cabinet policy was clear. Nothing was to be done to provoke her. Wavell thought this policy quite misguided and from his first moment in Cairo was secretly organising daring and imaginative schemes for the discomfiture of the Italians in Libya and the Horn of Africa, in which sabotage and the fomenting of patriotic rebellion were ingredients.

Friction with the Embassy soon arose over the activities of the Middle East Intelligence Centre, an organisation chartered by the Committee of Imperial Defence in 1938 to collate information for the benefit of all three Service Commanders in the area. In charge of MEIC was a Colonel Walter Cawthorn,[3] an Australian of engaging personality, but described in confidential Foreign Office memoranda on the situation as 'an extremely ambitious and comparatively young Indian Army officer, very anxious to find favour with General Wavell, and consequently inclined to push against the Embassy'.[4]

Wavell resisted promptly and vigorously all attempts on the part of the Ambassador, Sir Miles Lampson, to undermine the existence of the MEIC, and as he had the Service Ministries behind him, the Foreign Office gave ground. The papers in the Public Record Office reveal the intensity of the Foreign Office dislike for the Centre, and record Lampson's obstructive attitude. 'A monstrous organisation creeping into political activity' was how it was seen in London and strenuous efforts were made to do away with it by Lampson's Whitehall cronies.[5] General Wavell's objection to its abolition was attributed sourly to the fact that Colonel Cawthorn and his staff acted as intelligence officers for him, and were exceeding their brief.

Among the men with whom Freya in Cairo renewed acquaintance was Reginald Davies, formerly Adviser to the Alexandria Municipality, whom she first met in the winter of 1937–8 when on her way to Hadhramaut with the Wakefield archaeological expedition. He was now Area representative of the Ministry of Information in the Middle East, and responsible for the dissemination of the flood of guidance on the broad outlines of British policy which emanated from the Foreign Office. As the senior M of I appointment in the Middle East Area, Reginald Davies was in some sense Freya's superior, though she was seconded from the M of I to the Aden government as Stewart Perowne's assistant.

Whether it was he who introduced Freya to Cawthorn of MEIC, or whether it was through Sir Kinahan Cornwallis that the link was made, the upshot was that before Freya left Cairo, she had committed herself to do a job for MEIC once she reached Aden, and it was fixed up with the connivance of the London office.[6] So from her arrival in Aden she was operating on two levels, and keeping secret the plans that were being made for her in Cairo by an agency already at loggerheads with her own Service. Neither Perowne, nor Sir Bernard Reilly, the Governor of Aden, was informed of the plan until after Freya's installation there. Somewhat taken aback, they none the less agreed to the loan of her services, though Perowne held out for two months' use of her first.

The scheme outlined to Freya in Cairo centred on the independent kingdom of the Yemen north of the Aden Protectorate. It was a country Freya had long wished to see. Its Red Sea coastline faced the Italian colonies in the Horn of Africa, in dangerous proximity to the narrow passage from the Indian Ocean into the Red Sea. Freya was aware of the tortuous intricacies of its relations with Aden from her attempt to gain entry into the territory in 1935; and her fluent Italian, coupled with her reputation for daring and enterprise, made her a desirable accomplice in any scheme for clandestine observation proposed by MEIC.

In Freya's luggage she carried some cans of Ministry of Information newsreel and documentary film destined for Aden. Was it she who suggested showing the film in Yemen, as a counterstroke to the Italians' virtual monopoly of publicity in the Red Sea area? She was good at throwing out ideas, and the gesture would be in keeping with the pugnacity of her anti-appeasement crusade, a vindication of her belief in action.

Freya reached Aden in the second half of November, and

was immediately put to work by Perowne turning the Reuter news agency telegrams into standard English, ready for translation into the daily Arabic radio news bulletins. These were broadcast on loudspeakers every evening to the crowds thronging the main square of Crater, the business centre of Aden. Hardly had she arrived than she was writing to the M of I in London that her visit to Yemen was planned in two months' time. On 8 December she wrote to Cornwallis, criticising the Cabinet policy of doing nothing to provoke the Italians into abandoning neutrality.

> The fault is not here: our hands are tied and we have to sit still under every Italian infringement of gentleman's and every other agreement. Now that seems to me quite idiotic . . . I hope to go up to the Yemen in seven or eight weeks' time if this is possible to manage. The idea is to sit there, visit harems, rectify rumours, and alter the atmosphere as much as one can from the standpoint of female insignificance, which has its compensations. Sir Bernard Reilly and Stewart Perowne have both agreed to this with their usual broadmindedness. I shall enjoy going immensely. Of course I may not be able to do anything at all. Everyone says that it is immensely difficult.[7]

Perowne had preceded Freya to Aden in August 1939, to take up his duties as government Information Officer, supervising the distribution of open or 'white' propaganda in the shape of news bulletins and talks relayed by the BBC, and in pamphlets and leaflets printed by the government. At first everything went smoothly between the pair. The Aden office consisted of themselves, an English secretary, and a handful of young Arab translators and copy writers, whom Perowne had recruited and trained. Their office looked out across the bay and its shipping, and Freya had two rooms on the terrace above it for her private living quarters.

She was very happy, she told her friends, doing pleasant work with pleasant people. Perowne was very much the boss, and Freya found him a wayward but fascinating experience; she was content to fall into her allotted role as his assistant, and to take his direction. They worked together harmoniously, she explained slyly to their London chief, Professor Rushbrook Williams, when he paid them a visit, because both Perowne and she agreed that woman's place was in the background. She told Sydney Cockerell:

> In the evening when the office is closed, I have sherry brought out on my terrace and we talk of the day's doings or anything pleasant we can think of, and people come dropping in. I find it agreeably restful not to be responsible. I don't honestly think that I care one little bit who gets the credit as long as the work is done.

In a few weeks, she added, she would be uprooted to do more arduous work, for the machinery was to be put in motion after Christmas to detach her from Perowne's side. 'I am getting awfully *dependent*. Stewart likes bossing and organising and I find it rather pleasant to sit and watch him,' she confided to her mother by the next post. In the restricted society of Aden they were thrown together a good deal, and Freya enjoyed appearing at parties and dances on the arm of the most amusing man in the colony. Any party Stewart attended, so people said, was bound to be a success.

The majority of wives of the resident community had already gone, evacuated home with their children, and Freya frequently danced the night away at Government House parties and Garrison balls. She walked and rode and danced and displayed the dresses her mother Flora posted down to her from still-neutral Italy, and generally enjoyed to the full the social resources of the winter season in Aden. Her verve and social stamina, and her hats, earned her the wondering admiration of the Garrison population, to whom she was an entertaining novelty. One young couple, the de Lotbinières, who were rather taken up by her, received the impression that there was 'something up' between herself and Perowne.[8]

Perowne travelled about his parish whenever occasion offered; this included Jibouti, the allied French Somaliland colony on the African shore of the Red Sea. Long recognised by the Aden expatriates as an outpost of French sophistication, it was a magnet for people seeking a change from the staid respectability of a British colony. During Perowne's absence Freya had charge of the office, and ran the daily operation in his place. During these absences she had leisure to think. Her informal upbringing had left her untrammelled by insular prejudice. She soon noted the disadvantages inherent in the conventional attitudes of the ruling race, in which convictions of racial superiority played a part, and where the female was automatically subordinate to the male. She was to have ample time to reflect on them in the coming months.

The plan to send Freya up to the Yemen was set in motion during Christmas week. The granting of the necessary permit to enter what was in effect a closed kingdom was negotiated by Colonel Lake, the Political Secretary, an old acquaintance from Freya's previous two visits to Hadhramaut. Maurice Lake was a spare, reticent bachelor; like the Governor, Sir Bernard Reilly, he was a long-serving Indian Political appointment, whose career in south-west Arabia had opened in 1912, in the days when the Ottoman Turk and his German friends were the danger, and the Yemen was an Ottoman fief garrisoned by Turkish troops, and a threat to Aden. Lake was an experienced political agent, with a fingertip awareness of the system of pressure and conciliation by which an objective is attained in Asiatic autocracies. Freya received her briefing from him in the course of a week's excursion into the mountainous hinterland of Aden to visit the Amir of Dhala, in a party consisting of Colonel Lake, Perowne, herself, and the young de Lotbinières. It was for her the culmination of her long campaign to *do* something about the Italians, and tangible evidence that she was being taken seriously by men engaged, at however great a remove, in the manipulation of events in the Arab world.

On 1 February 1940 Freya crossed the border of the Aden Protectorate to the Yemen's Red Sea littoral, then went 202 miles up the only motorable road inland from Hodeida to the capital city of Sana'a, some 6000 feet above sea level on the central plateau. She made the journey in a Ford van with an Arab driver, her servant Isa and a cook found for her by Perowne, and two mechanics to minister to the vehicle and to the portable cinema projector and screen she carried with her, along with cans of newsreel sent from London. She also had a bundle of shawls and chiffon scarves, embroidered with gold and silver thread, to give as presents; these were bought in the Aden market with the £100 subscribed by her sponsors towards the incidental expenses of her trip.

This trip was arranged to overlap a visit by Colonel Lake to the Imam a month later; frontier rectification was under discussion. Freya's entry to Yemen was arranged on the grounds of health. Her age and appearance, and her scholarly interests, fitted comfortably into local stereotypes of missionaries and schoolteachers, and made acceptable her identity as a tourist. Her brief was to counteract the monopoly of Italian influence in the country by the showing, if possible, of newsfilm, and by introducing alternative interpretations of events in conversation.

This she did cleverly by titillating the interest of the female dependants of the leading families of the Yemen, sequestered in their harems, and glad of the distraction of a social call from the few foreign women in the country. There were two women doctors in Sana'a, one Italian, one British, attached to their respective medical missions, and Freya used their favoured position to gain entry for herself to the households of the leading men. The practice of medicine was a recognised route by which a Christian or Jew could obtain entry and employment in a closed Islamic society, and both Italy and Britain utilised this to maintain missions in the country. The two countries collaborated jealously in the running of the country's medical services, in which the Italian contingent far outnumbered the two Britons on detachment from the Protestant mission in Aden.

Yemen in 1940 was an independent Arab kingdom, secretive, aloof, shut away on its lofty plateau in medieval seclusion. Such foreign influence as was tolerated in the country was in the hands of the Italians, in the shape of the medical mission and individual doctors scattered at strategic places about the country. By far the largest foreign colony was in Sana'a, a group of some dozen Italians attached to the hospital and consulate. It was the British aim, if not to wean the Imam from his policy of friendliness towards the Italians, at least to ensure that nothing detrimental to Aden's interests should occur. Any indication of the way the wind was blowing in Sana'a would be useful. To sit as an unsuspected observer, absorbing all the gossip of the town, was work for which Freya was well suited, and which she enjoyed. It was what she had done in Hadhramaut. It suited a combative element in her personality which found satisfaction in scoring off her Italian rivals – Fascists always in the new-speak of propaganda.

Sana'a was a strange and claustrophobic place in which to be, a walled city of tall, stone-built palaces and tenements seamed by narrow, dusty alleyways, at night lit only by the lanterns of the watchmen, but not unfamiliar to one who had experienced Hadhramaut. The romance of her situation, alone for nearly two months as an official government guest, her personal servants her sole intermediaries with the wholly male authority of the Imam's court, stimulated her imagination. She was never presented to the Imam; as a woman she was not regarded as important enough, or of any diplomatic significance, and as the need for a holiday and change of air was among the reasons advanced for her presence in the Yemen, this reinforced the notion of her harmlessness. She had a good deal of time on her hands, which she used to keep up her large correspondence. Her lively, vivid accounts of her daily life there earned the admiration of the friends and colleagues who received them, and two articles for *The Times* further enhanced her reputation as a daring traveller and informed reporter.

Whatever may have resulted in the long term from Freya's arrangements with MEIC, the immediate impact of her arrival in Sana'a was deeply satisfying. The British presence there was modest and self-effacing compared with that of the Italians. Its main function was ophthalmic, and the young eye-surgeon was a member of the Keith Faulkner mission in Aden. Freya described the medical staff as:

small, Christian, and urged to conciliate at all costs; it went
to the Fascist tea parties (where there was the only good
tennis court) and tried the hopeless task of persuading Arabs
that medicine alone is the business of medical missions. The
Yemen, which only heard Italian news, and anyway does not
believe in discarding from weakness, thought Democracy was
losing the war.[9]

Freya's cinema show opened up alternative considerations in
a country regarded by the Italians as their own particular oyster,
giving food for gossip and speculation in a society whose rulers
alone were linked by wireless to the news of the outside world.
To the spoken word she added the impact of the moving image:
the fighter planes swooping, the battleships in their armoured
might cutting through the thunderous seas, the Germans scut-
tling their pocket battle-cruiser *Graf Spee* in Montevideo Bay.

It had been Freya's confident belief, based on her previous
experience of Islamic life, that once she reached Sana'a the
harems of the ruling family and its chief ministers would be
opened for her to show her films. And so it turned out. Freya's
nights were spent in the houses of the leading families of the
kingdom, giving private shows to each household in turn, for
convention decreed that no male outside the immediate family
could intrude in the privacy of the individual harem, however
freely the womenfolk might visit among themselves. She would
explain in Arabic what was happening on the film, turning up
the volume so that everyone could enjoy the noise of guns and
bombs, and she let the children play with the microphone once
the show was over, while she folded up the portable screen
and packed up the projector. Tea and sweetmeats were served
and the film was talked over until, like a conjuror whose entertainment is at an end once his props are dismantled, she would
be returned down the flights of steep stone stairs to the small
discreet door at the side of the house, where her servant waited
beside the ancient vehicle which had been sent to convey her
to and from her lodging.

The skill and panache with which she brought off this adventure redounded greatly to her credit in official circles on her

return to Aden, and enhanced her reputation in the world of political warfare. How much her fire-eating willingness to be of use in the complicated exercise of dishing the Italians on their own doorstep was sheer pugnacity and the desire to get a blow in first, or whether it had more serious objectives, is impossible now to say.

Freya's little arrangement with Cawthorn was possibly nothing more than a useful identifying of the personalities of the Italian mission, and their likely roles. She could bring back her own observations, and gossip picked up in the small European community living in the country, but she was not anxious to compromise herself in the eyes of her hosts, and was wary of attempting anything more. Colonel Lake would have better options at his disposal than anything Freya was likely to produce.

The conquest of Ethiopia had made the Italians perhaps over-confident of their ascendancy along the Red Sea coasts, while instinct warned the Yemen's ruling family that their country might well be the next to be taken over. Freya's modest cinema, with its newsreels and innocuous documentary portrayals of Ordinary Life in Britain (these were a great success in the harems), provided an enjoyable counteraction to a threatening influence at no cost to the Imam, who was perhaps pleased to see Italian pretensions receive a check without any intervention on his own part.

Her cook was a Yemeni, who like many others had found lucrative employment in Aden. He attended the royal *majlis* every day, the traditional occasion when the Ruler makes himself available to his subjects, and a court open to all is held. In the egalitarian tradition of Islam, this is a forum of comment, and for the passing of news among the many different ranks of society assembled. Here the courtesies of Freya's visit were regulated, the arrangements for her meals, and for those of her guards: three soldiers quartered on the ground floor of the small house she had been allotted in the old Turkish quarter of the town, where the European community lived. Secluded at the top of the house, she received there the courtesy calls of officials come to enquire for her well-being, formal attentions

which relieved the tedium of everyone's days, and provided
Freya with the opportunity to do her bit for the democratic
cause, and to produce the sallies and witticisms at the expense
of the Italians which would be passed on in the labyrinthine
recesses of an eastern court.

The pay-off for these triumphs came somewhat later, and in
a very disagreeable way. Upon Italy's entry into the war, in
June 1940, Freya's mother Flora and their old family friend
Herbert Young were arrested in Asolo by the Fascist authorities. It was his house, later known as the Villa Freia, that Freya
was to inherit after his death in 1941. They were held in great
discomfort in the common jail at Treviso for a month, with a
further month's exile under surveillance in a village in Apulia,
before Italian friends negotiated their release, and they were
allowed to return to three rooms in the upper storey of Herbert's house in Asolo, by now requisitioned for evacuees.

Herbert Young was eighty-six at this time and died some
months after his return home, while Flora Stark was seventy-
nine. She was permitted to leave for America in 1941 after
Herbert's death, and was taken into the house of her friend
Lucy Beach, the well-to-do American who, in 1925, had revived
the *tessoria*, the small silk-weaving workshop in Asolo of which
Flora Stark became the eventual owner and which Freya
inherited after her death. Like the majority of American expatriates, the Beaches returned home at the outbreak of war in
Europe, and it was in their house in California that Flora died
a year later in 1942.

Freya was unaware of these developments until she came up
from Aden to Cairo in July 1940, and was not prepared for
them. She had believed, as they did, that two such elderly and
long-established residents were unlikely to be harassed by the
Italian authorities. The news came as a very great shock, doubly
disagreeable when it was found that the arrest was inspired by
the Fascist head of the Italian mission in Sana'a, who had not
failed to check back through his own intelligence sources on the
antecedents of the middle-aged Italian-speaking Englishwoman
who had dropped a stone into the quiet pool of the Yemen.

The accounts of the expelled Italian Consul in Aden of her

social prominence and her broadcasting activities there also filtered back to Asolo, where it was commonly believed she was a spy. Whatever had resulted, or was believed to have resulted, from Freya's visit to Sana'a, the counter-stroke was swift, and cruel, and could be construed as a warning to Freya not to meddle. As it happened, Flora Stark, with admirable self-possession and resourcefulness, looked after herself and Herbert Young, and was arranging for them both to go to America when he died. Freya, cut off now by war from communication with Italy, was powerless to do anything for her mother, and it was Flora's influential Italian neighbour at Maser, the Contessa Marina Volpi, and Flora's son-in-law, Vera's husband Mario di Roascio, who arranged matters for her, and sent her safe to America in 1941.

Freya had been assiduous in courting a visit from Stewart Perowne while in Sana'a, but without success. A scheme for him to come up to join her for a ride back to Aden came to nothing, hardly surprising when entry permits were so hard to come by. Perowne's interest in her was practical and pragmatic to a degree she apparently did not appreciate, and this was to have embarrassing consequences.

By the time Freya left, she had had enough of Sana'a. She told Perowne:

> I am so glad to have been here, living the life of the town for six weeks, for it really does make one realise the oriental histories, the constant intrigue, secrecy, rumour, caprice of it all. But how can one live in such an atmosphere? I took a ride out in the afternoon, and it was delicious to be outside the walls, and see people ploughing their fields, and the pleasant green patches of corn catching the sun . . .[10]

It was as if the strain of the adventure was beginning to tell on her. She had stirred up a hornet's nest in the Italian community, whose leader angrily challenged to her face the innocence of her activities in the Yemen, so that she was ostracised and made conscious of the Italians' dislike of her. She came back

to Aden by ship from Hodeida, 'the expense of which I have to
pay if you please,' she told Jock Murray, unable to face the
return journey overland, because she was on the verge of collapse, 'exhausted by the *very* strenuous time I had had there,
hardly ever less than seven or nine hours' hefty Arabic per
day, and often a cinema show in the evening.'[11] Despite these
complaints, she settled to correcting the proofs of her fourth
book, *A Winter in Arabia*, the account of the Wakefield
expedition of 1937–8 to Hadhramaut, which were in her mail
at Hodeida, while awaiting a passage.

Freya's stock was high on her return from Yemen, and her
self-confidence proportionately enhanced. 'My expedition to
Yemen appears to have been a success, and I have the happy
feeling of having done one useful piece of work however small
– a definite little twist seems to have remained in opinion there,'
she wrote on her return to Aden, though a fortnight later she
was acknowledging that her newsreel operation – against Perowne's instructions she had left £160 worth of equipment behind
to maintain the service – had been closed down the day after
she left.[12] These however were local irritations. From London
she was invited to become godmother to the son of Alan Lennox-Boyd, a future Cabinet Minister. Her co-godparent was
Winston Churchill.

Freya returned to Aden to the last whirl of the winter season.
A large box of clothes arrived from her mother at the end of
April. She was delighted. 'The only one I *daren't* wear is the
pink which is just twenty years too late in the day! . . .'[13] The
war was coming closer to Aden, but the gaiety continued. Her
relations with Perowne were a source of coy private speculation
which invaded her correspondence. 'So *tantalising* of you to
say that Stewart *likes* me and not to say why,' she added in a
PS to her mother on 29 April. 'The fact is *nothing*, the *reason*
everything in these *matters*!!' It was as if some quality in him
exercised a fascination which made his capture ever more
imperative. This in turn acted as a stimulant to him; like two
lively horses they vied with each other in the gallop of high
spirits and fun to which he introduced her.

This was the social side of their relationship. The working

side was another matter, and here things were not always so smooth. They did not necessarily agree on the presentation of their material. Freya had her own ideas, and during Perowne's absences aired them in correspondence with London, writing over his head to Rushbrook Williams, and sending her observations on the Yemen direct to Lord Lloyd, the new Colonial Secretary, and a London acquaintance. This was the sort of thing that had earned Gertrude Bell a good deal of enmity among younger officials of the Iraq Mandate in the 1920s, and perhaps it was responsible for the element of irritation and tendency to snub that Perowne now began to display towards Freya.

As the Germans swept over north-western Europe, Freya was intensely patriotic and unflinching in the face of the worsening situation. Ideas, schemes, suggestions were promoted with all the energy and persistence of committed belief. When the threatened hostilities with Italy drew closer, she pressed for the co-opting of local volunteers as air-raid wardens and police auxiliaries in Aden. What did it matter, she argued, if they were less efficient than might be desired, or that they did things in a different way? The point to keep in view was that people who were actively committed to the British side would experience a feeling of solidarity and increased self-esteem in their relations with their rulers. The way to obtain friendship, she suggested, was to treat others as friends. It was by confiding difficulties that you obtained sympathetic support, not by pretending they did not exist, or by rejecting as meddlesome intrusions any offer of help from people outside your own particular experience.

Freya's insights owed as much to her relations with Perowne as to Jeremy Bentham. Perowne, she felt, monopolised all the important roles and left little for others to do as a share in the common task, except in a menial capacity. This was short-sighted. Freya, throughout her life, obtained much practical support from people whose generosity and goodwill responded to just such approaches as she now sought to introduce to the job of public relations.

In June, with the reality of war with Italy upon them, the existing propaganda directives from London were useless, and new talking points had to be thought out. Some 1000 pamphlets

on *Why Italy will not come into the War* were burnt. Perowne
all along had tended to this view, and bet twelve bottles of
vermouth that the Italians would not fight. Freya was more
pragmatic. She made her will and bought enough face cream to
last the duration. She pressed all the more anxiously her idea
of utilising volunteer enthusiasm to generate loyalty to Britain's
cause. '*I* think that the only sound propaganda in this sort of
time is to ask people to *do* things for one,' she wrote to the art
historian Tom Boase on 7 June, three days before Italy declared
war. She saw this as calling on a reserve which had as yet
hardly been tapped.

> The desire of average people to *give* rather than to *receive*
> . . . There is . . . a natural and almost universal generosity
> that makes people glad to be asked for sacrifice and service;
> and we have rarely appealed for such things outside our own
> race. Now we have a tough time ahead and it is not certain
> that the appeal of power will be at our command; we may
> have to rely on what we can do without the adjunct of success.

Her suggestion was

> (a) that we keep our local population *busy doing things for us*,
> so as to encourage the affection that is lavished only on the
> receiver of benefits in an unjust world; (b) that they should
> do them as far as possible in their way rather than ours so
> as to avoid any inferiority complexes. If we can arouse the
> feeling of service, we can count on loyalty in difficult times.[14]

Freya was worried, she explained to Harold Ingrams, who
as Acting Governor was drawn into the dispute, lest she was
not pulling her weight in the matter of work; that Perowne kept
her to routine office duties, at which she was bad, instead of
allowing her to do what she was good at, that is talking to
people, especially Arabs.

It was her conviction, nurtured by her family's Italian sympa-
thies, that the Italians as a nation were not wholeheartedly
behind Mussolini, and that the Fascist regime was a domination

by only one element in the population, and would gladly be discarded by more moderate elements were they given encouragement. Out of her correspondence with Rushbrook Williams, her chief in London, came a suggestion that Freya should go up to Cairo to talk over ideas for anti-Fascist propaganda at an M of I Area Conference in July 1940. This was something Perowne could hardly refuse. There was no inkling then that she would not be returning to Aden.

In charge of anti-Fascist activities, overt and covert, in Cairo was Colonel C. M. Thornhill, CMG, DSO, an old regimental friend of General Wavell. He had recently been sent out from London by the Special Operations Executive with Christopher Sykes, whom Freya had already met in London in the winter season of 1938–9, as his assistant. To them Freya explained her ideas. Her fluent Italian had been used in Aden to assist in the interrogation of some Italian naval prisoners of war. This encouraged her to believe that skilful handling of prisoners might 'bring over' the many she claimed were at heart opposed to Mussolini's regime and the German alliance. On 8 August 1940 a pamphlet was circulated under Thornhill's and her name, *A Memorandum on Anti-Italian Propaganda in the Middle East.*

The idea in it of a Garibaldi brigade, as it was later called, was to surface again in Freya's career, but it never really got off the ground. The Italian community in Egypt was staunchly pro-Fascist; the prisoners formed Fascist groups in the prison camps and bullied the non-Fascists. The element of patriotism in the captives was in excess of what had been predicted, and fear of reprisals probably kept others silent. However energetically Freya promoted the idea of re-educating prisoners to act as a fan of anti-Fascist scouts in the event of an invasion of the Italian mainland, in 1940 the scheme was still-born. An interview was arranged for her to present her ideas to General Wavell at GHQ. The encounter was hardly a success. Freya's propensity to hero-worship made her shy, and the General, notorious for his silences, merely listened while Freya outlined her scheme to him. A raid on the hinterland of Genoa – the country of her own youth and upbringing – to encourage the anti-Fascist element in the population, was what she suggested. Wavell listened impassively, and closed the interview with the laconic remark: 'I have no troops to spare.' But the idea stuck, and he later asked Peter Fleming to look into it. Fleming turned it down, and moved on to sabotage activities in northern Greece.

An echo of the idea, relayed by Colonel Donovan,[15] the American presidential observer who was in Cairo that winter and whom Freya met, may have sounded in the Americans' use of Mafia connections to prepare the way for their landings in Sicily in 1943, and in the orchestration of the partisan uprisings in north-west Italy in 1944. By a particular irony Freya's surviving Italian nephew, a boy in his early twenties, was killed at that time in a partisan skirmish with the Germans, fortunate perhaps to escape capture and the brutal reprisals exacted as the Germans withdrew towards their own frontier.

Once she arrived in Cairo for the M of I Area conference, Freya was soon launched. 'Everyone I *know* seems to be in Cairo, and mostly in GHQ, of which there seem to be dozens,' she told Sir Sydney Cockerell on 24 July. The diplomatic options had run out, and military necessities predominated. General Wavell's enhanced status as the only commander still confronting the Axis in a theatre of war ensured a more receptive attitude to his needs than had hitherto prevailed.

TWELVE

BIRTH OF THE BROTHERHOOD

It was the reappearance in Freya's account of her wartime career of names already familiar from the 1914–18 war and its aftermath that focused my interest in her involvement in the Middle East politics of World War II and how this affected her status as a literary figure. I received a sense of closely guarded, tenaciously held schemes to maintain and expand British influence, however much lip-service was being paid to the sovereignty of individual states. It was a fortunate conjunction for Freya that her summons to Cairo in the summer of 1940 should coincide with the emergence of the hitherto low-profile General Wavell as a major player in the only theatre of war in which Britain still had a presence. She came into the orbit of a military commander alert to the advantages of the unorthodox approach, and prepared to back its implementation in situations where more conventional solutions were unenforceable.

Freya's meteoric rise to prominence in wartime Cairo, when she hobnobbed with the great figures of the Middle East scene and formed exciting new social connections in their entourages, had about it, for those with a historical perspective, something of the quality of the *déjà vu*. The factor in common was the career of Gertrude Bell, traveller, archaeologist and government servant, who died in Baghdad in 1926, two years before Freya herself appeared on the Middle-Eastern scene. The two never met.

Freya never cared for being bracketed in people's minds with

Gertrude Bell (1868–1926), the last exponent of the grand style of travel in the Middle East, with its backing of wealth and influential connections.[1] Recognition of her own individuality was what Freya sought in coming to the East, not being linked to another 'as a sort of Siamese twin'. But the association was inevitable, for she replicated a generation later, in a modified form, the activities of the older woman. Seen in the context of Gertrude Bell's role in the Anglo-Arab politics of World War I, as the victors formed new kingdoms and republics under League of Nation Mandates, out of the Arab provinces of the defeated Ottoman Empire, Freya's own career as an Arab expert falls into place. She was recruited for service in 1939 by men formerly associated with Gertrude Bell, colleagues in the Arab Bureau and at the Cairo conference of 1920, who had all been actively concerned in the making of the Hashemite Kingdom of Iraq, and the setting up of its first Arab administration in 1921.

There are aspects of Wavell's early military career which have a bearing on some of his strategies and subterfuges in the North African campaign of 1940. He experienced at first hand the pre-1914 Russia of the Tsar and, as a War Office Russian expert and former Military Attaché on the Russian Caucasus front in 1916, was concerned in the abortive attempts after the Bolshevik Revolution to set up independent White Russian commands in the south of the country. At an impressionable period of his life he witnessed the collapse of a ruling class at the hands of determined ideologues. It left him with an awareness of the political factor to be taken into all military calculations, and of the value of propaganda in preparing the overthrow of systems.

Wavell was not a newcomer to the Middle East. He had commanded in Palestine during the 1937–8 Arab uprising against Jewish settlement under the Balfour plan, but his first experience of the area dated from even earlier. In 1917, as a staff officer, he was attached to General Allenby's Egyptian Expeditionary Force when it defeated the Ottoman Turks in Palestine and drove them back through Syria to their ethnic frontiers. Ten years later he published a detailed analysis of the World War I campaigns in Egypt, Sinai, Palestine and Syria. He admired Allenby, whose biography he wrote.

This body of experience made him unusual as a soldier, less the direct man of action than the reflective Chief, brooding over schemes that were imaginative and bold, and responsive to what was original and daring in individual personalities. He was more catholic in his choice of instruments than was usual in the military man of his period. Tucked away in the recesses of his mind was a file of people who by some quirk of circumstance had registered themselves with him as likely to produce a useful innovation. These could then be summoned dramatically to his side if an occasion for the use of their particular talent arose, a private following protected by his personal authority, favoured retainers at a chieftain's court. The Long Range Desert Group in Libya, the Chindits in Burma, were among the products of this discernment.

Under Wavell's command the contention that propaganda and subversion were aspects of a single subject was endorsed. The summer of 1940 in Cairo for the British was a period of accelerated preparation, and of making bricks with very little straw. Many of the deceptions practised by Allenby in Palestine were updated. They were put into effect by Dudley Clark – alias Major Galveston, alias Colonel Croft-Cook – a gunner colonel who served with Wavell in Palestine in 1938, and then went on to formulate and put into action the training and use of Commando units.

Wavell was not squeamish about the use of deception, or of the outright lie, which according to Dudley Clark was so precious that it needed to be concealed by a bodyguard of truth. Ninety per cent of doctored information, it was laid down, should be verifiable by local spies and informants as true, so that the deceptive ten per cent might slip through unperceived.

Once Western Europe fell to the Germans and Churchill came to power, more attention than hitherto was paid in London to the uses of propaganda. It led to the setting up of the Special Operations Executive (SOE) to co-ordinate all subversion and sabotage against the enemy overseas, while another organisation, the Political Warfare Executive (PWE), an amalgamation of certain elements of the Ministry of Information, the BBC and SOI, the secret and subversive side of SOE, enabled covert or 'black' activities to exist under the cloak of the Ministry of Information.

A British military man is not expected to meddle in political issues, and this aspect of Wavell's personality did not endear him to the Foreign Office. It led to a duplication of effort and proliferation of rival intelligence agencies in Cairo which bedevilled relations between the diplomatic and military communities during the first years of the war. This was only relieved when, under pressure from Wavell, a Minister of State with authority to make political decisions was sent to the Middle East in 1941. It was under his official wing in Cairo that Freya's Brotherhood was finally lodged, though the impetus for its formation had come from the military and its distant godparent was Wavell. This may explain his continuing interest in her, and her ardent personal loyalty to him, and the double standard it fostered in her relations with her official colleagues.

Unlike the British, whose innate reticence found propaganda distasteful, the Germans were generous in their distribution of wireless sets to local Axis sympathisers, and their broadcasts to Egypt and the Levant beamed from powerful transmitters in Italy, Turkey and North Africa were topical, scurrilous and poisonously effective. They were also very funny, very black. The official British line was much more solemn and, following Ministry of Information directives, stressed the undemocratic and therefore un-Islamic nature of totalitarianism. Great play was made with this over the local broadcasting systems, and items of theological nicety were debated with the scholars of al Azhar University in Cairo, to show why such forces of evil could never succeed.

Wavell distrusted the realism of the existing Embassy appreciations of the forces at work beneath the glittering surface of wealthy Levantine life, and was not impressed by the Embassy's information service. This was too hidebound and defensive in his view. The Spanish Civil War had seen the systematised undermining of loyalty in beleaguered cities. The fifth column was a potent fear, and the General was alert to it. Although the entry of Italy into the war in June 1940 cleared the air, and known Axis agents could be expelled from Egypt along with the diplomats, he preferred to form his judgments from his own sources. That is where Freya came in.

Freya's war was all to do with people, and its value resided in the impact of her personality on her selected targets. Although Oral Propaganda was the official name for 'whispering' or the passing of SIBs (from the Latin *sibillare*: to whisper) – the top secret code name for this technique – Freya preferred the term 'personal propaganda' or Persuasion, as implying it emanated spontaneously from the individual alone. Its declared object was to fortify and organise pro-British feeling at a time when a German triumph seemed inevitable and no-one was very anxious to be identified with a losing side.

Freya's scheme for the creation of a clandestine network of pro-British sympathisers throughout the Middle-Eastern lands, novel though it might appear to some, would not have been so to Wavell, a man familiar with the Bolshevik use of strategic deception after 1917. Then a fake organisation of anti-Bolshevik patriots known as 'The Trust' was elaborated by Lenin's Chief of Intelligence, Feliks Dzerzhinsky. Controlled by the OGPU, it penetrated the White Russian émigré networks, and effectively convinced Allied Intelligence that the overthrow of the Bolsheviks was imminent, and that intervention from abroad was not required.[2] It enabled the Revolution to be consolidated internally, without serious interference from counter-revolutionary groups which, ineffectually sustained by the Allies, were picked off one by one by the Bolsheviks or driven into exile.

Freya records with amusement the suggestion her Brotherhood was inspired by a Bolshevik model,[3] but it was the similarity of the idea, and the scope of the plan, that possibly impressed Wavell and formed the basis of his admiration of her talents.

Freya's own explanation in later life, when we talked together, of her relations with the military, was that the Services were more adventurous in their thinking than the Foreign Office, being more open to novel ideas and untried experiments. That was as far as she would go. When I asked Elizabeth Monroe, head of the Middle East desk and Freya's London link at the Ministry of Information, she was adamant that the Ministry was Freya's sole paymaster during this period. One incident she did recall, however, was an attempt to foist a payment of £50 on to the Brotherhood's account, which was disallowed. 'Would you believe it,' she remarked incredulously, 'it was supposed to be the fee for some actor or other to pop up during a Nazi broadcast and shout the Arabic equivalent of "Gairmany calling!" during the transmission!'

I said nothing. Here was an unbridgeable gap, which could not be reconciled. It recalled the indignation of Sir Basil Newton, the outgoing British Ambassador in Iraq in 1940, when he discovered that anamorphic cartoon drawings of pigs and jackals, which when tilted revealed the features of Hitler and Mussolini, were being distributed in the bazaar from his Embassy. He did not feel such scurrility, he complained stiffly to Sir Horace Seymour at the FO, was either useful or enhancing to the standing of the British mission, nor was it in keeping with its dignity or reputation for seriousness and probity.

How much, I wondered, did Freya enjoy and seek a double identity, and lend herself – with or without her employer's connivance – to one-off schemes fostered by Wavell's penchant for romantic adventurers, and the blind eye turned on their activities? Freya was modest; she never thought of herself as a heroine, but she did aspire to the company of heroes, and was impressed by the aura of reckless daring attached to their exploits. Her admiration expanded in proportion to their easygoing acceptance of herself as one of themselves in spirit.

A report by Squadron Leader Hindle James of MEIC on 2 January 1940, of a conversation with a Cairo newspaper editor, was perhaps the germ of the idea that Freya was called on to put into action. Pro-British news items planted in local newspapers were useless, said the Egyptian, as their provenance was always suspect and their information discounted. What was needed was a counter-propaganda skilfully introduced by sources free of all suspicion of local British influence. Hindle James' report was immediately shot down by Sir Miles Lampson, and the suggestion lapsed. The editor in question, snorted the Ambassador, was well known to the Embassy as a scallywag, and was probably seeking a source of income for himself.[4]

Lampson was a very tall, overbearing Englishman of the old John Bull type. His years of experience in Egypt as negotiator and signatory of the Anglo-Egyptian treaty of 1935, which bowed to nationalist aspirations and replaced his post of High Commissioner with that of Ambassador, gave him a good deal of leverage in the struggle between soldiers and diplomats over the use of information in the Middle East. His personal standing with Churchill was high. The Prime Minister was impressed by his forceful personality and pugnacious instinct, and this was a factor Lampson deployed with skill in the long and acrimonious dispute with London that followed the arrival of Wavell's Command HQ in Cairo in the summer of 1939, and that led to the eventual appointment of a Minister of State in 1941.

It was Colonel Illtyd Clayton of the British Middle East Office, the GHQ Political Intelligence think-tank, a younger brother of Sir Kinahan Cornwallis' colleague, Major Gilbert Clayton, at the Arab Bureau in World War I, who approached Freya at the M of I Area Conference that summer with the suggestion of a 'whispering' campaign in northern Arab lands to counter Axis rumour-mongering and alarmism. 'Whispering' after the fall of France had achieved something of the topicality that the fifth column achieved after the Spanish Civil War. 'After all,' Freya wrote on 27 August to Rushbrook Williams in London, 'if the Germans whispered Leopold [of Belgium] from his army and France from her pledged word, we ought to be able to do something with people who are on our side already in their hearts.'

The location first suggested by Colonel Clayton for the experiment was Iraq, where German intrigue was rife, and a pro-Axis uprising was feared by the intelligence agencies. This plan was short-circuited at the last moment by Sir Miles Lampson, who insisted that the need in Egypt was greater. So the *Ikhwan al Hurriyah* or Brotherhood of Freedom had its beginnings in Cairo in the winter of 1940–1, under the personal patronage of the Ambassador, and was funded on an *ad hoc* basis for the first eight months of its existence by the Embassy's Publicity Section. Its name aped not only that of the *Ikhwan al Muslamin* or Moslem Brotherhood, the secret pan-Arab nationalist society established in the 1920s, but echoed the *Ka'aba al Hurriyah* of John Buchan's World War I tale *Greenmantle*.

Freya's job was to be largely *talk*, day in, day out, wherever she could gain an entry, or persuade a suspicious or unconvinced audience that she represented a serious option. Her appointment to Cairo in September 1940 was, in some measure, a result of the rivalry between Lampson's Embassy and Cawthorn's MEIC. She herself did not know until she had accepted her assignment who her new master was to be. Colonel Clayton's original suggestion was to borrow her from Aden for six months, something that appealed to Freya, who had already been revolving ideas in Aden for a transfer northwards. She jumped at the proposal, and wrote enthusiastically to her Director, Rushbrook Williams, supporting it, while saying nothing to Perowne. The idea of a pro-British whispering campaign across the Middle East, she told Rushbrook Williams, began with Colonel Clayton 'and has, as you know, been endorsed by practically everyone who knows what is happening in all the north Arab lands; but the details are left to me with the most generous confidence . . .'

In other words, the elaboration of a working plan was to be her contribution. It was a challenge too important to pass up, and she accepted it eagerly, with one stipulation, that she return to Aden while her posting was arranged, to pack up and clear the decks there. The soldiers were not too happy about this, they wanted to get the scheme going quickly and with no fuss, but she got her way. Freya liked to try out ideas on people before finally adopting them. She wanted to use the experience of what she regarded as manageable old friends in Aden as a sounding board.

It did not turn out like that. It seems not to have occurred to her that Perowne might resent, or Harold Ingrams, now Acting Governor of the colony, be affronted by her lack of consultation, or that her defection might put a strain on existing operations. The airy confidence in her colleagues' willingness to further her career regardless of their own interests was ill-founded. Both men were exceedingly angry; Perowne's simmering distrust of Freya came to the boil, and he telegraphed London in an attempt to block the transfer. Freya was outraged by this. She saw it as a betrayal of personal friendship. She had only returned, she told Ingrams stiffly, to explain her action – dictated by patriotic necessity – out of consideration for Perowne's feelings, and their particular friendship. Now, since he had made clear that he was indifferent to this, she felt no further compunction in leaving, and tendered her resignation.

Freya's need to justify herself was always strong, and she would press her arguments with all the fervour of an emotional nature. 'If Stewart is going to be so rude about me, he'll have to marry me,' she scrawled angrily on one of the papers that passed between the three.[5] Perowne, the son and grandson of Anglican bishops, had the conventional values of his public-school upbringing. Among these was a dislike of humbug. Freya lacked any guiding principles other than those she put together for herself. This perhaps accounts for something that troubled more sensitive associates, a lack of cohesion between her public persona and her private actions. It was the 'little rift within the lute, that by and by will make the music mute'.

On her way up the Red Sea to her new job, she was still debating whether she had been right to abandon Perowne. Sir Sydney Cockerell, now established as her guide and confidant, following a visit to Asolo in 1938, was her sounding board. She wrote on 7 September:

On the *pro* side were 1) the knowledge that I can do far more useful work; 2) the usefulness of a double salary just now; 3) the intuition that as soon as Aden gets dull and out of things, I should be left and Stewart go away! On the *con* side, the regret at leaving Stewart and the feeling he will never forgive me, and this is made more so by the fact that he has started a new broadcasting scheme there which is rather much for him alone. I hope he may get away too and then will be alright, for Aden now will I believe settle into a backwater while all our energies concentrate on Egypt . . .

What does not go down of course is that a mere female should
be able to go off and get £1200 a year for the asking, and
both Stewart and Harold have been at ludicrous pains to miss
no chance of telling me that merit, mere merit, had nothing
to do with it . . .

By the time Freya left Aden she and Perowne had in fact
patched up their differences and their joint efforts had crystallised into the following plan. The recruitment for the Brotherhood of Freedom was to be:

1. Entry by oath, and absolute secrecy.
2. Payment of small entrance fee and subscription towards
    cost of weekly bulletin (this to help illusion that this was
    participants' own show).
3. Election of new members to be unanimous, and guaran-
    teed by two existing members. No military personnel to
    be accepted.
4. Obligation accepted to assist any foreign member in any
    way.
5. Attendance at weekly reunions where the material to be
    whispered would be given out, and short training lectures
    given to the recruits.

What was visualised was a nucleus of people sympathetic to
the British who met informally once a week to discuss the
war situation. Tea-parties were Freya's preferred means of
association, a sensible choice in a Moslem country. Once
installed in Cairo, in a smart little flat in Zamalek, she presided
over mixed gatherings of Egyptians of many different backgrounds and a few sympathetic Britons fluent in Arabic, or
whose social importance conferred distinction on those
attending the party. She was an adroit tuft-hunter, and harnessed this skill for the benefit of the Brethren. 'It is quite
scandalous how little our people have done to get themselves
known and a little liked in a strange land,' she wrote to Cockerell
in February 1941. 'I am gradually drafting in the more enthusi-

astic, but it is no joke to find anyone with *time* to spare for two weekly committees.' Fraternisation of the races was an essential object of her plan. Often pretty young women of recognised social standing, whose friendly charm contributed to the pleasantness of the occasion, were roped in to help.

Freya's scheme was based on confidentiality and the formation of small circles of like-minded sympathisers, each recruiting his agreed quota of contacts, and thus building up a network of cells, each secret from the others yet linked by the chain of information 'whispered' at the weekly meetings.

The 'cell' scheme – the mechanics of the affair – was grafted on to her earlier perception in Aden of the need to make people feel useful and important by playing on their desire to have a role, and thus cementing their loyalty to their rulers. Indeed the volunteer Air Raid Precautions (ARP) personnel in Aden in 1940 had been recruited under the slogan 'The Brothers of Freedom'. The 'committee' – an emotive word associated with progressive movements throughout the Moslem world – was to replace the system of bribery and favours previously employed, and to form the nucleus of an ever-expanding circle of contacts, influenced by the topics passed on for discussion at the weekly reunions of the members. Freya was later to describe her creation as an instrument, 'a machine of public opinion which we can influence from our position at the centre'.[6]

In later years, when Freya's and Perowne's relationship had soured irretrievably, and there were rival factions among their friends, there was speculation as to who *really* invented the Brethren, and as to how much was owed to Perowne. On this, Christopher Scaife, who succeeded Freya as Controller of the organisation in 1943, although a friend of Perowne, was forthright. The credit should go to Freya. It was her imaginative flair, he believed, based on her reading of the history of the Assassins for her travels in Mazanderan ten years previously, that produced the idea of a secret society. It inspired the amalgam of ideas and perceptions that she put together to form the concept of the Brotherhood; but perhaps the ground had been prepared earlier by W. P. Ker's friendship with John Buchan, and by her father's liking for the shilling 'shockers' that chronicled the adventures of Richard Hannay and his friends. Freya's vision of a pro-British secret society whose spiritual force would sweep across Asia and confound the Nazi intrigue was *Greenmantle* in reverse.

Harold Ingrams in Aden was another possible influence. Ingrams' much acclaimed peace-making initiative in Hadhramaut at the end of the 1930s owed something to General Lyautey earlier in French North Africa. The penetration and study of the secret religious fraternities of the Sahara, and awareness of their political role, formed an integral part of Lyautey's pre-scription for 'the smiling face of colonialism', sympathetic but efficient rule. The mysterious speed of the Saharan *marabouts'* communication by word of mouth was a subject likely to crop up in the informed conversation that Freya so enjoyed and was so good at promoting.

Freya's originality was that she turned existing propaganda situations inside out. Instead of courting the goodwill of the clients, she boldly assumed that the goodwill was already there, only awaiting the opportunity of being put to practical use. It was the move from defensiveness, already pinpointed by Wavell as the weakness of the existing official publicity, to attack. Freya's tactic was to give everyone the benefit of the doubt. She radiated a beaming conviction of the natural willingness of all right-thinking people to ally themselves to the cause of truth as enshrined in the Democratic option. Her unthreatening appearance and air of naive trust made her difficult to reject. There was thus a bias to the concept of the Brotherhood from the start which attracted serious-minded people, and which owed nothing to the men who had tossed the scheme into Freya's lap and told her to get on with it. She herself was to describe it as 'something built on Christian as opposed to Official lines, not only workable but infinitely and indeed alarmingly successful . . .'[7]

It entailed the mobilising of whatever personal goodwill existed between individual Britons and their circle of local acquaintances in the conditions of their daily existence. People were recruited to sound out their Egyptian friends with a view to starting informal discussion groups where current events could be talked over in an atmosphere of friendly interest and detachment. 'It is essential . . . that our propaganda should not be centred in obvious places only, such as Embassy, Institute, etc. but should spring up from all sorts of intangible sources so as to offer no definite target . . .'[8]

In effect, this was a cashing in of reserves of personal friendship, patriotically placed at her disposal by people whose relations with Arab and Egyptian colleagues were genuine and unforced. The foundations of the Brotherhood were built on the co-operation of such men, whose understanding and sympathy were based on long years of residence in the host country. It was through such men that the first Egyptian recruits were obtained.

The recruitment of this support was Freya's task on transfer to Cairo. Here she was helped by Reginald Davies who, although sceptical about the Brotherhood idea, co-operated loyally in finding collaborators for Freya's scheme. Lulie Abu'l Huda, who became Freya's first assistant, was produced from his own Area Information Office. A young, good-looking, aristocratic Palestinian girl, with an Oxford degree, she became an immediate favourite, and accompanied Freya everywhere.

Freya, meeting him for the first time in 1937 when he was Adviser to the Alexandria Municipality, had found Reginald Davies very entertaining: he told her he had encountered Jesus Christs thirteen times in the course of his Sudan Political career, and that most of them had ended by being hung.[9] But in 1940 her own messianic vision was beginning to take hold; it irked her that she should be listened to 'with a smiling but incredulous indulgence . . . and told to make the experiment if I pleased'. But she swallowed the affront and got on with her plan. She saw her creation like wildfire overtaking the East, and she demanded total faith. Any scepticism was an insult, stored up for future settlement. Reginald Davies himself always believed that the demotion of the Cairo Information Office in 1941 from Area to purely Egyptian jurisdiction was in some way due to an adverse report from Freya on its functioning.[10] She was consulted informally by Anthony Eden after he flew out to Cairo in February 1941 to push through the scheme for the ill-fated British military intervention in Greece.

Freya first learned who her patron was to be at a luncheon party at the Embassy, to which she was taken by Reginald Davies, who was putting her up, to be introduced to Lampson. The Ambassador broke the news to her himself. It was altogether an exciting day. She had now entered a privileged world in which decisions were taken and implemented with gratifying speed. Instead of hanging about like everyone else waiting for a passage to Aden, a seat in a bomber flying south was found for her at short notice.

At this same luncheon party Freya met for the first time a tall, fair, good-looking young woman, Pamela Hore-Ruthven, who had a job at GHQ as PA to Wavell's Director of Military Intelligence, Brigadier Shearer, and had thus escaped repatriation with other wives. She was part of the Embassy set. Her husband, the Hon Patrick Hore-Ruthven, was an officer in the Royal Fusiliers, and a kinsman of Sir Miles Lampson. A poet, and early volunteer for the Long Range Desert Group, he was to die in 1942 at the age of twenty-nine, as a prisoner, from wounds received in a raid on an Italian base. The two women took to each other immediately. Freya was elated and in form, and so impressed the younger woman that she accompanied her back to her quarters to help with the hurried packing, while the absorbing discussion of ways and means of influencing opinion continued.

Pamela Hore-Ruthven was the daughter of an Anglican canon of the Church of Ireland and already the mother of an infant son. He was left at home in safety while she, in the period of the phoney war, along with other young wives, joined her husband in Egypt prior to Italy's entry into the war. The favourable impression the two women made on each other continued on Freya's return from Aden in September, and on 1 January 1941 Mrs Hore-Ruthven resigned from her job with Brigadier Shearer, and moved over to full-time employment as Freya's assistant at a salary of £600 p.a.

Her good looks and charm were assets that Freya later boasted were invaluable when Lampson was interrogated by anxious Egyptian politicians as to the true function of the *Ikhwan al Hurriyah*. Then she would be sent to attend luncheon parties at the Embassy, or to call on the Prime Minister, Hussein Sirry Pasha, in his office, to reassure him as to the essential sincerity of the organisation, more readily appreciated when detailed by such a messenger. 'My Pamela's golden hair and blue eyes and charming way'[11] were held by Freya to make up for want of Arabic, while the enthusiasm of her belief in the Brotherhood gave Pamela hope 'of enlisting all the Hussars in Cairo to work for it in their spare time!'

THIRTEEN

IN THE CAIRO SWIM

Freya, on transfer to Cairo, was better off than she had ever been before, with all her expenses of installation covered, and with entertainment, salary and living allowances greatly in excess of anything she had previously enjoyed. 'I am as well as can be,' she wrote to her mother from Cairo on 19 January 1941, 'and living in great comfort; two servants, a car, a lovely flat, and I have bought two carpets and a Persian picture. Everyone is nice to me and I go to all the nicest parties. My car is a great amusement . . .' But a week later she was telling Perowne that her flat was *so cold* she was spending a few nights with Momo Marriot in her lovely warmed house. 'I do like luxury,' she wrote, 'though not to *own* it myself . . .'

Momo Marriot was a friend of Perowne's, the wife of a battalion commander in the Scots Guards, serving under Wavell. She was the daughter of the Jewish American millionaire, Otto Kahn. Her mother, the very wealthy Mrs Otto Kahn, was with her in Cairo for the season. Freya became very friendly with Mrs OK, as she was known in the smart set, and stayed with her later in America; Freya's post-war friendship with Bernard Berenson came through this connection. Momo was a dazzling American hostess whose parties in cosmopolitan Cairo were much in vogue. They had a worldly raciness rather different from anything Freya had previously experienced, and she cultivated eagerly the fashionable new friendships she formed there.

Freya's feeling for drama was excited and stimulated by the

novelty of her experience. 'Everything is strangely jostled,' she told Jock Murray at the beginning of March, 'khaki, and Paris hats two years old, the chitchat of Cairo and the convulsions of the world. I am, I suppose, one of the rather few people inclined to see life like this even in ordinary times, so that war seems to me not less but more real than ordinary life; just a making evident of what is always there . . .'

The Cairo of which Freya now became a part still maintained its pre-war standards. Much of the legendary glitter of its war-time personality derived from the peculiarity of a situation in which a non-belligerent country, such as Egypt, acted as a transit zone and headquarters for the British forces facing the enemy in the western desert. Cut off, except at top level, from easy communication with the outside world, it became an increasingly closed society which fed upon itself. The Egyptian royal court and the large foreign communities of Italians, Greeks and French formed the cosmopolitan backdrop to the essentially provincial, even parochial, British community, depleted of its wives and families, which formed around the Embassy and GHQ.

Pamela Hore-Ruthven and Freya twice spent the Christmas week at Luxor in the Lampsons' party at the Palace Hotel, holiday gatherings at which business could be discussed discreetly with senior Service guests in the course of donkey-rides across the desert to visit the temples, or while dancing the night away in the hotel ballroom, under the eyes of Egyptian notabilities amazed at the vigour with which the Ambassador demonstrated his stamina on the dance floor, and at the high spirits and good looks of his young wife and her friends. Freya in this company would have seemed to onlookers a chaperone to young women whose husbands or lovers were absent in the desert. With Pamela in position at Freya's side, easy and informal monitoring of the Brotherhood organisation could be maintained and undesirable tendencies checked at source.

This was the period when Freya's hats became notorious. Now that she had some money, and was emancipated from the control of her mother's taste by the closing of the Mediterranean, she was able to indulge her own ideas in dress. This was easy in Cairo, full of clever polyglot dressmakers and *modistes*. Freya's letters frequently refer to the acquisitions she is making, and the effect they are having on the cocktail round.

Freya and her outfits were a joke seized on readily by men glad of distraction and tomfoolery in a period of stress, and Freya played it for all it was worth. Her success was founded not so much on her work – there was always a reservation about that even among those privy to its secrets – but on her willingness to bat the ball along in the pursuit of amusement, and the tonic effect of her personality on men burdened by responsibility and amused by something innocently quaint in her eager, uncritical acceptance of themselves and their capacities.

Freya had one particular hat which excited much comment and smiling attention, which she recorded with satisfaction to her friends. It was a pale blue cartwheel, with the hours and hands of a clock embroidered on the brim in pink braid. The clock hands were set at five and seven – the *cinq à sept* of boulevardier farce, the discreet, intimate, early-evening hours when a man can visit his mistress, secure in the knowledge that her husband is visiting his. Freya's obvious ignorance of the significance of this emblem was what contributed to her cult among the dandies of GHQ, as she stood preening in their midst, delighted with the attention.

The joke about Freya's hats was taken up by Wavell and the people about him. Her seven new hats were later given as his reason to see her when passing through Baghdad on his way back to the East from a London conference in September 1941. Should he return Freya's valentine with embellishments, perhaps a hat for her? he enquired in 1944. That a man so notoriously silent and difficult in society should make such an exception towards Freya contributed to the gossip surrounding her. It was rumoured he bought all her hats. Some even suggested he must be in love with her. Such notoriety did not displease Freya.

The practical work of setting up networks of Brotherhood sympathisers, and card-indexing members, took time to arrange.

In Cairo Freya had no access to cadres of volunteer recruits as in Aden, where she had pushed for the recruitment of ARP personnel among the native population as a means of cementing loyalty. She had to rely on others to make the initial connections. Her first recruits were two second-year students from Fuad I University sent to her by a friend of Perowne, a lecturer in English literature at the university. This was Christopher Scaife. He was sympathetic to the idea of the Brethren from the start. He had taught at the Fuad I University for eleven years, and was fluent in Arabic and Italian, but in 1940 was preparing to don uniform and depart to the desert as an officer of the Senussi levies, raised among the followers of the exiled Libyan head of the Senussi religious confraternity, who now lived under British protection in a villa in Zamalek.

The two Egyptian students came to tea in Freya's flat, and she began her mission with them. To enforce the notion of disinterested attachment to ways of producing a better world through constitutional means, she adopted a comfortable, encouraging manner, and a high-minded idealism attractive to young minds. She described the two students as earnest and young, anxious to help 'democracy' in some way. Democracy was the card, so ran the M of I propaganda directive,[1] to be played against Axis totalitarianism, not loyalty to existing political structures, or to British commercial interests.

Freya's brief was to penetrate the unexplored world of the poor and the striving, of small shopkeepers and government clerks, of university students from rural backgrounds, of municipal employees and primary schoolteachers, and the whole seething ant-heap of life in Cairo and the Delta towns. As each of the original committee's recruits began to form a committee of his own, the organisation began to spread. One group of middle-aged government officials, assembled around Mr G. Murray of the Egyptian Desert Survey, sat in an office near Bab el-Louk. 'We had Coptic cells in the huge working-class suburb of Shubra, and one of our student brothers began to form cells in every district in Cairo among the poorest, the sweepers and tiny shop men and artisans. I gave these a coffee party: two from each cell came and sat in my flat overlooking the Nile, and made speeches in turn, and I was surprised at their good sense and the interest they took in affairs.'

A small weekly bulletin of information issued under Freya's direction was central to the programme. A sympathetic Cairo journalist in his spare time would translate Freya's verbal analysis of a situation, and this would form the matter of next week's discussion in the individual groups. In it she outlined the arguments to be used to counteract and answer the doubts and rumours current among the Brethren, collected and reported back during the week. Freya was intent, not on giving orders, but on inspiring faith, and the patient and plausible good sense with which she replied to stumbling and imprecise formulations of common anxieties and ambitions were the basis of the experiment.

At New Year 1941 Freya's Brethren numbered 400, and Freya was glad to have Pamela Hore-Ruthven and Lulie Abu'l Huda to deal with the filing, and to assist with the technique of reasoned reassurance in answer to questions raised in the groups. Within the week, a counter-argument or alternative interpretation could be given to any matter, true or false, that preoccupied the minds of Freya's clients. In this way, it was also possible to monitor the impact of Axis propaganda on the masses and devise a counter-strategy. This was the working end of the business. The women spent their time visiting the committees, answering questions, presenting arguments wherever a contact could be made. The object, Freya told Sydney Cockerell, was to have a membership of 20,000 by the end of 1941, but in the event the figures stood at 3000–3500 when in January 1942 Freya handed over the Egyptian networks to Christopher Scaife, now invalided out of Tobruk and active service, prior to her moving to Iraq. The solid work that engineered the great expansion of the movement in Egypt took place after she left, with the appointment in February 1942 by Scaife of Ronald Fay as full-time Director of the Egyptian operation as soon as he took control of the Egyptian network.

Freya's feeling about her committees crystallised fairly early on in the experiment. She told Perowne in a letter of 26 February 1941:

I go to Baghdad for six weeks in a fortnight's time, leaving poor Pamela to deal with committees, of which we now have 524 members. What a *nightmare* and how I begin to hate democracy but don't, don't say this abroad. I don't really, but I feel the Committee is just too much with us. I long for a camel or even a donkey. There is a lovely feeling of spring about, all the fields full of young flax or corn or beans or flowers – a war or an office seems monstrous . . .

She kept at it, however, long after the first euphoria had subsided. Her creation was the raft that supported her financially, and gave her the entry, however peripherally, to the society she loved and rejoiced to be a part of. This society ebbed and coalesced in response to the fluctuating fortunes of the desert war, but Cairo itself remained the same, a city given over to pleasure and entertainment, and glittering social occasions where enormous quantities of Mediterranean food, supplied by French and Italian and Greek grocers, were devoured in settings of gilded Levantine splendour.

At the apex of this society were the Lampsons, 'Sampson and Delilah' to the inner circle of ADCs and staff officers at GHQ.[2] The tone was set by the pretty young Ambassadress and the cool beauties of the Embassy set. As the Germans turned their attention to the Balkans, exiled governments and royalties gathered in Cairo and added their quota of romance to the scene, while Cabinet ministers and chiefs of staff made flying visits to confer, and their comings and goings added to a flattering sense of participation in great events.

Freya during this period lived on two levels, the one gay and social, the other difficult and demanding, a drain on her moral energy by humble people casting about for assurance of better things to come amid the limitations of their ordinary lives. She was soon complaining to her friends of the burden of the task she had assumed. The projected expansion to 20,000 members of which she boasted to Cockerell daunted her. 'How can I run a machine that size? It makes one in love with the idea of quiet obscurity in one's garden for the rest of one's life . . .'

This was a theme to which she was to return throughout the

period of her association with the Brethren. A week later she told Cockerell, 'I have got over my third attack of 'flu but feel very much below normal strength with about twenty committees that look to me as their spiritual head: nothing in the world is so tiring as mere amiability, when it's one's job. I can understand the harassed looks of ADCs . . .'

'The casualness with which we take our Positions when we have any must give perpetual shocks,' she remarked to Perowne. Freya was in love with the easy, upper-class manners and uncomplicated natures of the people with whom she was mixing.

One feels no-one can be much better than the best of our aristocracy; so conscientious, so anxious to play their part rightly, so self-reliant, so careless of all voices except that of their own conscience – and so refreshingly direct. I am always surprised that I seem to fit so easily into a world with which after all I have so little to do – but I suppose we do share the same values, interested in outside things and not so much in oneself, and that is perhaps fundamentally aristocratic.[3]

Freya was entering middle age in an accelerating rush of social activity. There was no distinction in her mind between her different roles, they were two sides of the same coin, proffered for the same end. However much she might complain in her private letters of the strain of her work, when wheeled out on show in Embassy circles to entertain and impress transient VIPs she was on the top of her form, confident and uplifting. Everyone, but everyone, must be enthused to work for Democracy. She celebrated her forty-eighth birthday at the end of January with champagne cocktails for 180 people.

It will be an Undemocratic party for a change, with all sorts of Corps Diplomatique, army, the editor of *Ahram* . . . so I shall be awfully poor for two months and unable to pay my motor car instalments. Not that this worries me as Mr Rust of the garage is a Brother of Freedom, she told Perowne in February 1941. Sometimes a note of excited silliness invades the Firbankian details of her activities.

I *wish* you could see our committees. Prince Aly Khan in a Persian committee in the Muski, surrounded by fountains playing and goldfish, is too lovely, and the seventy ladies (recruited by Lulie Abu'l Huda) are a small operette in themselves . . . Pamela says she has never done such entrancing work in her life . . .

A good deal of this replicated her audience's own snobbery, but it also satisfied Freya's craving to be associated with what was successful and admired, especially with the glamour of high endeavour and risk of life thrown in. She didn't aspire to youth and beauty for herself, or the dignity of titles and high position, but she did want to be accepted as one of the gang by the bereft and lovelorn young women and the gay, inconsequential young men serving around the Command Headquarters. It was a kind of vicarious living, an emotional fulfilment that made for happiness. Circumstances swept Freya up into a riot of fun and frivolity such as she had never before experienced. She was in love with a whole society, rather than with any individual, though as is in the nature of humans, particular individuals would embody the whole transient experience, and became the object of special affection and admiration

In the middle of January 1941 Freya wrote to two of her friends, Sydney Cockerell in London and Lucy Beach in California, that she had had the Wavells to dinner.

A quiet dinner party, only six of us . . . and we had a quiet and frivolous evening and talked about Samarkand, and he quoted a lovely poem by Oscar Wilde about those remote places . . . He is the most modest man in this world, and no one would think he had just brought off one of the biggest victories of the war.

The intimacy, growing over a period of ten years, is charted by the collection of letters she received from him, which were handsomely bound up for her in a red leather volume by her publisher, along with those of W. P. Ker. It is not an extensive collection, about forty items, including a few from his son Archie John, nor does it contain matter of significant interest.

The letters are mostly pleasant acknowledgments of letters received, often very belated. Freya seems to have written on average three letters to his one, and an impression is gained of a civil, patient man catching up with overdue private correspondence, in moments of relaxation snatched from the pressure of busy official life.

The series begins modestly enough with a holograph note from Wavell to Miss Stark, dated 28 December 1940, thanking her for her congratulations on the successful military operations in the western desert and signed 'Yours very sincerely'. This little bridgehead was expanded by Freya with the dinner party referred to above, which established her as an individual in Lady Wavell's eyes, though the upkeep of the friendship remained with Wavell. It was he who replied on behalf of them both, thanking Freya for the gift of an ivory box, which she sent them as a present jointly subscribed with other friends, after her first stay with them in India in 1943. The correspondence ends with a letter of 18 April 1950, written from his sickbed – 'the first for 20 years'. It is written to 'Dearest Freya', and finishes 'with love to you both' – for Freya was by then married to Perowne – and signed Chief. In it he spoke of the epic defence of Tobruk, which he compared to Belisarius's defence of Rome.

Throughout the series, the tone never varies. Friendly, candid, it is largely to do with his preferred interests, literature and history. It gains momentum from 1943 onwards, when his military career ends and he becomes Viceroy of India; it is as if her supportive loyalty was valued. There are occasional moments of self-revelation, but never confidences, only a gradual expansion of intimacy to take in family news, worries about his son, groans about the increasing demands of regimental, civil and academic chores. Despite her many invitations, he never visited Asolo. She was a pen-friend as much as anything, someone to whom he could communicate his thoughts on congenial topics, a relaxant rather than a stimulant.

Communication with Wavell, his ADC Bernard Fergusson
once said, was like a game of golf. You hit the ball down the
fairway, and it never came back. But every now and then, some
spark of reciprocity was ignited, and then it became a game of
tennis, fast and furious, as in a reply at the end of 1949 to an
enquiry from Freya about notable military marches. She
received an immediate response. Wavell fired off a long list of
memorable feats, as if a bottle had been uncorked, and the
contents gushed out. 'Xenophon was the first book I ever read,
and found it mercilessly dull, as all my schoolmaster was interested in was syntax. When I saw the ground I realised how
exciting and interesting it might have been . . .'

This was perhaps the trigger for Freya's subsequent interest
in military topography, leading the way to her tracing in *Alexander's Path* (1958) another of her heroes, Alexander the
Great's journey to the East and to his premature death.

PART FIVE

MRS FREYA STARK
1941–1952

FOURTEEN

THE BAGHDAD SIEGE

In the early spring of 1941 Freya left Cairo for a tour of Iraq. The Egyptian Brotherhood was put into the care of Pamela Hore-Ruthven, to manage as best she could. In Baghdad a change of government heralded a stiffening of local attitudes over the country's treaty obligations, which were similar to those of Egypt; nationalist stirrings were encouraged by a well-orchestrated German propaganda offensive and the intrigues of their agents and sympathisers in the country.

Freya arrived in Baghdad on 24 March where she found Vyvyan Holt,[1] the old friend who had helped her on her first arrival in Iraq in the 1930s, now Oriental Counsellor at the Embassy, and Sir Kinahan Cornwallis, newly brought out of retirement to take over as Ambassador. He was isolated in the worsening crisis, with no government to whom to present his credentials, but Lady Cornwallis filled the interval by spring-cleaning the Embassy.

Holt sent his love, Freya told her mother on 21 April, 'very overworked, and pleased to have me about in a harassed sort of way'. They went riding together, so he could give her the background to the events now gathering momentum. Freya's standing was rather different now from the time ten years previously when she was first making her name in Baghdad. Then Cornwallis had been a senior government Adviser, close to the ruling family through his king-making role in the Arab Bureau, while Holt was a circumspect army officer with a good command of Asiatic languages, seconded from India for intelligence duties and engaged in building up a wide network of informants. Of them all, the change in Freya's circumstances was the greatest; from being a not-very-welcome anomaly in local society, to whom Holt eventually held out a helping hand, she now dealt with both on equal terms, as a valuable auxiliary in good standing in the intelligence world.

Such a change in circumstances might be forgotten by the men, and put aside in the camaraderie of the war effort. Women were different. Lady Cornwallis did not particularly care for Freya. She had been headmistress of the government school for girls in Khartoum, before marriage, and had an old-fashioned concern for protocol, and a sense of ambassadorial dignity. There were few concessions to wartime informality on her part. The Cornwallis style was very different from that of the worldly Lampsons in Cairo, and however well thought of Freya might be by her husband, Lady Cornwallis was not prepared to countenance too much familiarity.

It was a very tense period for the British community in Iraq. The war in the Libyan desert was going badly, the evacuation of Greece had begun. The Regent of the country, Prince Abdul'illah, was smuggled out in his pyjamas to the RAF base at Habbaniyah, concealed under a rug arranged over the knees of the American Ambassador and his wife as they drove in their official car out of Baghdad, and was then flown to safety in Jordan. The little King and his relatives were prisoners in their palace, Cornwallis and his Embassy more or less marooned. 'I am so glad to be here in the middle of the mess, but oh! *why* do we get to such a pass and, in a country which really *is* in the hollow of our hand, allow both Army and Press to be against us?' Freya fulminated at the beginning of April to Pamela Hore-Ruthven, but two weeks later in a letter to Jock Murray a more realistic attitude prevailed.

Things here are what you might call in a rather volcanic state – and one has the unpleasant feeling of being aliens in an incalculable land. One brother in each camp is the policy of most families. The present Government is generally considered in German pay – but of course it will be obviously to their interest to work in with us, so I am all for conciliation if possible; even *if* Germany were to succeed at last, there would be very little left of Iraq when she did so.

Freya hated the alteration in the atmosphere she experienced as a propagandist for what might be a losing cause. 'You can't think of the difference between propaganding the people who *like* you and those who are all wobbly towards the other side,' she told Perowne. She felt ineffectual and depressed, a Don Quixote tilting at windmills, in the face of proliferating rumours spread by Axis sympathisers, poisonously calculated to shake Arab confidence in any British future.

At the end of April a slight stabilisation in the political situation opened the way for a visit to Teheran, and she seized the chance to get away. She spent less than a week there but . . . 'It was exquisite to breathe the mountain air, to see the *dasht* in flower, and the snow-slopes above; and larks in the sky – and all the quiet life going on in the big half-empty land.'

Such refreshments of the spirit were very necessary to her, and served to keep private fears and anxieties in some sort of control. These anxieties did exist. She feared being trapped off base and without diplomatic protection by a German *coup*. Possibly her mother's brief but unpleasant experience in Treviso jail the previous year warned her of what to expect should the Germans, through their Iraqi and Persian puppets, succeed in taking over the Middle East. She was too easily identifiable, and possibly had been too cocksure in her challenges to known Axis sympathisers, to escape reprisal.

Meanwhile, armed rebellion broke out in Iraq on 1 May, led by four generals of the Iraq army known as the Golden Square. It began with an attack on the RAF base at Habbaniyah. Despite a signal from Cornwallis to stay put in Persia, Freya made her way back by train to Baghdad on 2 May, in time to be the second-to-last person to enter the safety of the Embassy compound, now isolated under siege conditions by the conspirators of the rebellious Iraqi army. Some 380 people were crowded into the compound and garden fronting the river.

Lady Cornwallis had already loyally submitted to evacuation, taking with her the rest of the English wives and children, first to RAF headquarters at Habbaniyah, then to Basra. There were no special privileges for Freya, who shared a dormitory with seventeen other women: Armenian, Jewish, Greek and others with claims on British protection. She did not enjoy the experience and in self-defence busied herself looking after the contingent of native employees cooped up in the compound. There were some forty-five Indian clerks, Kurdish grooms, Persian gardeners and Iraqi houseboys; these latter in the cool inner sanctum of the Residence produced properly served meals with polished silver and glass on the table, and flowers freshly picked each day by the gardeners, while outside the motley throng of dependants did their laundry and prepared and ate their meals according to the tenets of their various religious faiths.

Among the Embassy personnel incarcerated in the compound was a colonel seconded from GHQ Middle East, and attached to the Embassy's Publicity Department. A former Anglican monk from Nashdom Abbey, Adrian Bishop, was officially designated as Services' Liaison Officer, but actually ran the clandestine SOE operations. The enforced intimacy of the besieged, cooped up within the sunbaked confines of the Embassy compound in temperatures which reached 115 degrees in the shade, tested the quality of their nerves and humour. Freya attached herself to Bishop, whom she found supportive and kind, as well as amusing and intellectually stimulating. They used to stroll together in the garden, reading the Latin psalms in his breviary, as a relief from the stagnant air and dim light of the shuttered and sandbagged interiors. Freya disliked what she called the 'Lucknow' atmosphere generated by the defensive precautions of the Military Mission harboured with them, and deplored bombast and any expression of revengeful rancour. She preferred lighthearted badinage and insouciance on the model of Wavell's household in Cairo.

She took comfort from the gratitude of the forty-five native dependants for the attention shown them, and in the occasional salty exchanges she managed with the policemen guarding the river approaches from a small boat stationed below the terrace.

These were contacts fortifying to her spirit, an affirmation of essential human solidarity. Iraqi soldiers of the rebellious army who took over at the gate guardhouse were less amenable to her advances. Every day a list of needed supplies, negotiated by telephone through Vyvyan Holt's close friend the Iraqi Minister of Foreign Affairs, was presented to the guard for purchase in the market. Freya constituted herself the upholder of feminine morale in the compound and, determined herself to die with her lipstick on, persuaded the other women to join her in indenting for cosmetics, shampoos and other female necessities. It was a hook baited to lead to conversational openings with the sentries and a picking-up of gossip, but she miscalculated. A surly NCO intervened with an angry shout. 'What's it for?' he cried. 'What's its use? You are all going to be shot anyway . . .' Freya paled, her military escort noted, at this rebuff, and beat a subdued and thoughtful retreat from the barbed-wire perimeter.[2] She did not attempt further approaches.

The Secretariat congregated in Vyvyan Holt's cool office to listen to the news on the radio concealed there. Freya took her turn with the Information people to monitor the broadcasts, and infiltrated Holt's office, under the plea of illness and debility 'lying during the day on Bishop's bed under my Kurdi rug, pleasantly engaged with *Alice Through the Looking Glass* and with Bishop and Holt to talk to'. Freya's cultivation of a civilised lifestyle, devoted to good talk and the contemplation of nature as a corrective to more alarming emotions was an additional tax on Holt's patience; Freya was turning his office into a boudoir, he complained. On his continued telephone access to the Foreign Ministry depended the welfare of the besieged.

Freya's conversion to the promotion of the young Iraqi effendi – the urbanised and upwardly mobile product of the Mandate's educational policy – as the target for long-term schemes to maintain British influence in the area, was initiated during the Baghdad siege. The consecrating influence was Adrian Bishop. He saw the danger to the future of Anglo-Iraqi relations in terms of failure to capture the imagination of the modern educated Iraqi population, unlikely to tolerate indefinitely the rule of a puppet royal family installed by the British, and protected by them. The contrasts between wealth and poverty were too extreme, and the spread of secular education too rapid to be ignored. The need, he advocated, was to forget the Regent Abdul'illah and his clique, the tribal rulers of vast tracts of country, with whom the British missions maintained such friendly social contact as they practised, and the Jewish million-aires, and to concentrate instead on winning the confidence of the less glamorous middle classes, the junior army officers and NCOs, the high-school and university students with whom the future lay.

This was the message Freya promoted via the ear of Corn-wallis. It added impetus to her crusade to expand the Brother-hood. She was willing to work in Iraq, she told Cornwallis and, given a free hand with the Iraqi army, undertook to bring it round to the cause of Democracy in two years.

During this month of captivity Freya consolidated her position with Cornwallis. As a fruit of her conversations with Bishop, a report was produced for his consideration under Bishop's and her name, on the growing force of nationalism among Arab youth, and the need – and the way – to make this nationalism friendly to the British. This type of joint effort was very much Freya's preferred vehicle for launching ideas. She was happier to be associated with, rather than propose, ideas which might or might not prove acceptable. It could be seen as a prudent provision of a get-out clause in an adverse situation, a staking of a claim in a successful one.

The future of relations with the Arab world was a topic end-lessly discussed by the besieged as they whiled away the tedium of captivity, and exercised their minds on how to break through the wall of inaccessibility to local feelings that the British had contrived for themselves by their policies. In moments of confi-dentiality Cornwallis sometimes deplored this situation to Freya, while taking the evening air in the garden, or lingering over the bridge table at the end of a wearying day. It was a topic of some moment. In 1941 the end of empire was not conceived of by the men on the spot. British troops landed in the Middle East with the belief that they were on British soil, won for them by their fathers in the campaigns of the 1914–18 war. They were a citizen and Dominions army, born of parents for whom the Empire was a birthright, ignorant of and indifferent to the aspirations of the people among whom they found themselves.

Winning the war against Germany was the priority, an approach which suited the pragmatic national temperament, and discouraged theorising. It was a necessity that overrode all other considerations. Freya's difficulty was to integrate the advantages of this obdurate element in her countrymen's thinking with a realistic awareness of the aspirations of the Arab world. It was a task too hard for minds more solid than her own.

Faced with an irreconcilable choice, Freya went off at a tangent. The psychological mechanism for overriding what was distasteful came into play, racking up the argument, like a gear change, in a smooth transition to the exposition of an idealised relationship between imperial rulers and their client states. Whereas Bishop was gloomy about the future, depressed by the intractability of the forces stirring in the modern generation of Iraqis, Freya was optimistic. The conviction that the present situation of armed rebellion, dangerous though it was, might yet be the chance, the very last chance, to restore relations with Iraq to their primitive simplicity and good feeling, fired her with a persuasive energy that made her a heartening and invigorating companion in a difficult situation.

She held doggedly to the belief that any resentment on the part of the Iraqi people at the humiliation their army would inevitably sustain at the hands of the British, still the most powerful military force in the area, could be switched against the Germans. These, now occupying the Balkans and swarming into Crete, had fanned the Iraqi revolt but had not followed up with any solid support. The anticipated landing and drive through Vichy-held Syria to the oilfields was a threat which never materialised, though it dominated the planners' minds until the German attack on Russia and invasion of the Crimea at the end of June showed their assessment of enemy intentions to have been at fault.

Freya deplored any expression of rancour or recrimination on the part of her fellow-prisoners. Far better to treat the rebellion as an unfortunate intrigue by violent and misguided men, to be tactfully put aside once order was restored. No diminution of confident belief in the underlying loyalty of the country was the best way to cement it. Faith must be shown in traditional Arab chivalry. These views were argued with all the force and fluency at her command. They impressed Cornwallis, anxiously casting around for means to retrieve a compromised situation.

It was to take a generation for the disenchantment of the East with the West to be acknowledged by the colonial powers. The rethinking of their relations with former clients was difficult for people on the spot; too much of their own life had already been invested in the situation. An emotive idealisation of personal relations became the refuge of one type of temperament, while a sour resentment that of another. Many of the people to be affected suffered a deep inner affront at the proposition that their careers had been motivated by self-serving ambition and a liking for privilege.

Only the very clear-sighted as yet accepted that in all Middle East countries the British tended to be identified with the oppressions of a corrupt and inefficient ruling class, whom their garrisons protected, and on whom they were obliged to rely – so ran the argument – in default of alternatives capable of running the country.[3] Commercial as well as political considerations required this. There was the oil interest with its concessions negotiated at government level, and the big commercial firms maintaining large expatriate communities in Egypt and Iraq. Unlike the Germans, whose commercial relations with their clients were pushed through by hard work at bazaar level and punctual deliveries, the British adopted a grander, more autocratic approach, as befitted the heirs of the East India Company and the Egyptian Condominium, and were careful about whom they admitted to their clubs.

The last imperial generation of Britons in the East was largely the prisoner of its own creations. There was an inability to conceive of any alternative to a system in which it played such

Above Herbert Young's villa, built on the ramparts of Asolo. Freya sold the property after the War.

Top right Robert Stark, a portrait by Flora.

Centre Flora Stark, aged 19, a watercolour portrait by Edwin Bale, Robert Stark's tutor at the Kensington School of Art and Design.

Bottom left Freya, aged 11, by Robert Stark c. 1904.

Bottom right Vera Stark, Freya's sister, born 1895. She died of blood poisoning following a miscarriage in 1926, leaving four young children.

Opposite page, top left Venetia Buddicom, early 1920s. *Above left* Freya in 1915, aged 22. *Left centre* Colonel Gerald de Gaury as a young officer of the Hampshire regiment. *Bottom left* The British Ambassador and his staff outside the British Embassy, Baghdad, 1930s. On the extreme right is Captain Vyvyan Holt, the Oriental Secretary.

This page, top Venetia Buddicom and Freya (under umbrella) trekking through the Syrian Hauran, 1928. *Above* The young Margaret Jourdain, poet, translator of French Symbolist writers, writer and journalist. *Above right* Freya, aged 40, outside the Royal Geographical Society, having received the Back Memorial Prize, 1933. *Right* The Australian dilettante painter, Herbert Young. A talented amateur photographer, he passed on his skills to Freya, and gave her her first camera. Helped by Robert and Flora Stark, he built and laid out the house and garden at Asolo, later known as Casa Freia. Freya inherited the property on his death in 1941.

Above left Harold Ingrams, British Adviser to the Kathiri and Qu'aiti Sultans of Hadramaut, taking the submission of rebellious tribesmen. *Above right* The guest house outside Shibam where Freya was so ill. *Below* Hureidha, the scene of *A Winter in Arabia*. *Bottom left* The Wakefield Archaelogical Expedition, 1937-38; Elinor Gardner, Gertrude Caton Thompson and Freya (in flowered dress). *Bottom right* Doreen and Harold Ingrams with Meryem Besse.

Top left Sir Sydney
Cockerell in June 1951,
ten years before his
death. Former Director
of the Fitzwilliam
Museum in Cambridge,
bibliophile, man of
letters and the best of
friends, he admired
Freya and was used by
her as unofficial editor
and general factotum.

Top centre Christopher
Scaife, actor, singer,
poet and university
lecturer in Cairo and
Beirut. He took over
Freya's Brotherhood of
Freedom in 1943, when
she left for a lecture tour
in America.

Top right Field Marshal
Lord Wavell, whose
penchant for romantic
adventures fostered
Freya's wartime career
and facilitated her early
return to Italy in 1945.

Right Captain Vyvyan
Holt arriving in Berlin
after his release from
captivity in North
Korea, 1953.

Far right Lulie Abu'l
Huda, Freya's first
assistant with the
Brotherhood of
Freedom, Cairo, 1940.

Bottom the Hon. Mrs
Pamela Hore-Ruthven
with Sir Arthur
Longmore, Luxor,
1941.

Above The wedding reception at John Murray's at 50, Albemarle Street, London W1 after Freya's marriage in 1947 to Stewart Perowne. This was after a private ceremony at St Margaret's Church, Westminster, attended only by three witnesses. Freya's dress was a brilliant green – an auspicious colour in Moslem eyes – and her flamboyant appearance caused one guest to remark she looked rather like an Xmas cracker. *Below left* Freya and Asolo's parish priest, the Monsignor who was a friend and ally of her mother. *Below right* Jock Murray in 1954. Freya's discoverer, editor, mentor and friend, he nursed her career and made her famous.

Right Lunch in the garden of the Villa Freia, mid-1950s. *Below* Tracing Alexander's path, descending the gorge of Mount Climax above Kemev, on Turkey's Southern Shore.

Above At the Castle of Mey Caithness: a visit to the Queen Mother. Freya wears a red hat. *Below* A picnic in the Taurus, an excursion in the Consular landrover while researching Alexander the Great's route through Asia Minor for her final series of travel books on Turkey in the 1960s.

a gratifying role, its modest rewards coming from the sense of work well done rather than from former shameless shakings of the pagoda tree. The self-congratulatory innocence of this belief made its rejection by its beneficiaries the most disappointing aspect of the Nasserite revolutions that were to come in the 1950s.

Freya was not untainted by this egocentricity. Her criticisms of the ruling race were of style rather than content. It was their lack of tact that aroused her indignation, not the fact that they ruled.

I see my friends rising to more and more responsible positions, till it seems to me I know almost everyone who is guiding the machine of the Middle Eastern future . . . There is something very enthralling about this work, trying to build here and there some little step of permanent material where ideas and dreams, however infinitesimal, are woven.[4]

The negative aspects of the British presence in eastern lands was something with which she had collided on her arrival in Baghdad in 1929, and the gossip and lack of understanding she suffered then had coloured her feelings about the stuffiness of official attitudes. But the larger concepts of imperialism had her vote. She was an Edwardian in outlook, for whom revolution presaged not liberty and opportunity, but terror, anarchy, the overthrow of all that made life pleasant and sweet. Disorder, and the threat of disorder, alarmed her. Like many people in the 1920s, she had admired Mussolini for his firm handling of threatening industrial anarchy, and for the trains that ran on time, until family discords and the new friends she was making in the 1930s persuaded her she was entering the wrong box.

Freya liked to be right. She also liked to be taken seriously. Here in Baghdad in the heightened tension of a siege, she was close to Cornwallis, and could influence him. The element of push in her perhaps led to her making claims for her Brotherhood which actuality did not entirely justify, while Cornwallis, preconditioned by his friendship with Gertrude Bell and his admiration for her capacities, was perhaps prepared to accept

Freya rather more at her own valuation than was wise. You could say she projected a larger vision, where communities co-existed in harmony, and where the desire for better things found expression in honest government and public service from a young generation won over by friendly and disinterested guidance from their old friends, the British.

That, in later years, became her public stance on her work in the Middle East, and was what perhaps she came to believe the Brethren were about. The manipulation of opinion by its system of contacts, the passing of news and misinformation, and the usefulness of the weekly bulletin as a gauge of public opinion, were obscured by a charismatic sense of mission which impressed some, and produced indulgent disbelief in others. Freya's imagination was fired by a vision of a network of Brotherhood cells spread over the Middle East, friendly to Britain and willing to be guided to a higher concept of nationalism than the mere ousting of a political rival. She clung to the image of fraternal solicitude and reciprocity with all the idealistic conviction of one whose own experience of family life had been stormy and far from ideal. She saw her Brotherhood as a means 'of bringing together gradually all men of good faith in a common effort, where the personal sense of inferiority, the frightful snobbishness of races, may vanish once for all . . .' I found this identification of the evil to be combated illuminating.

The upshot of these conversations was that on 4 June 1941, after British and Jordanian forces had crossed the desert and raised the siege of Baghdad, Cornwallis sent an urgent request to the Foreign Office:[5] 'for the particular task of publicity, propaganda and direct relationships with Iraqis, especially the tribes, the best material available as any blunder or false move on our part may undermine advantages already secured.' For this purpose he recommended that Perowne (from Aden) should be placed in charge of all these activities with Holme (from Jerusalem) as Press Officer, and Bishop (already in Baghdad on loan from GHQ Cairo) and Miss Stark assisting Perowne in Public Relations. Miss Stark, he said, was willing to work here. 'Sympathetic tact' and a light touch were important to the work, and he recommended that the existing team, with the exception of

Bishop, be disposed of as temperamentally unsuited and with the wrong outlook, and not liked by the Iraqis. In this restructuring of the publicity side of the Embassy in Iraq, many people recognised the influence at work.[6]

Freya by now had already left for Palestine en route to Cairo. On the afternoon of 3 June she and Bishop were lifted out by plane with Cawthorn of MEIC, Colonel Clayton and other advisers who had come over to confer, and reached the King David Hotel in Jerusalem in the dark, in time for dinner, and champagne afterwards in the Regence nightclub. 'The whole of Cairo seemed to be packing its kit to cross into Syria for a war which opened next morning with an old-fashioned cavalry charge.'[7] This was the combined Free French and British attack on the Vichy French in Syria, which led to the occupation and securing of that country by the Allies. Freya, released from her month's captivity, was back in the swim with a splash.

Once the Iraqi rebellion had collapsed, Freya's friends in GHQ ME were anxious that she transfer there at once to set in motion a Brotherhood scheme. Lampson, in Cairo, however, was difficult about the suggestion, and uncooperative. 'Miss Stark's organisation in Egypt,' he huffed in a telegram on 7 July 1941 to the Foreign Office (copy to Cornwallis), 'comprising 70 committees with 1100 members cannot be left without guidance.' 'Miss Stark may spend some time in Baghdad but I cannot relinquish Miss Stark for permanent attachment to your staff,' was his reply to a direct request from Cornwallis.

The competing claims of the two Ambassadors provoked Mr Moore Crosthwaite at the Foreign Office to minute 'that their Excellencies are fighting over stolen property, as it is understood from Professor Rushbrook Williams that Miss Stark is anyway on loan from Aden.' In the event, she continued to shuttle between Iraq and Cairo during 1941, and only in February 1942 was she officially accredited on a temporary basis to the Baghdad Embassy as a Second Secretary; she was based there until her resignation in July 1943 to go to America.

Freya was never an administrative empire-builder. Rather the Brotherhood gave her access to confidential areas of wartime diplomacy in the Middle East, something she had angled for since the Munich crisis of 1938, which fed her self-esteem and set her apart from the associates of her earlier, humbler days in the East. With chameleon-like virtuosity, she adapted to her new circumstances.

She told Cockerell from Cairo on 14 January 1941:

> I met a charming man, Colonel Donovan,[8] who is travelling about as observer for President Roosevelt . . . He was at a dinner and birthday dance at the Embassy – such a *pretty* party, candles and a great table with silver buckets of roses at intervals all down it and silver plates to eat from. Everyone wore their best dress and we had a number of young guards-men looking very smart and Napoleonic in their dark mess clothes. We danced in the drawing room among Chinese treasures and flowers and it was one of the pleasantest par-ties I have been to. Colonel Donovan agreed that one must take a long war as quietly and simply as one can . . .

Freya's instinctive preference was to influence indirectly, through the manipulation of other people's ideas; her own pre-war celebrity as a traveller and writer gave her the impetus with which she moved in official circles while it cloaked her private motivations. On a more mundane level, this excused any little financial peccadilloes that might occur along the route, and perhaps explains the blandness of her self-assurance, and its baffling impenetrability, when challenged by more pedestrian minds.

From the time of her appointment to Cairo Freya sought for a man to front for the Brotherhood, and to run the adminis-trative side, leaving her free to concentrate her energies on evangelising. She hated the pettifogging detail of office adminis-tration and lobbied hard for Perowne, who enjoyed bossiness, to take over the job. It would be difficult, she confided, for any woman to make an impact on a male-dominated society obedient to Islam: 'You know how little ice our sex cuts in the oriental mind. I think if we want to make a really big thing out of it [the Brethren] a more impressive standard bearer is required.'[9] But she failed to draw Perowne. He had no intention of playing second fiddle to Freya in Cairo, whatever the blandishments proffered.

It was not until December 1941 that Freya got what she described as her 'supreme Man'. This turned out to be Christopher Scaife. In January 1942 he was appointed Area Controller of the scheme, and liaison officer to the Minister of State's office, under whose cover the Brethren with other elements previously sheltered by the Information Service now nestled. Freya on paper became Scaife's subordinate, but a device was arrived at whereby she retained salary and allowances on the same scale as his. She was designated Sub-Area Controller, as well as Director in Iraq, where she was now setting up a similar operation to that in Egypt. Perowne, lobbied for successfully by Freya, had already preceded her there from Aden to take charge of Public Relations in the Embassy, in response to Cornwallis' request for his services, after the Iraqi rebellion had collapsed.

An attempt by the bureaucrats of the Minister of State's office to scale down Freya's salary to two-thirds of the equivalent male remuneration – the standard practice at that period when women were employed – produced a notable row. Freya complained vigorously to Sir Kinahan Cornwallis, and threatened resignation. The affair was smoothed over. In acknowledgment of her status as initiator of the Brotherhood scheme she obtained parity of earning with the official Controller, and she insisted on, and obtained, complete freedom to conduct the campaign in Iraq as she desired, with only nominal supervision by Scaife. He, however, as titular head of the organisation, had to negotiate the yearly funding of the operation with the Minister of State's office, something that Freya's often notional system of accounting did not make easy.

Freya was quite funny about this. She told her mother:

I feel the items are like wild shy animals which I have to trace in and out of their elusive columns. Christopher [Holme] in Jerusalem was awfully pedantic while I was trying to make that d–d budget conform with his . . . couldn't see why I had

classified a typewriter (bought) under the heading of telephones; they all seem to me the same sort of mechanical
idea, and telephones were the only heading that had any
money left . . .

Throughout 1942 the effort for the British to keep up spirits
was exhausting, in the face of repeated military setbacks in
Libya and the Balkans. It drained energies already depleted by
the heat, and by the nagging fear of a German invasion of the
Middle East through Turkey or Syria. This fear, Freya told me,
was the daily accompaniment of her life at this period. She
never left Baghdad without wondering if she would ever return
to her comfortable house there. Two small suitcases of personal
effects were kept permanently packed for sudden flight. A letter
from Wavell possibly reflects these preoccupations. 'There will
always be room for you in our house,' he wrote kindly from
Delhi, and this was comforting. She missed the good-natured
friendliness of his household in Cairo, now transferred to New
Delhi where Wavell was appointed Commander-in-Chief, India,
in July 1941; in Baghdad her relations with colleagues were not
always happy, as her letters at that time make plain.

Throughout the worst period of the war, between 1941 and
1943, Freya promoted the expansion of her Brotherhood with
tireless energy and messianic conviction. She saw no reason,
she later wrote, why the organisation should not spread to
every town and village in Asia. She was eager to push on to
new territories. Her tonic enthusiasm, and her fund of gossip,
as she flitted about legations and consulates and High Commissioners' households, was a cheering distraction in a period
of gloom. But with the Allied landings in Sicily and the movement of the war on to European soil, such undiscriminating
enthusiasm presented danger. In the view of the district Political
Officers it exposed the organisation to infiltration by elements
intent not on democracy but on the deliberate overthrowing of
existing political institutions – the monarchy and parliamentary
government – once the occupying armies withdrew.

Adrian Bishop's SOE team, clandestinely stitching together

stay-behind networks, was sceptical of Freya's optimism; they trawled at a different level from Freya, among students and urban political activists rather than village headmen and 'tame' tribal leaders, and were not always happy about what they brought to the surface. Perowne, as head of the Embassy's Public Relations Department, sheltered both Bishop's and Freya's outfits under his official wing. These were to some extent, especially after Bishop's accidental death in the summer of 1942,[10] divided by irreconcilable political viewpoints. Freya instinctively held to the established centres of power as the target for manipulation; the younger men were open to newer alternatives. Bishop's team inhabited a large, rambling Arab house, with two courtyards, sprawling along the bank of the Tigris. It was well away from the British residential area – on the wrong side of the tracks, as it were; no woman, so it was gossiped among the Embassy womenfolk, ever crossed its threshold, where Bishop reigned supreme.

Adrian Bishop was a life-enhancing figure for his friends. He appears in the memoirs of several, including those of Sir Maurice Bowra, the Warden of Wadham College, Oxford, whose closest and most reckless friend he was in the 1920s; and in the archaeologist Seton Lloyd's recollections of Bishop's establishment at the South Gate in Baghdad, during 1941–2, of which he formed a part. He and Bishop were interned with Freya during the Embassy siege. All who knew Bishop are agreed on his ability, which was a gift Freya shared, to liven up any gathering at which he was present. Resembling Oscar Wilde both in appearance and style – tall, heavy, ugly – and coming from the same level of Dublin society, talk was his supreme gift.

There was always a certain amount of mystery about his antecedents. Herbert Frank Bishop – he was known as Frank in his family – was the son of a maltster in John Jameson's distillery in Dublin, and of a Protestant Ascendancy mother. Sent to Eton, where the name Adrian was attached to him, he was sent down early for a homosexual scandal, but went on to King's, Cambridge, to take a degree in classics. A self-proclaimed hedonist with a darker, more depressive side to his nature, he was convinced, and sought to convince others, that most orthodox opinion was a conspiracy against enjoyment conducted by Philistines and Pharisees, who sought to destroy what they themselves did not understand. Debarred from returning to Dublin by threatened police action over an earlier indiscretion, after a spell with the Anglo-Persian Oil Company he drifted about central Europe and the Balkans, a remittance man kept afloat by friends and family, until early in the 1930s he finally decided to take up residence in Berlin because it was cheap.

This period ended in 1935 when, back in England, he suffered an attack of *encephalitis lethargica* or sleeping sickness. It produced in him a religious conversion which, while not altering his personality, completely changed his life. Convalescing in a farmhouse at Uffington, near Oxford, nearly penniless and supported by friends, he joined the circle of John and Penelope Betjeman. Shortly after, he became a novice at the Anglican monastery of Nashdom Abbey, and took the name in religion of Brother Thomas More – Brother Tom to his lay friends. With the outbreak of war he requested release from his vows and in 1940 he was commissioned for army intelligence duties and posted to the Middle East in 1941.

Described to me by Professor Lloyd as a refugee from Isherwood's Berlin, Bishop exercised an immediate fascination on Freya. Sir Maurice Bowra has remarked on Bishop's particular quickness in seeing others as they saw themselves. Freya herself adjusted quickly to any company in which she found herself, so who most reflected who when she and Bishop were together is an interesting conjecture. It must have been like entering a hall of mirrors. Freya in 1961, writing of this period, mourned the loss of this 'dearest, gayest and deepest of friends', but Seton Lloyd recalls that Bishop was always a little patronising about her. If she held forth too much about her own affairs he was likely to interrupt with, 'Now little Freya, if you will keep silent for some minutes, there will be a prize for you . . .'

Freya's Brotherhood in Iraq never enjoyed the success it did in Egypt, its members remained depressingly below the target figure, but the house at South Gate was seen by its occupants as a magnet for young Iraqi intellectuals and an outpost of progressive liberalism. Co-opted by Aidan Philip, a resolutely left-wing recruit of Bishop's from his Anglo-Persian Oil Company days, these were set to work on a variety of social-welfare projects aimed at introducing a wider practical understanding of how government worked. How much the idealism of these programmes was a vehicle used by doctrinaire political activists awaiting their opportunity is open to surmise.

Much of this activity, regrettably down-market in Freya's view, was in the spirit of the British Army Bureau of Current Affairs' adult educational programme that prepared the way for the Beveridge Plan and the post-war Welfare State in Britain. Open house at South Gate once a week provided, it was claimed,[11] a milieu of serious thought for young Iraqis unspoilt by crude propaganda. This ivory-tower approach aroused Freya's scorn; she wanted mass conversion at grass-roots level by populist appeal. Whether either approach proved ultimately beneficial to its clients is a moot point; the middle age of Freya's 'Young Effendis' was passed either in exile of one sort or another, or under regimes less friendly to the relaxed atmosphere they so enjoyed at South Gate. Several suffered arrest and imprisonment, two were publicly hanged, one for the murder of King Abdullah of Transjordan in 1951.

Freya herself inhabited a comfortable modern bungalow in the Alwiyah residential suburb, where the amenities of Anglo-Indian life were faithfully reproduced in a Babylonian setting. Once installed here Freya deputed domestic administration to her assistants, of whom she now had two. Pamela Hore-Ruthven, retrieved from compassionate leave with her husband, was charged with the furnishing and decoration of the house and, for the sum of £600 squeezed out of a grudging HMG by Freya, produced a pretty feminine interior, charmingly different in its fresh white paint and pale pink and grey colour schemes from the usual wartime billet. A staff of servants, cook, cleaner, gardener, sewing-woman, looked after the household. Vyvyan Holt, dragged there by Freya to admire the finished result, was deflating. 'I can only see the tax-payers' money in it,' was his comment.

Pamela retired once the move to Baghdad was completed, and returned to Britain to have a second child, of whom Freya became godmother. Her place was taken by Barbara Graham, a driver with the Spears Mission to the Free French forces in Syria, whom Pamela recruited in Cairo; she brought Freya's car over the desert from Palestine on appointment, and was constituted purse-bearer to the establishment, charged with the overseeing of Freya's comfort. Freya viewed her assistants as a means of sparing herself stress, so that she could devote herself wholeheartedly to promoting the Brotherhood. Modelled on the ADCs of senior military personnel, they were expected to answer the telephone, arrange Freya's social calendar, run the office and the house and, on tour, to look after Freya's comfort.

The journey-money on tour was handed over to the accompanying assistant by Freya, rather as some grand Victorian might hand over the care of her jewel-box to her maid. The responsibility to a newcomer, unfamiliar with the country and the language, was daunting. Freya was not sympathetic to inexperience; she expected her people to cope with whatever was thrown at them, and didn't welcome interruption. The lady's-maid aspect of the job and Freya's driving impatience were hard to take; after six months, Barbara Graham resigned. Another assistant, Peggy Drower, the daughter of Lady Drower, Freya's early protector in Baghdad in 1930, arrived in 1942. Having had a childhood in Iraq, she was familiar with the country and the language and became Freya's right-hand; and eventually took over the revamped Iraqi Brotherhood under Christopher Scaife, when Freya resigned in 1943.

The house in Alwiyah was roomy and comfortable, the style in which Freya lived lavish and grand. She entertained constantly with a host of friends, English and Iraqi, in and out of the place. In private, Freya complained to her mother about the cost of it all. She was always careful about money, her assistants recalled; they were expected to work wonders on very little. To offset her expenses, Freya took in lodgers, the first, Lady Ranfurly, a Cairo friend of Pamela's, and like her with a husband a prisoner of war. She was PA to General

'Jumbo' Maitland Wilson, Wavell's overall Commander of British troops in Egypt during the successful winter of 1940, and now commanding an occupying army, PAI force, protecting the supply lines from India and the Persian Gulf to Russia. A second paying guest, Nigel Clive, a young yeomanry officer being prepared for SOE work in Greece, joined the household in 1942. He recalls a gay, carefree, pre-war style of life, with horses brought round by their grooms to the door for early-morning rides, servants handing around trays of cool drinks under twirling fans, and easy access at the dinner table for a young man to the leading figures of the local political scene.[12]

Freya, riding out with her group of attendant admirers each morning, dancing with the top brass in the Baghdad nightclubs, calling on the Iraqi Ministers and the Palace harems, infused her companions with energy and fun, and presided over her household like Kipling's Mrs Hauksbee in Simla. She was careful about her choice of intimates; she tended to make her friends among people who could be useful, and homed in instinctively on the prominent and the glamorous, rejecting all that was seen as dull, ordinary and commonplace.

Perhaps this aroused resentment in lesser minds. There were pinpricking administrative queries about her expenses; full housing allowance was disallowed by Cairo once it was discovered she was charging rent to her PGs. Her accounting was sketchy, often a last-minute improvisation. To minds pedantically alert to irregularities, it was not a satisfactory situation, but one difficult to alter. The rumoured reports of her influence – that she had friends in high places – warned people off. There were rows with Perowne about money; who controlled the cheque book was the point at issue in one furious scene. Freya won. At the first sign of any trouble she flew straight to Kinahan Cornwallis; this perhaps accounts for Lady Cornwallis' distaste, seeing in this an exploitation of her husband's good nature. Despite, or perhaps because of, Freya's promotion of his talents to Cornwallis, relations with Perowne followed the pattern of the Aden rupture. Like other of her early friends, who had known her in simpler circumstances, he was not prepared to be patronised by Freya. Distrusting her blandishments, he preferred the more intellectually rigorous male company to be found in the SOE mess across the river at South Gate.

Freya believed jealousy of her social success since leaving Aden coloured his attitude to her work. Perowne's view was that she neglected her duties to further her social ambitions. 'But she was never there!' was his explosive response to my enquiry as to what exactly she did in Baghdad. An analysis of times spent on leave – excluding short local leaves and forty-eight-hour breaks – from her office in this period, always on grounds of failing health, shows she spent one month in Palestine in 1941, two months in Cyprus in August/September 1942, and two months in India and Persia in February/March 1943.

Freya's adulation of Wavell inclined her to programme her career in terms of military rather than diplomatic priorities. Her household was modelled on the informality and youthful high spirits of Wavell's domestic establishment in Cairo, and the liveliness of the Lampson circle, a glamorous interlude whose loss was regretted by all who had once experienced it. Baghdad by contrast was stuffy and provincial, and games of ping-pong with the Iraqi royal ladies or bridge parties with the Cornwallises were no substitute for the glitter of cosmopolitan Egyptian society.

Having Hermione Ranfurly in the house kept Freya in touch with her former Cairo friends. Shortly after her return from leave in Cyprus a suggestion came from Wavell, early in December 1942, through General Maitland Wilson. Would Freya be prepared, if she could be spared, to spend three months in India sifting through Italian prisoners with a view to selecting reliable anti-Fascists for use on the Italian mainland once the Allies had landed? If yes, he was to arrange her dispatch as a military priority to Delhi.

Freya was thrilled. After eighteen months mostly in Iraq she was restless and longing for change. Merely the idea of a landing in Italy filled her with excited anticipation. She longed to know what had happened to her property there. The Villa Freia was hers, she knew, bequeathed to her by Herbert Young, but how would she find it? From now on, getting back to Italy was her private priority and Wavell's offer was a move in the right direction. Without further consultation she accepted it in principle and then tackled Cornwallis.

The Ambassador, she told Christopher Scaife, on to whom she moved next, accepted the importance of the offer, and her temporary assignment. Scaife passed the buck to the Minister of State's office, and Freya went joyfully ahead with her plans. Privately he expressed the view that she was 'flighty' in abandoning her employment in Iraq at a time when every effort was needed to consolidate the effect of the gains in North Africa and Russia on Arab opinion.

Freya from the start was mysterious and evasive about her Indian mission. What had been a suggestion was presented as a summons. Top security was the card she played, and the overriding authority of Wavell as C-in-C, India. It was a disagreeable shock when the Minister of State's office in Cairo made difficulties. More precise explanations were demanded. There was a loud angry row over the telephone to Cairo, and permission to leave was refused. Freya was furious. Cairo's bull-in-the-china-shop insensitivity, she told her private correspondents, had destroyed a wonderful opportunity for her to experience India in 'country-house comfort' under the wing of the Wavells. A sense of betrayal added to her disappointment; she suspected she was the victim of spiteful intrigue and a repeat of Perowne's performance in Aden, when he tried to block her transfer to Cairo. Predictably, illness declared itself, never precisely diagnosed, but enough to procure concern. Her mother's recent death in California was taken into account. Three weeks' leave for a private visit to the Wavells was offered by Cairo. Her miserable appearance as she drooped about her business evoked contrition, and her staff begged her to accept the offer.

Her spirits restored, before leaving she gave a grand dinner party for the Iraqi Prime Minister, Nuri As Said, General Maitland Wilson, Air Marshal de Crespigny, the Iraqi Director of Police, and assorted ADCs, where they all enjoyed themselves being critical about the Free French administration in Syria. Such evidence of Freya's status in ruling circles impressed the Director of Police, who willingly made over the former German social club premises, a prominent centre of Nazi propaganda, now closed down and discredited, for the use of the Brotherhood. This was something Freya had long angled for, a conspicuous demonstration of the decline of German influence; her sense of theatre always favoured such gestures, though their effect might be short-lived. It was embarrassing for the Embassy to discover at war's end that no record of rent paid or agreement with the municipal authorities on the terms of occupation existed. A large bill for arrears of rent was received from an angry Arab Municipality, and had to be met by HMG, but by that time Freya had already left the Brotherhood behind her.[13]

Freya left for Basra on 4 February 1943 en route to India. Shortly before her departure a letter had arrived from the M of I in London, raising the suggestion of a six-months' lecture tour in America. This had already been offered and refused while she was on leave in Cyprus during the previous summer; now she felt she could leave Iraq with a clear conscience in the near future, for the Brethren were in good hands, the tide of public opinion was turning, and the organisation would not suffer from her temporary absence.

On the day of departure she forwarded the M of I letter, with her reply, to Cairo, indicating that though she was prepared to abide by her superiors' decision, she would welcome the opportunity to spend some months in America, not only for the propaganda value of the mission, but also to settle up her mother's affairs and to inspect her property in Canada – her father's fruit farm in British Columbia – unvisited since 1930.

In this way her detachment from the Middle East was set in motion.

FIFTEEN

A SOLDIERLY FAREWELL

From the moment that Freya knew her visit to the Wavells in India was agreed, she was determined to turn it to advantage by a private speculation. This was to buy a car in India, drive it back through Persia to Iraq and then sell it at a handsome profit. The wartime curtailment of imports, and government requisitioning, had produced an overall shortage of private transport and a vigorous black market fuelled by enormously inflated prices existed throughout the Middle East. It was combated, not entirely successfully, by local government decree and the field security police. The export of any private vehicle from India was strictly forbidden.

In June 1942, during the worst reverses in the western desert when Tobruk fell and German invasion through Syria was feared, Freya sold her own private car, brought with her on transfer from Cairo to Baghdad, to the Embassy car pool for £500. She thus prudently, in a period of uncertainty, capitalised on an asset for which she received a petrol and mileage allowance from her employers. It enabled her, somewhat grudgingly, to send 500 dollars (£125) to her mother in California, while the rest went to swell her savings, patriotically invested in War Loan. The success of this manoeuvre encouraged her to repeat it. The financial sleight of hand appealed to one who never believed in paying more for a thing than she had to and who delighted in getting something for nothing. She was apparently unaware of any likelihood of bureaucratic interference with her plan.

She discussed this openly in her letters to her friends. It was a sort of game, a projection of her 'gamine' personality, which made good copy for more circumspect admirers and effectively veiled the calculation that underlay it. The prospect of an easy profit thrilled her. She was confident that Wavell would support the adventurous element in her plan and lost no time in sounding him out. 'He is a dear about it all,' she wrote within two days of arrival in Delhi '. . . he would never stand in the way of anyone *doing* things . . .'

She told Cockerell:

I hope in two to three weeks to get back overland by Persia if I can manage it. I have a great hankering for the spaces of Asia with no committees and just a *chaikhana* (teashop) to rest in when night comes . . .

Freya's hunch about Wavell proved correct. A first-hand report on the functioning of the eastern supply route to the new Russian ally could be construed as a useful enterprise, but even more interesting would be confidential diplomatic gossip about Russian political activities along the sensitive border lands of Persia, Afghanistan and China.

Freya's friend, Sir Clarmont Skrine, a Central Asian expert first met in the 1920s in Bordighera, was now Consul-General in Meshed, the northern terminus of the East Persian supply route. Here he was well placed to observe the activities of Britain's new Soviet allies and to study the problems of sending war supplies to the Russians in Transcaspia, an area familiar to Wavell from World War I. Freya's plan was to talk over the Persian situation with Skrine before going on to Teheran to discuss the possible expansion there of her Brotherhood, while en route for Baghdad.

In the gossip-ridden upper echelons of ME wartime society, people were curious as well as impressed by Wavell's patronage of Freya. There must be some hidden element in it, they felt, and this enhanced her status in the minds of the uninitiated. Wavell was a man notoriously difficult in terms of commonplace sociability. He had no small talk, remaining dauntingly silent in company, a terrible ordeal for women seated beside him at dinner parties and crushed by their inability to breach his reserve. Freya's warmth, friendliness and spontaneity made communication easier for such men. She presented no obvious threat and was not cowed by silence. Wavell, for all his air of impassivity, was susceptible to the sprightliness of a witty woman and enjoyed such company. Freya was not the only woman with whom he corresponded. Her status as a published author helped her, for he had something of the same exaggerated and uncritical admiration for *literati* as W. P. Ker had for Alpine guides, an unworldliness that fostered the protective devotion of those admitted to his intimacy.

Mutual admiration is a good basis for friendship but it can be dangerous for the less level-headed. Perhaps Wavell's favour fostered Freya's growing belief in her own singularity, while what he really admired was her optimism and resourcefulness rather than her intellectual capacity. 'The great gift of vitality,' he wrote to her in August 1944 '. . . is to my mind the most attractive quality that man, woman, poet or writer can have . . .' Vitality was something so native to Freya that she did not recognise it in herself, and this confused people.

Punctually at the beginning of March 1943 on completion of her three weeks' leave in Delhi, Freya began her return journey to Baghdad. Her plan was in motion. 'The F M had a faraway benevolent look when I suggested it,' she wrote to her Baghdad household as the resources of the C-in-C's establishment were mobilised to assist her. A car was found for her by Peter Coats, Wavell's Military Secretary, 'a sumptuous 24 hp Plymouth', for which she paid £1000, she wrote. It was supplied with extra spare tyres and tanked to the brim with additional cans of petrol – all valuable commodities virtually unobtainable by a private person – by a zealous sergeant of the Royal Army Service Corps. Charles Rankin, another of Wavell's staff, negotiated an export permit for the vehicle from the Viceregal Foreign Secretariat, something normally unobtainable for a private person in a period when government of India regulations against black-market irregularities were strictly enforced. Freya's application was backed by an official note, signed by Wavell; a permit

was issued on the understanding that the car would, at the end
of its journey, enter the official car pool in Baghdad.

She was provided with a driver to take her via Lahore to
Quetta. En route, she detoured to Simla, where she first saw
the Himalayas. At Quetta she was joined by an acquaintance
whom she had run into in Delhi. This was Johnnie Hawtrey, a
close friend of Sir Philip Sassoon, the former Air Minister.
Freya had met him earlier in Iraq through Gerald de Gaury; he
was now on the staff of RAF HQ, India. Formerly Inspector of
the Iraqi Air Force, he and Freya had spent an evening together
in a party at a Baghdad nightclub. An agreeable bachelor with
Iraqi friends in the Regent Abdul'illah's circle whom he was
keen to see again, he fell in readily with Freya's suggestion to
join her on what seemed an amusing adventure easily manageable on a short local leave.

An experienced motorist, he did the driving, and they reached
Meshed on schedule, following the supply route from Quetta
via Zahedan northwards towards the Russian frontier. The drive
took several days, over 800 miles of gravel roads kept open by
Baluch and Pathan labour gangs, guarded against brigandage by
the Indian army and supplied by rations brought up from India.
The two travellers were put up in consular households and army
posts on the way and were a welcome interlude to their hosts,
marooned in such barren surroundings and pleased to discuss
their experiences with a sympathetic listener, thus providing a
rationale for Freya's journey.

Arrived in Meshed, they were entertained by the Skrines in
the spacious surroundings of the Consulate. Freya enjoyed four
days of sightseeing and good talk, during which she was shown
round the famous Shi'a shrine of the Eighth Imam Reza, a glittering treasure house of Persian art rarely shown to foreigners,
and a focal point of Shi'a religious fanaticism. This was a privilege arranged for her by her host which Freya was fully qualified
to appreciate.

Less happy was the news, just as she and Hawtrey were
about to start on the last leg of the journey to Teheran, that
the road was breached by spring floods for a distance of three
kilometres and would remain impassable for several days.

Despite her host's efforts to persuade Freya to wait for the all-clear, she preferred to backtrack to Zahedan and take the Kerman road to Ispahan.[1] This was a town she had long planned to visit, the capital of medieval Persia, with many famous surviving buildings. There was also a Consulate where she could profitably sound out the expansion into Persia of her Brotherhood.

This change of plan entailed a detour of some 1200 miles, adding up to a total journey time of nineteen days, instead of the week or ten days anticipated when the journey was originally planned. Freya wrote that she enjoyed the detour immensely and found it a great rest to look at one desert after another and have no-one about who wanted to be told about Democracy. Hawtrey saw his leave evaporating under the demands of Freya's sightseeing. By the time they reached Teheran anxiety about overstaying his leave, which had been somewhat grudgingly sanctioned by his Air Marshal, was paramount and he lost no time in fixing himself a lift on an RAF plane about to leave for Baghdad. This plan misfired when the aircraft failed to start and another day was lost while efforts were made to get it going.

Hawtrey's defection put Freya in something of a quandary, and possibly explains her next action. As a civilian, Hawtrey explained, she was not eligible for military transport and would have to wait and catch a BOAC plane if she wanted to fly. She was nervous of continuing the journey on her own without the protection of a male escort, and she did not want to pay an air fare. Quite apart from the driving, she did not relish the prospect of being waylaid and robbed. Car tyres and accessories, let alone vehicles, were at a premium on the black market; something that made a solitary private car travelling out of convoy a target for banditry. If she lost her car, she lost her investment, and though it might be argued it was bought for official use, and should be indemnified, she would certainly lose any profit she might hope to make. Persia was a sovereign state, despite its occupation by Allied troops, and Freya, as an attaché of the Baghdad Embassy, landed on the doorstep of Adrian Holman, formerly Oriental Counsellor at the Baghdad

Embassy and now moved to Teheran. Holman himself had always enjoyed Freya; they were locked up together during the Baghdad siege of 1941 and he had an amused appreciation of her life-enhancing qualities. He and his young wife were glad to put her up. The Holmans in Teheran had an Armenian chauffeur, Armencar, on whom they depended as their domestic right-hand man. When Freya asked casually if she could enlist his help in something about her car, they agreed readily. This was at breakfast and, without enquiring further, Armencar was instructed to look after Miss Stark when he had finished taking Holman to his office and his wife to the Services club she helped run for Allied troops.

Freya's decision to sell the car and take what profit she could without risking loss on the final stage of her journey was already taken. What she needed was help to find a buyer. This Armencar supplied. In no time at all two Persians were produced. The absence of papers was no deterrent. The deal was completed over a glass of tea, the money paid in cash, and the car driven away before lunch. The first the Holmans knew of the transaction was the excited appearance of their driver in Betty Holman's canteen, clutching a bundle of notes which he begged her to put in the safe for him. It was £500, his pay-off for fixing the sale of the car, an enormous figure at that period for a man in his position. Disconcerted and surprised, she telephoned her husband. The sum of £5000 was the figure quoted for Freya's sale.[2]

Forty years later this episode was the most abiding recollection of Freya's wartime activities among the people I interviewed. She herself bluffed out the situation with cool effrontery, disclaiming any awareness of transgression. To the Holmans' astonished enquiries, she gave no answer. The car was gone, driven off into the bazaar, there was nothing to say; she simply smiled her quizzical little smile and changed the subject. 'But I put it all into War Loan!' was her bland self-justification when tackled later by Christopher Scaife and Gordon Waterfield.[3] Her composure stonewalled reproach into silence; people could not really believe one of their own kind could be so irresponsible, or so disingenuous.

The scandal was muffled, submerged. There were other more pressing matters to attend to, and Freya's little gamble came off. But it did her no good. Sir Reader Bullard, the Ambassador in Teheran, let it be known quietly that he did not want to see Freya about his Embassy again.[4] He was an old-fashioned diplomat, experienced in Eurasian affairs, and respected for his probity. Several people felt they had been taken in, their good nature exploited. The story trickled out over the years. Freya's playing into the hands of Axis propagandists in Persia, busy attributing food shortages, inflation and the black market to Allied military occupation, was genuinely shocking to the average Briton. It compromised Holman and the Teheran Embassy in a transaction contrary to its own regulations, and though Freya might seem to have got away with it, the incident was not forgotten, and it tarnished her reputation among the old hands.

The impasse at Teheran was solved by an impatient brigadier, stranded like themselves on the airfield. He commandeered a car to drive himself, an ADC and Hawtrey to Baghdad. Not to be outdone, Freya persuaded him to fit her in too, and was crammed into the back seat. By driving through the night the party reached Baghdad on 10 April. Freya had been absent sixty-five days.

Hawtrey's attempt to ditch Freya in Teheran did not go unpunished. Writing about her wartime activities, Freya in 1961 skipped lightly over this episode. 'The history of my car caused some scandal, for I sold it for a splendid profit as soon as I got to Teheran, having omitted (by ignorance and not intention) to get the diplomatic permit to which I was entitled.'[5]

She and Hawtrey, she added, divided the profit of the car sale between them. Was this pique, or the need for a racy flourish to round off the adventure and imply an intimacy greater than existed? It is difficult to say. The rapid wartime friendship with Hawtrey was not maintained; despite subsequent invitations, he never looked Freya up in Asolo. He died in 1954, collapsing suddenly at San Remo, en route by car from Iraq to retirement in England.

Freya owed money to Hawtrey from the journey. She liked

to pick up amusing things on her travels, trinkets and jewellery
for herself, or things for her house. She was not always prompt
in settling loans. On her instructions, after some correspondence, Hawtrey was finally repaid from the Brotherhood's
funds, after she had left Baghdad; the money came from a
secret reserve fund and would not show on the books.[6] The
unravelling of this and other transactions, on taking over the
entire Brotherhood in 1943, may account for Christopher
Scaife's private opinion that some of the Baghdad household
furnishings packed up and dispatched to Asolo at war's end on
Freya's instruction were 'perks' paid for by the Brotherhood.

Once the second battle of El Alamein was fought and won,
and the war moved on through North Africa to the landings in
Sicily, Freya's interest in the Middle East diminished. Her
instinct was to follow the drum, and get out. She was glad to
be shot of the Brethren, the American tour would give her new
options, and after one last hectic tour of all her parish, she
left Cairo by air on 12 August 1943 for London and her new
assignment. She had no intention of being left behind in a backwater. She had set her sights on Italy.

On closer examination, as I dug deeper into the record, Freya's
Brotherhood proved to be a good deal less disinterested and
less altruistic than she pretended. Her work was never secret,
she claimed; there were never any financial bribes. It was not
planned, she told me in Asolo, that it would ever be more
than a useful temporary expedient. She was unimpressed by
its development from a purely anti-Nazi counter-propaganda
role to its final identity as a cultural organisation. *Her* scheme
was a model exercise to produce a desired effect, the stiffening
of pro-British sympathy and confidence in the war's outcome
at a time when Britain stood alone. This was the language of
practical men of action, soldierly talk that brushed aside the
softer implications of elder brothers helping younger ones, a
favourite metaphor employed by Freya to push home arguments
to humble auditors.

I found the contradictions difficult to swallow. Was I being
given a doctored truth? I remembered a warning given me by

my neighbour, Ifor Evans,[7] when I told him of my interest in Freya. 'Oh, you couldn't help but like Freya!' he exclaimed. 'She had her own way to make in the world. Mind you, you had to be careful with her. She was devious. You had to watch what you told her, you never knew where or how it might be used . . .'

My uneasiness was fortified by a paper I unearthed in the Public Records Office, an M of I document, Paper No 536 of the Overseas Planning Committee, dated 3 October 1944. In the matter of personal contacts it said:

Oral Propaganda was now part of the Publicity Section, and quite separate from the *Ikhwan* or Brotherhood. Agents are paid and work through committees with a certain amount of secrecy. They have contacts with preachers in mosques, schoolmasters, businessmen, café frequenters, journalists, deputies and society people. They foster Anglo-Egyptian relations by tea parties, dinners, etc at which prominent Egyptians are brought into contact with officers and men of HM Forces, and members of the British colony.

The *Ikhwan* has deliberately shed its 'secret' character, and in Egypt as in Iraq it has become a means of interesting its members in social welfare, and generally fostering their nascent sense of civic responsibility.

It was difficult to reconcile this material with Freya's own account of the Brotherhood written on her return from America in 1944. If there was nothing secret about the *Ikhwan* how could the Oral Propaganda element have been hived off to continue its clandestine activities independently?

Much of Cairo's hectic gaiety in the early wartime winters derived from the privately acknowledged fact that without a local logistical back-up from the Egyptians the army in the desert could not function. It took twenty-six Egyptians, so General 'Jumbo' Maitland Wilson calculated, Freya told me, to put one fighting soldier into the battle line.

The need to keep up Egyptian spirits and confidence in 1940 as the Italian army in Libya moved slowly towards the frontier

with Egypt was the task of the Ambassador, and the domestic
atmosphere of gaiety and confident high spirits generated in his
household, and in Wavell's, was the model for the rest of the
British community, designed to keep local enemy agents guess-
ing. It was the reality that underlay all Freya's professions
towards her clients of friendliness, affection, well-wishing and
disinterested benevolence. In Freya's thinking altruism and self-
interest were always closely linked. 'Put it like this, turn it like
that, and you'll have them eating out of your hand,' was her
cry when hammering out an argument. To hold people or events
in the hollow of your hand was a metaphor often used; it produced a painful impression on more sensitive associates. The
difference between her advertised and her private pronouncements on the Brethren – 'Freya's little Brothers' as they were
smilingly referred to on the cocktail round – jarred. 'The poor
little effendi does so badly need a helping hand, and so rarely
gets it, and is so touchingly grateful,' is a sentiment often produced in her letters. The element of condescension in these
utterances pained associates whose liking for the people they
recruited was genuine and unforced.

She made no secret to her own friends of her boredom with
the routines of committee work. She visualised her clients at
the war's end, she told Jock Murray:

> sitting all over the country in their little assembly rooms with
> chairs all round the walls (the best velvet at the top and
> gradually decreasing towards bareness as they reach the
> door); little tables always toppling, and hideous ashtrays first
> made to advertise whiskey or tobacco; and round them and
> behind them all the Effendis in imitation tweeds, in imitation
> silk ties, in imitation European shoes, with imitation Euro-
> pean minds, and nothing genuine but the precariousness of
> their financial arrangements and a dim longing for a better
> world where the imitation virtues may suddenly turn out to
> be genuine after all. I have a sort of maternal feeling for all
> these people. They *do*, however imperfectly, want better
> things, and there is such pathetic gratitude for the mere fact
> that one is interested in their thoughts and wishes. I think

by the end of the war some sort of instrument will have been made – a body of opinion friendly to Britain and anxious to build something for its future; a sort of *receptacle*, and I only hope that someone will be there ready to pour in a suitable mixture. I shall have done my job and will look around for a quiet life, far – *ever* so far – from committees![8]

Freya possibly never understood why such sentiments could offend, and why uncritical applause should be denied her by the very men she most wished to impress. The dedication of her book *East is West* in August 1945, 'To my friends the Young Effendis . . . wishing them well', was received with lifted eyebrows by former associates, aware of the very different tone adopted by Freya in private conversations.

A belief was current among Freya's male admirers that she enjoyed nothing more than danger and discomfort. 'Freya put her head round my door this morning,' noted Sir Miles Lampson in his Diary for June 1941 after the lifting of the Baghdad siege. '. . . looked in excellent health and spirits . . . seems to have enjoyed herself thoroughly. She's a great girl . . .' he added appreciatively. 'A glorious experience; you would have given anything for it,' was the report of Bill Bailey of SOE, caught at the start of the rebellion distributing anti-Nazi pamphlets in Baghdad, and given a rough time by the mob during his captivity. Wavell wrote to her from Assam of 'nice wild uncivilised dirty happy mountainy men . . . you would have enjoyed it thoroughly . . .' Nothing in Freya's personal habits substantiated this belief. There was an element of wishful thinking in people's readiness to take her at face value, a surrogate adventurer for themselves. Women tended to associate Freya more with bubble baths and beauty treatments, and excited acquisitions from *couturier* houses. Daphne Fielding recalled staying after the war at the Paris Embassy with the Duff Coopers, and Freya being there and making a great to-do about attending the dress shows, 'and coming back after all the fuss with the kind of oriental confection she habitually wore . . .'

Her letters often dwell on fortunate purchases made in times of stress. The Munich crisis of 1938 was the occasion for an eye-catching hat, snapped up in Paris while Freya was on her way to London. It had a garland of pink and yellow ostrich plumes around the brim, tilted over one eye, and a red plume drooping down the back. Italy's entry into the war was marked by the acquisition of six boxes of face-cream, the last in Aden – enough, she hoped, to see her through the duration – while Japan's in 1942 galvanised her to pick up the remaining three little silk washing frocks in Baghdad, and nine pairs of silk stockings. The raising of the Baghdad siege in 1941 was celebrated on arrival in Cairo with three new hats 'each gayer than the other'. One was the famous cartwheel with its embroidered clockface, another, red, had a *bouquet champêtre* sprouting out of the pinnacle of its crown.

Freya never fell into the trap of Gertrude Bell's particular emotional enthralment with the Arabs; hers was reserved for her own compatriots and for a very special element in them too. Her deracinated upbringing, more Italian than English, perhaps explains the sense of marginality, of not belonging or not fitting in with ordinary English people, which colours her recollections of herself as a pre-1914 student at London University, or clerking in censorship in 1916, and briefly as a VAD with a British Red Cross hospital unit in Italy in 1917. She was too insecure, the struggle to establish herself had been too hard, for her to throw herself away in reckless pursuit of a dream, and to give her life in service to an ideal. She clung to her Devonian roots, and the sense of Englishness this gave her, and it delighted her when through her own talents she was accepted into the company of the men she most admired, the fellow-countrymen who *did* things, the men who were bold, resourceful, patriotic, and who discreetly controlled the destinies of other races with no vulgar thought of self.

This was the last, late flowering of the imperial ideal, into which Freya won her way. But she was late at the fair; the period in which to enjoy its prestige and facilities was already limited. Between 1933 and 1945 Freya made her considerable reputation as an expert on Arab affairs but, unlike Gertrude Bell, she knew when to cut her losses and get out. It is this willingness to let go, to change, to take another course, that makes her such an absorbing and fascinating study. In 1945 she was by no means finished; her twilight was still more than a quarter of a century away.

Once Freya had achieved the social recognition she craved, she adopted the views of the people with whom she now associated without question, content to be accepted into the intimacy of the ruling elite. What she liked was the insouciance of a privileged upbringing and the cheerful high spirits that went with it. Her patriotism was never in doubt, but the sincerity of her professions of friendship towards the Arabs was. 'We know Freya is paid to be nice to us,' remarked the Iraqi royal ladies, secluded in the Palace harems but sensitive to the nuances of personal relationships. George Antonius, the historian of the Arab awakening and a leading figure in pan-Arab nationalist circles, refused at the end to receive her; she was considered a lightweight, and insincere. Freya settled the score for this rebuff in the final volume of her biography with a belittling remark on his death.[9]

On signing off from the Brotherhood in 1943, Freya wrote to the incoming Minister of State:

When we have produced this band of friendly democrats we shall have fulfilled our wartime task. We shall have fashioned a powerful instrument which is not British and can therefore continue without offence under non-British governments. Its fundamental principle is that it is not based on bribery of any kind, but is intended to be beneficial and to obtain co-operation by persuading that it is so. This and the treatment of the idea of Democracy and Freedom as an essentially religious idea explain, I believe, its comparative success in a most difficult year.

Her little system of 'cells', she explained in the report sent by request to R. Casey, the new Minister of State, in April,[10] was based purely on democratic propaganda, with the minimum of British participation. Its aim was to introduce the concept of Westminster-style parliamentary democracy to the emergent educated classes. In Egypt there were less than half a dozen British in the whole show which now had over 20,000 members, and in Iraq it was the same, although there the numbers stood at less than 6000, half the number promised in 1941.

This is because the people we are angling for are the ones who have been or are or might at any moment become ardently nationalist, and the object is to combine their nationalist feelings with a pro-British bias . . . The object of this propaganda is rather a long-term one, devoted to a time when we may have to do without our Political officers etc, and almost certainly our armies, when even the British Institutes *may* sound too foreign in the eyes of Eastern governments, and when a nominally Iraqi, Egyptian, Persian organisation unobtrusively bound to us, may be our only means of influence among the population in general.

The differing interpretation of the Brotherhood's purpose advanced by Freya on different occasions is confusing. To her sponsors it was a machine of public opinion to be influenced by its operators from their position at the centre. To members of the Iraqi government she was insistent that the Brotherhood was *not* a political instrument, and as such barred under law, but a non-political cultural organisation whose object was to foster the democratic principle apart from all party politics, and therefore permissible to soldiers. It was the Iraqi government's refusal to countenance Brotherhood proselytising in its army, she told Cornwallis in May 1943,[11] that accounted for her failure to deliver the 10,000 members promised him in 1941. Now, on the verge of departure in 1943, she regretted any acquiescence in the Iraqi decree and urged Cornwallis to engineer some way around the impasse.

Freya apparently saw nothing incongruous in preaching freedom of choice as a religious necessity while advocating Machiavellian strategies to keep popular feelings docile and in control. She found it monstrous that her Brotherhood should be accorded the same status in Iraqi eyes as the defunct Nazi publicity organisation, now driven underground. It affronted her that Britain, the dominant power in the Middle East, of which the Brotherhood was covertly acknowledged to be an instrument, should acquiesce in its relegation by the Iraqis to the status of yet another foreign vehicle for political intrigue, and not intervene on her behalf. It was a personal affront which enabled her with good conscience to abandon 'her little Brethren' and, like the heroine of some picaresque romance, be off to fresh fields and pastures new, confident that other opportunities would open for her.[12]

SIXTEEN

WAR END AND MARRIAGE

In early 1943 the Nazi policy of gas-chamber extermination of the Jews was as yet not widely known. The Jewish issue then was still the 1939 British government White Paper on Palestine advocating the restriction of Jewish immigration under the Balfour plan to a population of 500,000, half that of the native Arab population. Further entry should then be halted to allow this influx to be digested, and only be reactivated with the acquiescence of the resident Arab majority.

Opinion in the American Jewish community was split between Zionists and moderates. The Zionist campaign for unfettered immigration to Palestine was concentrated on the discrediting and overthrow in American minds of the British White Paper, something not difficult in view of the almost total ignorance of the transatlantic public on Middle East affairs. The Zionists shrewdly calculated on arousing anti-colonial American opinion against the intransigence of the British attitude.

Freya's dispatch by the M of I to America was part of an attempt to mitigate the effects of this general ignorance, by sending lecturers – academics and other experts – across the Atlantic to tour America and put the British case. Britain's policy was presented by the Zionists as legalistic, pettifogging and essentially anti-Semitic, and showing evidence of hidden colonialist intentions, aimed at the nascent Arabian oil industry; this had been belatedly inaugurated by American money and know-how, in response to wartime needs to supply the US

Pacific fleet. The taking over of the subsidising of Ibn Saud as the guardian of the Holy Places of Islam from the hard-pressed British, and the exploitation of the oil resources of his kingdom was a diplomatic *coup* for the Americans which led to bitter jealousy in the oil community.

Freya's own view of how best to counteract this situation was through personal connections and private meetings with selected audiences, small influential gatherings where a personal impact could be achieved, rather than meetings open to the general public. This was always her way. She aimed to present the Arabs as *people*, and to implant the notion of a common humanity.

She stayed with Mrs Otto Kahn on arrival in New York and through her was introduced to wealthy cosmopolitan Jewish circles, politically moderate, hospitable and intelligent. These were the kind of people Freya liked, and got on with. The journalists who interviewed her, and the highly politicised, tough, vocal women's luncheon gatherings, at which she spoke, were a novel and not altogether agreeable experience. She found the American reporters' likening of herself to a fictional female sleuth or an *agent provocateur* laughable and droll, but she did not fail to pass it on to her friends. As with her jaunty hat-brims from under which peered out a shrewd bright eye, there was an innate *coquetterie* in her relation to truth that encouraged the notion that there was more to her than met the eye.

The Zionist lobby was a different matter. She reported to London that she was a particular target of its counter-propaganda, and that her public meetings were plagued by Zionists who followed her around the country and challenged her remarks. There was a combative element in her personality, she admitted, that sharpened her tongue in these polemics, but the persecuting rabbis were tenacious, and she could not shake them off.

In due course reports on her progress around America filtered back to parliamentary circles in England. Questions were asked in the House, and the innocence of Freya's mission was defended. *The Times* reported on 27 April 1944 that Mr

Geoffrey Mander asked the Minister of Information if he would state the purpose of the visit of Miss Stark to America; and for what period and at what expense this visit had been arranged by his department. Brendan Bracken, the Minister, replied that Miss Stark was a member of the Middle East staff of the Ministry of Information. She was granted leave of absence in order to visit America to deliver lectures at the invitation of the Oriental Institute of Chicago. Her salary and travelling expenses were being paid by the Ministry and because, since her arrival, she had been invited to speak by other public bodies, the date of her return was not yet decided.

Mr Mander then asked if the Rt Hon Gentleman could give an assurance that there was no foundation for the statement that Miss Stark had gone out to spread pro-Arab propaganda.

Mr Bracken replied that he would certainly give that assurance. Miss Stark was a distinguished scholar who had been followed through the United States by a number of persons anxious to traduce her, and 'I wish to put it on record that she has nothing to do with propaganda for the Arabs or anyone else.'

Mr Keeling, a Conservative MP, with whose wife Freya was friendly, and at whose London home she often stayed, here chimed in with 'Would not the Rt Hon Gentleman agree that she is one of the greatest authorities on the Middle East and is a most admirable person to represent British culture in America?'

On the next day, the twenty-eighth, Geoffrey Mander wrote to Sydney Cockerell, who had been to the House at Question Time to see him, to thank him for the copy of Freya's *Letters from Syria*, which Cockerell had left for him. 'I put the Question,' he added, 'because the Jews are very much worried about the sending by the Ministry of Information of Freya Stark to America. She talks very interestingly no doubt about Arabs, but apparently never mentions the Jewish National Home, or the fact that there are any Jews in Palestine.'

In the ripple of interest that followed the parliamentary exchange the *Evening News* gossip columnist reported on 26 April that friends of Miss Stark scoffed at the suggestion she had gone to America to do pro-Arab propaganda. Miss Stark, he was told, was by long odds the most distinguished authority now living on the problems of Arabia. Sir Ronald Storrs, associated with the raising of the Arab revolt in 1916 and subsequently Governor of Jerusalem and of Cyprus (where he had Government House burnt about his ears by indignant islanders), poohpoohed the suggestion that she was anything else. It was news to him. 'I have known Miss Stark for years and years and the idea that she is grinding axes for anybody seems to me not only baseless, but ridiculous.' Sir Sydney Cockerell was equally emphatic. Miss Stark, he said, 'knows the Arab world as very few people have ever known it. She speaks about it not as a propagandist, but as the leading authority on it.'

The reporter completed his piece – entitled 'A Woman who Knows' – by describing Freya as small, brown-haired, completely unpretentious, a gifted woman with a widespread reputation as a conversationalist. 'Her tongue is pungent and brilliant and all sorts of celebrities, including Lord Wavell and Lord Halifax, are numbered among her friends,' while, he added, her enterprise as an explorer had been recognised by the Royal Geographical Society with its greatest honour, the Founder's Gold Medal, awarded her in 1942.

Freya did not enjoy America very much and complained constantly in her letters of exhaustion, and the strain her programme imposed on her. She was sick of the Zionists, and shocked by the oil men, she told Elizabeth Monroe, and longing to be back in England. But the trip was not without its compensations and enabled her to complete some private business of her own.

She stayed for a week with her mother's old friend, Lucy Beach, in California to collect the bundles of her own letters to Flora and to go through her mother's papers and possessions, in the intervals of giving talks to friendly gatherings organised for her by Mrs Beach. Continuing north to Canada she spent a week at Creston, British Columbia, doing the same for her father's papers, untouched since his death in 1931, while inspecting her inheritance. Lucy Beach took her to the cemetery at La Crescenta where Flora is buried, where she ordered a gravestone for her mother, but at Creston she was saved a similar expense. Robert Stark's ashes on his instructions had been placed under a rocky outcrop of the hillside overlooking the Kootenay Lake and the mountains beyond, a last gesture of solidarity with Nature, and his own beliefs.

The idea of her 'childhood book', the autobiography for which Cockerell was badgering her, was not absent from her mind. The retrieval of her letters to Flora was an important element in this, and was followed up in Canada, while staying with the Governor-General, Malcolm MacDonald, the author of the White Paper on Palestine. There she looked up her hitherto unknown first cousin, Arthur Stark, a Federal Government telecommunications employee, the son of her father's brother and neighbour in Creston, Playters Stark. The sight of a Government House car with its chauffeur, waiting importantly in his suburban street, Art Stark later told me, caused quite a stir among his neighbours. The cousins took tea together, and talked over family history and their fathers' lives in Creston, but no mention of this episode is made in her published correspondence.

She spent two months in Washington at the end of her tour arranging contracts for a book suggested by Dr Brandt of the Oriental Institute in Chicago, the original hosts for her tour; it was published in New York as *The Arabian Isle* and in London by Murrays as *East is West* in 1945, and was intended to encourage a popular understanding of the Arab background to the Palestine question as a counter to Zionist propaganda in both countries.

Circulating on the Washington diplomatic cocktail round, Freya attracted the attention of the Pentagon Middle East experts, and was invited to talk to interested parties in the War Department. She was quizzed for over two hours by a group of some thirty people, drawn from all the Services, followed by a similar meeting with the Office of Strategic Studies (later the CIA).[1] The Americans, with their long-established and respected educational establishments in the Middle East, had good connections among their alumni. A pool of such young men was drawn on for the American equivalent body to the

British Middle East Office. Many of their uniformed experts were members of missionary families, born and brought up in the East and fluent in the local languages, while others were diplomats.

Freya assured London that she had been very careful and let nothing slip regarding the actual mechanics of the Brotherhood operation, in deference to Foreign Office sensitivity on the subject. The Americans' dominant preoccupation, she reported, was Communist intrigue in the Arab world by the Russian ally; she was asked again and again if they were active among the young people. Freya discounted this, but it was evident her hosts thought her optimistic. The idea of treating the menace 'in a homeopathic way', by introducing controlled doses of democratic idealism through the Brethren, was not received with any enthusiasm; at bottom there seemed a humiliating conviction that the British could not make themselves liked anywhere 'so that if anyone else comes along we are more or less done for; of course no-one said this, and in fact may not have consciously thought it, but the whole structure of their theories is built on this assumption . . .'[2]

With well-founded prescience, she warned against underestimating the influence of their educated Arab protégés on American government thinking: 'It means that their information is that of young men inclined to be antagonistic to the people in office and to spread the feeling, if we are not careful, that Britain is the bulwark of the old fogeys. If the USA ever came to look upon itself as the champion of the young progressive Arabs as against the reactionary governments supported by Britain, it would be largely through the agency of these effendis in office . . .'

Freya in America was running up against the same scepticism regarding her view of future Anglo-Arab relations as she had found so *wrong* in Iraq in the previous year. It made her angry and suspicious of others' motives but it did not shake her faith in the competence of herself or the people with whom she identified. The past for her was not a foreign country; the future was. She saw progress in terms of conciliations, modifications of existing programmes, but with the same guiding hands always on the tiller. It was as if her vision was contracting, she could not imagine any other outcome.

At a much deeper level was the threat to her own reputation. She was used now to the uncritical acceptance of her fitness to pass judgment on anything touching on Arab affairs. The Pentagon questions were on the same awkward lines as those of Adrian Bishop's young men in Baghdad, and evoked instinctive rejection. What she particularly disliked was any suggestion that she was over-optimistic; it undermined the whole edifice of her proclaimed belief in the perfectibility of human nature and its susceptibility to gentle persuasion in the right direction. The bland emollience of this message was what made her admirable and encouraging to some people, and maddening to others.

'*You* are a kind of arch-fiend of propaganda,' wrote Lionel Fielden, Director of Public Relations, Allied Control Commission in Italy in 1945, in response to a query from Freya as to whether *East is West*[3] gave too kind a picture of the British Raj. She was disconcerted and bruised by the dismissive attitude of the younger generation to the achievements of their seniors. He went on:

> You do (or appear to) really act on perfectly equal and equable terms with the desert and its people and if any Raj could be as amusing and intelligent and friendly as you – well, it should take charge of the world. But I kick violently when you say that Englishmen are 'loved' abroad, and I don't believe it . . . Take away from an Englishman his money and position and power and how many really 'adore'? . . . I am quite certain that all your books do good and I think you've done one of the finest bits of work of our generation [presumably the Brotherhood] – you make everyone, including yourself, lovable! It can't but do good. But I personally feel your spectacles are very rose.[4]

To dryer and more acerbic natures she could appear self-deluding. Any such suggestion was dangerous to her equilibrium. She had a need to trust and be trusted, anything else was upsetting, a disturbance at the deepest interior level.

If Freya's actions influenced the outcome of the war in the Middle East to the extent she came to believe (helping to save the Middle East for Democracy) they have been edited out of the official record, where little trace of her remains. She hoped her favourite godsons would take the torch from her and light the way into the future, but in the event it was the Americans who picked out the kernel of her message, and recognised the value of what they called a 'hearts and minds' programme as an alternative approach in the promotion of their own national interests.

The overrunning of the Nazi concentration camps by the advancing Allies in 1945, and the immensity of the Displaced Persons problem at war's end, put paid to all hopes of moderation on the part of the Zionists. Humanitarian feelings throughout the world were outraged at newsreel footage of British troops refusing landing rights to battered Jewish immigrant ships limping across the Mediterranean towards Haifa. Film of survivors of the concentration camps being landed under British naval escort in Cyprus and trucked away under guard to detention camps did nothing to enhance American sympathy for Britain's position on Palestine. In 1948 Britain abdicated its responsibility as Mandatory Power and the Arabs and Jews were left to fight it out for themselves.

The rundown and discrediting of British pretensions after the decision was taken to quit India in 1947 gathered momentum with astonishing speed once the process was set in motion, but in the spring of 1944 no-one envisaged such an outcome. Freya came back from America at the end of June; the invasion of Europe had begun. Her post-war persona was now established for the public record by the questions raised in the House of Commons and reported in Hansard and newspaper summaries of them. The endorsement of her qualifications as a scholar and Arabian expert by a coterie of elderly admirers faithfully fulfilled her own recipe for successful propaganda. 'It is my firm conviction, after nearly four years of propaganda, that the way to make people believe a thing is to make them say it themselves!' she had told Elizabeth Monroe on accepting the assignment to

America. 'If we get a selection of the right people saying what
we want them to say about the Arabs, to their own compatriots,
it will be less spectacular but far more effective than if we say
it ourselves.'[5]

In August, she went down to Devonshire, where she spent
some weeks with her girlhood friend, Dorothy Varwell, now
the widow of Sir Maurice Waller, HMG's Inspector of Prisons,
and Dorothy's sister at Thornworthy, outside Chagford. This
was the neighbouring property to Freya's father's house, Ford
Park, where he lived from 1902 until his departure to Canada
in 1911. Here, resigned from the M of I, and now a private
person, she completed *East is West*.

This return to Dartmoor and to scenes and people
remembered from summer visits to her father before 1912, in
the heightened tension of the landings in Europe, stimulated
Freya's associative powers and enabled her to join elements
from the Varwells' established country life to the more frag-
mented recollections of her parents' activities around Chagford
at the turn of the century. The idea of the 'childhood book' of
which she had written to her mother, though dormant, was not
extinct, and she utilised this lull in events to absorb atmosphere
and mood and to research the past. A sister of her mother,
Meta Stark, was living in Torquay at this period and was possibly co-opted to fill out what Freya had learned in Ottawa from
Arthur Stark, but these are conjectures.

Freya's ambition in 1944 was to get home to Asolo and
reclaim her property there, but Allied progress in Italy was
slow, the crossing of the Apennines held up. The D-day landings
and advance into France occupied everyone's attention that
summer, while V-bombs discouraged visits to London. Freya
was back in town, however, for the winter. She was rather in
the doldrums, her book finished, no job, everybody harassed
and preoccupied, and no opportunity appearing as yet of a return
to Italy. Lord Wavell, now Viceroy of India, was the means of
extricating her from this impasse. He was turning over an idea
for Lady Wavell,[6] he wrote, to enter into friendly relations with
the politicised Indian ladies through the philanthropic institutions
supported by local Indian initiatives. Would Freya undertake

the planning of this friendly approach, which should be informal
and unassertive and directed at opening channels of communication rather than imposing authority? If so, a *lakh* of rupees
would be allotted to the project, Freya would be fed, housed
and transported at government expense for six months; she
would have a free hand and her salary would be commensurate
with what she earned in the Ministry of Information.

One of Freya's assets was the ability to accept temporary
dislocation of plans. This quality of *elasticity* was something she
had decided to adopt as early as 1929.[7] India was not Italy, but
the longest way round is sometimes the shortest way home.
Freya accepted Wavell's offer but with one stipulation, that he
would ensure her return to Asolo once Venice was liberated.

Freya landed at Karachi in February 1945 after the usual
slow and uncomfortable wartime journey, and arrived in New
Delhi to find the Wavells away on a flying visit to London.
She was allotted a suite in the vast pile of Lutyens' viceregal
residence, with a tall 'House' bearer, the scarlet viceregal
emblem blazoned on his spotless white dress, to be her personal
attendant. Cars, drivers, a small aeroplane with its pilot, were
placed at her disposal. She was to contact his Military Secretary, Wavell wrote, or his aides, when in need of anything.

Lady Wavell, stopping over in Cairo on her way back to Delhi
and happy to be again in the livelier Egyptian scene, wrote
perfunctory apologies for her absence on Freya's arrival, while
sending her the list of contacts and introductions in the Princely
States which Freya had requested. It was an open sesame
to the wonders of India. Freya flew around Rajputana in her
aeroplane, and to Mysore and Hyderabad, and south to Travan-
core. Lady Wavell's introductions ensured she saw India in
style, the only bore was the work. Freya's business was to
visit the institutions which Indians were running for themselves
– the welfare and charitable work common to all religions – and
to express Lady Wavell's sympathetic interest in their doings.
This was something of a novelty in Anglo-Indian society, and
the Edwardian District Visitor aspect of the approach perhaps
went unperceived. Among the younger Indian women Freya
found it hard to adjust to the atmosphere of co-operative effort

and team spirit required by the project; she preferred the
elegant upper-class women she met in the Princely States, and
did not care for organised committee women. She was thrown
into the arms of philanthropy, she wrote, 'for which I have a
natural repugnance unless its stern features relax into some
sort of human face.'[8] What she really enjoyed was the wonder
of India itself, the colour, the pageantry, the palaces, fortresses,
ruins of martial confederacies and dismantled empires, and the
prestige of being part of the viceregal 'House'.

After two months she came up with a plan for a group of four
women – two Indian, two Britons – to tour the country on a
regular basis on behalf of the Vicereine. 'I feel sure that if you
can keep half a dozen of the right sort in touch with all these
young and emotional people you will see quite a strong and
friendly feeling in two or three years' time,' was her recommendation. Lady Wavell had a disconcerting way of closing her eyes
and dropping off into a light slumber whenever Freya sought
to engage her attention in the project; she was very content to
let someone else arrange it all. It was Wavell who had pushed
the idea, possibly inspired by Freya's Brotherhood, but it was
already too late.

Freya wrote to her friend Moore Crosthwaite at the Foreign
Office on 20 May:

> My work here will be handed over on 15th June. I call it very
> clever to persuade any Government to find a *Lakh* of rupees,
> and the only reward I ask is to be deposited on the Lido
> aerodrome (Venice) in a month's time.[9]

On the same day she wrote to another friend:

> Soon I hope with a clear conscience to sit in Asolo and forget
> politics, and write a book of philosophy, quite small and easy
> and intended for all the world. I shall call it the art of getting
> old, and it is the art I mean to cultivate.

Wavell found time to visit her bedside to chat with her while
she was laid up with a foot injury; this delayed her departure

and enabled her to witness and photograph the Simla conference with the Indian leaders. Faithful to his undertaking, Wavell had written personally to Field-Marshal Alexander in Italy to facilitate Freya's return to Asolo, and a telegram was duly received from Allied Headquarters 'ordering' Freya to report to Venice. On 12 July she started her journey home. Northern Italy was under Allied Military Government, with separate Occupation Zones. Venezia and Treviso came under the British. Freya flew from Karachi to Cairo as the solitary passenger on a Sunderland flying-boat, spent a few days there seeing friends, then flew by night to Rome, arriving on 20 July where she spent a week. Her presence was viewed with mixed feelings by the Allied Military Government of Occupied Territories (AMGOT) authorities. She had jumped the gun, arriving as she did under military auspices; no civilians, no foreign residents would be granted permission to return to Italy until months had elapsed and some sort of order was restored in the chaos following the German surrender on 2 May.

There were no trains, the only transport was that of the occupying forces. She got a lift to Treviso, and next day hitched a ride on an army lorry to Asolo, to find the Villa Freia shabby but intact, and her mother's maid Emma answering the door bell in a white apron, with Caroly, her mother's secretary, behind her.[10] It was very nearly six years since she had left the house in October 1939 on her journey to the war.

From India Freya had lobbied friends in the Foreign Office as hard as she could, seeking any PR job which would justify her return to Asolo. She still hoped to be employed permanently by the Foreign Office. She wrote from New Delhi on 28 March 1945 to Victor Cunard, a pre-war neighbour in Asolo and now in the Foreign Office's Political Intelligence Department.

He [Wavell] has promised to send me when Liberation comes [to Italy]. I shall be glad to put my hand to anything you want after giving a week or two to my own surviving affairs. Does this suit you? If so . . . let me know whom to get in touch with out there and to expect my arrival otherwise there might be difficulties. Will be glad to do anything you and Major Rayner want – preferably in the north where I feel I can be more useful. I might easily be there before summer ends . . .

In May 1943 she had confided to Cockerell that she would think of it with great interest if she were 'asked to go on in diplomatic'[11] for she appreciated the advantages of a regular salary. But now she drew a skein of wool over such practicality and wrote to the Wavell household in India bemoaning the new burdens laid on her. Reinstalled in the Villa Freia, she now received a temporary six-month assignment – later extended to a year – visiting and reporting on the provincial reading centres being opened under Foreign Office auspices in the British Zone to provide newspapers and periodicals to the news-hungry Italians. There was considerable anxiety in London lest a Communist victory in the impending free elections, the first since the Fascists assumed power in the 1920s, should push Italy into the Russian sphere of influence. Freya was recruited to tour the Zone and, under guise of monitoring the reading centres, to use her familiar blend of persuasion and uplift to spread the message of Democracy and the individual's right of choice. This gave her access to an official car, petrol and rations in the difficult first year of peace, and a sterling allowance of £100 per month plus £200 p.a. for entertainment allowance, very useful in the devalued state of the Italian currency and with the black market the accepted way of life for the private person.

But it was not permanent. She had hopes of the British Council, but that too failed, though she got some lecturing jobs from them. The appointment of Reginald Davies, her old M of I superior in Cairo, as Finance Officer to the Council in 1943, later advanced to Assistant Director-General with responsibility for the financial restructuring of the Council in 1947, perhaps did not help. It was not until early in September 1947 that she received final notice of the termination of her contract from the Foreign Office, and was forced to accept that no continuation of a career as a government servant was available to her. 'Too old' was the unofficial explanation, but Sir Reader Bullard's comments on the incident of the car in Teheran may have influenced the decision.

It came at an awkward moment, for under the War Reparations scheme she had embarked on repairs and expensive improvements to the Villa Freia and had allocated £250 to her Italian niece Cici, her sister's daughter – now her sole-surviving close relative – for the repair of her other property at La Mortola. Money was flowing away. Her literary career had not as yet regained momentum. Her mother's *An Italian Diary* had been pushed through by Cockerell with a foreword by Freya, but she had delayed commencing the autobiography which Cockerell and Jock Murray were urging her to undertake. In spite of their advice she wrote instead what she described as 'a clear and simple exposition of her Everywoman philosophy, an easy picture of the values she believed in . . . vague and mystical and not agnostic at all'. This was *Perseus in the Wind*, begun at Asolo in March 1947, and published as a small book of essays in November 1948. It was dedicated to two of her godsons, and dealt with such topics as Service, Happiness, Education, Beauty, Death, Memory, Love, Sorrow, Courage and Old Age. It was immediately popular, reprinting in six months, her most successful book. It appealed to troubled people facing up to the bleak post-war world bereft of the comforting assumptions of their own upbringing. 'Here was someone who had *standards,*' they felt and this was helpful, a reassurance that all that had been familiar was not lost.

Freya was sensitive about 'her little Benjamin', as she described the book, but as was her habit, distributed it freely among her friends. Murrays may well have been uneasy about the venture; a tendency to uplift was an ominous indication of a change in their author's style.

Stewart Perowne had remained in Baghdad when the war ended but she had kept in contact and he spent three weeks in Asolo in June 1946 en route to leave in England. His appointment as Oriental Counsellor at the Embassy came to an end in 1947, and at Freya's warm invitation he again passed through Asolo in May. His dedication in Baghdad to stage-managing the young Iraqi King's public appearances on the lines of the British royal family's had produced a second-hand landau from Buckingham Palace and new uniforms designed by himself for the mounted royal bodyguard in the carriage processions instituted for formal occasions. This musical comedy effect, so different from traditional Arab procedures, elicited the designation 'Perownia' from a passing American journalist, while the flamboyance of his written reports, replete with every kind of historical reference and analogy, were to amaze researchers and scholars when the PRO archive was opened thirty-five years later. His influence on Freya's political thinking at this period should not be underestimated.

Now, Freya wrote, he was in very good form, and full of Baghdad gossip but, like everyone else, unsettled and uneasy about his own future with a Labour government in power in London, and the cutting back on imperial commitments commenced. Freya, hanging on herself for news of her own, was warmly sympathetic. She wrote in July, asking for his news:

It is so disheartening to work for HMG. One would think there would be a real welcome for you after all your years of successful work. I am sure they want you, very soon, and then will be all smiles and favours, but meanwhile it gives a chill to the spirit and takes all the *joie de vivre* out of one's work . . .[12]

There was a horrid basis of envy, she feared, for the feeling of pinpricking insecurity they were both experiencing. She could acknowledge this in relation to him, but pride would ensure that whatever anxieties she might experience on her own account she would keep to herself. It was as if she suspected that payment was being exacted for the triumphs of the past when, riding high, she could afford to deride and evade the petty restrictions of bureaucracy. Now it looked as if those chickens were coming home to roost.

In September, in rapid succession, came the news of her rejection by the Foreign Office, Perowne's telegraphed news of appointment to the West Indies and a proposal of marriage, and her acceptance of it. They were married privately on 7 October 1947 at St Margaret's, Westminster. She was fifty-four, he was forty-six. The whole decision had been made and implemented in a month.

Freya's impetuous acceptance of Stewart Perowne's proposal dumbfounded her closest associates. In 1947 people's sexual proclivities were still part of their private lives and were not talked about openly in general society. Certainly no-one among Freya's friends seemed able to warn her of the pitfalls of marriage to a homosexual. There was a bland, stonewalling obtuseness about her response to such attempts that baffled and astonished those who made them, and it was this, as much as the marriage itself, that fed the gossip and surmise that surrounded the event.

Her appearance of starry-eyed delight convinced others, as well as apparently herself, that here was a fairy-tale ending to a long romance. Some concluded that her inability to understand what they hinted was a quaint kind of innocence, an aspect of her personality that contributed to its uniqueness. Others interpreted her decision as a belated determination to experience sexual life. This was a view that reduced to locker-room crudity a complex and protracted process whereby fear of loneliness, aversion to literary drudgery, and affronted ambition were fused into a solution which was demonstrably helpful to both parties.

For a man ambitious to rise in the restructured Foreign and Colonial Service, a wife was now a necessity; any hint of deviant inclinations was suspect as opening the way to blackmail and scandal. For Freya, not only did it ease the smart of rejection by the Foreign Office, but it had the gratification of producing a rabbit out of a hat, and showing her detractors that she could do without their favours.

Freya had rather grown accustomed to the well-oiled functioning of grand official life and perhaps missed the flurry of ADCs and people to do things for you that it provided. Marriage to Perowne was a means of reactivating her influence in those circles through a husband whose butterfly brilliance impressed her and in whose future career she believed. Whatever doubts both parties experienced were put aside, though each confided in private to mutual friends feelings of anxiety as to whether the other was *really* quite good enough for them.[13] Freya never doubted that strings could be pulled to effect their return to the Mediterranean from the Caribbean, and in this she was right. Perowne was posted to Cyrenaica as an Adviser in early 1950, and she accompanied him. To the superficial observer it would appear that the marriage was producing the very benefits – a comfortable home at Asolo and distinguished literary connections matched with the importance of a senior official position and the pensionable salary that went with it – that suited them both, and that by pooling their resources they were reasserting the glamour of their own past.

The inside story was different. The news of the intended marriage was received with incredulity by their friends, and ribald laughter among the couple's Iraqi associates. 'Does he have to marry her?' roared the Regent's uncle as he leant out of the London Embassy's window to verify the extraordinary news with a passing acquaintance. Even the Regent's bodyguard, accompanying their master to London, was in on the joke.[14] A host of suggestions, many scandalous and farfetched, enlivened the gossip which surrounded the event.

Freya's triumphant entry in 1947 into the dignity of the married state was more an assertion of status than the recognition of a soul-mate. The marriage was a calculated risk, the flurry of sexual titillation that accompanied the event a red herring. If the marriage was a success, her influence would be maintained through Perowne; if it failed, he could be discarded. Five years, Freya told me, was what she privately allotted to the experiment and if it was not working by then it would be better to cut their losses.

Some native element of caution in her own assessment of the marriage may have coloured this view. The Caribbean was not the Mediterranean and Freya did not find the local British business community to her liking. She found them dull and unrewarding. She was only interested in Society – and English Society at that – with a capital S; this was already turning the

islands into a winter playground, and its members were the
only people she considered worth knowing.

She wrote to Gerald de Gaury on 19 March 1949 from
Barbados:

> We are here in grandeur in Government House . . . [where]
> one avoids solitude without obtaining company . . . though I
> creep away to Ronnie and Marietta Tree and the nice simple
> life of the rich whenever I can. It is *absolute* agony to me to
> hear God Save the King being struck up when entering a
> concert room, etc. *Much* prefer a dust storm on the Tigris
> . . . *Please* don't repeat all this – Stewart of course loves it
> and is full of brilliance and benevolence and depressingly as
> if intended to be a colonial governor . . .

She followed this up on 8 April with, 'Stewart is governing
his island *pro tem* and it means a fearful lot of general amiability.'
She was self-conscious about her appearance and disliked being
snap-shot by the local press as she planted trees and handed
out trophies.

> I *like* people, but I like them much better when I can look
> on in obscurity and not be looked at myself. I always thought
> this a normal reaction but here is Molly Huggins from Jamaica
> staying with us, lecturing, visiting, baby welfare, rallying girl
> guides, calling everyone darling, smiling beautifully and com-
> pletely at home in the limelight. How enviable! Yet I still
> think the world is nicer when looked at than looking.

The Barbados sugar planters and businessmen showed little
awareness of her distinction, literary or political, while her
public role as the wife of the Deputy Governor failed to gratify
her. While Perowne enjoyed the pomp of provincial eminence,
and entered into the protocol with zest, Freya resented her
secondary duties as his wife. Their competing egos clashed in
their public life. Freya complained that Perowne sulked if she
enlivened the conversation at her end of the dinner table, and
was cold and snubbing to her, both in public and in private.

For his part, Perowne was 'officially embarrassed' at Freya's insistence on departing from traditional attitudes to the native Barbadian population, by attending their chapels and attempting to repeat her Brotherhood successes. Within six months Freya was letting her old friends know that all was not well in her marriage.

Lack of marital tenderness on Perowne's part, and his treatment of her as nothing other than a subordinate partner in a marriage of convenience, was later advanced by Freya to explain her decision to terminate the relationship.[15] The emotional pain of rejection was cited, though some felt an element of indignation at being, as it were, short-changed sexually was paramount. Whether recollection of a previous event, thirty-six years ago, when her engagement was abruptly terminated by her Italian fiancé, contributed to the upswelling of distress she exhibited to intimate old friends on making her decision is anyone's guess. Freya's emotionalism is well documented. Her ability to believe what she wanted to believe, in defiance of reasoned argument or explanation, was known to her close associates. Once aroused, and her emotional charge deflected into it, it is possible that recollection of past injuries made rational discussion or objective counselling impossible; this polarised opinion among the couple's associates as to the rights and wrongs of their brief marriage and gave rise to more gossip.

What none of their circle, including Freya, anticipated, was that Perowne's career as a colonial official should be prematurely terminated in 1951. His post as Adviser in Cyrenaica was eliminated when the former Italian colonies in North Africa were amalgamated to form present-day Libya, and the rundown of the Colonial Service got under way; at the age of fifty he accepted, without demur, redundancy with three months' paid leave and a pension.

From Freya's viewpoint his usefulness as a husband now ceased, and little further attempt was made to resuscitate an already failing union. She had no intention of supporting his lifestyle by her literary labours. In the spring of 1952 it was ended by a mutually agreed divorce. But this was long after

Freya had become thoroughly disillusioned both with official life and her husband.

'I don't want ever any more to do Public Things. I want to make a Good End,' she wrote to Nigel Clive from Paris on 18 December 1951.

In 1972 Freya was made a Dame of the British Empire. This disposed of a troublesome problem of nomenclature, following her short-lived marriage. From now on there was no need to define marital status when she reverted to her maiden name. As Dame Freya Stark she could dispose of the stigma of spinsterhood and celibacy and appear before the world independent of any other prop to her self-esteem. That the sexual experience implied by her married state was important to her is underlined by her choice of the style *Mrs* Freya Stark when the marriage broke up. It was as if the status of married woman was something she had long craved, and was reluctant to forgo, while the husband was relinquished with cool determination and without any great fuss.

PART SIX

DISINTERRING THE PAST
1893–1927

SEVENTEEN

GODPARENTS AND A COUSIN

Once Freya's early journeys, her recognition by the geographical societies, her first literary successes, her wartime activities, were understood, I was still left with an unexplained hinterland of over thirty years – and these included her adolescence and girlhood – with which to get to grips. The linking of the personal motive, embedded in family relationships, to the evolution of the famous figure in Asolo presented baffling complexities. The apparent absence of documentation for her early life[1] – her collected *Letters* begin when she is already in her twenties – and the dearth of surviving witnesses made it difficult to get beyond Freya's own presentation of herself. Nobody seemed to know anything concrete about her antecedents, other than what she had indicated in *Traveller's Prelude*.

In an attempt to break through the veil of unknowing in which I seemed to be enmeshed, and to form some understanding of the past through the places in which the Starks had lived, I toured about Italy – La Mortola, Dronero, Bellosguardo, Asolo. My own experience of provincial life in the Trentino before the war helped me here. Later I went down to Devon to visit Torquay and Exeter and drove to Chagford to find Ford Park, the house her father completed in 1902 on the outskirts of the little town. This plays an important part in Freya's story of her youth. She told me it was her real home.

It is an awkward, irregular building, a roomy family house well sited just below the lip of Dartmoor, with no immediately apparent means of entry. The long drive zigzags up from a steep, empty country lane through ragged plantings of pines. The first sight of the building is dominated by the huge, oversize window of the sculptor's studio Robert Stark built for himself, facing the carriage drive, with a bargeboarded smaller aperture above for his wife's work-room. The actual entry to the house is an inconspicuous door set in the wall of an adjacent yard.

The property now belongs to the Duchy of Cornwall, and is leased to tenants. It has the reputation locally of being haunted, the occupant told me. Some children were playing about the verandahs and mossy stone steps when I called. It could have been Simla: a rusticated woodwork verandah, overhanging balconies, uneven levels, rhododendrons and pines. The windows are small and deep, set back between slabs of granite; other irregular granite shafts support the balcony across the front of the house. Creepers climb and cluster about the wooden balustrades. The house is pushed back on its site against the hillside, with shrubby growth crowding on to the small stable yard and outhouses at the back. There are three large rooms, the drawing-room with its gleaming parquet floor, an adjacent dining-room, opening off through an arch, and the nursery above the drawing-room where Freya and her sister slept. The rest, with the exception of the big studio room and a large kitchen, are poky and utilitarian. There is a lot of varnished deal wainscotting. It is a house in the Arts and Crafts idiom, so nothing is set square; fireplaces occupy angles, doors and windows appear in unexpected places.

It is not a house, it seems, that keeps its tenants long. It could be lonely and in winter perhaps forbidding in its silence and isolation, shut off from its view by the tall growth of pines planted in lines across the hillside. Seen on a pleasant summer's day the neglected garden, its small pond and stream the focal point of a sunken grassy dell, had a sunny Edwardian stillness but was essentially dull. It is the standard period 'gentleman's hobby' planted up with specimen shrubs and trees.

Italy was also a little deflating. I reached Dronero on a cold late autumn day with a flurry of snow across the rich brown farmland of the Piedmontese plain. I was seeking the formative background of Freya's adolescence and early maturity, from 1903 until 1920, when she and her mother Flora moved down to the Riviera coast at La Mortola.

The shoaly reaches of a green, snow-fed river separate the little town, speckled black and grey on its steep hillside, from the flat plain. A narrow street twists up past dark, arcaded shops and tall, shabby shuttered houses, and a big gaunt, yellow brick church on the edge of the bluff overlooks the wide river and its battlemented stone bridge. A wreath, and an inscription on its wall, commemorate the execution of two partisans.

It is a small place; everyone must have known everyone else's business, I felt. There was an atmosphere of stagnation and dourness. What a distance Freya had travelled from this unpromising beginning! What a death in life it could have been for her mother, accustomed to the gregariousness of cosmopolitan studio life and sociable by nature!

Freya's sister Vera was married to Mario di Roascio in Dronero's church in the spring of 1913. She was just eighteen. Prior to the ceremony she was received into the Roman Catholic faith. Her husband's family were of sufficient importance in their locality for the service to be conducted by the Bishop of Salerno, a kinsman. Robert Stark came over from Canada to attend the ceremony. In Vera's engagement photograph she looks smiling and confident.

She died in 1926 at the age of thirty-one, and lies in the Dronero cemetery in the di Roascio family vault under an overpowering funerary monument. A grieving lifesize figure is flung against a rocky boulder, into whose surface are inserted in brass the names and dates of the occupants and their wives. Among the Italian alliances the name *Stark* strikes an incongruous note.

Her eldest son was lost at Stalingrad, as one of the Italian brigade sent by Mussolini to fight on Germany's eastern front and marched into captivity as a Russian prisoner of war. Despite efforts on Freya's part, he was never traced. The road to the cemetery bears the name of her youngest son, killed in a partisan skirmish with the Germans in 1945. At the junction of the main road with that to the cemetery some workmen were moving about in the empty shell of a modern factory building erected on the river bank. It was the only sign of an industrial activity in the town; Flora Stark's and her son-in-law Mario di Roascio's legacy to his surviving child, Freya's niece, Costanza Boido (known as Cici), and, according to Freya, bankrupted by her ex-husband's bad management, was now passing into new ownership.

Back on the coast and wandering in the emptiness of the Hanbury Gardens at La Mortola, I got another insight into Freya's life in the 1920s and of the gradations of English society on the Riviera. Freya wrote so idyllically of the beauty of the then undeveloped coastline and the charm of her little property and the life lived there, that my actual sight of the place was a disappointment. It is an ugly white structure with no view, bang alongside the railway line, patched together piecemeal, and unexpectedly large.

L'Arma, as the property is called, is a narrow two-and-a-half-acre strip of land at the foot of the La Mortola promontory on the Italian side of the frontier with France. This was bought in the 1860s by the Hanburys, a wealthy English manufacturing family who formed the huge and splendid garden that bears their name; the sloping hillside descends to its rocky headland in terraces stocked with plants and trees collected by a seafaring relative. Freya's tiny smallholding, then the lowest level of an already existing flower farm, nestles up close under the lee of the Hanburys' hillside and is separated from a small pebble beach recessed between rocky outcrops by the main railway line from France. Trains erupt from the tunnel under the Hanbury Gardens and thunder past the back door of the house in an awe-inspiring rattle and vibration of sound.

Nowadays the olive trees she planted to screen the mouth of the railway tunnel from view are grown huge and ancient, their limbs straddled arthritically, like Rackham illustrations. The house faces inland to the rocky mountain crests dominating the coastal road; the tall stilts of the overpass from Ventimiglia to France cut across the foreground view, so the property is now sandwiched between two sources of sound, the railway line and the motorway. By a particular irony the eventually hated name of di Roascio is on the notice-board that indicates the turn-off from the main road, for Freya transferred the property to her niece, Cici, after the war, while reserving continued access to it for herself. It is now administered as part of the di Roascio family estate.

Freya, in her autobiography, records the long-running feud the Starks conducted over a right of way across the tip of the headland, and of difficulties about access for bathing off her grand neighbour's rocks; gestures of self-assertion on the part of new arrivals not on the calling list of the established Hanburys, whose sixty years of benefactions to the local community in the shape of schools, drinking-fountains and employment were exercised with magnanimous Victorian philanthropy. What a small, angry spot of resentment must have festered in that ungainly building beside the railway line, that Freya should feel impelled thirty years later to plant her derogatory little dart.

The old cemetery at Menton gave me another feel of that vanished life. The doves were settling for the night among the pines and cypresses that ring the terraces crowded with memorials to dead Russians, English, French, Germans, Swedes and Americans, who ended their days here after quiet invalidish decline. Looking out from the topmost terrace in the fading glimmer of twilight to the illuminated town below, the promenade a glittering line on the distant seafront, I was astonished to come across a sort of outsize Gothic hutch in some stone composite material, prominently sited.

It was the family vault of the di Bottini de Ste Agnes family of Dronero, who figure prominently in Freya's account of her growing up in Piedmont in the period of World War I. There they all were, Gabriel, Achille, Clothilde, the old parents, the wife, the grandparents, on to all of whose lives the Starks had impinged momentarily some seventy years ago. As in life, the family hung together even in death, unlike the ephemeral Starks, scattered about the globe.

It seemed in some sense a message. I received a hint, an indication of something lacking in Freya's history. There was an element of contrivance, of a knocking together of things to make an impression. The simplicity was not real, it was all effect. I began to understand W. P. Ker's dry remarks in his letters to Olivia Horner on the increasing elaboration of L'Arma's interior arrangements. But it still did not help me to any proper insight into Freya's antecedents or how she arrived at her fame.

I was rescued from my condition of despondency by a third piece of luck, just as Francis Edmunds had illuminated the 1920s and Wilfrid Blunt's offer of Cockerell's box of 'Starkiana' had come to my aid for the 1930s. I read Hilary Spurling's biography of the novelist Ivy Compton-Burnett,[2] as a matter of general interest, and found it explored comprehensively Ivy's relationship with the once well-known expert on seventeenth- and eighteenth-century English furniture, Margaret Jourdain, a formidable arbiter of decorative taste in the 1920s and 1930s and Ivy's companion and friend from 1919 to Margaret's death early in 1951.

This triggered something in my mind. Margaret's 'dry, biting sparkle of wit' is briefly referred to in a footnote to Freya's account of her own chrysalid period, before she struggled free in the late 1920s from the carapace of lethargy and semi-invalidism that encased her, and spread her wings for flight. In Freya's autobiography nothing more is said about Margaret, while her *Letters*, published in the 1970s, do little other than record their first meeting in 1916 and her own dislike of Ivy. I wrote to Hilary Spurling, who generously replied that her researches into Ivy's life included Freya among the several younger women who, with Ivy, came under Margaret's influence during World War I and its aftermath. She gave me dates extracted from Margaret's diary of stays of seven to ten days' duration at the couple's Kensington flat in the period when Freya was preparing her first venture to the East in 1927, and on her return from subsequent adventures; Margaret and Ivy also visited her in the 1920s at L'Arma. It indicated a greater intimacy than Freya had cared to admit.

Freya first came to Margaret Jourdain's notice in 1916 when, broken and humiliated by the collapse of her Italian engagement, the girl was sent to the protective care of her mother's old friend, Viva Jeyes, in London and Miss Jourdain was summoned by Viva to help get her on her feet again. She was well known in her circle as more of a goad than a comforter to those in distress. Her forceful nature brooked no repining or sinking under misfortune and she exerted herself to find solutions for the sufferers, aiding them to use their talents, however hopeless their situation might seem.

As much as Professor Ker, so often celebrated in Freya's written and spoken reminiscences, Margaret Jourdain influenced Freya's literary development, showing her the practicalities of journalism and encouraging her somewhat indecisive movements towards independence. In these circumstances it seemed rather ungenerous of Freya to disclaim any such influence, and to be unhelpful to Ivy's biographer. This reluctance to acknowledge debts of gratitude to influences on her career was not confined to Margaret Jourdain. It was rather the same with Cockerell's biographer, Wilfrid Blunt, when he too approached Freya regarding his subject. Freya was not to be drawn, and did not welcome his approach. 'Rather a tiresome woman,' was his comment. Again, her ardent friendship with Venetia Buddicom, begun on the Riviera in the early 1920s, which for thirteen years was so important to Freya, is written off in two paragraphs in her autobiography *The Coast of Incense*.

If Ivy's characters speak, as it has been suggested, in Margaret's tones, Freya's own laconic utterances, her Freya-isms, derive from the same source. She borrowed quite a lot from Margaret, but did not acknowledge it; Ivy's greater capacity, while it might echo the tone, made out of her own observation and understanding something original and all her own.

It was perhaps this greater capacity that kept Freya from taking Margaret over in her autobiography, as she did W. P. Ker. Ivy's personality, so quietly and implacably applied, was difficult to challenge, a more refined egotism than Freya's own. One could admire, but must not touch, on pain of Ivy creating a diversion of an irritating but unassailable kind, guaranteed to cramp any intruder's style.

It was not so with Ker. No proprietary jealousy was evinced

by his family, with whom Freya remained on good terms after his death, and who were practically helpful to her. In later life, when Freya was famous, she resurrected the memory of W. P. Ker, claiming him as a godfather. Like her father, he was incorporated into her legend. She liked to dwell on his tender sensibility, particular to herself. As time went on, this was expanded into a mysterious empathy only denied its natural conclusions by the difference in their ages – he was fifty-three and she eighteen when their real friendship began in 1911 – and by his sudden death in 1923. Ker's connection with Freya and her mother spanned only the last twelve years of his life. It is after the fiasco of her broken engagement in 1916 that his general interest in her deepened into greater intimacy. He was on excellent terms with Flora Stark, whom he admired and with whom he corresponded. He was practical in his concern for Freya's well-being after such a shock and he provided a steady, unsentimental support in getting her back on her feet.

Despite his formidable scholarly reputation, Ker was a man of no intellectual pretensions. 'Which of us,' he asked, 'alone in a waiting room with a copy of Shelley's verse and the latest *Strand* magazine would not pick up the *Strand* first?' The hothouse atmosphere of the aesthetic movement and its mannered and contrived literary style, in which Margaret Jourdain's literary career had commenced, was alien to him. His preference was for the well-told tale of adventure, full of human incident. Scenery alone could not make up for want of life in a story, he said; only plot and characterisation supplied that. Here he instinctively put his finger on what was to prove Freya's weakness as a writer: the stretching of her material to substitute philosophising and fine writing for genuine experience.

It was when looking into his papers, and reading his obituaries, that I realised that however important W. P. Ker might have been to Freya, she was only one aspect of his life, one element in his meticulous arrangements of his duties and time. His private letters are largely to do with train travel and mountaineering expeditions; he hated anything to do with 'personal talk'. Freya's letters to him may not have been kept.[3] It was as if by conscientiously filling up his days with service towards others he might truly be part of that Real World after which he hankered, and so keep at bay the disquieting thoughts and intimations of futility that troubled so many of his contemporaries at the turn of the century.

Ker practised *hilaritas* as a duty of his pedagogic profession, and had no time at all for *tristitia*, which he regarded as spineless and self-indulgent. Looking at the fierce, bitten-back line of his mouth, and the hard, piercing stare of his photograph, I wondered at what cost this solution had been reached. He was a more robust personality than Freya suggests, much given to declaiming Miltonic verse in a strong Scottish accent amid the fume and smoke of late-night gatherings of university debating societies. This led his colleague A. E. Housman to note: '. . . for malt does more than Milton can/To satisfy God's ways to man'. It was felt, Ifor Evans later told me, among those who had known Ker, that the loss of his influence on Freya at so early a stage of her literary career was unfortunate. He might have kept her closer to the matter in hand and checked the tendency to inflate, rather than examine, received ideas. There was nothing mystical about Ker. His leaning was towards the concrete, and he hated anything that was 'up in the air'. His true contribution towards her formation was his scholarly insistence on thoroughness of preparation, for despite his fastidious antiquarian affectations and prejudices, the Real World was, in his words, hard to beat. This preference for actuality informed all his communications to his students. 'The prime object of the imagination is not to invent, but to discover, not to soar away but to penetrate, not to discredit ordinary perceptions but to deepen them . . .'

John Buchan's novel *Huntingtower*, which tells the adventures of the Gorbals Diehards, is dedicated to W. P. Ker. Dickson McCunn, the middle-aged Glasgow provision merchant and unworldly innocent, whose capacity to recognise Romance in the most unlikely circumstances triggers the plot, is believed to be modelled on him. Consulted by Buchan on the feasibility of Hannay's traverses of mountainous Skye in *Mr Standfast*, Ker's austerely deflating response, 'Ye travel unco' free in the Coolins', ensured that Buchan in the next adventure stuck to the topography of Carrick and Galloway, familiar from his own tramping holidays as a university student.

From the start of their acquaintance Freya envied Ker's godchildren; she was jealous of their particular status and longed to be one of that elite. The element of wishful thinking in the relationship surfaced early; Ker became her 'honorary' godfather. In later years, when he was long dead, and only recalled by the 'April children' and a few old students, he became her 'godfather', *tout court*, so that the mantle of his distinction was wrapped protectively around Freya's association with love of mountains, and mountain climbing, though Ker himself was a mountain traveller rather than a mountaineer. However, once started, in middle age he undertook programmes that would have taxed a much younger man. He did not approve of such feats for women, and did not encourage them. Freya's only two big climbs were made after his death, in 1923 and 1924.[4]

As a climber Ker was dedicated to the austere spirit of the Alpine Club, and other than particular colleagues and godchildren, his preferred companions were the professional guides, for whom he had an exaggerated respect and admiration. Freya records his refusal to shake hands with one whom he deemed to have failed to live up to the high standard of responsibility expected of this elite. He learned their personal histories, and delighted to feel himself accepted into their professional intimacy. That his heart should fail from one minute to another at the start of a climb, and that he should be buried at Macugnaga in the Italian Alps, in a small cemetery where families of guides are his companions, was felt by all who knew him to be the Perfect End.

The desirable perfection of this end was one recognised by Freya too, as anyone who encountered her in Nepal in the early 1980s would know. Then the recollection of W. P. Ker was uppermost in her mind, and she spoke repeatedly about him, on camera and off. Her 'godfather', his opinions and example, were a running accompaniment to her experiences, often repeated.

It is a very small cast of relatives that appears in Freya's autobiography, and with the death of her mother Flora in 1942, the older generation of them virtually disappear as an element in her story. Freya appears to have taken what she needed out of her parents' papers when she was preparing her autobiography, and then disposed of them. Her relatives, apart from the set-pieces on the two grandmothers, are soon dismissed. Her mother's three sisters – 'hopelessly emotional, impossible and always in financial straits' – disappear after the barest of mentions; one does not even learn their married names. It was only indirectly, through Cockerell's papers, that I learned that an aunt, her mother's younger sister Meta Stark, was still living in Torquay in 1943.

A baffling wall of selective editing shuts off the hinterland of Freya's life from view until 1950, and the publication of *Traveller's Prelude*. This was the source, I found, from which all general information about her was derived and, try as I might, I could not at first find any independent way back into her past. It was as if I had entered a maze, its hedges towering sombre and enigmatic in the sunbleached stillness surrounding some shuttered villa on the Venetian plain.

It was not until 1984, when Freya was ninety-one, that a flurry of promotional activity in Italy by an ambitious provincial official, aimed at placing Asolo more in the mainstream of cultural tourism, gave me another thread (besides Margaret Jourdain) to lead me still further back into Freya's growing up in Italy in the decade prior to World War I. Hitherto Italian recognition of her had been confined to an honorary citizenship of Asolo, prudently bestowed by its Municipality on Freya's reappearance there at war's end in 1945, when she claimed her inheritance of the Villa Freia. It was a tactful exercise in public relations made with a view to laundering Asolo's reputation with the Allied Military Government officials now running the country. Asolo had been designated Military HQ of Mussolini's armed forces in the last phase of the war, as the Germans withdrew northwards towards their own frontiers: the Villa Freia was requisitioned for the use of the general in command of the Fascist forces. The town's gesture of reconciliation to the daughter of a victim of Fascist oppression was made at a time when her good offices with the AMGOT authorities were being anxiously sought.

Now, nearly forty years later, Freya was perceived as a 'living treasure' whose fame might again be useful to the town. This new initiative resulted in a scheme for a public banquet and the ceremonial offering of the keys of the city to Freya. Ostensibly to commemorate the distinguished Englishwoman's long association with the town, the real aim was to promote cultural tourism.

Freya lent herself gladly to the project, pleased with the attention. Invitations and publicity material were sent out by the Municipality to all her grandest English friends. The band of the British Household Cavalry was flown in to play in the town piazza, paid for by a local bank. The promoters rather hoped that Freya's great friend, the English Queen Mother, would grace the ceremony. Photographs of the two elderly ladies, much the same in size, arm in arm and wearing not dissimilar hats, figured prominently in the publicity material, but she did not materialise. Freya, however, enjoyed the occasion, flanked by a supporting cast of old and new friends, eating everything put before her and beating time with her spoon to the music of the band. Small knots of puzzled Britons wandered around the town, uncertain of what the show was about. It was on this occasion that her Canadian cousin, Arthur Playters Stark, the son of her father's brother, Playters, his neighbour at Creston in British Columbia, first came into public view. Unrevealed to her closest friends, the two had been in correspondence for some years and she had included him in her list of invitations. It was Malise Ruthven, Pamela Hore-Ruthven's younger son, and Freya's godson, who brought us together.

Art Stark, when we met, turned out to be a small, chirpy, russet-coloured widower in his late seventies, similar in physique to Freya, with bright twinkling brown eyes and a friendly and unpretentious disposition. The family likeness was strong. He was a retired Canadian Federal Government communications employee. The cousins had met once previously when, during her 1943–4 lecture tour of America and Canada, Freya came to take tea with her relative and to talk over family history.

*   *   *

The personality of his uncle, Robert Stark, remained as elusive in Art Stark's recollection as it did in others' accounts of Freya's parent. He couldn't find much to say about him. He doubted, he said, whether as a boy he was even aware that his uncle had a wife and daughters in Italy. They were never spoken of. To a young boy knocking about the place out of school Uncle Bob was rather a shadowy presence; he was bald, he recalled, and polite, uninterfering, mostly reading or sitting sketching in the window of his wooden ranch house.

This confirmed impressions from other sources. A man of no social pretensions whatsoever, according to his daughter, he preferred the company of 'simple' people, and animals. The provincialism of his Devonshire upbringing in voice and manner was retained all his life.[5] 'Very retiring', 'insignificant', are comments that have come down in the Olivier family, from recollections of the 1880s and 1890s, when he and his wife Flora were members of the same group of watercolourists assembled around Edwin Bale, or working at the Studio Delacluze in Paris.

Art Stark also filled me in about his Uncle Arthur, for whom he was named, the oldest of the three Stark brothers of that generation. Trained as a doctor at the Edinburgh Infirmary, he appears never to have practised. A keen ornithologist, he had travelled widely in pursuit of this interest. His nephew possessed his notebooks, filled in meticulous copperplate with his ornithological observations. He also had a set of *Birds of South Africa* on which Dr Stark, MB, was at work when his life was cut short at the age of fifty-three by the first Boer shell to land on Ladysmith; it exploded outside his hotel and blew off his leg. The work was completed at his executor's request by W. L. Sclater, MA, FZS, the Director of the South African Museum, Cape Town, and appeared in three volumes in May 1901, published in London by R. H. Porter, Cavendish Square.

As frontispiece to Volume I is a portrait photograph by Messrs Dinkson of Torquay of Dr Arthur Stark. It shows a glossy, well-set-up figure in Norfolk jacket, stiff high collar and billycock hat, a watch-chain glinting under the high-buttoned coat. There is an impression of vigorous hirsute growth, as in a well-trimmed holly hedge, allowing a big, blunt nose, large ears, and alert foxy eyes to emerge convincingly from the carefully barbered thickets of beard and side whiskers.

I was delighted at this sight of a Stark in his native plumage. At last I felt I was getting an idea of Freya's male relatives, who so far had hardly appeared in her story. Her father's second brother, Playters Stark, Art Stark's father, is mentioned only as a rough, rude man, whom her mother Flora did not like. This must have made for difficulties at Chagford, where Playters Stark and his family lived at Southill, a now gentrified thatched farmhouse just down the lane from Ford Park.

On retirement Art Stark became interested in his family tree and compiled a chart of his relatives and family connections from papers his father had brought with him to Canada. Of this he kindly sent me a copy. It was my first break in my exploration of the Starks' family history and it enabled me to establish the relationship of Freya's parents, Flora and Robert Stark, as first cousins and the dominance of two families, the Starks and the Wilkinsons, in the record, since a brother and sister pair of Starks married a similar pair of Wilkinsons in the 1840s.

Both Starks and Wilkinsons are scantily recorded in the late eighteenth century around Torquay and Taunton, their respective places of origin, but emerge into documented clarity after 1815. The limited repertoire of surnames in the four generations of forebears recorded showed a pattern of marriage within kin groups, something not uncommon among Quakers and other dissenting sects. It implied a narrow range of social contacts, a defensive alliance among minorities anxious to retain coherence and afraid of contamination by outside influences. The linking factor in the early Stark-Wilkinson marriages was the Salem Chapel, Torquay.

Freya's ancestral history, as it unfolded in leisurely communications from Art Stark in Canada, bore an unanticipated resemblance to that of Ivy Compton-Burnett, as examined in Hilary Spurling's biography of Ivy. Although Ivy was ten years older than Freya, their backgrounds were similar. Both women came of rural stock – 'the agricultural class' moving up at the beginning of the nineteenth century from illiteracy through nonconformist Dissent, small shopkeeping and Victorian self-help to professional status at the end of the century. Both families were aided by marriage with others who rose from similar beginnings into prosperity through the conjunction of shopkeeping and radical politics, Ivy's mother being a daughter of an autocratic and controversial Mayor of Dover, and Freya's grandmother a daughter of the first Mayor of Exeter to be elected after the Reform Act of 1835, a popular figure dedicated to the public exposition of biblical prophecy, a licensed victualler and a prominent Chartist.

In both women the smooth upward movement towards the decorous respectability of the Victorian ideal was distorted by something individualistic and irreducible in the previous generation. Ivy's father compromised his hard-won position as a medical man by embracing homeopathy, of which he was a distinguished and well-rewarded practitioner. He left an ample fortune largely invested in property around Brighton, much of it in back-street rentals and speculative development. The Starks' emergence from obscurity was similar. It came about from dissenting religious convictions no more socially acceptable to the established Church of England, with its close connection with the ruling class, than homeopathy was to the medical profession. In Freya's father this led to an eventual rejection of all pretensions to class identity, and the abandonment in middle life of England for the egalitarian self-sufficiency of the settler's life in Canada.

In both Freya and Ivy this element in their background seems to have been felt as something that debarred them from the mainstream of their contemporaries' life, and though they chose to suppress this, it left scars. Misconceptions about their background passed unchallenged, as if they feared the snobbish Edwardian discrimination against the stigma of 'trade' in their families' recent history. Freya evoked a cultivated dilettantism and a country gentleman's well-funded security in her parentage which was certainly an artistic touching-up of the truth, while Ivy's novels are set with one exception in similar households and suggest a native familiarity on the writer's part with their occupants' manner. The exception, *Dolores*, was published in 1911, at Ivy's own expense, and remaindered eight years before she and Margaret Jourdain met. It was not a work on which she looked back with pleasure, and fourteen years elapsed before she wrote another.

In reality, for both Freya and Ivy, their formative experiences were a world away from that of their imagination; they had a basis of recently acquired middle-class prosperity and social attitudes defensively rooted in the provincial past. Their inherited culture was moralistic, material and self-assertive, while their imaginative response to an ethic based on altruism and aristocratic ideals made them particularly susceptible to the appeal of personalities that seemed to combine both without detriment to individuality or social acceptance.

EIGHTEEN

THE STARKITE INHERITANCE

It was after my meeting with Art Stark that the key to Freya's origins at last turned in its lock, and I had to rethink my first acceptance of the aura of Establishment grandeur that surrounded her personality. From lack of material I now moved into a phase of plenty. The threads of the story were being drawn together but the pattern was still unclear. Freya's compartmenting of identities, her evasions, her embroidering, were baffling. Through what new labyrinth of the emotions was I being led? What had started as desultory curiosity about a wartime episode was taking me into a vast hinterland of shadowy motivations, strange inheritances, Protean transfigurations. How was it all to be interpreted? Freya's private history, as it came into view, insistently provoked the question: how much was adopted, how much was inherited? What actually was her individual contribution? If Cockerell's papers had shown me how fame was achieved, Art Stark allowed me to see what the spur to it had been, hidden in the perplexities of parental lives begun in the middle of the last century.

Robert and Flora Stark, Freya's parents, were born respectively in 1853 and 1861. Their parents were mid-Victorians. They themselves matured in the 1870s, at the high point of late Victorian culture, while their daughters, Freya and Vera, were born in the 1890s and had an Edwardian childhood. The thread of documentation traced back through four generations led into the Victorian age and beyond, to the late Georgians, the Reform Acts and the beginning of the modern era.

The family's rise from obscurity began with Freya's great-grandfather, the paternal one, Robert Stark (1788–1854), who had an undertaker's business at Lower Braddons Road, Torquay.[1] He was born on 17 April 1788 at Chelston, Cockington, a once-rural parish now included in Torquay's urban sprawl. His family belonged to 'the agricultural class' and he was baptised into the Church of England on 9 May 1788. He had a varied career and achieved some local notoriety as a lay preacher, the founder of a dissenting sect known as Starkites. 'As a boy of nine or ten he was impressed by religious ideas derived not from the Liturgy but by hearing the Scriptures read in a peculiarly solemn and beautiful manner by the Rev Thomas Kitson. His family believed that it is to the impression thus received that his intense love of Scripture later developed.'[2]

After leaving school he was placed in the office of a local lawyer, Mr Cosserat, as a clerk. Here, although never articled, he acquired a practical knowledge of the law, which he used to his own and his friends' advantage, when he became agent for the Carey family at Torre Abbey and was active in local politics. In 1814, at the age of twenty-six, he married a Miss Peggy Cowell. Three years later, with his wife, he was baptised into a sect of Calvinistic Dissenters. They attended a Baptist chapel in Torquay and adopted the views of the high Calvinistic party – the Plymouth Brethren – as preached in Plymouth. At the same period William John Playters Wilkinson in Taunton, Somerset, a grocer and tavern keeper, was marrying and beginning his own family of ten children, two of whom, a son and a daughter, married into Robert Stark's equally large family.

From the close study of legal documents and the teasing out of exact meanings Robert Stark moved to the study of the Scriptures, and succeeded in persuading himself and others that he had overcome many apparent difficulties, often considered stumbling-blocks to a right understanding of the Bible, which by some mysterious process of reversal in his mind became so many helps to it instead.

In his own account, written as letters to his friend Mr James Murray, he tells how about the year 1825, in default of the expected preacher, he was asked to speak one Sunday at the

Baptist chapel he and his wife attended. He spoke first in the morning then, for the evening, in order to refresh his thoughts, took down his Bible and allowed it to fall open at random to the sixteenth chapter of Matthew, which he began to read. On reaching the nineteenth verse, which speaks of giving Peter the keys of the Kingdom of Heaven, he experienced some sort of mystical illumination – he speaks of the words striking his mind like a flash of lightning – making the connection that Peter, with the first key, opened the grand mysteries of the Heavenly Kingdom to the Jews on the Day of Pentecost, and did away with the straitjacket authority of Mosaic law. Fired by this understanding, he spoke at length that evening to the congregation. 'Some were overwhelmed with delight, while others hardly knew what to say; such novel interpretations confounded them and they grew perturbed as to where it would lead them.' A jealousy arose, he says; the deacons sent to Plymouth for aid in restoring the primacy of the Mosaic law. This was of no avail. Robert Stark was convinced that his interpretation was correct, and that the righteousness of the Gospel was not the righteousness of the law of Moses. That was first given to the children of Israel alone, while the second law given by God in Christ was extended to all nations.

A fortnight later Robert Stark again spoke in chapel, this time to make a brief comment on Galatians 3. As soon as he began to speak, a relative of his rose up and walked out of the chapel, followed immediately by his wife. There was an embarrassed pause: as the reading of the text continued, first a deacon, then another member of the congregation rose and left. Robert Stark then challenged anyone else who wished to leave to do so now; his own mind was firm, he wrote, his face as it were a flint. No-one did, but on leaving the pulpit he was assailed by one of the remaining two deacons with the words, 'The peace in this church is broken.' On that he said he would disturb them no further, but would withdraw from the congregation and speak from his own house in future, where he would receive all who wished to come there to hear him and to investigate the Scriptures.

Robert Stark's defection from the strict Baptist community and the uproar this created in the small fishing port of Torquay and its environs had a deleterious effect on him. The animosity and spite of his detractors and the accusations of heretical and indeed satanical practices levelled at him, so the Memoir recounts, produced a low nervous fever – a breakdown of some kind – aggravated by a decline into typhus in its severest form. Delirious for several weeks, it was not thought he would survive. His enemies saw this illness as a judgment, designed to put a stop to his wickedness; but he recovered, strengthened not only in spirit but in physical health as well, so that until two years before his death in 1854, he enjoyed better health than he had done before this event. According to his daughter, he showed no malice towards those who had turned against him and reviled him. His convictions remained firm as a rock, he reported, and the more he studied the word of God the more he found to convince himself that he was right, and his beliefs in harmony with all Scripture. So intense was this belief that he often said that if everyone else in the world were opposed to him, he could not change it.

The *Torquay Directory* of August 1854 supplies some facts about Freya's ancestor. It had

the painful duty to record the decease of one of the oldest and most valued inhabitants of this town, Mr Robert Stark, which occurred at Harefield on Wednesday morning, 9th August, after a lingering illness. For upwards of forty years Mr Stark had taken an active interest in the public business and Institutions of this town, of which no-one took a more enlightened and interested view. As the agent of Torre Abbey during many years, he never allowed the interests of the manor to supersede those of the public, and the impartiality and moderation which he displayed in our local contests gave a weight to his opinions which was equally recognised by all parties. He had been one of the original Improvement Commissioners and a member of the Local Board since the introduction of the Public Health Act until the election in 1853, when he resigned in consequence of failing health . . . a vote of condolence to his family was unanimously passed at the last meeting of the Board. His religious opinions were original and peculiar, but not to the extent which his opponents sometimes represented; whilst his unblemished moral character showed that vital Christianity, although differing in externals and that which is comparatively non-essential, is ever productive of the fruits of faith.

One of the oldest established tradesmen in Torquay, he was of an active and persevering character in business and in general parochial matters, from as far back as 1821 protecting the town's interests and aiding its prosperity. On the introduction of the Old Torquay Local Act, in 1835, when Torquay began to emerge from embryo into greatness, Mr Stark was among the first elected Commissioners . . . On the formation of the Newton Abbot Union, under the New Poor Law in 1835, he was elected Guardian of the Poor for his parish. Always known as a conscientious Dissenter, he 'searched the Scriptures', formed independent opinions and fearlessly proclaimed them.

The turning point in Robert Stark's career as a preacher was the publication in 1836 of a *Dissertation on Prophecy* by the Rev Dr Lee, Professor of Arabic at Oxford University. This made a great impact on him and strengthened confidence in his own interpretation of the Scriptures. He was introduced to the book by W. J. P. Wilkinson (who became Mayor of Exeter in 1837), already deeply concerned with the correct interpretation of Scripture. The two men had shared a friendship based on the similarity of their views since 1832. The Mayor throughout his life held regular public meetings to examine and interpret the Scriptures.

Persuading Mr Wilkinson to accompany him, Robert travelled up to London and spent the day in discussion with Dr Lee. They returned to Torquay reassured as to the validity of the beliefs they shared. This seems to have been something Robert Stark needed, shaken by the persecuting attacks of former friends, and by their repudiation of his spiritual illumination. His self-righteousness restored, he spoke every Sunday to an increasing congregation, which soon overflowed the room he rented from the Freemasons for the weekly meeting. His style as an orator was plain and open, his argumentative powers formidable, but always conciliatory and friendly. Eventually he had the satisfaction of buying the original Baptist chapel from which he had been expelled in 1825; in 1839 this was replaced by a new stone building subsequently twice enlarged, built by subscription from his congregation of whom the older Wilkinsons, now retired from Exeter to Torquay, were important members. It was named the Salem Chapel, but it did not long survive the death of its leading figures, Mayor Wilkinson in 1849 and Robert Stark in 1854. With their passing the Starkite message began to lose its authority; in the next generation the congregation dwindled, and the building eventually became the Torquay School of Science and Art.

The *Memoir of Robert Stark of Torquay 1788–1854*, issued at the time of his death, was reprinted at the *Directory* office, Torquay, on 17 April 1904 when Freya was eleven. Its reissue was decided on by surviving members of the preacher's family 'prompted thereto by an enduring and loving memory of his noble life, which to them, and also to many friends, has been a source of gratification and a lifelong comfort. A further object,' continues the Explanatory Introduction, 'is the hope that the younger generations by whom the Memoir may be read, will be influenced by the example of so true, earnest and active a life, which was in all things influenced by a sense of duty, and guided by the dictates of conscience.' Included in the pamphlet is the following list of Robert Stark's publications.

A Divinely Commissioned Ministry

A Diagram (with a Key to the same)
Showing the Order and Course of Divine
Revelation

What is Truth?
A Reply to the Rev John Walker,
Catholic Priest

The Scripture Term
The End of the World or Age

Eleven Letters on
The Doctrine of Regeneration, addressed to
The Right Rev the Lord Bishop of Exeter
(the late Dr Phillpots) in the year 1849

A Letter to the Rev Dr Wiseman on
The Power of the Keys of St Peter
Showing that there is no Successor either of
Peter or of Paul.

On the eventual sale of the Salem Chapel by his descendants
it was stipulated that a marble tablet, placed as a tribute by his
friends, should remain on the walls of the new School of Science
and Art. It read:

This Tablet is erected by the Christian Congregation of this
Chapel as a testimony of respect in Memory of

ROBERT STARK

of Torquay, who was called to end his career on the 9th
August 1854 in the 66th year of his age.

During a period of Thirty years he voluntarily stood forward as a fearless Lecturer on Gospel truths, in which he
faithfully adher'd to the Fulfilment of the Saviour's Prophecy
of the Second Advent at the destruction of Jerusalem; and
end of the Jewish economy, with its covenant of works; and
the perfect establishment of the Gospel covenant of faith,
liberty and life.

As a believer he lived, and rejoiced in this great salvation,
and in his sufferings experienced the rich consolation of resting on the Fulfilled Promises of the Gospel; and cheerfully
longed for the happy hour, to be for ever alone with the
people of God.

May every reader possess this heavenly experience!

A lithograph likeness of Robert Stark, dressed in the fashion of
the 1830s, is printed in his Memoir. He looks a genial card,
with his glossy quiff and whiskers; there is something confident
and alert about his smiling regard. The heavy features repro-

duced in his descendants are there – the blunt nose, large ears, ugly mouth – but also the bright eye found in Freya and Art Stark. What was he, I wondered, some sort of barrack-room lawyer, up to his elbows in local politics? His facility for self-promotion was phenomenal. Letter-writing was the means employed, a constant salvo of communication fired off out of the blue to chance acquaintances and complete strangers, proffering arguments and offers to call to discuss the merits of his ideas in person; these he sent to clergymen of all ranks and denominations, impervious to snubs, often inviting them to public debate.

Religious nonconformity allied to small shopkeeping and radical politics was a well-established conjunction in the political history of the late Georgian period. Cathedral towns like Exeter were dominated by the Cathedral Close and by the agents of the local territorial magnates, until the Reform Acts of the 1830s let in new men like the Wilkinsons and Starks. Blocked by the established hierarchies, these had to find new local initiatives on which to expend their energies. This coincided with the railway boom, and intensive speculation in building and development. I seemed to have stumbled into some Barsetshire scenario of sharp lawyers' clerks and slippery land agents, of ambitious development projects and local tradesmen promoting small fishing ports into seaside resorts. The mixture of business acumen and religiosity in Freya's ancestry seemed a stereotype of Victorian cant.

The first defector from Victorian self-advancement in Torquay comes into view in the 1850s. This was William Stark, the third son of Robert Stark of the Salem Chapel, and the father of Flora Stark, Freya's mother. I could learn very little about him, but if, as seems likely, he only quit Torquay about the period of his father's death, he was a man approaching forty when he settled in Italy, having formed there an infatuation for Madeline Schmid, a German governess employed by a princely Roman family, whom he married. I have been unable to trace any record of this marriage. Perhaps the oblique reference to his father's 'domestic afflictions' in the original preface to *A Divinely Com-*

missioned Ministry refers to what must undoubtedly have been a heavy blow, the defection of a son from the narrow Starkite community accreted around the personality of his parent.

The Schmids were Rhinelanders in origin, farmers from around Trier. They were an able race. Madeline Stark's father was a professional portrait painter who attained some success in the small princely and ducal courts then existing in Europe; one of his patrons rewarded him with the minor title of Chevalier. This Chevalier Schmid married the daughter of French émigrés, members of the Princesse de Lamballe's household, refugees who fled across the Rhine to Germany in the Revolution of 1791, where they supplemented a living as music teachers in the provincial backwaters of their exile by selling the produce of their vegetable garden. Like many victims of revolution they carried with them the recollection of better days and past distinctions, an unsettling inheritance for descendants born to insecurity and falling fortunes.

A brother of the Chevalier also made his way in the world. He had a position in the Austrian administration of the Grand Duchy of Tuscany, then a Hapsburg possession. The talents of this branch of the Schmids were rewarded with an aristocratic *von*, and it was through them that a post as governess in a princely family of the Papal nobility was found for the Chevalier's daughter. The seventeen-year-old Madeline Schmid was dispatched south from Germany, and journeyed alone to Rome to take up her duties in the grand Roman Catholic household her relatives had found for her. There William Stark saw her one day, taking the air with her charges in the family's carriage, determined to meet her, and eventually married her.

William Stark did not make the mistake of bringing his bride back to his relatives in Torquay, but rented a villa at Bellosguardo outside Florence, and devoted himself, so the story goes, to painting in tempera, until his death in 1875 from the bite of a mad dog. A dedication to the arts was one way out for men and women who chafed at the conventions of their period. He left a widow and four daughters, the eldest of whom was Freya's mother, Flora Stark, born in Florence in 1861 and at the time of his death a girl of fourteen.

The marriage of William Stark and Madeline Schmid turned out to be something of a disappointment. He was of a jolly, sociable disposition, and careless about money; her favourite parent, it was from him Flora first acquired her handiness with paint-brush and tools. His wife despised housekeeping as middle-class and unintellectual and after the birth of four daughters retreated into mild invalidism and a good deal of lying about on sofas. She preferred reading history, Mommsen for choice, and the practice of her music to housekeeping. Her musical ability she passed to her daughters, though not to Freya, but a habit of reading and a sense of history was inculcated in her grand-daughter by Madeline Stark, along with an early familiarity with the myths, legends and fairy tales of European culture.

William Stark's death precipitated a crisis for his dependants. Money supplies dried up and bills accumulated. It seems that whatever income he had ceased at his death. Some sort of remittance man, he left no independent fortune. The villa at Bellosguardo had to be given up, leaving the widow and her four daughters no alternative but to turn to her own connections for assistance. Her former employers, the Rospigliosi family, and her own relatives, the Schmids, combined to provide a solution. This was to set her up in a small school in Genoa, where she could coach the daughters of the well-to-do local families in music and foreign languages, and generally apply a cultivated polish. This venture provided the initial contact with the Blanchi di Roascio family of Piedmont, into whose cadet branch in Dronero Madeline Stark's grand-daughter Vera was married in 1913.

During this crisis, the Devonshire Starks appear to have done nothing. The school in Genoa lasted into Freya's early childhood, until some atavistic impulse towards grandeur impelled Madeline Stark to expand into more imposing premises. This precipitated another financial crisis. The grand new apartment had to be given up, and the lease sold to pay bills. She became in her old age what Freya herself remembered, something that was shunted about between her daughters, the subject of distracted conferences between husbands and wives, an inhabitant, so Freya wrote, of gloomy lodgings at the end of long tram-lines.[3]

The presence of his mother-in-law in Robert Stark's domestic life may have contributed to his stringency in financial matters. An awareness of crisis and contrivance, of shabby pensions and obstinate old women, of painful interrogations by impatient husbands about money spent was an integral part of Freya's growing up. Freya in maturity, piecing together her recollections of her German grandmother years after her death, evolved a glowing picture of a woman unbroken by the disappointments of life, detached from petty cares and anxieties. She transformed her grandmother into a symbol of the triumph of Spirit over Matter, and the toughness concealed by the gentle grand manner, the passionate resentment of criticism, became a testimonial to wisdom and integrity. It was Freya's valediction to her past, a making over of what was undistinguished and shabby, the pearl formed from the piece of grit in the sensitive matrix of the oyster. In some sense it was a scenario for her own old age. Freya's grandmother glides out of her grand-daughter's story, unregretted, but leaving behind her intimations of spirituality in Freya which might have surprised her, had her own lofty spirit condescended to examine them.

The story of the German grandmother has something of the ironic pathos of all histories of decayed families, as if the sustaining recollections of past distinction were in themselves the instruments whereby the survivors perished. Dispatched alone at an impressionable age to a grand and awe-inspiring household in Rome, Madeline Schmid never accepted the realities of her marriage to a commonplace man insensitive, she felt, to the good manners and fastidiousness of mind which had been an asset in the aristocratic environment she inhabited as a young woman.

She retreated into a world of studied bookishness at Bellosguardo, where her daughters grew up untrained in all except literature, music and art. This abdication of responsibility was probably a first expression of the overweening egocentricity which in Genoa became the pattern of her old age.

There are parallels between the grand-daughter and the

grandmother. Freya adopted the affectionate manner that engrossed other people's service and attention, coupled with a passive acceptance of their concern. The programmed fostering of youthful idealism by exposure to only what is superior in literature and art is a reflection of her own indoctrination when a child, and was transmitted hopefully to godchildren and other young people in default of any children of her own.

It seems to have eluded her that her grandmother's stance of intellectual detachment from the practicalities of daily life was productive of a serene, egotistical indifference that maddened those attempting to protect her, and wore out their goodwill. Freya records that she was never without a book in her hand, and never too engrossed to put it down, but she goes no further. The retreat from actuality, the imperviousness to advice, are never examined, or the development of *folie de grandeur* acknowledged.

This was expressed in her grandmother by manipulative scheming, ostensibly for the benefit of others, that involved her daughters in tiresome and embarrassing explanations. These schemes were not so much personal dishonesty as devices to bolster up her own importance as an altruistic dispenser of favours and a channel of influence. Promises were made on other people's behalf and their financial credit invoked; this led to painful confrontations with the angry victims, until it was finally accepted by her daughters that their mother was no longer able to run her own life, and that they would have to look after her.

So far the family history of the Starks had been localised and identifiable, and quiet mornings in the Torquay and Taunton public libraries enabled me to follow the topography of Victorian urban development, and to trace the rise of the Stark and Wilkinson families through the local directories. Freya's paternal grandfather, John Cowell Stark, a brother of William Stark in Italy, had a furniture-hire business at 13 The Strand, Torquay, where he rented out items of household furnishing, bed and table linen, cutlery, candlesticks, at a shilling or so a week. A copy of an ornate business card detailing the articles supplied, and the list of prices, was sent me from Canada by Art Stark.

This grandfather died early, around 1860, while Freya's father, his youngest son, was still a small boy. The material situation of this generation of Starks was obviously improved, aided by marriages into the well-entrenched Wilkinson family of Taunton and Exeter. The Wilkinson women appear to have been the chief repository of the Starkite tradition in Torquay, where the pressure for conformity in the preacher's descendants was perhaps enforced by the inaccessibility of capital held in trust for long-lived widows, and by their control of the income. The widow of the first Mayor Wilkinson of Exeter lived on in retirement in Torquay to the age of eighty-six, while her daughter Anne, who married John Cowell Stark and was Freya's paternal grandmother, had over forty years of widowhood until she in turn died there around 1905, at the age of eighty-eight. She was the motivating force behind the reprinting of Robert Stark's Memoir in 1904, in association with her brother, Robert Carne Wilkinson. Also a Mayor of Exeter, married to Elizabeth Stark, the preacher's eldest daughter, he was another expounder of biblical truths, whose firm religious convictions were noted in his 1918 obituary, as well as his inability to see eye to eye with many of his day and generation. It is also recorded that he carried out his public duties with great dignity.

Both Freya's paternal uncles married within the network of their Wilkinson family connections, while Freya's father, Robert Stark, married his first cousin, Flora Stark, in 1878 when she was a girl of just seventeen and he a young man of twenty-five. A curious feature of this marriage is that the copy of the announcement, written in his mother's hand, makes no mention of William Stark's widow. It reads: 'September 23rd at St Mark's Church, Robert Stark of The Engadine, Torquay, to Flora Madeline, eldest daughter of the late William Stark, of Florence. Foreign papers please copy.' One can only assume that Flora's mother was not acknowledged by the Devon Starks, and did not attend the marriage.

In 1895, by which time Freya was born, her father's mother,

the widowed Mrs John Cowell Stark, had moved from The Engadine to Eccleston, another recently built villa on the Newton Road, adjacent to Torre railway station. This house figures in Freya's early recollections of childhood, for Robert and Flora Stark continued to make use of it for many years and the two Stark children were deposited there with their governess for long boring visits while their parents were busy elsewhere. Here the child Freya could watch, from the windows of the house, the comings and goings of the railway passengers at Torre Station. Their grandmother was to continue in ritualised authority in this setting until Freya was eleven or twelve and her father a man in his early fifties. Though this house has now disappeared, bulldozed to make way for a road-widening scheme, its atmosphere was imprinted on the sensitive child and recorded by her in maturity. Eccleston provided Robert Stark's children with their first experience of English life.

Freya's autobiographical account of her two grandmothers allows no doubt as to where her imaginative sympathy lay. The German grandmother, poor, aristocratic, peripatetic, intellectual and serene, is the one with whom she identifies. The Torquay grandmother, in contrast, is viewed with detachment, and Freya's account of the hushed formality of her household is tinged with condescension. But Freya's old age has been that of the Torquay grandmother rather than the German one. There was the same morning ritual at the dressing-table, a maid in attendance, the same discreet display of a well-ordered household, the same deference accorded the mistress of all these splendours.

Today, the once rural parish of Chelston and Cockington has been engulfed, like Torre Station, by urban sprawl, but St Mary's Church, where the ancestral Starks were christened and buried, remains and by diligent search a tombstone bearing the name was found by a visiting Canadian descendant.

It is not difficult to suppose that the Starks had some share in the development of the area around Torre railway station. Freya's own father's dabbling in property and the renovation and building of houses was an important element in Freya's early childhood. She herself had a commercial approach to house-ownership; it had to work for her. She was indefatigable in arranging seasonal lettings of the Villa Freia during absences, and leasing out L'Arma to finance her trips abroad, or allocating space to paying guests, either at La Mortola or at Asolo. Pages of her correspondence in the immediate post-war period are devoted to efforts to persuade friends to rent or buy properties she found for them in and around Asolo.

Freya told me that over the years Robert Stark built four houses and 'gentrified' – though she would have disclaimed the term – several more, a speculative total of about ten properties, none of which made a notably successful return on money invested. Indeed, she claimed, his ventures barely broke even, being assembled slowly and patiently in accordance with the precepts of Ruskin and William Morris. Like many similar couples today the young Starks would occupy the property they were renovating, between absences abroad, then move on to the next. Flora was an active partner in this work, undertaking the interior decoration, while Robert laid out the gardens. This pattern was already established when in 1897 Robert Stark bought 275 acres of land outside Chagford from the Rev Richard Follett. In the purchase document his address is given as the Log Hut, Chagford, a wooden shack on the lane up to Ford Park and Thornworthy. The purchase included Ford Park, Great Frenchbeer Farm, Little Frenchbeer Farm and Metherall Farm, small farmhouses which, over the next fourteen years, he either rebuilt or improved, twice mortgaging the estate for two-thirds of the purchase price.[4] As Ford Park, his most ambitious house, built on the site of an earlier building, was completed in 1902 without a bathroom, at a period when such an adjunct had ceased to be a luxury in a family house, his practicality as an architect may have left something to be desired.

Eccleston was inherited by Freya's father on his mother's death, and leased out until 1912 when, in the general liquidation of his assets in England, it was sold along with his Chagford properties to finance his new venture in Canada. Freya and her sister Vera were each given £2000 as investment capital from the proceeds of this liquidation.

Freya wrote rather dismissively of the Wilkinson connection in her account of her family in *Traveller's Prelude*; she implied an element of condescension in her grandfather John Cowell Stark's marriage in 1842 to Anne Wilkinson which nothing I was able to learn substantiates. Indeed, the Wilkinsons would appear to be rather more solidly established than the Starks. Wilkinsons (Wylkynsons) are recorded as Freemen of Exeter as early as 1484–5, but for present purposes their history begins in Taunton where William John Playters (or Playtus) Wilkinson in 1815 married Grace Blatch Cox, whose family were maltsters and ironmongers and, like the Wilkinsons, long-established worthies of the town.[5]

William John Playters Wilkinson himself was a retailer of beer and spirits at the Market House Tavern in Taunton, as well as being a grocer and importer of tea and foreign wines. A town Bailiff, he was a returning officer at the election of Members for the Borough of Taunton in 1818, but some time after 1823 he moved to Exeter, the local port of entry for dutiable goods, where the Wilkinsons had their bonded warehouse. Here he opened his own business in North Street, as a wholesale importer of wines and spirits, and entered local politics. The connection at that period between grog shops and radical politics may have influenced the outcome, for in 1837 he became the first Mayor of Exeter to be elected after the Reform Bill of 1835. A leading Chartist, he led the delegation from Exeter to the Hyde Park Rally of 1848. He lived to the age of sixty-two, dying in 1849, and was buried in Exeter's Old Cemetery under an imposing monument raised by public subscription, the hearse being followed to the graveside by a large portion of the local population. The last two interments in the family vault, as inscribed on the pedestal of the monument, were in the 1930s.

After the Mayor's death in 1849, his widow left Northernhay House, Exeter, and moved to Ash Hill Grove, Torquay, closer to the Starkite community and her married daughter Anne Stark. She died there on 5 February 1875. Her son, Robert Carne Wilkinson, married to Elizabeth Cowell Stark, carried on his father's business in Exeter and was elected Mayor in 1884, living on hale and hearty until his death in 1918 at the age of ninety-six. During his mayoralty an entry by his own son, Robert Stark Wilkinson, an accomplished watercolourist who exhibited at the Royal Academy, won the competition for the architectural design of Digby Asylum; the Drill Hall, Exeter, was also built by him.[6]

Among the documents sent me by Art Stark was the photograph of an engraved silver salver presented by admirers to his great-grandfather, William John Playters Wilkinson on 11 August 1841, to commemorate his birthday. It is inscribed 'As a testimonial of the high Respect and sincere Gratitude of attached Friends for his gratuitous labour of love for their education, in the Exposition of the Scriptures COMPARING SCRIPTURAL THINGS WITH SCRIPTURE.' Above the inscription is an engraving of a Bible, open at Revelation 5:5. On opening the Bible at this passage I read the following: 'And one of the elders saith unto me, Weep not: behold, the Lion of the tribe of Judah, the Root of David, hath prevailed to open the book, and to loose the seven seals thereof.'

This was my introduction to St John the Divine and I read on amazed. Many images familiar with casual everyday use made their appearance. There was the beast with the ten heads that sat on the seven hills, there was the heavenly city, with its gates of pearl, the scarlet woman flaunted in her colours. The images reeled by like television. Believers were saved, sinners cast into the pit, beasts crawled on their bellies, angels ascended, the elect were safe in heaven. It sounded mad.

I thought back to the stagnation of isolated Devon communities before the coming of the railway in the 1840s, and of the life of small farming folk tied to their acres, and at risk of pauperisation when their bodily framework collapsed. A picture formed, as in some journeyman painter's primitive composition, of literal-minded, hirsute Victorian congregations, men and women, clustered in their tiny chapels, spellbound by powerful preachers intoxicated by their own words. The 1830s in the West Country was a period of great distress among the agricultural poor, and considerable unrest. The frightening 'Captain Swing' machine-breaking and rick-burning disorders swept across southern England and alarmed the propertied classes, while the evangelical zeal of Wesley's followers undermined the authority of the Bishops of the established Church.

Spiritual unease gave rise to curious experiments in living, in which men and women participated – Simonianism and its offshoots the Lampeter Brethren in Wales, the Abode of Love at Spaxton in Somerset, the Irvingites in Bloomsbury. Many believed that a new social order could only be established through spiritual regeneration, but in the more bizarre manifestations of this belief, the flesh sometimes obtruded, as at Spaxton, where for many years the leader of the community lived surrounded by females whom he called his 'spiritual brides'. This upset the local farmers who refused to allow their wives to attend evening service.

This climate of spiritual unease and its accompanying religiosity perhaps explains the resentment with which Robert Stark's dismissal in 1825 of the Mosaic law in favour of euphoric optimism and charismatic universal Love was received in Torquay. To reject fundamentalist Bible teaching was seen as an invitation to godlessness and licence. In the simplicity of their beginnings and their Pentecostal enthusiasm, did the Starkites feel they were indeed a people apart, to whom God spoke through the medium of a designated mouthpiece, although threatened and persecuted by their enemies? Even in the casual remarks of genial Art Stark I received an impression that the Starks were conscious of being something special and that family pride was well established. Was the preacher Robert Stark's collapse into illness the reaction of a hyper-sensitive personality faced with an unexpected and bitter rebuff?

It was with a sinking heart that I accepted that there was a vast discrepancy between Freya's conjuring up of a family background of leisured gentility and acceptability among the landed classes and this strange inbred community of small-town radicals and individualists. I would have to rethink my ideas about Freya's reliability as a witness to her own past. Her not-so-distant ancestry was a good deal odder than I anticipated and I could not help thinking that there were many points of resemblance between her and her dynamic forebear, as his history unfolded.

NINETEEN

ASOLO AND CHAGFORD

Flora Stark's introduction in 1878 to married life in Devon was not a success. Perhaps insular wariness had already prejudiced her English relatives against William Stark's Italian family, whose history was made worse by its financial disarray, a judgment, it might be felt, for his defection from their own community. Perhaps, too, they were disconcerted by something unwomanly, to them, in Flora's participation in her husband's artistic pursuits, and in her lack of the conventional self-effacement of the young bride.

There is a photograph of Flora and one of her sisters among Freya's albums at Asolo, two good-looking, smartly dressed young women in a group with the senior Mrs Stark, her private nurse in attendance, in the garden of her Torquay home. Perhaps it records the wedding party of 23 September 1878. The two girls are brilliant in silks, and striking in appearance. The elder Mrs Stark's small, sober face looks out without expression from under her widow's bonnet. Clad in black, she is tiny and dauntingly self-composed, an icon displayed to the photographer's lens. Flora, in a dashing striped dress, a figure out of a painting by Tissot, is flung flamboyantly on a rug at her feet. One has to wonder what the effect was on the hushed routines of the Torquay household of that big, glowing girl, with her foreign ways and tomboyish handiness with paint-brush and tools. She strikes an incongruously vigorous, vivid note in the muted setting of an English autumnal garden in the suburbs.

The contrast between the Stark cousins' upbringing could not have been more marked, the one stuffy, deferential, restrained, the other negligent, eccentric and impractical. Flora early in life was introduced to insecurity, and the actuality of disaster, while Robert read books about the Wild West, and imbued the 'simple' life of trappers and smugglers with the glamour of the adventurous unknown, longing to participate in it.

These books were still in the house when Freya was a child, and were read by her. The schoolboy's yearning for adventure in the young man was translated into restlessness, and an inability to settle to anything for very long. All three Stark brothers seem to have suffered from this. Thus the role of amateur naturalist and landscape painter suited Robert Stark, something towards which Flora's own artistic inclination further encouraged him. She was the tougher, more resilient personality, and it was her dislike of Devon, its climate, and her relations, that within two years sent the young Starks up to London to make their way in the artistic life of the capital.

The working out of the relationship between the two cousins was to occupy many years and make for unhappiness all round. Eventually it settled into a mutual acceptance of incompatibility and an agreement to part company. It was twenty-seven years before the death of the senior Mrs Stark released the financial assets which enabled Freya's parents to come to some kind of a settlement and go their own ways, and these years were perhaps a harder apprenticeship for her mother than ever Freya allowed. The break was made in 1911, after a partnership of thirty-three years, when Robert Stark emigrated to Canada, and the future of their two daughters became Flora's responsibility.

But at first they seem to have been happy enough. Flora was a fine, handsome, affectionate creature, artistically talented, and well-trained musically. That she had some sort of romantic feeling for her young husband seems evident from the large pastel portrait she made of him in this first period of their marriage, which hung in Freya's sitting-room in Asolo. He sits in his velveteen clothes, his gun on his knee and his game-bag beside him, on a blue kitchen chair in some Devon farmhouse.

There is something alert and pleasing about his look, so that an impression is gained of a fit, wiry young man, keenly responsive to the artist.

Once arrived in London, Edwin Bale, Robert Stark's old tutor at the South Kensington School of Art, found a part-time job for him there teaching sculpture, while Flora attended classes. Bale painted a charming watercolour portrait of her, aged nineteen, singing and playing at a decorated piano in Alma Tadema's studio in St John's Wood. Bale was the catalyst, I saw, in all these developments. It was he who first drew Robert Stark to Italy to tour the art galleries with his fellow-student Herbert Young and to enrol at a summer school in Florence, when one can suppose the cousins first met. It was with Bale's help that the young married couple were now installed in lodgings in London. Bale was a man who made his own way in the world by his talent as a professional watercolourist, exhibiting regularly at the Royal Academy and Watercolour Societies between 1870 and 1883. He gave up painting on marriage to a well-to-do American widow, Julia Dalton, to become Art Director of Cassells, the publisher, a position he held from 1884 to 1907. He was the first Chairman of the Imperial Arts Council, founded at the time of the Boer War, and the forerunner of the present Arts Council. His stepdaughter Genevieve – the Viva Jeyes of Freya's story – was eight years younger than Flora, and a friendship formed between the two girls which was to last all their lives.

The Bale household in St John's Wood was Flora's introduction to London life in the 1880s, while Viva Jeyes provided the launching pad for her daughter Freya's subsequent more spectacular rise in the world. In the 1880s Flora's musical abilities came in useful; she played the piano and sang at the literary and artistic gatherings. Her youth and freshness, her good looks, intelligence and vitality ensured her a favourable reception, and there seems no doubt that socially she outshone her husband.

When Freya first visited her father in Canada in 1928 she described his life there as 'very Bret Harte';[1] had she had more insight into her parent's history she might have cited Edward Carpenter instead. This apostle of the Simple Life was a major influence on Robert Stark's decision in 1911 to leave his family and at the age of fifty-eight to emigrate to British Columbia as a settler.

At the turn of the century 'Back to the Land', 'Back to Nature', 'the Simple Life', were all popular terms to describe what was essentially an anti-industrial impulse whose basic premises were a return to the country and the simplification of daily living burdened by the oppressive elaboration of high Victorian culture. It was now that cycling, walking and camping first became popular. There is a whole associated literature of taking to the open and sleeping under the stars, all reflected in Robert Stark's upbringing of his children. Houses such as Ford Park in 1902 were designed with special balconies so that beds could be pushed out for healthy open-air slumber.

The seedbed of the Back to Nature movement was among intellectuals and social reformers. It fostered nostalgia for the innocence and simplicity of country life and filtered down to the Edwardians ('resident trippers' in the pejorative rural phrase of the time) in the fashionable new interest in garden design and weekend cottages built in the vernacular idiom. Love of the countryside was established as an article of faith, a reversal of the eighteenth-century horror of the tedium of rural life. One aspect of this, among the new immigrants to the countryside, stimulated by a revived interest in country traditions, was a mystical substitution of Nature for conventional religious belief. This influenced children's literature well into the new century and formed the background for many Edwardian childhoods. Much of Freya's recollection of her upbringing falls into place when seen in this context.

Freya's parents began marriage in 1878 eager to identify with what was fashionably progressive. In sociological terms they were third-generation urban, for whom the recent past held no romantic interest or charm; rather it was something to reject and disclaim. They did all the things their 'advanced' contemporaries did, bought bicycles and rode about the countryside progressively clad in natural wool and bloomers, and joined colonies of artists doing similar things on both sides of the Channel. Robert Stark was all for the open air and the open road, and gladly swapped his inherited culture for an equally dogmatic pantheism, enshrined in Nature worship. This was no individual eccentricity, it was a response to current moods, popular at home and on the Continent among people reacting against the stuffiness of a conventional upbringing.

In England two figures in particular were important at this period in showing the way back to the bosom of Nature, the one, Richard Jefferies (1848–87), very English in the rapturous purity of his response to fresh air, clear light and the landscapes of southern England. A self-educated novelist and naturalist, he came of small farming stock in Wiltshire and became a popular author in 1877 when *The Gamekeeper at Home*, originally contributed to the *Pall Mall Gazette*, was issued in book form. This was followed by *Wild Life in a Southern County* in 1879, and *Bevis*, an idealisation of his own childhood, in 1881, books in which the poet interpreted Nature, while the naturalist studied her with passionate accuracy.

If Jefferies led the way back to the Wild Wood and its mysteries, Edward Carpenter (1844–1929) was the apostle of economic survival as a smallholder. Both were men of Robert Stark's generation. Carpenter, a mathematician and college tutor at Trinity Hall, Cambridge, took orders and became curate to F. D. Maurice, the Christian Socialist associate of William Morris. He now became friendly with a married labouring man of his own age, Albert Fernehough, and the farmer who employed him. These offered a new ideal – 'a life close to Nature and actual materials, shrewd, strong, manly, independent, not the least polite or proper, thoroughly human and kindly, and spent for the most part in the fields and under the open sky.'[2]

In 1879, when he was thirty-six, Carpenter moved in as a lodger to the Fernehoughs' cottage, to begin writing Whitmanesque poems, 'Towards Democracy', and three years later bought seven acres of land at Millthorpe, south of Sheffield, and set up a market garden, in response to what he felt was his personal need for physical labour in the open air to restore his overstressed constitution. Here an ugly, utilitarian brick house was built for Carpenter and the Fernehough family, who were co-opted into the experiment. The wife and daughter looked after the domestic side of the enterprise, while the two men worked the land and sold the produce from a stall in the local market. It was the Simple Life to which Robert Stark aspired when he took a young farm couple with him from Chagford to Canada, and set up a joint household in a four-roomed prefabricated wooden ranch house at Creston, British Columbia in 1911.

Freya's father never again worked as a painter or sculptor once he reached Canada in 1911. He was then a man of fifty-eight. It was as if his creative stamina was limited and he preferred instead to find in physical labour the solution to whatever perplexities he experienced. The adventurous spirit of his young manhood, when he travelled widely with his brother Arthur, shooting and collecting ornithological specimens and eggs, did not mature into any sustained ambition. It was a life punctuated with episodes of entrepreneurial energy, but unproductive of any major success.

Carpenter's socialist writings made him a cult figure, and his admirers tried hard to turn him into a sage, a charismatic figure at whose feet they were eager to sit. This he very sensibly declined to allow, for he was homosexual. In a period when the trial and disgrace of Oscar Wilde marked the limit of public tolerance of fashionable decadence, he sought to make the condition of deviant sexuality, or Uranianism, as he called it, respectable.

After *Civilisation: its Cause and Cure* appeared in 1889, a text-book for the Back to the Land movement in which he developed further his ideas on the return to Nature and simplicity, *Love Comes of Age* in 1896 and *The Intermediate Sex* in 1908 chart the emergence from the closet. In casting off his class background – symbolised by the giving away of his dress-suit – Carpenter also shed conventional attitudes to sex. Both books plead the need for tolerance and understanding of sexual varieties and needs, and showed many troubled homosexuals how to come to terms with their condition. In 1898 he set up an independent household with a young working-class lover, who remained with him until his death at the age of eighty-five, in 1929.

How much Carpenter's advocacy of free love and personal relations that were unconstrained by laws or conventional expectations had to do with the break-up of Robert Stark's marriage one cannot say. It took some thirty years for the two Stark cousins to acknowledge that their ambitions were irreconcilable, and to agree to part company. Robert Stark held on stubbornly to beliefs which, followed to their logical outcome, led to the breakdown of family life, when Flora refused to commit herself and her daughters to a settler's life in the backwoods of Canada.

His obituary in the Creston weekly newspaper describes Robert Stark's success as an orchardist in 1921 and 1922 when, at the Empire Exhibition fruit shows in London, he acquired four gold, one silver and a bronze medal, as well as ten special prizes. He was active in backing all moves to promote the interests of the fruit industry in his area and was on the agricultural committee of the Creston Board of Trade. One of the prime movers for the East Creston irrigation system, in his last four years of life he was making a name for himself as a producer of daffodil and tulip bulbs for export.

The obituary also records that in private life the good turns done to others less fortunate than himself won for him the well-deserved respect of the whole community. This came as rather a surprise to me. Freya implies that he was only too prone to be taken in by glib lame ducks and that his unbusinesslike nature cost his dependants a lot of money.

The buttresses to Freya's self-esteem in youth were successful older people. Her upbringing explains this. She was rarely with companions of her own age, there was only her younger and more passive sister for company. To win applause set the seal on her own self-approbation; Freya as a child exacted attention from her parents' friends and enforced their participation in her imaginative games and preoccupations. That the adults should respond was part of the liberated ethos of the period, a revolt against the strictness of their own Victorian upbringing. The belief that children should be seen and not heard was going out of fashion in progressive circles.

The original impulse towards a simpler life had come from John Ruskin in the 1870s, developed by William Morris in the next generation and formed into a new aesthetic. It is the sympathetic link between Freya and Sydney Cockerell's own young manhood. Both Ruskin and Morris were heroes of Cockerell's youth, to whom he attached himself in the performance of various voluntary secretarial duties. In him, throughout his long life, there remained this strain of idealism, the elevation in default of conventional religious belief of artistic truth and beauty and simplicity to a sort of Holy Grail, to be sought with passionate sincerity, and recognised when found.

Freya's own youth was spent among people who all, in their different ways, were believers. They believed in Art for Art's sake and the worship of Beauty if they were artists, and in Futurism and modern technology if they were Italians like her brother-in-law Mario di Roascio, or in a diffused humanitarian socialism if they were feminists like Flora, and in the superiority of the Real World to the Ideal if they were Professor Ker. Irony or scepticism rarely coloured their viewpoints, and Freya grew up in a world where belief was acted on to the best of everyone's ability.

The difficulties between Flora and Robert Stark possibly began with how the children were brought up. Robert Stark was not an aggressive man, but he was tenacious of his views, and subversive of what he disapproved. Flora, at the age of seventeen when she married, was uncritical, enthusiastic, talented, with bouncing energy and high spirits. Of what happened in the succeeding thirteen years of childless marriage there is no clue. Freya never offered any explanation of this, which was followed by the birth in rapid succession of three children, in 1891, 1893 and 1895. It suggests an active sexual life on the part of parents who were progressive enough to employ contraception, or an attempt to cement, through parenthood, a marriage which for unexplained reasons was breaking down. The evasiveness and dissimulation of Freya's account of her own and her parents' lives is centred on the sexual aspects.

Perhaps the death of Flora's first child in 1891, the year of his birth, sobered her, though when Freya was born in 1893 her arrival was unlooked for and premature; she was a seven-months baby, very small, for whom nothing was prepared. The birth took place in a Paris studio where the couple were living while attending classes at the Académie Julien, and the two men in the neighbouring studio, Herbert Olivier and Herbert Young, went out to buy a layette. Herbert Young startled the shop assistant on being asked how old the child was by stammering ingenuously, 'Half an hour,' a good story later used by Freya and attributed to her father. Cockerell painstakingly traced it back through Herbert Olivier's wife to its real source.

Concern for the Stark children on the part of friends was something that accompanied the household from its earliest days. Flora's slapdash exuberance and her pleasure in studio life may account for this. The children had to fit into their parents' lives, carried about on their migrations as an animal shifts its cubs from one territory to another. They were extensions of the parental personality rather than particular individuals; more sensitive understanding was slow in coming.

Freya's babyhood in Asolo began when she was about a year old. Her parents rented rooms there so as to be on hand to help their well-to-do bachelor friend Herbert Young rebuild the small house on the ramparts of the hilltop town he had bought in 1887 from the local priest. Freya's sister Vera was born in 1895 and the Stark children throughout their childhood were regular visitors to Herbert Young's house there. The dramatic circumstances of Freya's premature birth in Paris, and the coincidence of a shared birthday, made him a special property of the child, while his own delight in schoolboy tales of adventure was rekindled by the books he presented at Christmas and birthdays to the children. Sitting on the floor, with an arm around each sister, he would read his old favourites to them by the hour, something that rather bored Vera, while Freya's vivid imagination seized on the dramatic aspects of the story and saw knights in armour, dragons, pirates and all the other ingredients of romance as elements of an imaginary world in which she was chief.

The making of Herbert Young's house and garden at Asolo, which was to form such an important element in Freya's history, is well documented, for like many painters of his period, he was interested in photography, and used it in his work. He built a darkroom in his studio, and developed and printed his photographs. In time he passed these skills on to Freya.

Among the carefully bound volumes of Freya's own photographs is a collection of Herbert Young's records of Asolo and the neighbouring small towns as they were when he first came there in the 1880s. They are selected from the hundreds of negatives Freya found in a drawer in his studio in 1949 and had printed with a view to making a book of them.

It is the background against which the earliest scenes of Freya's life are deployed. The life of the people is geared to the pace of their oxen and mules, slow-moving, rustic and organic, expressions of a reality which gave a texture to the life of the countryside which no modern conservation can hope to match. There are many pictures of the rebuilding of the house and the making of its garden and of the circle of friends who met there, and who stayed for long weeks at a time. The interior of the house is recorded, full of polished-wood surfaces, woven draperies, large hand-made pieces of furniture, ceramics and paintings. It is dark, sombre, solid, for the Arts and Crafts influence of the South Kensington School had shaped the taste of Herbert Young's generation and William Morris had imprinted their imaginations with an ideal of the Simple Life devoted to artistic pursuits, in surroundings of natural beauty.

It might be assumed from the photographic evidence that this was the Starks' native environment, but the reality is different. Even Freya admits that for a couple so devoted to artistic pursuits, her parents spent a lot of time in lodgings or in small ugly houses which they were either rebuilding or renting.[3] Between 1892 and 1897 both the Starks sent in work to the Royal Academy – landscape and genre scenes from Italy – but the addresses they gave were Robert Stark's mother's house in Torquay, or Chagford on Dartmoor, or the studios of painter friends in London. They were never property owners in Asolo; they came to help Herbert Young make his house artistic and comfortable, and to advise on the garden he was making on the hillside, where the remains of a small Roman theatre formed a little knoll. Whether the relationship was on a professional basis is not disclosed.

Seen against the background of the small Renaissance town, the life of the foreigners seems protected and idyllic. They have imported their own style and make few concessions to local ways. Herbert Young and Mrs Olivier play the cello and violin together, face to face on solid wooden chairs, in front of an open fireplace. The men wear Norfolk jackets and tweed knickerbockers, the women the waisted hour-glass jackets and long skirts of the period, with big hats pinned to their heads. Good-looking Herbert Young – Giovanni to his friends – his trilby hat set straight on his golden curls, stands before his easel with his paint-box slung around his neck, and paints yet another view of the blossoming fruit orchards creaming down to the plain below. Robert Stark, also in a trilby, dandles the chubby befrilled and petticoated infant Freya on the terrace. Only the poet's son, Pen Browning, round-faced and corpulent, who dabbled in property and had found the house for Herbert Young, wears an Italian straw boater tilted over his eyes, and looks jolly.

The Stark children appear regularly throughout the series. The two little girls are always together. There is something a little solemn, a little constrained, in their manner, as if they are on their best behaviour. They are dressed alike, and look up seriously into the camera lens, or concentrate dutifully on their books or their game of chess, though Freya is also recorded making a derisive face at the camera. Sometimes they are draped artistically in Greek tunics or Japanese kimonos, at other times they are posed naked among the flowers, shrimpy little creatures, with great mops of thick curly hair.

As they grow bigger, they are in England on Dartmoor where hand in hand with their father they walk out across the moor, their pinafore dresses fluttering in the wind. Then they are back in Italy, in Belluno, or later on in Piedmont where they appear planted in bleak upland settings, or posed on boulders, vast folds of mountain rimming the horizon. Herbert Young used to

bicycle over from Asolo to visit them in Piedmont, a ride of
several days across the Lombardian plain, and the record continues up to and beyond the accident that befell Freya there in
1906, and which necessitated the shaving off of her thick luxuriant hair.

Robert Stark's fidelity to his own intellectual discoveries and
his determined adoption of ruralism as a way of life at the turn
of the century led the family first to Surrey and finally home to
Devon and to Arts and Crafts experiments in house building
and landscape gardening. The concept of the master craftsman
designing every detail of a building was adhered to conscientiously, something Freya was to follow with somewhat uneven
results when she turned to house building in Italy in the 1960s.
The children were allowed within limits to run free, and this
perhaps accounts for the concern for them evinced by Flora's
friends. In their father's view, individuality was all that mattered. Artistic and intellectual skills were not to be forced on
a child, but fostered only if they manifested spontaneously in
the course of its development; the child itself was not to be
turned into a performing monkey by mechanical training. Nor
was there to be any baptism or religious indoctrination; when
the child was old enough it could choose its own form of worship.

Such an absence of direction was something Freya rather
basely held against her parents in adult life; though the sheltered
nature of her upbringing and the lack of outside companionship
undoubtedly contributed to the idiosyncrasy of her fullblown
personality. Physical skills, however, were encouraged. Perhaps Robert Stark would have preferred his girls to be boys,
for he brought them up as such. He taught them to ride, to ski,
to swim, exercises at which Freya never excelled, while from
early childhood they were trained to accompany him on his
tramps and cycle rides about the countryside, and to be shown
the delights of field and hedgerow. *His* children were to be
brought up in the freedom of a natural environment, little animals socialised only by patience and kindness. Freya records
instances of silent sympathy when she was punished, mute
associations in which he took her hand as she stood, tear-stained
and obstinate in a corner, refusing to apologise for some misde-

meanour. Smacking and punishment had no effect on her other than to increase her stubbornness.

The German grandmother's influence on the upbringing of her grand-daughters was in the ascendant in the early years. Flora had a German maid in the Paris studio; then a German governess appeared. German was the earliest language of the nursery. Madeline Stark's views in matters of child care, and the upbringing of daughters, were important. After all, it had been her profession, and the feeling that in William Stark she had married a husband socially beneath her reinforced the value she attached to good manners and a good appearance. The tone of voice inculcated, the fastidiousness of mind displayed, were quite different from Robert Stark's Simple Life and a pantheistic response to Nature. Interest in wild life in southern England meant nothing to his mother-in-law, whatever it did for him.

The battle between the parents for the supremacy of their differing viewpoints intensified when they moved from Surrey to Devon where Robert Stark joined his brother Playters in a nurseryman's business, Stark Bros, Chagford, specialists in conifers and rhododendrons. This was not a reassuring association for Flora. She found her brother-in-law unsympathetic, while from the early years of her marriage she retained an aversion to the stuffiness of Starkite society in Exeter and Torquay.

William Stark's daughters had grown up in Italy unaware of their father's antecedents. The aristocratic associations of their mother's family were more important. To Flora, on her first introduction to Torquay, her Stark relatives were less than congenial; she found them stilted and provincial after the easier manners in which she had grown up. The return to Devon in 1897 was a compromise she would have preferred to avoid. But Flora had no money of her own and consequently no independence; in the final outcome she had to follow her husband's decisions.

The failure of the Stark parents to present a united front on questions of upbringing had its effect on Freya once she grew out of infancy. It taught her to edit her responses. Her inability to stomach correction, a trait that remained with her all her life, seems to have begun early. The first lessons in reading and writing were begun with the German governess. In old age, this woman figured largely in Freya's recollections of her childhood. She seems to have been the focal point in the parents' conflicting views on what constituted a proper upbringing for their daughters. Freya always said she was sadistic. She left when the child was eight, to be succeeded by a young Italian who remained with the family until Freya was fourteen, when all pretence of formal education ceased and Freya educated herself by correspondence course and omnivorous reading until she entered London University.

The German governess, in Freya's account, was a sentimental fool who formed an emotional attachment to Flora. German notions of correct upbringing for children placed importance on modesty of manner. Children and young people were not expected to demand attention, or to be rude and answer back. Fraulein's attempts to instil discipline and manners into her charges evoked the subversive spirit in Robert Stark, who disapproved of any form of artificiality in human relations.

His emphasis on the male virtue of daring, with the screwing up of nerve to meet a challenge, was underlined by a system of reward when the children performed satisfactorily. Sleeping out on summer nights on the lawn in front of the house was encouraged; resting on the bosom of Nature was believed to promote a healthy and harmonious disposition. The girls were not expected to panic at the nocturnal sounds of the Wild, rustling and stirring in the undergrowth and uttering its unpredictable grunts and cries. A solitary traverse of a copse or spinney, still and shadowy in the twilight, would earn a tip for a child bold enough to venture it.

As they left childhood behind Robert Stark's impatience at any physical ineptitude, combined with a fiercely competitive spirit at games, reduced Vera early on to silence and self-effacement. Dispatched alone from Italy as adolescents in 1907 and 1908 to visit him – now a quasi-stranger – at Chagford, the girls were expected to join in his sporting activities, and to follow hounds on the ponies he bred and broke for them. It is perhaps not surprising that they aroused comment and curiosity when they appeared in the hunting field in cut-down breeches of his own, so that their sex was in doubt, at a period when the side-saddle and the riding-habit were the conventional equipment of the horsewoman.

But it was his financial stringency and strictness in practical details that most frightened and disheartened them. To bring a pony in hot from a gallop excited his wrath. Vera suffered from anxious timidity in his presence, but Freya, a tougher spirit, learned how to withstand her fear and get around him. He was difficult about money and it required courage to approach him on the subject. Freya in 1911, at the age of eighteen, overdrew her pin-money allowance of £40 a year by about £10 and, desperate under the pressure of this debt, finally screwed up enough nerve to tell him. In those last years when he was alone at Ford Park, Robert Stark picnicked rather than lived in the house. He had a bed moved down to his ground-floor office, a narrow deal-boarded room sandwiched between the dining-room and his studio, where it shared the space with his desk and seed catalogues and account books. It was a truer expression of his personality than Flora's long drawing-room with its gleaming floor, copper bowls, lustre and silken shawls and cushions. Freya records her sense of stunned relief when he accepted the debt without comment. 'He pushed an island among the papers inch deep on his desk, to rest his cheque book on. It was almost as overwhelming as a revelation of omnipotence.'[4]

Freya was self-conscious about this aspect of herself. Fearlessness once lost, she noted in her journal on New Year's Day in 1929, as by a tumble out sledging, was difficult to regain, and the effort to get it back showed her the advisability of never letting herself get out of practice. It explains many things in her life. She forced herself to take risks as a test of nerve, first climbing in the Alps after W. P. Ker's death, then venturing into lawless territory, perhaps even accepting the sexual implications of marriage. Contrary to her admirers' beliefs, she did not enjoy danger for its own sake, but some natural resilience in her make-up, a vitality independent of intellect and will, ensured that the actuality of danger would be met with instinctive courage and coolness, whatever nightmares of anticipation invaded the imagination beforehand. She herself has said that the delight of mountaineering is the passing through fear to the absence of fear, which is where the reward lies. I couldn't help thinking there was something punishingly masochistic about this dedication to the extreme situation.

TWENTY

DRONERO AND ST JOHN'S WOOD

In the 1890s, when the Robert Starks took up residence there, Chagford was no longer a small farming community, it was a developing holiday resort with a scattering of large, often recently built houses in the vicinity. An early arrival was the Victorian landscape painter Alfred Fripp, whose fine, stone-built manor house Easton Court, just outside the town, was inherited by his daughter Mary Androutsos some years before the Starks arrived in Chagford. She was a childless widow and rather 'took up' Flora, so that a friendship formed which survived all the subsequent displacements of the younger woman. 'Aunt Mary' was a regular presence in the formative years of the Stark girls, a channel of introduction to a society other than the local community.

Flora Stark gravitated naturally towards this. Her vivacity, good looks and social talents attracted people to her. Her women friends remained constant, while she never lacked other admirers. Perhaps it was her vitality that drew towards her people who welcomed the element of decisiveness that she brought into their lives. A gust of good-hearted, Teutonic forcefulness comes through all her communications. Even the pet names the mother and daughters bandied about so cheerfully in their correspondence – Pips, Bumps, Biri, Grassig – have an un-English sound, alien to the sobriety of the Starkite community.

The loss of Ford Park and its life of recognised status and

comfortable independence loomed large in Freya's mature evocation of her upbringing. In old age, Ford Park, when I asked her, was claimed as her proper home. Yet the record does not substantiate the recollection. Mrs Mary Androutsos is listed in the County Directory at Easton Court in the 1890s; Robert Stark only appears at Ford Park in 1902, and in 1903 Flora and the children were installed in a rented villa in Piedmont, after a winter spent in the grandmother's house in Torquay. The children were not to see Ford Park again until 1907 and 1908, when the two adolescent girls were sent alone on visits to their father there, being met and looked after by Viva Jeyes on their passage to and from Devon through London. The second visit was in winter, and they arrived at Ford Park, late at night, unheralded and unexpected, to their father's irritated surprise.

After 1903, Mary Androutsos followed Flora into her self-imposed Italian exile. She was affectionate, artistic, muddled, imprudent, always in financial difficulties, but she took the girls off Flora's hands for long periods, and afforded them some relief from their life at Dronero. To Freya's surprise, she preferred Vera to herself, and took a particular interest in the girl's development; she believed the child needed a more careful fostering than she was receiving, and would benefit by removal from her sister's dominance.

Flora's eventual abdication of Ford Park and her position as Robert Stark's wife may have caused her no regrets, but it hurt Freya. Writing to Cockerell from Cyprus in 1942, she could think back to the few years of childhood spent in Surrey and Devon as a sort of earthly paradise, a haven of security and a real home. It was an emotional recapture during a period of danger and stress of a world in which adults were kindly Olympians. The serpent, Freya could see, that drove her out of this Eden was her brother-in-law, Mario di Roascio, and his baleful incursion into their lives, she told Sydney Cockerell, was the only thing she regretted about the past.

The young Italian came to England through the agency of Flora's mother and her school in Genoa, in 1900 or 1901, and was passed on to the Robert Starks by one of Flora's sisters, married to a social-settlement worker in London. A short, bouncing, energetic university student, he was at an age when young men are sent abroad to improve their languages and to widen their knowledge of the world. Robert Stark took him about with him, tramping and riding around the countryside and explaining his afforestation contracts and building work to him. They got on well together. Both were practical men, and the visit was a success.

A year or so later, Mario joined Flora Stark and the children for another visit, this time while they were summering in the Dolomites after a winter spent by the Starks in lodgings at Asolo. This was in 1902, when Freya was rising ten, and the children were in the charge of a young Italian governess. He was to make himself useful escorting them on their walks, while he practised his English.

In 1903 the Starks, following their usual practice throughout Freya's childhood, rented a small villa for a temporary stay, this time in Piedmont in the north-west of Italy, where the di Roascios had property. The Blanchi di Roascio family was one ennobled at the time of the unification of Italy in 1861 by a king whose origins were in Piedmont and Savoy. The title of Count descends in the senior male line of the family; Mario was the younger son of the second holder of the title, the cadet of a family whose head lived mostly in Rome.

The family's place of origin was Dronero, a straggling, medieval hill-town which lies in the elbow of the Maritime and Cottian Alps, on the edge of the Piedmontese plain. Perched on a bluff overlooking a pale green river, it is twelve miles from Cuneo, the local market town. Though they did not realise it, Flora and the children were to remain there for another sixteen years.

As was by now the pattern of their domestic life, Robert Stark came out at intervals to join his family there, then retired to his own occupations at Chagford. Flora meanwhile, as was also usual, assembled around herself her sisters, their children and family friends. She kept up her painting, and took an interest in what was going on about her.

The break-up of the Stark marriage was precipitated by the death in Torquay of Robert Stark's mother in or about 1905. Once their mother's estate was settled, her two surviving sons began planning emigration to the Dominions. This was not something that appealed to Flora Stark, and she instinctively looked for a way out. It presented itself in the shape of a manufacturing enterprise in Dronero, on which young Mario di Roascio had recently embarked. In tune with the Futurist ideology finding expression in northern Italy at this period, he planned to turn the site of a small local basket-making enterprise into a modern factory, powered by turbine-driven electricity from the river. In it he would produce coir-matting, doormats and carpets.

Flora was impressed with his ideas. The design and dyeing aspects of the work appealed to her bent towards craftwork. Without telling her husband, soon after the family was installed in Dronero, she lent di Roascio £1600 as a short-term loan to modernise his investment, and began to take an increasingly active interest in the enterprise. How such a sum came into Flora's hands is never explained. Either in some mysterious way money trickled through to William Stark's descendants, when long-lived Stark widows died off and capital was dispersed, or this was part of a capital sum, set aside by Robert Stark to support Flora and the children while the gradual disposal of the older generation's property continued, and plans went ahead for emigration.

Freya in later life believed her mother was taken in by di Roascio, who exploited her unworldliness by pandering to her artistic bent. She bitterly resented the engulfing of Stark – and by inference, her own – money in this venture, and this was built into her dislike of her future brother-in-law. The money, once invested, was soon swallowed up, and short of bankrupting Mario's enterprise, there was no way of taking it out.

No-one told Robert Stark in England of his wife's action. When I asked Freya, in Asolo, why this was so, she replied tartly, as if it was self-evident, that the truth would have upset her father. I was surprised; this was rather at variance with her more sentimental portrayal of her parent in her autobiography. By a cruel irony, it was Freya who inadvertently was the cause of her mother's imprudence being revealed.

*   *   *

One day in January 1906, just prior to Freya's thirteenth birthday, when new machinery had been installed in the factory, the children and their governess were invited to inspect the innovation and to share in the triumph of the achievement. Mario showed them around. No independent report of how the accident occurred survives, but it seems a draught from a revolving steel shaft caught a tress of Freya's long loose curling hair and she was snatched up, her head ground against the shaft, her feet floating horizontally in the seconds before Mario snatched her free. Running repairs were effected on the spot by the local doctor who stitched Freya's eyelid back in place, but something more was needed for the head wound, where a whole clump of hair had been wrenched out. Mario arranged for her to be moved to Turin where a new technique of skin-grafting was used to patch her head. Her mother's entire attention was devoted to comforting and sustaining Freya through the ordeal of the very painful dressings she had to endure.

Some thirty years later, with her first literary success, Freya submitted herself secretly to plastic surgery in London and had the scars about her eyelid and brow removed,[1] though faint residual marks about the eyebrow and temple were still just discernible in old age. The bare patch on the side of the head where the clump of hair caught in the machine was torn out remained, and was a source of chagrin to the girl and an element in her resentment of Mario di Roascio. He was privately held responsible for the disaster. Sydney Cockerell, probing in 1942 into Freya's history, was told by Lady Lawrence, a neighbour of the Starks in Asolo, that the cruel accident in Dronero was made worse because 'instead of stopping the machinery the idiot subsequent brother-in-law pulled her down, thereby scalping her'.[2] Mario's incompetence and Flora's mistaken confidence in him became an article of faith in the circle of Freya's English friends. This episode perhaps contains the kernel of her abiding dislike of her brother-in-law, which she proclaimed in 1950 on the last page of *Traveller's Prelude*.

Freya's accident and the partial disfigurement that resulted gave her a special status among the adults surrounding her, which the slow painful process of skin-grafting enhanced. Her

mother hung over her in anguished concentration and devoted
the entire force of her powerful nature to overcoming the shock
Freya had sustained. Her parents put aside their differences
during the crisis and after two months her father came out from
England to be with her in Turin when Flora returned to Dronero
to look after Mario's factory.

Everyone was kind and concerned for the poor little girl,
whose thick luxuriant hair was shaved off to enable the surgeon
to work effectively. Gradually it grew back into short curls
which mitigated but did not entirely conceal the skin-graft on
the side of the head where no hair grew. Her mother made her
cotton bonnets, edged with lace, which tied under the chin, to
hide the disfigurement until it was hoped nature would repair
the deficiency; and in doing so she perhaps inadvertently
implanted in the child a self-consciousness about her disfigurement that Freya never overcame. It is a strange thing that in old
age Freya resurrected these bonnets. They were of a singularly
unbecoming pattern and drew attention to her head; she liked
to wear them informally about the house, where they added a
grotesque element to her appearance that photographers were
quick to seize on.

Up to the accident her sister Vera, who was placid and pretty,
had been the 'good' child of the family. Now Vera was eclipsed.
Freya monopolised everyone's attention, while Vera withdrew
gradually into silence and loss of spirits. For Freya the transition
from the hardiness of her upbringing by parents who were
inherently healthy and strong, to constant anxious attention and
sympathy was a revelation, intoxicating to her self-esteem. She
felt herself the most important person in the family, as her
mother's anxious care concentrated itself on her to the exclusion
of everything else. Despite the pain she endured during the
dressing of her wounds as the skin-grafting proceeded, Freya's
accident enshrined for her a blissful period when she was envel-
oped in the warmth of her mother's personality and could command her entire attention. It set up a pattern in her relationships
with people she loved that made her a demanding friend.

As the years went by and Flora became increasingly involved
in di Roascio's business, and Vera drifted towards marriage and

maternity, Freya's own disappointments and frustrations turned inward and sought a counter-balancing security in a dreamy absorption in the books provided by her German grandmother or found in her mother's bookshelves. Narcissus, rather than Eros, presided over these reveries. It was hard for her, so much cleverer and quicker than her sister, to understand why she had been passed over, once Vera's engagement with di Roascio was agreed in 1912; she rationalised this as due to her damaged looks. In Italy a girl was expected to marry young; Vera conformed to the Italian pattern and was married and a mother before she was twenty, while Freya was left on the shelf.

Freya's nature was proud. It was now that assuaging compensatory devices perhaps first came into play. Her mother was no use, she had promoted Mario, a betrayal externalised in Freya's accounts of her own jealous adolescent attempts to rival him. These took the form, first of protecting Flora from di Roascio's demands on her attention, and secondly of saving Vera from being absorbed into his Italian life. Both episodes ended in defeat,[3] with the sisters sobbing their hearts out in each other's arms in bed; Flora off to the theatre with di Roascio in one case and Vera about to be baptised into the Roman Catholic Church and married to him the next day in the other.

The similarity of both scenes was odd and set me wondering about the reliability of Freya as a witness in the story of her youth. Why did Mario have to be such a villain? There is an element in Freya's account, a vehemence of dislike held on to for so long, for which allegations of financial dishonesty, unsuccessfully substantiated in court, are hardly sufficient to account. An affronted sensibility hides itself in many disguises. Freya as a girl loved and longed to please her mother. She wanted to fall in love and be married like everyone else, as her mother wished for her, but the men she fell for were always much older than herself. Those who figure in her account of her young womanhood, W. P. Ker, Bernard d'Hendrecourt, the di Bottinis and the Bianchieris, were middle-aged, while Guido Ruata, her only documented suitor, was in the same age group as her brother-in-law, eighteen years older than herself.

Her father's withdrawal from his daughters' lives after they arrived in Dronero contributed to Freya's emotional confusion. In those important years Freya had no-one except her mother with whom to fall in love. Her jealousy of Mario di Roascio put him out of contention. Never having attended school, she had never experienced, or had the opportunity to observe, the 'crushes' of younger girls for their seniors, or for their teachers. Freya's 'crush' was her mother, when in 1906 the full force of Flora's personality was focused on her daughter, torn and damaged by the accident in Mario's factory.

What brought about the final showdown between the parents in 1906 was Flora's loan of £1600 to di Roascio, either disclosed to or discovered by Robert Stark during his visit to Freya's hospital bedside. Despite the availability of capital after his mother's death, he did not make up Flora's loss and returned to Chagford once Freya was discharged from hospital. From now on Flora, at the age of forty-five, was on her own, dependent on her own exertions to maintain her household and very hard up. Perhaps her husband thought this would bring her to heel, but he miscalculated. An early economy was the Italian governess who after seven years with the Starks was passed on to an American family in Asolo. Freya continued to educate herself by reading omnivorously and took a correspondence course with a view to attending a summer school in Switzerland. She was coached for this by her German grandmother, who was imported to be with the girls while Flora worked full-time as manager at the factory and Mario travelled about developing the sales network. This scheme came to nothing as Robert Stark refused to provide the fees.

It was at this period that Freya's dislike of Mario di Roascio took more detailed form, as he extolled the advantages of practical training in things like book-keeping and housekeeping to the girls. Vera was dreamy and didn't take too much notice, but Freya resented it. She hated her mother's involvement in the factory; she hated the hold it had on her attention. After the intoxicating period following her accident when all her mother's concern was focused on herself, it was difficult to resume the detached life of the schoolroom, especially as, with the departure of the governess, the schoolroom no longer existed.

Freya at fourteen and fifteen was too immature to have any understanding of her mother's needs. She only saw her own. That Flora could obtain a satisfaction and a sense of achievement from her work was beyond her comprehension. To comfortably off Edwardians like Herbert Young and the family's London friends, Flora's determination to be independent appeared unnatural. The association with di Roascio offended their sense of propriety and they 'feared the worst', so that even mild Herbert Young, so Freya said, in 1913 abstained from suggesting Vera be married from Asolo, something that Flora had confidently expected would be offered.

In 1907 Flora finally turned to her friend Viva Jeyes in London for advice on how to obtain for Freya the education she clearly needed and deserved. Mrs Jeyes consulted her friend Professor W. P. Ker, who had the Chair of English at University College, London. Freya was introduced to him at Viva's when passing through London with her sister in 1908, on a visit to their father in Devon. Ker suggested London University as a possible solution. If she matriculated as an external student by correspondence course a way forward would be open to her. Dronero remained Freya's home. In this shabby little backwater the Stark girls grew up, Freya working conscientiously at the correspondence course arranged for her on Professor Ker's advice by Viva. Her eager mind welcomed the opportunity to increase her intellectual development and she enjoyed the work. In 1911, at the age of eighteen, she came to London to live with Viva while she attended college.

Professor Ker expressed no further interest in the girl until she entered the matriculation class at Bedford College. This class, subsequently discontinued, enabled students irregularly educated, often abroad, to supplement their external course with a final year's supervised work in London. Accepted in 1912 at Bedford College as an undergraduate to read English, in her second year Freya switched from literature to history but she never completed the course as war came in the summer vacation of 1914 and she did not return to England from Italy.

Viva Jeyes' friendship with the Starks dated from the earliest period of the marriage of Freya's parents. An American by birth, she had grown up and married in the interlocking literary, political and artistic circles that were so influential in pre-1914 London society. Her husband was Harry Jeyes, deputy editor on the conservative *Morning Standard* newspaper. A slim, beautiful, golden-haired girl and woman, widowed in 1911 and childless, she was well-off and independent and shared a house in St John's Wood with her old stepfather, Edwin Bale, Robert Stark's tutor at the South Kensington School of Art in the 1870s. Retired in 1907 from the Art directorship of Cassells' publishing house, he was still involved with the Arts establishment of the capital.

Viva was Honorary Secretary of the Women's National Anti-Suffrage League, founded in 1908 by Mrs Humphry Ward, the best-selling popular novelist and pioneer social worker, when Votes for Women first became practical politics. An effective speaker, Mrs Ward travelled about the country lecturing public audiences on the issue of women's suffrage, which she opposed. *Persuasion* was one of her key concepts, and this note of calm rationality was an aspect of the women's anti-suffrage movement which contrasted with the increased stridency and violence of the militant suffragettes.

Freya, when she came to London in September 1911 to live with Viva, was drawn into these concerns. She accompanied her to committee rooms and was introduced to Mrs Humphry Ward. She was sent out to canvass for the League and attended a monster anti-suffrage rally at the Albert Hall in February 1912, a boisterous affair with much heckling and abuse from the suffragettes and their sympathisers. She was introduced to Lord Cromer, leader of the anti-suffrage parliamentary party, by Viva. What with this and the literary men of an older generation whom she met at Viva's dinner table, or encountered in the course of afternoon calls among her circle of friends, the girl was being brought forward and polished in a way her own more provincial relations could not supply.

Mary Ward was a grand-daughter of Dr Arnold of Rugby; her uncle was Matthew Arnold. Through Viva, Freya at an impressionable age was introduced, however fleetingly, to people by nature and upbringing resistant to the snobbery of wealth and aggressive philistinism, whose manners were simple, whose ideas were clear-cut, and whose educational formation was idealistic and public-spirited. The household in St John's Wood was a world away from that of Freya's previous upbringing; now she was experiencing 'a cool, sequestered, upper-class existence', something she recognised and for which she was grateful. Her own background with its financial constraints and embarrassing eccentricities had no place in the Jeyes' household's smoothly running, well-maintained domestic arrangements. Viva was conscientious about Freya, as well as affectionate and kind; people assumed she was Freya's godmother.[4] Such careful consideration was rather a novelty for the girl; there wasn't too much of it around in the busy, pressured household in Dronero, dominated by the expanding needs of Mario di Roascio's business and harassed by Flora's lack of money and time.

With Viva, Freya experienced a life that was quiet, comfortable and secure, protected by the conventions of the society in which she found herself. That measuring up to such a standard might be something of a strain to one introduced late to it is sometimes hinted in Freya's recollections. She described Viva in 1913 as already rather old-fashioned, careful about chaperonage and strict over promises, engagements, or even casual remarks, but Freya knew where her bread was buttered and profited from the experience. She was tactful where the slangy, emancipated, cigarette-smoking products of the new girls' schools and colleges might be brusque and offhand. An affectation of mannishness was fashionable in such circles. 'The New Woman is neither a lady nor a gentleman' was a phrase of the period. She listened intelligently and modestly to dinner-table conversation and learned how to draw her partners out by adroit questioning. They tended to be older men and kindly disposed towards Viva's little protégée. Young men were more rarely encountered.

*   *   *

The decision by Robert Stark to sell the Ford Park estate was taken in 1910, and emigration to Canada in association with his brother Playters planned and put in hand when the elder brother went out to Canada and bought adjoining ranches for himself and Robert Stark at Creston in the Kootenay district of British Columbia. Devon Ranch, of approximately fifty acres, the elder brother's property, had an already established eleven-acre fruit orchard, while Robert Stark's thirty-acre Broken Hill Ranch was cleared but mainly unplanted.[5]

The family was briefly reunited at Ford Park in 1911. Freya recalls it as a happy time. The parents were relaxed and satisfied at the resolution of their problems; the separation was agreed amicably, and it was left to Flora to empty the house on completion of its sale to the Duchy of Cornwall. Flora reactivated old neighbourhood friendships; the girls enjoyed the companionship of young people of their own age. In the summer of 1912 the sale of Ford Park was finalised, and Flora came over from Dronero with the two girls, now aged nineteen and seventeen, accompanied by Mario di Roascio and his mother. The young people rode about the moors, and the two mothers came to an agreement on the formal engagement of Vera to Mario. Only Freya remained overlooked and alone.

With his departure in 1911 Robert Stark may be said to have ceased to exist as a parent for his daughters, except in Freya's mind. Thereafter he only appeared occasionally in England, or in Italy, as for Vera's wedding in 1913, and at the beginning of World War I and at its end, when he was persuaded to buy for Freya the flower farm at La Mortola, which became her and her mother's home in 1920. His policy towards his family was one of emotional detachment, and an unwillingness to be embroiled in their concerns; as soon as his business was completed he lost no time in getting back to Canada. He had little or no interest in maintaining old friendships or associations, something to which Freya clung with limpet-like tenacity.

TWENTY-ONE

ENGAGEMENT AND AFTERMATH

What no-one in St John's Wood or Dronero anticipated was that once war broke out in 1914, Freya would reject any thought of further education and express a spirited desire to join a voluntary organisation and nurse soldiers. All the young women of her age in England were doing such things, and Freya wanted to be like them. In the uprush of patriotism war work became acceptable even in families whose daughters hitherto had been kept at home until marriage.

In Italy such emancipation was distrusted. Freya's wish to become a VAD worried Flora and outraged Mario; only as a nun could a woman retain her respectability in such an employment! There was no patriotic precedent for a well-brought-up girl to endanger her reputation by exposure to the immodesty of hospital nursing. The country was neutral and it was only after Italy's entry into the war in 1915 that the Duchess of Aosta gave the lead to upper-class women to join the Red Cross organisation. But Freya persisted and eventually Flora gave way. A compromise was arrived at. It was Flora's old friend Mary Androutsos who found the solution. She was friendly with the Ruata family of Perugia, a well-known family of physicians, and it was through the head of the family that a place for the girl was found at a clinic in Bologna where his son, Dr Guido Ruata, a bacteriologist, was a member of the staff.

Freya went to Bologna to start her nursing training in November 1914. By her twenty-second birthday, at the end of January

1915, she was already infatuated with Guido (Quirino) Ruata. Her 'crush' developed rapidly under the simpering encouragement of the Italian girls she was now meeting, and the careless chaperonage of her landlady, a retired English governess with whom Flora had placed her daughter for safety. It was fanned with well-meaning ineptitude by Mario, who made it his business early on to sound Ruata out as to his intentions. Ruata replied that he had none.

Freya attributes her own recognition of her detestation of her brother-in-law to this episode. Bologna was the first time Freya lived away from the protection of her family and friends; news of what was happening there soon reached Dronero and confirmed Mario's fears of Freya's likely imprudence. She was falling between the two stools of the conventions of her Italian upbringing and the casualness of English manners. Soon she would have no reputation left!

Meanwhile, in Bologna, Freya's silent, stage-struck adoration was having its effect on Guido Ruata. He began to take notice of her. The tenuous social connection between their families facilitated this, and he took to calling on her at her lodgings. Long, intimate talks followed, often late into the evening. Alerted once more, Mario acted. His sister-in-law was not some little Miss to be trifled with; family honour and the conventions of the arranged marriage entered into it.

Perhaps there was more to Mario's intervention than Freya in her account of events admitted. Ruata was a man of thirty-eight whose longstanding affair with an Italian woman had just broken up. A concert musician, she had terminated their liaison and gone to America, leaving Ruata to pick up the pieces. Under renewed pressure, Ruata capitulated; Freya's clinging infatuation and naive trust was balm to a spirit wounded by rejection. He and Freya were formally engaged at Easter 1915, a binding agreement in Italy, and it was expected that they would marry that summer.

Freya's romance, the only fully validated one in her life, and its collapse, took place over a period of little more than a year. Italy entered the war on the side of the Allies in May 1915 and Ruata was called to the colours in the medical corps. Freya pined at the separation but gave up her training and returned to Dronero to prepare her trousseau. The atmosphere there was not favourable to her romance, for Mario disapproved of Ruata and did not support the engagement, though Flora, eager for her daughter's happiness, threw herself energetically into the preparations.

Freya wrote daily to Ruata. Matters dragged on through the autumn, while her sister's first child died as an infant. In this sad and anxious time Freya was ailing and uneasy. As winter set in, she was found to be suffering from mild typhoid, later aggravated by pleurisy and then pneumonia, all serious illnesses at that period. Her convalescence was slow, and that further delayed the marriage. In the late spring of 1916 Viva Jeyes made her way out from England to Italy, and took Freya off to convalesce at Alassio.

By now wedding plans were advanced, a house for the couple had been found, and furniture designed for them by Flora was being made. Presents were arriving, and in June Freya wrote to her father and Professor Ker about dates and arrangements.

Abruptly, at this late stage, Ruata wrote to Freya at Alassio breaking off the engagement, offering no explanation other than that it was not her fault. Freya was devastated. Impervious to all advice, and accompanied by the anxious Viva, she insisted on going to plead with him. It was useless. He was obdurate, and Freya returned to Dronero in a state of emotional collapse. Early in August she was sent from Italy to Viva in London, and was there when news of Ruata's marriage to his former lover was relayed on the family grapevine. Freya bore up very stoutly under this, but Flora Stark behaved badly, descending on the mortified Ruata family in Perugia to make an angry scene, and being difficult about the financial costs of unscrambling all the preparations for the marriage. It was as if her rage and resentment at the injury done to Freya could only be expressed by making things as awkward as possible for Ruata. He himself finally appealed to Freya in London to call off her mother's lawyer, and this she exerted herself to do. It was a bitter humiliation to the girl that her romance should end in this unseemly fashion, and it opened up a rift in her confidence in her parent.

She was mortified and humiliated by her mother's rage against Ruata. She herself behaved well, with dignity and forbearance. Her mother's un-English behaviour was a source of pain and distress. 'You seem unable to understand what it means to have the memory of the happy days smirched over. Nothing, nothing could have hurt me like this,' she wrote. This note of angry despair persisted until Flora's intemperate emotion was brought under control, and Ruata was left in peace. 'There are things too personal and sacred for anyone to tamper with, and you had no right to spring this misery on me without my knowledge,' Freya cried.

Freya wanted to waste no time over spilt milk, she was concerned for her own reputation and dignity. By January 1917 she was writing to her mother, 'I am so glad of what you write about the gossip *à propos de moi* . . . if I have forgiven what he had done to me, you can forgive what he has or hasn't done to you. If he speaks well of me, that is all that matters, as that is all that concerns our good name . . .' The sooner the matter was definitely closed, the sooner she would be able to begin to try to forget. 'You are wrong to think I do this for Quirino (his pet name): I do it for myself. You do not seem able to understand that the hurt all this is to me is far greater than any satisfaction . . .'

From now on Freya's attitude to her mother was more detached and though the affectionate surface of the relationship remained, an ascendancy was established that found its expression in a conscientious loving subservience on Flora's part. This in turn masked Freya's own dependence on her mother. The intricate emotional knot that bound the two was reinforced rather than diminished by this apparent shift in the pattern of dominance within the relationship, for no other lover, no husband, appeared to complete the weaning away of Freya from her dependence on her mother's energy and supportive affection. But it left her vulnerable to new influences, and her tendency towards sudden infatuations was not diminished.

Freya, writing about her youth, refers to several such incidents. She claims they are early examples of her recognition of the quality of excellence in others. She was humble in her adorations, seeking no tangible recognition or awareness, content with the proximity of the admired object. It was the type of yearning, self-hypnotising infatuation that demands no response, something familiar to all prominent personalities; Freya herself in turn was to receive similar attentions from her own fans.

In its extreme form, when it steps out of the victim's control and assumes a reality of its own, this obsessive condition is recognised by medical science as de Clerambault's Syndrome. The French psychiatrist whose name is given to the syndrome described it in 1942 as *psychose passionelle*. He pointed out that the delusions of passion, the conviction that some secret understanding exists between the object of passion and oneself, is produced by the individual will and imagination in reveries or daydreams, and differs from paranoid delusions. These come unsolicited, from outside the personality, often in the shape of whispers, voices, commands that must be obeyed. In de Clerambault's view, 'pure' or sentimental infatuation is a symptom of disorder, rather than a cause. The condition is a self-rescue by the victim from the depths of contempt and humiliation which derive from insignificance. De Clerambault emphasised that the principal source of *erotomania* is pride rather than love. The condition evolves from pride, leading to desire, to hope, and hope spurned may be replaced by spite.

Once Freya, crushed and dejected in spirit by the humiliation she had experienced, was installed in her house, Viva turned for practical help in getting the girl on her feet to those two of her friends most likely to be of use. These were Professor Ker and Miss Margaret Jourdain, at that period a freelance journalist and book reviewer. The news of Ruata's marriage in November 1916 reached Freya at Viva's and put an end to any secret hopes she might have harboured of a reconciliation. It was a spur to activity and through Margaret Jourdain strings were pulled by Viva and Professor Ker, first to get Freya a job in Censorship, and then to engineer her eventual acceptance as a VAD with the historian G. M. Trevelyan's Red Cross ambulance unit on the Italian front in Gorizia. This was something Freya had set her heart on. It was a way to get back to Italy and to her mother. Viva used her connections with Mrs Humphry Ward, Trevelyan's mother-in-law, and Professor Ker wrote to Trevelyan himself, to promote her acceptance into his much sought-after unit. All Freya wanted now was to lose herself in war work.

'The dear Professor came with Miss Jourdain to dine last night,' Freya told her mother immediately after her arrival at Viva's on 16 August 1916. 'I think he rather expected to be alone and would have preferred it . . .'

The start of Freya's friendship with Margaret Jourdain is established by this date. It was the older woman's fortieth birthday so she was just old enough to be Freya's mother, while Ker was a man of a previous generation and thirty-five years older than Freya. Now Miss Jourdain's impact on the girl was more novel and exciting than Ker's, already familiar from Freya's introduction into Viva's household in 1911 when he used to include her in the theatre and supper parties for his many godchildren which he delighted to arrange. Throughout the next three years Freya attached herself humbly to him and, though not one of his students, she haunted his lectures at University College and with shy silent determination infiltrated the tea-parties at his rooms in Gower Street to which they were invited.

Freya responded to the bracing quality of Miss Jourdain's personality with gratitude. Already recognised as a translator of the French Symbolist writers, a published poet and author, Margaret Jourdain belonged to the early generation of university women, going up to Oxford on a Lady Margaret Hall scholarship in 1894 to read classics. To a far greater extent than was ever acknowledged, she influenced in practical terms the development of Freya's career as a writer. Margaret always believed in hard work as the solution to anyone's problems; she had no time for wan repining, and its accompanying apathy. One had to cut one's losses and get on with life. In 1916 she gave the girl work as a research assistant, taking her to the British Museum, showing her how to use the Library and the card index. This was the way to mug up a subject, and was the tool with which she was fashioning her own future career. In wartime this career was dormant, but she was to emerge in the coming decade as an arbiter of decorative taste, and a respected expert on English furniture and decorative arts of the seventeenth and eighteenth centuries.

She kept herself in precarious independence by translating, reviewing, and turning out articles for Fleet Street and the magazine market. Her reputation for scrupulous accuracy derived from quiet mornings spent in the British Museum with pencil and notebook, a technique she passed on to Freya, who in time introduced her godsons to similar tasks. Margaret was singularly free of personal vanity; the element of hackwork in this employment was accepted without rancour and celebrated with ironic humour, a down-to-earth approach refreshingly unusual in the greenery-yallery school of aesthetics in which her literary career had begun. In 1916, however, like most university women, she was employed on government work, and in receipt of a regular income.

Freya at the age of twenty-three was impressed by the older woman's vigorous and iconoclastic spirit. It fascinated as much as it perturbed her, a seductive insight into another, more stimulating intellectual life than that in which she had grown up. Its effect was to lead her to aspire to a career as a woman of letters and to start to look about for suitable subjects to write up from the security of a home with her mother, once the war was over. Margaret's mocking puncturing of hitherto accepted beliefs jolted her complacency, it was so much more dashing and spirited than her own soulful yearnings.

> Fifteen Horace
> Sixteen Tom Paine
> Seventeen Plato
> Nineteen Montaigne
> And when I look back
> To say the truth
> I stand aghast
> At the age of youth

was Margaret's deflating reminder to the girl in 1917 of how stodgy and pedestrian her efforts to educate herself must seem to more assured and brilliant minds. In letters to her mother she was soon outlining schemes for the future, in which journalistic freelancing in antiquarian pursuits, on the model of Margaret's own career, was eagerly promoted.

Such schemes did not meet with the Professor's approval; her lack of a solid foundation in the classics would prove too much of a handicap for her, he wrote. His own belief was in a wide-ranging exposure to every type of literature and a patient waiting upon the Idea, which must arise inwardly to be valid, and not be plucked from the discoveries of others. Nor did he believe in reworkings of other people's material.[1]

Freya's upbringing was too sheltered for her to recognise that it was not so much her own individuality as her type that attracted the attention of the older woman. Young, traumatised by Guido Ruata's rejection, yet still undaunted and responsive, she embodied just those aspects of the unfairness of life that always touched Margaret's heart, and produced towards younger women a protectiveness expressed in forceful encouragement and a refusal to allow them to slide away into any sort of negation of living. Clever, sensitive girls broken in spirit by family problems, illness, bereavements, difficulties of any kind, were taken by the scruff of the neck, as it were, and shaken into life again.

She was patient, underneath a brusque manner, with her lame ducks. She trained them to work systematically, was never sentimental. Indeed, the most formidable aspect of Miss Jourdain derived from the very absence of this quality.

Tart of tongue, caustic, categorical, vehement, argumentative, often cuttingly funny, she was excellent company, the centre of an energetic social life and a prime source of professional contacts in a field cultivated until recently only by amateur antiquarians. This ensured her the attentions of a ceaseless supply of young men making their way in the museum and furniture world, eager to accompany her on country house visits, and to sale rooms and auctions.[2]

To the end of her life there was never any lack of such young men to take her out to lunch, to amuse, to gossip and to pick her brains, something she tolerated with good-humoured indulgence. The parallels with Freya's own subsequent performance are not far to seek.

It seems likely that Freya's involvement in the early 1920s with Vicomte Bernard d'Hendrecourt, an elderly aristocratic French picture-dealer, came through Margaret. After W. P. Ker's death in 1923 Freya seems to have looked for a surrogate relationship with d'Hendrecourt, who visited occasionally at La Mortola, but with practical objects in view. Freya made herself useful to him by reporting potential buying targets among her acquaintances along the coast and earned a fee of £100 from him for smuggling an Italian primitive across the French frontier.

Freya's apparent inability to recognise the deviant sexual impulse and the many disguises it can assume was later in life to make her appear astonishingly naive, even silly, to more detached observers. She took the attention of men brought up by their families to be pleasant and helpful to women as tributes to her own femininity, never apparently conceding that it was perhaps the absence of sexual threat on her part that made this possible. She liked to discuss with her women friends the eligibility of such men as possible husbands. This lack of the sexual dimension in no way interfered with her power to entertain and to fascinate. In later years these ephemeral episodes of mutual admiration would be mused over and incorporated in the cast of phantom lovers that peopled her legend.

Perhaps she was not so unworldly as she liked to appear, and a sense of her own unworthiness – for whatsoever reason – made her grateful for masculine friendship and recognition, if for nothing else. The muffled implications of homosexuality and particularly of bisexuality were not a topic of general discussion in the 1920s and between the initiated and the uninitiated extended a range of possible misunderstandings baffling in its complexity. Even so, it is remarkable that Freya should fail to make the connection on their visits to the Riviera between the Vicomte and his young protégé, David Horner, the 'orchidaceous

youth' who was to become the lover and long-term companion of
Osbert Sitwell after d'Hendrecourt's death.[3]

David Horner was a relative of W. P. Ker's favourite godchild, Olivia Horner. Freya records him making up a party at
L'Arma with Olivia, Venetia Buddicom and Mervyn Arnold
Foster in the summer of 1926, and of herself visiting d'Hendrecourt at Evian, when he was taking the cure, with the young
man in attendance, before his death from cancer in Paris in
1928. Freya writes of this death with restrained emotion in
Traveller's Prelude. Whether or not she recognised the situation
for what it was, she was seeking to enter a game of blind-
man's-buff in which she would inevitably have been the dupe,
had not d'Hendrecourt's illness and death supervened. This was
a situation which was to be repeated at intervals throughout
her life and suggests a predisposing factor in her emotional
make-up whose origins are tantalisingly obscure.

The Vicomte was part of Margaret's world of wealthy patrons
and secret benefactions which to Freya was both exciting and
challenging, the participants glamorous and intriguing. It is perhaps here that her native aptitude for taking chances was first
consecrated, when she delivered d'Hendrecourt's purchase
over the French frontier to him, hidden among the luggage of
an unsuspecting household visitor. This world of dealing and
elegant chicanery had all the elements she found so fascinating
in the *Arabian Nights*. Risks stimulated her ingenuity. She
delighted in evading the rules, whether it was smuggling coffee
beans through the frontier customs at La Mortola, or using a
camera surreptitiously to take a forbidden photograph on the
Bosphorus. These were not tricks she learned from her father
or from W. P. Ker, both of whom detested any sort of irregu-
larity. Freya found it amusing to slip a packet of coffee, unknown
to him, into Robert Stark's pocket on a shopping expedition to
Menton, and to 'watch him pass the barriers with a conscious
innocence that no-one could query'.[4] It was this air of innocence
that did the trick, and Freya soon became adept at simulating
quiet unconcern in a tight corner. It contributed greatly to her
success in future adventures.

There was nothing Freya enjoyed more than making a fool

out of well-meaning simpletons buoyed up by their own self-importance. She had a whole repertoire of stories in which, her corsets stuffed with illegal currency, false-bottomed suitcases concealing smuggled antiquities, or filled with dutiable goods, she was helped on her way by customs officials and frontier guards oozing protective indulgence towards someone so helpless and so insignificant, and so grateful for their condescension.

How Freya laughed when she retailed these adventures! And how everyone laughed with her! Like the elderly spinster sleuths who figure in detective stories, the unwary might dismiss her as harmless. Her fondness for embroidery, as she sat quietly stitching away while minds were being made up, perhaps fostered the illusion. Only the alert twinkle of her small eyes – 'clever little eyes' was how she herself described them[5] – might give the show away, but this was mitigated by a pleasing frankness of manner and a friendly approach.

Nowadays Margaret Jourdain is recalled chiefly as the companion and friend of the novelist Ivy Compton-Burnett, whose reputation as an original talent, after slow beginnings, was only fully established in the 1940s. But in October 1919, when Margaret moved into Ivy's flat as a lodger, she was the interesting figure, while Ivy, a dim, disregarded young woman, barely known by Margaret's circle, sat about the flat eating chocolates and doing nothing; to Margaret's clever friends the essence of mediocrity and dullness. Few realised that it was Ivy's comfortable private income that supported the household.

That Margaret should choose such an outsider for her lifelong companion was a source of chagrin to established friends, among whom were other contenders for the position, more suited, in their own opinion, by circumstance and upbringing for the privilege bestowed. They couldn't understand why Margaret should select someone so silly and skittish, when not actually silent and dim, and in their own view rather common.

Perhaps Freya experienced a similar disappointment when she returned to London in the summer of 1919, and found her position of protégée usurped; she was possessive in her relations with people she admired, and did not like to share.

But Ivy, like her vegetable namesake – 'poison Ivy' in the words of another outmanoeuvred favourite – was tenacious and difficult to dislodge, and Freya, on the principle that something is better than nothing, conceded precedence. Though the two younger women might not care for each other – 'that dull Ivy Compton-Burnett' is a comment of Freya's from the 1930s, after a visit in the couple's company to Vita Sackville-West at Sissinghurst – in the 1920s Freya was careful to include Ivy in invitations to L'Arma: 'You of course is you and Ivy; she can now reach the beach with no giddy heights to overlook, tell her.' The letter is undated, and was found stuffed in among Margaret's papers given to the Victoria and Albert Museum at her death. She was notoriously careless about her paperwork, scribbling notes and accounts on the back of used envelopes and odd scraps of paper, as if she despised their importance. Perhaps she resented the plodding financial necessity that had forced her to bridle her Pegasus, and compensated by a lofty indifference to its rewards. She was not fussy about where money came from; a job was a job, and she could take it or leave it without loss of self-esteem. That she should be exploited and underpaid by 'the trade' was nothing to her, rather it underlined her refusal to align herself with the shopkeeping ethos.

In later life Ivy could be very funny about Freya. She had a terse wit, and her powers of observation were formidable. She explained to Robin Fedden[6] in the 1950s that Freya, having spent much time among Italian peasants and Arabs, was inclined to treat her friends with unconscious imperiousness. People were expected to come to her, not she to them. This was exemplified, in Ivy's experience, by her habit at home at L'Arma, when emerging from her morning seclusion, of summoning people to her presence by loud calls rather than by seeking them out.

It seems unlikely that the intimacy was retained after the 1930s, though interest in Freya's career did not diminish. 'Of course he had to get married,' Ivy remarked to Rose Macaulay, apropos of Freya's marriage to Perowne in 1947. 'He's homosexual . . .'[7]

None of those admitted, men and women, to the intimacy of

Margaret and Ivy's friendship in the coming years ever seriously thought of them as practising lesbians. It was somehow impossible to imagine. Something austere and self-contained in the household and its atmosphere was a world away from the passions of the Sackville-West circle or the fashionable *saphisme* of the French feminists. It had a dignity and reticence peculiar to itself, as of a celibacy welcomed for its own sake.

On both Freya and Ivy, Margaret was to prove a subversively liberating influence, but if there was any rivalry for the older woman's affection, Ivy was the undoubted winner. Margaret's feeling for her was deep, tender, protective, you might almost say maternal, and it never faltered. Freya's lesser need, buttressed as it already was by her own mother and her circle of older friends, had to yield to the other's greater urgency. Freya and Ivy remind me in that early period of a pair of monstrous mythological twins being suckled by a wolf-mother. Margaret stands over them, stubbornly obedient to her instinct to nourish and protect, tugged at and harassed by a horde of other cubs, eager to participate and elbowed aside by stronger egotisms.

The Jourdains came of Huguenot stock of a line of what Margaret described as 'the middling class of people' of education and taste, not grand, not rich, but cultivated and intellectually alert. They were the seedbed, she claimed, from which generations of the English gentry had sprung, each to foster in its time the domestic art and literature of the period. Such an ancestry was lacking in the Stark and Compton-Burnett history, and both Freya and Ivy would have liked to possess it. It was a talisman which rendered its possessor immune from self-doubt and feelings of social inadequacy. Gerald de Gaury had a story of driving back to Asolo with Freya from a grand cultural event in Verona in October 1951, when she discoursed on the topic of civilisation and of the essential role of 'the middling class of people' in sustaining it. Perhaps Margaret's death earlier that year had stimulated recollection of the theme which she presented as her own discovery.

One does not need to be an active participant to be influenced by the example of others. That comes later. What Margaret's circle offered for Freya's consideration in the 1920s were single-sex 'partnerships' and 'platonic' unions between men and women based on mutual interests and a need for companionship. Often the link was a man killed at the front; marriage to the sister of a lost wartime 'pal' was not uncommon at this period, a legitimised expression of feelings perhaps not otherwise acknowledgeable, a transfer in which both sought relief from grief and sense of loss. Several of Margaret's set belonged in this category.

Freya adopted quite a lot from Margaret, a dry, caustic wit which surfaced as she in turn became admired and courted. It led her too to romanticise the hardship of her own early years, for poverty has an appeal to those who have never known want, while conferring distinction on those who manage to transcend it. All her life Margaret depended on better-off friends for anything extra to the subsistence level of her own economy. She never lacked admirers happy to supply this; a succession of wealthy women, Levantine and Jewish millionairesses, helped her out, glad to make use of her taste and discerning eye and the company she provided, a barter system which Freya in turn adopted.

She also adopted Margaret's cavalier attitude towards bills and accounts, which did not go down well in the wartime Ministry of Information. There, advised by Elizabeth Monroe that something rather better was expected than scribbled notes on the backs of envelopes when indenting for travelling expenses, Freya tossed her head and replied curtly that in her youth her family was too poor to afford more than beans or potatoes at any one meal. She had decided then, she said, that as an artist she would never allow herself to take seriously anything to do with mere money. With that, she swept grandly out of the room.[8]

TWENTY-TWO

DRONERO TO L'ARMA TO ASOLO

Freya's experience as a wartime VAD was brief. After six weeks' training at a civilian hospital in Cricklewood she was sent out from London to Italy at the beginning of September 1917. Eight weeks later, with the collapse of the Gorizia front under Austrian attack, and the retreat to Caporetto, she was evacuated from Udine along with the rest of her unit to Padua, but elected not to be repatriated and was disbanded and back in Dronero by the beginning of November. She wrote an account of her experiences on the retreat, and submitted it to Trevelyan, but he did nothing other than acknowledge it politely. It can be found in *Traveller's Prelude*, where she included it in her account of her two months' war service as a VAD.

Freya spent the last year of the war at home, co-opted by a friend of her mother, Clothilde di Bottini, to help organise Dronero's civil hospital on a military basis in anticipation of the casualties expected in the summer campaign of 1918. But these never came. Instead an influenza epidemic that ravaged Europe at this period arrived in the autumn and carried off hundreds of local people and refugees from the war zone. Within a few days Freya herself fell ill, and retired to bed, overwhelmed by the misery of it all, while the war in Italy ended on 4 November 1918.

The friendship between Flora Stark and Clot di Bottini developed during the war in the general relaxation of social barriers of the period. The di Bottinis de Ste Agnes were a relic of the old French-speaking Piedmontese nobility, made Italian by revision of the Franco-Italian frontier in 1850; they antedated the di Roascios, only recently ennobled under the House of Savoy when Italy was finally united in 1861. The family consisted of aged parents in a shadowy, dilapidated family mansion in Dronero, with two sons away in the army, and an ugly excitable daughter, trapped into spinsterhood by the need to care for her senile mother, personal eccentricity and lack of dowry. For Clot di Bottini, like many other daughters of her class, the war was a liberation, and she escaped into patriotic Red Cross work and hospital nursing once Italy joined the Allies.

She was of a lively, amusing, enthusiastic nature, and formed a fervent admiration for Flora, which was expanded to include Freya when the latter arrived back in Dronero at the end of 1917. This admiration found expression in plots to marry Freya to one or other of her brothers, which flattered Flora's social ambitions for her daughter but received little assistance from the men concerned. The tantalising possibility of such a match was pushed on by Clot's inventiveness and need for excitement. Nothing came of it. The di Bottinis were an old race, dwindling towards extinction. Only one brother married, manoeuvred into a family alliance by a matchmaking relative after his mother died in 1925, a disappointment for Freya carefully explained away in her own story.

Freya was twenty-five when hostilities ceased in 1918, another of the cohort of unmarried daughters living at home, bereft of possible husbands by the death-toll of the trenches. The stigma of this condition was made worse in Italy where failure to marry off a daughter often led to consultation with a matchmaker or consignment to a convent. This was doubly painful to Freya in Dronero, where a realistic appreciation of the devaluation of a girl's marriage prospects by any physical blemish was under-lined by Vera's marriage, while the elder sister was passed over. Her father, over from Canada in December 1918 on business of his own, perhaps imagined that, in picking up a small property on the coast at La Mortola, rich in soil washed down from the terraced hillside and safe at sea-level from frost and hail, he was putting Freya in the way of independence by the same dogged persistence and labour as he practised in Canada. He cannot have spent much on the property, a few hundred at most, for the sterling exchange rate was very favourable, nor did he stay to see her settled in. He did not feel at ease with his family, and was eager to return to his own life in Canada.

Whatever her father may have believed in 1918, Freya never intended actually to *work* the flower farm for herself. She saw her little property as an investment, not as a way of life. A peasant couple was employed for that, and a shack built for them at the entrance to the two-and-a-half-acre property. Nor was there any question of making do with the house as it was; it had to be enlarged and modernised. The building works dragged on into 1921. Freya was employing her own labour and was soon in difficulties over money and in managing her workmen.

Her brother-in-law came down from Dronero to sort out the water rights, always a problem on that coast. Freya's supply passed through the Villa i Fauni, on the hillside above L'Arma, whose purchase was negotiated for her parents' old friend the painter Herbert Olivier by the Stark parents at the same time as L'Arma was acquired. His improvements to his property were a source of some discord between the new neighbours; and eventually he installed two storage tanks on Freya's property, to reduce complaints over her water rights.[1] A couple of laying hens, a goat, a cow were sent down on different occasions from the di Roascio farm at Dronero, along with other produce, to help out the housekeeping; but the money problems accumulated. These were at the root of the disagreement that eventually arose between Freya and her brother-in-law. Much of Freya's trouble came from her unwillingness, or incapacity, to take charge of her newly acquired independence, and she sought about eagerly for someone to take the burden of its management off her shoulders, so as to leave her free to pursue her own interests and social life.

The first person she tried was her father. If he could be persuaded to give up Canada and come back to develop L'Arma for her instead, she wrote, and they put their capital together, there would be more than enough income for them all, Flora included, to live on comfortably. What Flora thought of this idea is not recorded. What Robert Stark thought is all too clear. He had absolutely no desire to return to a domestic existence whose aspirations were so out of tune with his own. The notion that his Canadian property was worth £6000 was quickly dispelled, and the sum £4000 substituted, with an inevitable loss on the transaction if sold prematurely. He was not to be budged. In April 1921 Freya was still trying.

> I would *much* more happily do without a large income and have you these few years sooner. I would not say this if it meant real poverty for us all . . . I wouldn't mind selling therefore, dear old Pips. If I were strong enough to come out and really help you it would be different, but as it is I'm afraid I'm no good for real hard labour. I have been knocked about these last seven or eight years and seem only to be good for an ordinary kind of life. I feel you are hesitating because of me, as Vera is well off and settled in life, but I do want you to feel how *very* little – nothing at all – it matters to me to have more than just enough to be quiet on. That we should certainly have, and anything beyond that isn't worth comparing a minute with the joy of having you again.[2]

Vera's prosperity and settled life and status in Dronero, with husband and children about her, was by 1920 in sharp contrast to Freya's situation at L'Arma where, harassed by the problems of an income insufficient for the style to which she aspired, she was thwarted by the obstinate refusal of her father to give her further aid. Not getting her way never did Freya any good; it provoked angry resentment and self-justification, discharged in a grand turmoil of the emotions, often on some tangential issue. Her single-minded concentration on her own needs edged milder natures into compliance. She had a child's persistence in getting her own way. Elizabeth Monroe once explained to me that if Freya had by mistake ordered a dozen more linen table napkins than she needed, you inevitably found yourself buying them.

Now, she decided, she must have help at L'Arma, and, in default of her father, her mother was the obvious solution. Freya in London in 1917 had already debated her future[3] and decided that a home with her mother was the answer. Flora would be there to run the household and oversee the flower farm and Freya would be free to pursue her literary ambitions.

It did not lessen Freya's resentment of the changed circumstances in Dronero that it was Flora's energy and commercial acumen that had built up the di Roascio prosperity and enabled Mario to take a government job in Turin, where he and Vera spent the war. Flora's management of Mario's interests during his absence had been exemplary. She took the minimum out of the business for herself, seeing this as her contribution to the war effort, as well as a measure of her devotion to her family's interests. Most family rows are about money. In the Starks' case it was the value of Flora's services to her son-in-law's enterprise. Freya, struggling with workmen at L'Arma, felt that if anyone needed Flora's help now it was herself, and this fuelled her resentment of what she saw as exploitation of her mother's gullibility and good nature. Farther back still was the rankling awareness that di Roascio's prosperity derived in part from the injection of Stark capital (in the shape of Flora's £1600 loan, and Vera's £2000) into the factory in its early days. Freya had protested in vain against the writing in of Vera's capital as dowry in the marriage settlement.

Flora Stark had many admirable qualities. Whatever the disappointments of her married life she kept silent about them. Her guilt over Freya's accident, and her anxiety for her future, operated to Freya's advantage. It gave the girl a moral ascendancy over her parent which she did not hesitate to use. Flora, after Freya's accident in 1906, cut her losses and accepted nothing from Robert Stark for herself. She became a devout church-goer, active in parish welfare. At the period of Freya's illness in 1915, when pneumonia following on typhoid threatened danger, she became a Roman Catholic, quietly and in private, telling no-one. She found a comfort in religion which her family perhaps despised, but it led her to a satisfying habit of service to others. Her sympathetic awareness of the difficulties in her work people's lives translated itself into practical assistance to them; it earned her their loyalty, and a great deal of respect in Asolo, where she spent the penultimate fifteen years of her life.

Freya always hated Flora's involvement in Mario's factory. She hated the hold it had on her attention; she resented Mario's domination of her parent and what she saw as his shiftiness and dishonesty about money. But Flora herself did not complain, nor did she consider herself exploited. The indignity of her mother's occupation when compared with the more leisured life of Freya's English friends rankled. The absorbing humdrum shop-talk of Mario and Flora bored and alienated the daughters, and united them in a determination to get their mother out of Dronero. Freya's argument was that it would relieve Vera of an overpowering and pervasive presence; but it would also enable herself to win back from Mario an efficient manager to run her own establishment at La Mortola.

That Flora could derive satisfaction from her life in Dronero, and the scope it gave for her abilities, escaped Freya. She saw only her own need and set to work to detach her parent from Mario. But it would mean that Flora's upkeep would now descend on herself, something for which her own resources were entirely inadequate; this produced the idea in Freya's mind of bringing di Roascio to court for the restitution of Stark capital and the salary left in the business by Flora.

She tried this out on her father, when he came over from Canada in 1922 to exhibit fruit at the Empire Exhibition at Crystal Palace. His only advice before disappearing back to Creston was to get on with it if she insisted. Freya must be responsible for her own actions. Nor was Flora, on whose behalf the case ostensibly was being got up, any more helpful. She had no quarrel with di Roascio, whose support of herself and her daughters during the crucial early years of their residence in Dronero was not forgotten. Vera remained temperate and cool, and the family ties held. The drama that ensued had its basis in the emotions, but was played out in terms of money and property settlements. Freya was the chief mover in the long-drawn-out legal wrangle that began in 1922; she was left to battle alone with dilatory Italian lawyers, and against Mario's entrenched position in Dronero as a Fascist party member as well as one of a leading local family. It was a frustrating and embittering experience; she was convinced there was a conspiracy among the lawyers to prevent the case coming up for trial.

A decision was eventually given in 1926 whereby the capital remained, by mutual consent, in di Roascio's hands, in trust for the children, but a regular monthly sum of 1000 lira was to be paid to Flora for her contribution to the success of his enterprise. This was the year in which Vera was dying slowly, at the age of thirty-one, of septicaemia following a miscarriage, and in the general distress of this event, even Freya had not the heart to continue the feud. Despite her angry dissatisfaction, the terms were accepted, and Flora became Freya's responsibility, though with an income of her own from di Roascio.

This period of frustration and inhibited rage was to assume a significant place in Freya's history when she came to tell her story. It enabled earlier mortifications to be concealed by an altruistic defence of her mother's rights in a less obviously personal attack on di Roascio. To their English friends she appeared forlornly brave and beleaguered, a gallant little figure struggling to defend truth and fair play. It is no doubt how she appeared to herself.

Freya's need became an article of faith in the circle of her older intimates. The confiding simplicity of her manner evoked pity and concern and spurred them to provide practical solutions to her problems. Viva Jeyes lent her unspecified sums at this period, to tide her over the expense of improving and enlarging L'Arma and building the gardener's cottage. In October 1922 Professor Ker insisted on putting £300 into her English account, to ease her anxiety about her overdraft.[4] This loan was written off after his death.

Flora Stark put aside her personal reluctance and wrote privately to Robert Stark explaining the inadequacy of Freya's income, so that a furnished property in Teignmouth was put on the market in 1922, and the proceeds, something in the region of £5000, whether the whole or half is not clear, were put into

Freya's English account early in 1923. It came as a timely relief. Whether her sister Vera received a similar sum is not recorded, but the difficulties with Mario di Roascio about the repayment of Stark money invested in his business began about now.

Freya used the money received from the sale of the English property to buy War Loan, so her income was doubled, if not trebled, to £350 a year and any idea of personally slogging away at the flower farm was given up. The land was leased out to produce additional income, while the improvement and embellishment of the house went on, with Flora designing, painting and decorating the furniture and rooms and Freya instituting the regime of quiet, undisturbed mornings devoted to study and letter-writing that remained with her all her life.

Professor Ker retired from the Chair of English Literature at University College, London, in 1922 at the age of sixty-five, while Professor of Poetry at Oxford. He was given a farewell luncheon at the Connaught Rooms, at which 200 people sat down, among them Freya and her mother, Flora.

He died the following year, on 23 July 1923, while on a walking tour in the Italian Alps with his godchildren Olivia Horner and Dr Poldores MacCunn (one of the original April children), and Freya and her mother. Freya, the youngest, was now an active young woman of thirty. The weather was very hot and stuffy, she told her father,[5] with thunderstorms breaking themselves against Monte Rosa, towering above Macugnaga, where the Professor had booked rooms at the inn. The Prof, she added, did not care much for climbing any longer, 'so we feel rather like horses on a curb'.

Early on 23 July, Ker and the three younger women and a guide, Josef Bini, started off in starlight from the inn to climb the Pizzo Bianco, with a view to watching the sunrise flush Monte Rosa rose-red in the first light of dawn, a particular delight Ker was determined to share with his companions. Flora Stark remained below to spend the day sketching around Macugnaga.

At about 9000 feet, as they were about to rope up, Ker collapsed, and was dead of heart failure before he hit the ground.

The guide went down to fetch help, while the women waited beside the body for seven hours until a party of villagers arrived with a ladder to bring it down.

It was a shattering experience for them all. Included in the Ker Papers in University College library is the mute testimony of Olivia's pocket diary for 1923. For the week following the twenty-second, the diary is a blank. It is only when she is safely back home in Surbiton that the tidy record of daily events is resumed. Freya however utilised the services of the guide, engaged by Ker for the week, to climb the Matterhorn from the Italian side, then crossed into Switzerland to rejoin her mother and Viva Jeyes, through whom Freya had originally come to the Professor's notice, at Zermatt. It was to test her nerve, she later told Sir Sydney Cockerell, after the shock of WPK's death, and it was the first of the only two big climbs she ever attempted though she had made several smaller ones in Ker's company.

Her second climb was also associated with his memory; she climbed Monte Rosa in 1924, on the occasion of a Ker family gathering of friends at Macugnaga to visit WPK's grave, whose monument had been designed by Flora Stark. Perhaps these strenuous exertions helped assuage the pain of his loss, and the stringing up of nerve in the face of danger was a means of keeping regrets at bay.

By the time she was thirty Freya had arranged the pattern of her life largely to her own satisfaction – seclusion in the morning, sociability from lunchtime onwards. Flora still hoped Freya would marry, but nothing came of the various possibilities found for her by matchmaking friends. Asked once what she would most like to be, she replied, 'A widow'; hardly an encouraging response, but one which perhaps contained a kernel of truth. What Freya wanted was the status of marriage, but not its responsibilities. She rather liked the thought of herself as a gay little widow, she said, untroubled by financial anxiety and free to do as she pleased; it was a situation which in modified form she eventually achieved.

The 1920s were a critical decade in Freya's evolution. The

cracking of the chrysalis that was to release the moth began, despite the pathos of her account of a semi-invalid existence for three years 'nearly always on bed or sofa' between 1923 and 1926 when, using contacts made by her mother with retired Protestant missionaries in Bordighera, she took Arabic lessons to occupy her mind, with a view to obtaining a governess's post with a wealthy Middle East family.

After Professor Ker's death in July 1923, Freya was off in September on a gay and exciting journey with her new friend, Venetia Buddicom. Trekking with a donkey and guide from Provence to Andorra, this small adventure was the curtain-raiser to her future career. The old protected life under the lee of WPK's personality was over, and Freya was free to develop her own.

Events conspired to ease Freya's parting with her Italian associations. She lost two matrimonial targets at this period. In 1925 Gabriel di Bottini in Dronero married a cousin, while her neighbour, the elder of the Bianchieri brothers at La Mortola, whom Freya later allowed people to believe had been another possibility,[6] died unexpectedly, provoking a sense of loss that might have surprised him, had he been aware of it.

The stresses and frustrations of these tantalising relationships and the mortifications of pride they induced put Freya into hospital in the winter of 1924, when she was operated on for gastric ulcers. She recuperated slowly, and the years of misery and semi-invalid status that followed are associated with this.

It was a rotten time for everyone. She took out her dissatisfaction on Flora who, detached from her former busy life in Dronero, was drudging about under Freya's thumb, doing up L'Arma, and being bullied about the housekeeping. She herself, physically strong and healthy, had a bracing approach to illness; this did not make for easier relations with Freya. Perhaps it was awareness of this that prompted their old family friend Herbert Young to make his suggestion.

In February 1926 Freya received a letter from him in Asolo, making her the proposal which proved the cornerstone of her future life. 'Briefly it is this,' he wrote. 'Do you think you could carry on this Asolo property after I have gone permanently? I mean making it a home? If so I shall be delighted, because then I shall be sure that this dear place, where I have lived such a long time, and which is, in a sense, my creation, will not fall into unworthy hands, and be destroyed perhaps – a contingency that revolts me.'

If she agreed, he proposed making a will in her favour, leaving all his Asolo properties – houses and garden and furniture, etc. – to her, as she seemed the most proper person to inherit his 'earthly Paradise'. 'You have very early associations with Asolo . . . and I know you love the place . . . Of course, I don't want to tie you down here for always and always – don't I go away myself pretty often? But to have it and keep it as a home: not a place to sell – unless circumstances oblige you to part with it. I think that is pretty clear, isn't it?'[7]

Freya accepted. It was a wonderful solution, for herself, for Flora, for Herbert, who would now have an efficient household manager in Flora and company in his old age – he was in his seventies – while Freya would be free of her responsibility for her parent, just as her improved income from investments and the L'Arma property enabled her to exercise independence at last.

It is not hard to perceive in the installation of Freya and her mother in Asolo the colonisation of another's habitat by a stronger species; the Oliviers always rather suspected that Flora in some way got around Herbert and put the idea into his head. But perhaps Freya herself was the motivating force. She kept up her links with her parents' old English friends throughout the period of Flora's greatest involvement in di Roascio's factory, and Margaret Olivier latterly replaced Viva Jeyes as Freya's proxy parent in London, by whom she was put up as a semi-invalid on visits extending into weeks at a time.

The year 1926 ended another association with the past. Her sister Vera died in September leaving four young children, two boys and two girls. The sisters had seen little of each other in recent years, because of Freya's lawsuit with her brother-in-law. Flora was with her daughter at her death, but not Freya. Mario's children grew up as Italians and saw little of their aunt.

A niece of Flora's, a daughter of one of her sisters, came out to take Vera's place, and brought up the children. Through Flora, contact with Dronero was maintained, and the children were sent down to L'Arma for the sea-bathing in summer, but Freya was excluded from any real share in their management.

Now, at long last, impressed by Venetia Buddicom and spurred on by Margaret Jourdain's bracing influence, imbued with popular ideas of romantic travel, and of adventure on the lines of Kipling's *Kim*, Freya finally opted for Professor Ker's Real Life. It was 1927, and she was thirty-four years old. Her career as a traveller and her fame were about to begin.

PART SEVEN

THROUGH THE
LOOKING GLASS

TWENTY-THREE

MOTHER AND DAUGHTER

With Freya now installed in Asolo at the Villa Freia and her travel adventures about to begin, I had come full circle in my exploration of her origins. The threads that had come so opportunely into my hand – my meeting with Dr Francis Edmunds, Cockerell's painstaking assembling of such general information as he could extract from Freya, the influence of Margaret Jourdain, and Art Stark's researches into his family history – had all been followed up. Only one knot had still to be teased out: how to reconcile what I now knew of Freya's life and that of her parents with her own account in her autobiography *Traveller's Prelude*.

My difficulty centred on Flora Stark and her personality. At first I had accepted the mother as her daughter presented her, a somewhat troublesome liability whose enthusiastic unworldliness was apt to involve her family in predictable difficulties. Later, as I went deeper into the story, I began to look rather more carefully at such material as I had already assembled from the recollections of pre-war friends and acquaintances, and a somewhat different picture formed. A response dated early in 1945 from Countess Marina Luling-Volpi in Switzerland, to whom Freya wrote from Viceroy's House in New Delhi for news of Asolo and the Villa Freia, further alerted me. 'A little breath of Flora came to me with your note today,' she wrote, '. . . when I think how she sailed into that deplorable room [in the women's prison at Treviso] I am consumed with admiration

. . . All she ever did, she did for you . . . and I am sure that that dear place she loved so much will be saved – she will save it herself for you!'

Cockerell's magpie acquisitiveness was another help. He came to stay for several weeks at the Villa Freia in 1938 to select illustrations for a prototype coffee-table book, *Seen in the Hadhramaut*, a splendid photographic record of the extraordinary architecture of Hadhramaut, and of its people, assembled by Freya during the Wakefield expedition and published in November that year by John Murray in time for her lecture at the Royal Geographical Society.

Cockerell's diary records his first meeting with Flora on his June visit of that year: 'A tall, very charming woman with whom I immediately felt on the friendliest terms.' This good opinion was maintained throughout the remaining four years of her life and beyond. Cockerell worked hard to ensure the publication of Flora's prison diary and expanded memoirs in 1942, prior to her sudden illness and death. In the event, this was held over till 1945 on the advice of Sir Leonard Woolley, the archaeologist, now in the War Office intelligence section dealing with escapers from Occupied Europe, for fear of compromising people who had been helpful at the time of her arrest in Italy and subsequent release and departure to America. Discussing Flora's manuscript with Cockerell on 5 August 1942, Mr Bucknell, her solicitor and the recipient of her material and instructions, wrote:

> Almost the strongest argument for early publication is Mrs Stark's immediate need of money to repay friends the debts she owes them, but I do not suppose any of these friendly creditors are really pressing her but I know the relief to her would be very great if she found herself able to repay their generosity. Sir Leonard Woolley's arguments are, if valid, of a kind which would override personal considerations . . .

Flora's abiding concern during her last year of life in California was first to mitigate the role the Asolani might have played in the imprisonment that she and Herbert Young had endured in 1940, and secondly somehow to earn the money to reimburse her friends for the expenses they had borne on her account in bringing her to America. She was both surprised and pleased at the amount of enthusiasm her prison diary evoked and readily agreed to Sir John Murray's suggestion to expand her memoir to include her experiences in Piedmont and Asolo as what she described as 'a small industriel' (i.e. manufacturer) from the 1900s to World War II. She was completing and correcting these additional memoirs when her illness finally overcame her and she became too weak to continue.

On 20 November Mr Bucknell again wrote to Cockerell: 'The news of the death reached me through Lady Iveagh yesterday. I think that death in the end was a welcome relief from pain but a remarkable character has gone out of our lives and I am truly sorry to think that none of us will see her again . . .'

After her death, Lucy Beach got in touch with Cockerell through Mr Bucknell, to whom she sent copies of Flora's additional memoirs. Her letters to himself were kept by Cockerell along with those from others of Flora's friends. In an early letter Mrs Beach wrote:

Every time I read the manuscript of Flora's *Italian Diary* I am more and more amazed at what she accomplished – her courage, her initiative and her cleverness. She wanted to have her Italians understood, and she has portrayed them most sympathetically and honestly and, without in the least intending it, she has shown us her own wonderful character.

On 11 January 1943 she wrote again to Cockerell:

When you think she was sixty-six years old when she came to Asolo and started so lightheartedly this new and exacting work [the *tessoria*] and that she grew to be a power in the town with all ages and nationalities coming to her for help and advice! We have lost a great and dear friend, but she lives on in her writing and I hope earnestly that these writings will be published and will reach the right people and so help her Italians, as she longed to do, up to the very last . . .

Cockerell promoted publication of the complete memoir with unfeigned zest, passing copies of the material around to his circle of correspondents, and to Flora's friends. He called on and corresponded with Mrs Gray Granville, the Starks' old friend and neighbour on the Italian Riviera in the 1920s, and with Lady Waller, the Dorothy Varwell of Freya's girlhood friendship at Chagford, and also with Lady Lawrence, the Asolo neighbour who, like Sir John Murray, had encouraged Flora to write not only her prison diary but also about her life in Italy. This was something Freya was anxious to prevent;[1] she did not want Flora crowding her scene, for she feared her mother's pro-Italian bias might affect her own standing in political circles. Freya's letter to her mother in September 1942 about this matter is reproduced in full as Appendix B.

When published by John Murray in 1945, the diary was a slim little volume decorated with an engraving by Reynolds Stone, and with a foreword by Freya written in Devon in 1944 when she was staying with the Varwell sisters at Chagford. It was proof-read at Freya's request by Cockerell; she was anxious to get it published quickly. Only the diary of the imprisonment was printed, the ancillary chapters describing Flora's life in Dronero, which the Beaches found so interesting, and the period in Asolo up to Herbert Young's death, are omitted, and I have been unable to trace the missing material either in Cockerell's papers, in Murrays' archives or in the records of Flora's solicitor. He, at Cockerell's request, made several copies of the material consigned to him by Lucy Beach after Flora's death. On 13 December 1985 Jock Murray wrote to me regarding the missing sections of Flora's memoir. 'It seems it was decided to get Freya to include the important parts of Flora's two additional chapters in Freya's Foreword, but it does not seem from a re-read that this happened . . .' It is possible that some of Flora's background material was reworked later into Freya's own autobiography.

Freya's foreword to her mother's little book was in a sense a warm-up exercise for the evocation of Italian provincial life in the early years of the century that contributed so much to the charm of *Traveller's Prelude*. The tone is tender, elegiac; the sentences drop gracefully into place; the whole is washed in the golden light of affectionate recollection. Cockerell's papers contain a typescript of Flora's original prison diary. Freya always told people that Mario di Roascio did nothing to help her mother at this period, but Flora wrote that on 6 July 1940, having been rebuffed by the prison authorities at Treviso, he went straight on to Venice and began enquiries with the American Consul for a visa to America for herself and Herbert Young.

The letters from Mrs Gray Granville to Cockerell after Flora's death made me think more about the relative statures of mother and daughter. Minnie Granville had become friendly with the Starks at La Mortola in 1923, when she rented a villa from their neighbours, the Bianchieri family. Freya described her then as a widow, smaller even than herself, all hung about with little dangles of pearls and diamonds over Reville frocks, 'county and clergy and had never met anything artistic in her life,' but that she was charming in herself, artless, sensible, charitable and gay. 'No-one could have settled more happily into our casual sort of life; and for her it was a new horizon opening; she said she had never known how one could *enjoy* things before.'

Minnie Granville thanked Cockerell effusively on 19 July 1943 for a copy of Flora's prison narrative.

Dear darling, I can see her so perfectly dealing with those awful women – and always seeing Beauty . . . This account as you say puts Flora in a wonderful light. She was a far more really outstanding woman than Freya, but Freya will always make the most splash – however they are both most unusual and it is a privilege to know them . . . Freya's view of life is quite different from her mother's. There is much more self in Freya and yet if you wanted a simple thing like your passage – or your luggage found – Freya was the best!!!

On 23 July she followed this up, telling Cockerell she would be delighted to talk over the Starks with him.

I *think* Flora had more heart than Freya – but really both out of the way dears. Freya absolutely true! If she liked you she always did. I have worked for her quite a bit, whereas I *think* Flora worked for me! . . . I will keep the Diary till you come. Does she not write naturally! I know her so well with Italian girls . . . and I had an Italian maid myself! so I can enter into it all so well – dear Flora putting on 'the grand air' I have seen it and being so large and fine she did it so well! I was *very* fond of her . . .

The letters of Lucy Beach and Minnie Granville, when I found them among Cockerell's papers, revived recollections of fugitive impressions received on my second visit to Freya in Asolo. Most of what I then knew about her mother had come from Freya's pen, filtered through her own recollection. Her verbal communication was laconic. One did not get very far on the subject of Flora's artistic or domestic skills. Notoriously disdainful of anything to do with the practicalities of daily living, in old age Freya claimed never to have cooked a meal, or saddled her own pony, or washed her own clothes. Others, she indicated to post-war interrogators, were there to do this for her. She had little time for the merely domestic, family-orientated woman. An impression was received of a leisured, cultivated Edwardian background in youth which only her mother's intransigence had caused her to forfeit.

Nowadays, of course, there were difficulties. Even in Italy, she complained, servants were no longer easy to obtain or to keep. The flow of young girls from the surrounding countryside, eager to be trained in the well-to-do foreign households in Asolo, the commonplace of her mother's period, had long ago been transformed into factory hands and counter assistants, so that to obtain a woman of any calibre such as her present maid Floriana was indeed a triumph.

Lulled by this conversation, a staple of the well-to-do elderly coping with a reduced scale of living, I began to elaborate inwardly a view of faithful family retainers, devotedly protecting Freya's old age. On asking how long Floriana had been with her, I was rather surprised when Freya replied dismissively that Caroly had found her some months ago. 'Such a relief,' she added crisply, 'there'd been such unsuitable women before . . .'

'Caroly?' I asked, wondering where he or she fitted into the fabric of Freya's Italian life. Freya wasn't much of a one for making things easy for the unprepared. One was expected to be familiar with the events of her life. 'Why, my mother's secretary, of course,' was the impatient response. 'She looks after all that kind of thing. I really don't know too much about the details,' she added dismissively. 'She runs the *tessoria* now; my mother took her on and trained her as her assistant as a girl . . .'

It was Hilda Besse's remarks at Le Paradou that had originally drawn my attention to Flora Stark, and her *An Italian Diary* shown me there had sharpened my interest. Here in Caroly was a woman, trained in the 1920s to assist Flora in running her small silk-weaving manufactory, still actively supervising Freya's domestic comfort more than fifty years later. It was an encouraging testimonial to the success of that earlier relationship, whatever fall-out there might be among subsequent ranks of servitors. It indicated a more substantial legacy of personal devotion to the mother than the daughter had felt necessary to disclose.

I was taken next morning to see the shop and to be introduced to Caroly Piaser, while Freya set off alone on her daily walk. The Tessoria Asolana occupies a tall, narrow building sandwiched in a row of similar structures along what were once the ramparts of the little town. It is not far from the Villa Freia, sold by Freya in 1962 to cover costs incurred on building her new villa outside the town at Montoria, and now a conference centre and holiday rest home for the Treviso District Council. The shop had a small, shabby, neglected appearance, as if not much business was done there, but appearances deceived. The slow clacking of a loom upstairs ceased at Freya's imperious call, and hesitant grudging steps on bare wooden boards heralded a cautious appearance, peering over the banister. Caroly Piaser, a tall, haggard middle-aged woman, with a glum, preoccupied air, looked as if she could do without our visit. 'No talent for delegation,' remarked Freya dispassionately as she left me and set off on her solitary morning walk.

Caroly had little to show me. It was the off-season, and the shelves were bare. Looking about me to make conversation in my rusty Italian, an oil sketch of a fine, stately, white-haired woman caught my eye. It could do with a clean, I thought. Then I recognised it as the original of the photograph pasted into Flora's *An Italian Diary* shown me by Hilda Besse. It looked down on the dingy brown shop interior from a commanding position above the counter, and had an air of cordial, dignified geniality that was impressive. Upright, with a self-assured carriage and a deep, capacious bosom, the sitter looked confidently out of the canvas. Strong dark eyebrows barred the face, and were its dominating feature.

Observing my glance, Caroly brightened. 'Yes, that was Signora Stark, Freya's mother,' she answered, showing the first sign of pleasure at our encounter. 'Oh, what a wonderful, what a remarkable woman,' she continued. 'She was so good, so kind, she had such talent and ability.' Never, never could she, Caroly Piaser, ever think of her without regret, or heartfelt gratitude and respect for all the Signora had done for her and for Asolo. 'I feel for her like a daughter,' she said. 'She was like a mother to me . . .'

I came away from the shop pensively preoccupied and, turning up towards the crest of the town's hill, I followed at random a path zigzagging up the flank of a pasture. Above me, in the distance, a figure was crawling slowly towards the summit. It was Freya. She seemed very small and solitary as I watched her from below, careful not to intrude on her privacy; she walked so slowly now, she told me, she did not like to inflict her lack of pace on anyone else.

Arrived at the top she paused for several minutes, leaning on a stone wall to look over the view. The intentness and stillness of her concentration struck me. She appeared to be absorbing some spiritual sustenance from the panorama of dark mountain mass and glimmering plain, the intrusions of the absurd pepper-pot shapes of the Euganean hills poking up below in the middle distance like termite mounds. I later learned that the disappearance of familiar landmarks from her view – a first indication of cataract obscuring the wholeness of her vision – was a puzzle she was intent at this period on solving to her own satisfaction. 'An extraordinary thing has happened,' she told a caller. 'Montoria has completely vanished from the view . . .'[2]

I had been conscious of fluctuations in the emotional temperature during our visit to the *tessoria*. Freya's presence seemed to induce a certain wariness in Caroly; she did not appear too pleased to see us. Later, remembering this, Flora's portrait, the *tessoria* and the Villa Freia in such intimate relationship to each other, I wondered if the groundwork of Freya's present life in Asolo had been laid by her parent, and the status she enjoyed in the little town derived as much from the mother as from any personal quality attached to the daughter.

It was a novel thought. For most of her friends Freya *was* Asolo. But in the 1880s, when her mother first visited Asolo as Robert Stark's wife, the wealthy cosmopolitan Mrs Bronson and her circle of cultivated Americans had been the dominant foreign influence. Flora soon ingratiated herself in the Bronson household, by making herself useful accompanying the older woman on her carriage drives around the district. Writers such as the aged Robert Browning and the young Henry James had come to Asolo as Mrs Bronson's guests. For *them*, Mrs Bronson was Asolo while for scholarly Italians, the deposed Queen Caterina Cornaro of Cyprus, and her court, pensioned in Asolo by the Venetian Republic in the fifteenth century, and Eleonora Duse, the great tragedienne and the inspiration of d'Annunzio in the early years of this century, were the dominant associations. Freya, in this context, had little significance. Virtually unknown to the wider Italian public, her work was untranslated until towards the end of her life.

As I walked slowly about the empty, off-season streets with Freya, I remembered, we had been accosted occasionally by elderly women, scrawny hags from whose grinning, gap-toothed mouths emanated raucous salutations. Freya's response was courteous but restrained, in the repressive manner of the Edwardian *grande dame*. 'So sorry I couldn't introduce you,' she murmured plummily, as we disengaged ourselves from such an encounter. 'I couldn't quite place them – their names escape me. Some of my mother's work people, you know, there are many of them about the town . . .'

I felt rather dashed by the stateliness of her manner. It had about it a touch of the Lady Bracknells. Now it seemed my curiosity was bringing me even closer to the Gladstone bag.

Freya's book about her childhood and youth, *Traveller's Prelude*, in which she set out her portrayals of her parents, had a long, interrupted and difficult travail before it finally appeared in 1950. Eight years earlier, on 26 April 1942, Cockerell had written to Freya in Baghdad, asking specific questions about her career. Then, in response to his enquiries, she told him she had never been out of Europe before 1927, nor east of Italy, and that she had been a semi-invalid from 1924 to 1927, not always but mostly on bed or sofa. This illness, she said, was the result of war strain, or a residual effect of typhoid during World War I. Her invalid period was spent partly in Italy at La Mortola, and partly in London with friends like Viva Jeyes, in St John's Wood (where she first met Cockerell in 1933), or at the Herbert Oliviers, on Campden Hill.

She began learning Arabic at La Mortola, she told him, as a means of occupying her mind and the deciding factor in her adoption of the language as a study was the presence of oil in the area. She was convinced that its inevitable increase in world importance would offer as yet unidentified opportunities for the enterprising and the bold. This interpretation may have been a borrowing from the soldier-diplomat Gerald de Gaury, who befriended her in 1929 when she first arrived in Iraq. As a young officer convalescing from wounds in World War I, he occupied himself studying Arabic in a similar way and for a similar reason.

By the time Freya answered Cockerell's letter she had received her mother's wartime prison diary, a copy of which was sent by Lady Iveagh through the diplomatic bag. With this the idea of an autobiography began to take shape in her mind. On 31 May she wrote to her mother in California complaining of tiredness and of the uphill nature of her work. She longed, she wrote, to sit in peace and quiet and evolve a book again, 'a sort of childhood book', and she asked Flora to write down what she could remember of the family's history and to send her a copy. She herself, Freya confessed, knew very little about her antecedents and looked to her mother for assistance. This was perhaps the last service Flora was able to perform for her daughter.

The exchange of letters with Cockerell in the early summer of 1942 heralded the burst of creativity that found its release four months later while she was on leave in Cyprus. Sitting in the bracken under the pine trees, in the dry hot stillness of the Troodos mountains, she put aside the tribulations of her working life and lost herself in a vivid recapture of her childhood. The setbacks, the disappointments of her present existence were forgotten and the exile's homesickness for what may indeed have been an imagined past found expression in a touching evocation of a troubled growing-up. Once started, her recollection flowed. She wrote and wrote, page after page in a loose sprawling hand. One weighty packet went from the island, another was dispatched from Beirut. Both safely reached their destination, their arrival recorded by Cockerell in the little notebook in which he slowly filled in the chronology of her life. When typed the 150 pages of manuscript formed the first sketch of her future autobiography.

This welling up of memory was a release from the unbearable pressures of weariness, depression, loneliness and the struggle to keep up spirits when the likelihood of the Middle East being overrun by German forces assumed ever more threatening proportions. It was less a record than an outpouring, a testament to a kinder, more secure world than that which she now inhabited. The pathos of this disclosure in an outwardly tough woman of almost fifty was what first warmed me to her, it opened up such vistas of despair, combated by a stubborn summoning up of all that was happiest and best in her own life, to stand by her at the hour of peril.

Renewed confidence in the outcome of the war as the tide turned at Alamein, combined with an unanticipated sense of personal loss after her mother's death in November 1942, produced an exaltation of spirit that enabled Freya at last to see Flora 'not so much as a mother, but as a very vivid entrancing presence' whose departure would leave more of a blank than most people.

Cockerell was her refuge in this period of strain and uncertainty. She told him on 25 October 1942 that the draft of her story sent him from Cyprus had entailed far more labour than she had anticipated.

Some day I would like to edit and simplify and possibly write it as a book; as it is, it is just the naked truth and is quite unfit for publication, and I had not the time even to read it over and see if what I wrote gave the impression of what I meant. It seems to me a fallacy that the unstudied version of a thing is the more truthful: the elaboration of style is merely the attempt to get the truth out, hidden by the vagueness of human speech. My style at least is merely the effort to say a thing as I see it, first to see clearly and then to find the word for it, but this I had no time for and wrote like a tap . . .[3]

This first purging of emotion in Cyprus enabled Freya to turn more easily to the technical problems of shaping her story once the war was over. It was not until early in 1948, after her marriage to Perowne, that she wrote to Cockerell from Barbados saying, 'I have pulled out the autobiography you will be glad to hear, and mean to try and see if any work can be done . . .'

It was something she did not embark on willingly. She had rather hoped that with marriage she could relax, and write at leisure, to please herself. Now, her own dissatisfaction with her role as Perowne's wife, and a need for self-justification, drove her to seek relief in literary work. She and Perowne did not see eye to eye about the disposal of her earnings, which Freya regarded as entirely her own, or about the demands of their official position which Perowne relished and Freya despised. A letter of 13 January 1948 marks the first open divergence on this topic.

The only extra income that is likely to come to me is a book now and then, and that I *never will* devote to Ordinary Life! . . . Please never ask me to spend it on everyday existence, because I won't. For that we must share and share alike, and we shall be poor, but there it is!

When the first volume of autobiography appeared in 1950, it was hailed as her masterpiece. The three succeeding volumes, which brought her life up to 1946, never recaptured the intensity of feeling of the first and degenerated ultimately into a recital of events, of books read, of people known, the wonder of emergence from the chrysalis overtaken by polemical issues.

She has an odd way of telescoping or expanding time to suit herself. The collapse of an ardent friendship of many years' duration is disposed of in a couple of paragraphs, while pages may be devoted to musings upon philosophic abstractions, or evocations of the Historical Past. 'Freya can get three chapters out of peeling a banana,' was the comment of one disgruntled acquaintance. Her flair for self-dramatisation led her to the actor's preference for looking outward to the effect of the telling gesture, rather than to the poet's inwardness, something she rather confusingly told her mother in 1941 she considered 'a fundamentally aristocratic trait'. It enabled her to tell her story uninhibited by self-questioning or doubt, an extrovert account that was picturesque and entertaining, and fashioned with considerable skill.

Having in high dudgeon cut short her first visit to Perowne in Barbados, returning to Asolo in July 1948, she wrote to Cockerell about the autobiography from Vallombrosa, where she had gone to consult Bernard Berenson.

I have done four chapters . . . and have read them to BB, and he thinks I ought to do it on a quite different plan, not going straight, chronologically, but building it up more artistically to lead up to my own real life of travel and writing. I feel he may be right but it is an appalling thought . . .

She got around her difficulties by what the French writer Jacques Supervielle called 'the memory that forgets because it selects, and by its selection creates . . .' This device, redolent of a musing feminine passivity, was employed by the French novelist Colette in the early years of the century with considerable success. Freya reconstituted her growing-up by a use of emotional undertones and evocative descriptions not dissimilar to Colette's. It was a valediction and a clearing away of what had gone before, a defining of the past that enabled her at last to put it behind her. The artist's selective memory was at work. Like Eurydice at the mouth of the Underworld, her mother Flora and the past's reality receded as Freya looked back at her own youth.

TWENTY-FOUR

FATHER AND MOTHER

When Freya came to write about her two parents in *Traveller's Prelude* her mother was the harder to digest. 'My new chapter is so difficult,' she told Perowne on 8 August 1948, 'as my mother is so *improbable*! If I don't explain, it looks very *louche*, and if I do it is rather brutal.'[1]

Freya shrank from the personal, private aspects of her mother's life, and from the light this might throw on her own interpretation of her parents' marriage. In introducing a hint of sexual surmise over the relationship of her mother and the young di Roascio – something she conscientiously denied in the next breath – she projected her own tendency to infatuation on to her parent, while passing over and ignoring any hint of feminist idealism as a motivating force for Flora's domestic rebellion. In doing so she perhaps betrayed Flora's memory for it was taken for granted by her readers that Flora and di Roascio were lovers, and what Flora believed was a struggle for her own and her daughters' independence was reduced by Freya to a misguided and undignified surrender to a passion for a younger man.

In Freya's story, Flora sacrificed her family's interests over a period of sixteen years to her infatuation for di Roascio, living in a little Piedmontese town to be with him, devoting all her time, and much-needed Stark money, to his business, and by her unconventional behaviour exposing her daughters to comment and social ostracism.

To disclose such a story posed problems for Freya. Although she might appear to court it, she was sensitive to gossip and speculation. Social acceptance, perhaps as a result of unhappy experiences in youth, was always important to her. But Flora seems to have been impervious to such considerations. In Freya's view she deceived herself, and thought of her life in Dronero 'as business and the emancipation of women; and went on serenely secure in a technical morality, so that I have looked with suspicion on technical moralities ever since.'[2] Robert Stark, Freya's 'dear old Pips', however, is painted in as a dearly-loved and loving father whose memory she often invoked, much as she summoned up the ghost of W. P. Ker to preside over her old age. Her delicate and touching account of her childhood is a loving homage to him, a beautiful celebration of his unobtrusive respect for the natural world: the model, she indicated, for her own outlook on life.

Her *Letters*, published over forty years after his death, offset this idealised picture. The affectionate tone is there, but also a certain weariness. His limitations are recognised and his resistance to any form of coercion accepted. However much Freya may have wanted it, having once escaped his family, nothing was going to induce Robert Stark to return. Freya worked hard to forge links of emotional and intellectual reciprocity with him, sending him books and papers which interested her, but it was uphill work. 'Not enough adventure' was his terse dismissal of Gertrude Bell's account of her early travels along the Syrian borderlands in 1907. She sent him records for his gramophone – foxtrots and two-steps were what he preferred – and the shilling 'shockers' which were his favourite relaxation. His letters are flat in tone and deal with practicalities. He seemed more interested in possible new species of plants than in Freya's actual adventures. 'Freya is on her way back to the East exploring in the Alamut Country,' he wrote to Playters Stark in January 1931, 'she found a host of flowers over there . . . Have arranged with Department of Agriculture Ottowa so she can send any plants to them direct to have grown on and established.'

He and his brother were skilled horticulturists and in 1927

he moved from fruit farming into the more lucrative commercial bulb-breeding market, underplanting his orchard with daffodils and tulips. When the blooms were freighted to the Plains for the florists' trade, both the brothers' households busied themselves packing long flat boxes with this cargo.[3] Such aesthetic satisfaction as he needed he found in the contemplation of the view across the Kootenay Lake to the big mountain landscape beyond. He built a picture window in his four-roomed wooden ranch house for that particular purpose, and in his last years it was where he liked to sit, looking at the sunset.

He had a stroke in 1927, just prior to Freya's first departure to the East, but refused to have her alter her plans, vigorously rebuffing any suggestion that she should come out to Canada to nurse him. 'Coraggio, per Bacco,' he telegraphed. 'Go East: I am half cured.' With this uncompromising rejection of her presence, Freya started off on the travels that would make her famous.

From 1911 until 1950 and *Traveller's Prelude*, no-one else mentions him and, reading the book with hindsight, one might think he was an invention, a necessary victim, the inevitable dupe in a *commedia dell'arte* story in which his son-in-law, di Roascio, is Harlequin. His retiring nature made it hard to fashion more than a subsidiary role for him in the drama of the emotions on which Freya was about to embark in 1948. To admit the search for a father substitute would imperil the existing legend, the sentimentalised picture of 'dear old Pips' that was already part of her acknowledged background.

Freya's sentimental education was neglected in childhood, and she received little guidance on what constitutes sensibility. In part this was to do with the period in which she was growing up. The Edwardians, supported by ample reserves of cheap domestic labour, were discovering children as delightful pets, and a burgeoning literature developed in which the primitive quality of childhood was presented as part of the mystery and poetry of the childish state. What had formerly been moral delinquency was now natural high spirits, bridled but tolerated; there were no shadows in the child mind for these Edwardians,

all was whimsical, full of tenderness and reticent pathos, and
delightful humour. When so much charm was the order of the
day, how was Freya to explain Robert Stark's defection from
family life?

She got round her technical problems by editing her material
to suit her story line. This resulted in an element of ambiguity
that drew the attention of the reviewers. Philip Tomlinson in
the *Times Literary Supplement* hailed the book as an uplifting
reconciliation of past and present that has 'the allurement of
the mystery of fiction and the astonishment of fact'. Freya's
father, he wrote, 'is one of the grand characters in a story
packed with personalities. The mother, too, is striking, but
enigmatic to the end. We see the man, and understand him;
his wife, for all her charm, seems always a little beyond the
borders of our comprehension.'[4] The di Roascio factory and
Freya's bitter and unsuccessful struggle to recover the money
Flora invested and earned for it form the sombre background
to the girl's upbringing in Piedmont before the 1914–18 war.
The role of the factory in the story – 'the non-human personality, the family Moloch, which . . . sat in the background
devouring money' – and the frequent and telling references to
it are also noted by the *Observer* with some puzzlement.[5]

In Freya's account her father's failure as a parent was
explained as a sensitive shrinking away from marital incompatibility, aggravated by the rashness of her mother's conduct. The
burden of his loss could then be hung on Flora, so that at a
deeper level an idealised intimacy between father and daughter
could be sustained. But she did not stop there. She also implied
that Flora in 1913 pushed her daughter Vera, aged barely eighteen, into marriage with a man of thirty-five who, if not actually
Flora's lover, was generally believed to have been so by the
family's English friends. Why in the circumstances Robert Stark
should come from Canada to attend the wedding – the only time
he was ever seen in church, so his daughter wrote – is never
satisfactorily explained. Freya herself conscientiously denied
the imputation, but there is perhaps a clue in the delicately
written, sensitively evoked episode where Freya, at the age of
sixteen, becomes aware that di Roascio's increasing friendliness

towards herself is motivated by something other than his usual bouncing self-assertion, and has the instinctive foresight to snub his overtures.

In this way self-esteem could be maintained, and the humiliation of being passed over in favour of her younger sister is explained away. But that the mother should be made responsible for such an outcome implies a conflict of feeling on Freya's part too painful to acknowledge even to herself.

In reality, Freya's adolescent love affair was with her mother, not with her father, and the jealousy she experienced in this context set the pattern of her adult social life. Her father had in fact become something of an ogre by the 1900s, short-tempered and impatient. The real damage sustained by Freya in youth was not her accident or the loss of an English home but Robert Stark's self-absorption and his withdrawal so early from his daughters' lives. Freya entered adolescence with no-one except her mother to admire or with whom to fall in love, an uprush of emotion touched off by Flora's warmth and solicitude at the time of the accident at Dronero. To a child hungry for attention the concentration on herself of her mother's powerful personality was an intoxicating experience. It imprinted her with a grateful love of her own sex which assuaged what may also have been a secret fear of her own unlovability. That any attention, even punitive attention, is better than nothing is something learnt early by anxious children craving sympathy and affection.

Freya writes feelingly of this period in her autobiography. In the immediate pain and distress that accompanied the girl's skin-grafting treatment in hospital at Turin, Flora was Freya's chief support.

I can still feel the warmth and delight of my mother's presence. She now devoted herself to me, and I *discovered* her, as it were. Her love, which now became greater for me than for Vera, probably dates from this time when I was nearly lost. After about two months, [she continues rather strangely] my father arrived [from Devon], and sat for hours by my bedside, showing his affection by rubbing my arm gently, till he chafed it raw: I was too polite to ask him to stop, and perhaps dimly conscious that it made him happy to think he was doing something for me.

Freya's account of her love for her mother is a touching record of altruistic adolescent ardour.

My mother was now all my happiness. I adored her, and began to notice, indignantly, but without understanding, that nearly all her old friends had left her, or if they came once [to Dronero], never returned . . . I don't think my mother noticed: at any rate she did not care. She had no time to do so; she worked from early morning to dusk. She became someone not only to be admired, but to be protected. I spent half my time thinking out things to please her, and waited for her when she came home in the evening, helping her to wash and change. She was so used to these adorations that she took it all very easily – a thing always dangerous for any human being to do. But our love [i.e. Freya's love for her mother] went on for years, unquestioning, and gave me that warm background of affection [i.e. something to love] with which my life has always been provided in one way or another. Vera, far more independent in herself, looked on in a reserved way – as she had done with King Arthur, years before . . .

In Freya's accounts of her adolescence in Dronero with her mother and sister, the three might seem to have spent a good deal of time curled up in bed together, a defensive feminine huddle against the only predatory male in their vicinity, Mario di Roascio. But voluptuous intimacies – the entwined arms, affectionate embraces, sentimental poses, shared grooming – between women were an accepted part of Victorian life, lingering on into the new century, and only routed by the mannish affectations and brusqueness of the Edwardian New Woman.

Throughout her mother's life Freya's dependence on her for moral support was great. It was as if she needed an audience – a captive audience – whose applause would validate her own success, and this the mother supplied. Freya the performer, and the mother the accessory witness, was a unity that fed on itself, and a triumphant demonstration of the daughter's ascendancy over the parent. Perhaps it was the only way Freya could resolve the conflicts inherent in her relationship with her mother.

This relationship was possibly the single most important one in Freya's life, and the one she was least able to manage. She depended on Flora for all sorts of services, even when her own reputation as a writer was made and she had escaped into a success far removed from the early Italian years. Throughout Flora's life, when they were separated, the long lively accounts of places and people flowed from Freya's pen on an almost daily basis, a steadily accumulating store of correspondence understood by both to be a memory-bank for future use; meanwhile at home in Asolo Freya's work in progress was discussed and read over with her parent.

Flora saw to Freya's clothes. Freya's appearance was a subject of absorbing interest to both women and was discussed without inhibition. Her mother found the materials for her outfits and the clever little seamstresses to make the pretty lingerie that Freya liked, and to copy and make-over dresses sent out to Freya each season, parcels of which followed her around the Middle East and contributed to the fuss which attended Freya's descents on the households of her friends.

The intimacy of the correspondence between mother and daughter, extending over so many years, came as a surprise to pre-war friends when extracts were published by Freya in her old age. The affectionate tone was unexpected. They had not always received this impression of the daughter's relations with her mother and it required an effort of rethinking on their part to accept that Freya compartmented her intimacies so that no one person – except perhaps her mother – had access to all her life.

Freya wanted and needed to love. Her nature blossomed in response to others' recognition, but that was a reflection, a response with no organic life of its own. Whatever grew of herself, grew secretly, and in the dark. But once experienced, she sought again the sense of buoyant well-being and happiness that being in love induces. It was a need, an appetite, that demanded to be fed, so that when real relationships failed, imaginary ones were substituted, to induce the constant senti-mental excitement that was so pleasurable and gratifying, how-ever secret from others it might be. Out of this perhaps arose the disingenuousness that runs like a thread through her own autobiographical writings. She specialised in the *faux-naif*. This took in some, and amused others. Her spontaneity, and light-ness of touch in the writing, engaged people's sympathy. She was careful to claim nothing for herself; whatever interpretation others cared to make was not her responsibility, and this fed the romantic imagination of the armchair traveller.

It was a concealment and displacement of grief and resent-ment that was to permeate Freya's whole life. Emotions accumulated in one situation are discharged in another, a knock-on effect which confused people drawn into a too rapid intimacy with her and led to misunderstandings and disappointment. Much as in the abstract she longed for it, she could not manage a sustained intimacy at close quarters; her affection was best transmitted through a diffused sociability. The story of her life is sown with quarrels and breaches of relationships, almost always ardent friendships which begin enthusiastically and end negatively, sometimes in silence and neglect, sometimes in a blazing row. The latter was more common with women; her friendships with men were cooler and based on shared interests and admiration of her talent. 'It is easy to become cross with Freya,' Elizabeth Monroe told me in 1979, 'but difficult to remain so. She is such good value! Her intelligence is her great-est gift and asset, perhaps the explanation of her power to infuriate, and still to melt. It is her actual presence that produces the melting effect, all the men adore her . . .'

Freya's response to admiration was matched by an over-sensitivity which did not tolerate criticism or being taken for granted; spiteful reprisals soon followed. Applause, acceptance, meant much to her, it was immaterial from where it came. The important thing was that she – her individuality – received it, and in the mirror of other people's admiration she could perceive her own reality. It was this, far more than lack of looks, which probably accounts for her failure to form any lasting attachment. Many plain, forceful, intelligent women have made successful marriages, or formed a permanent partnership. Freya's need for attention, with its resultant injection of drama into her relationships, was something most people preferred to avoid when seeking a companion, but the worldly could enjoy Freya for her stimulating company, her well-stocked mind, her quickness of wit, gaiety and a quaint but entertaining shrewdness.

Her sexual bias was always a puzzle to her friends but her propensity towards infatuation inspired amusement rather than anxiety. No-one took it seriously. To the superficial observer it might seem that men were Freya's target, while women were of secondary importance, mere appendages of the important males, to be patronised, snubbed or ignored, yet this apparent predeliction for male company was possibly a smokescreen to disguise other inclinations, hidden even from herself. Physical beauty in women, itemised and extolled, was often recorded by Freya, while parallel good looks in men pass unremarked unless their possessors are indigenous inhabitants and, like the Queen of Spain, they can be considered objectively as asexual beings, having no lower extremities.

Her emotional history is one of persistent misinterpreted ardour and of tacit evasion by men, and of domineering relationships with younger women, culminating on their part with rebellion. The pattern of distortion was set in childhood by her father's defection; it was followed by her brother-in-law's choice of her sister instead of herself, while her blighted romance with Guido Ruata in 1916 had little to do with the war. It was embarked on while Italy was still neutral and with a man nearly twenty years her senior. She was a casualty of the sexual politics of people more sophisticated than herself, a bruising situation into which she blundered with all the force of a nature resistant to advice and deaf to all warnings. The resultant shock was severe. To her lack of social definition was now added the haunting sense of sexual rejection and together they combined to alienate her from the preoccupations of her contemporaries and led her to seek her satisfactions elsewhere. Intellectual compatibility and shared experience became the touchstone for her friendships. She had no time for the obscure and the commonplace; they were a potential contamination too risky for one in her own marginal situation. Only the successful qualified for her attention.

Perhaps her mother's well-meant attempts to disguise her daughter's cropped and stitched head, when she returned to Dronero from hospital, with the lace-edged cotton hoods, set up in the girl an instinct to conceal, to disguise her singularity. That would be a structuralist's interpretation of many puzzling aspects of Freya's adult personality. 'The scars got much smaller,' she wrote, 'but have always remained, and were a constant trouble, making me self-conscious and also no doubt spoiling such looks as I might have had.'

Here she deceived herself. Freya was a plain child, and grew into a plain young woman, while her scars were more apparent to herself than to anyone else. It was hard having a handsome, forceful, able mother, and a pretty, quiet, graceful sister, but that is the luck of the draw in families. Freya was rather like the Toad Prince in the fairy-tale, whose beauty is hidden like a jewel in his head, a vitality and intelligence redeemable only by another's recognition and pity. The need to obtain this became the mainspring of Freya's life, a need not always understood by associates impressed by the glamour of her own success.

Projection on to a faithless other of one's own failings is a common neurotic aberration. If Freya's capacity to deceive herself as to others' responses is remarkable, so too is her ability to reverse the implication of a situation. This made her very useful as a propagandist. So sensitive was she to neglect or rejection that the compensating mechanism was activated at a much earlier level of feeling than would be usual, and a screen of make-believe obscured painful reality from herself, as well as from others. Hence the belief that people were always in love with her, that loving affection and interest accompanied her every move. She disguised her possessive love for her mother in her love for a fictionalised father, but the distorted imprint of her sexual choice remained, something secret and unacknowledged, a bias towards love of women concealed by flirtatiousness and the need to captivate men.

It was in the captivation of the other sex, the holders of power whom a clever woman could manipulate, if she kept her nerve, that Freya's need to dominate found acceptable expression. She never wanted the responsibility of power, what she wanted was the secret satisfaction of having influence. It enabled her to claim success for ideas put into operation by others. It was a displacement, a disconnection between concept and execution, that perhaps accounts for the mystifications surrounding her wartime activities, and the speculations as to what she *really* was up to. It provided satisfaction to her vanity, and blunted her sensibility, so that people who fell foul of her found her overbearing and hard, lacking in sympathy and often devious.

This was the other side of the coin from the lively good humour and optimism she generally presented on show in public. Her skill in drawing people out, her interest in other lives, contributed to this impression of genial accessibility. Her persistence and courage as the tide of battle turned against the British in 1940 heartened wartime associates assailed by doubts and anxieties as the years of isolation, of lost battles and shifting loyalties followed the triumphant overrunning of Western Europe by the Nazis. Few looked beyond the courageous exterior, or speculated as to its antecedents.

She was impatient of criticism. Failure to get her way produced explosions of rage, or episodes of brooding sulks lasting several days, culminating in migraine or unspecified illness until conciliatory attitudes were adopted by those about her, and then the cloud of misery and depression lifted and her spirits rose with it. Targets for her ill-humour were often the husbands or lovers of particular favourites among the younger women whose friendship she cultivated, and whose company she aspired to. Possession of the Villa Freia was an ace card in the dreary post-war years of austerity in Britain; people were very ready to take up Freya's pressing suggestions for visits but, disappointingly, they shied off the various schemes she proposed for more permanent arrangements. These were to look after Freya in her declining years and share the upkeep of the household, first at the Villa Freia, then at Montoria, in exchange for the promise of ultimate inheritance of the property by the offspring of their choice on Freya's death.[6]

Whenever she was tired or depressed Freya craved for the warm feminine solicitude that finds expression in the little attentions that comfort a sickbed. Being ill and convalescing in other people's houses is a regular feature of her social life. It was as if she sought to recapture the grateful confidence and dependence of childhood invalidism and it is hardly surprising that as the years went by and things became less easy for what had been the leisured classes, several friendships wilted. Only very grand households, people felt, could provide the service and attention Freya exacted; lesser folk had no longer the time or the servants.

Freya never escaped this particular emotional enthralment. The shock of her accident in Dronero and the resultant quality of her mother's solicitude seemed to have imprinted themselves so forcibly that the only form of love she could recognise was emotional subservience responding to constant demand. Flora's personality was too strong a draught for a child who had not enjoyed a settled environment and all the varying relationships that go with it, but had been forced to concentrate herself hungrily on the limited options within her immediate circle. The family's early life, drifting in and out of the artists' colonies popular on both sides of the Channel, their children dragged around with them in care of a foreign governess, and kept away from the local children, fostered the attention-getting proclivities which were so marked a feature of Freya's personality, even when she had secured recognition and fame. She adored being fussed over by 'nice little nurses', was always in and out of nursing homes and hospitals, or taking cures at obscure spas. There were endless consultations with doctors and specialists over real or imagined illnesses, a constant preoccupation with health and appearance is part of her legend. Every adventure had its own drama of illness and the threat of death.

That Life should be lived as Art was something that Freya

absorbed from her reading as a girl in Dronero when, isolated for long periods from English life, she had little to do but read. At fifteen, that aesthete's guidebook, Walter Pater's *Marius the Epicurean*, was a powerful influence, read and re-read. It is Freya's heroic achievement that by painstaking attention to her own personal development she transformed herself in accordance with her belief. She made herself into a work of art, something built up layer by layer out of the accretions of her long life. She annexed and incorporated whatever impressed her. Her imitative faculty was strong. She was quick to catch the tone of a society, to subscribe to its attitudes, until another discovery overlaid it or another opportunity beckoned. She enjoyed operating at several levels concurrently; it all added to the fun. In this way a personality was evolved that was unique and entertaining, but also irritating and baffling in its variation. As late as 1948 she records rereading *Marius*, and finding her appreciation unchanged.

When I advanced this theory to her former husband, Stewart Perowne, he exploded. 'Work of Art, Work of Art,' he snorted, 'that woman's not a Work of Art, she's a Force of Nature!'

I had to laugh.

Freya at work, Gerald de Gaury, 1955.

TWENTY-FIVE

A BLITHE SPIRIT

Freya always enjoyed talking about herself. She was a fluent communicator, and excellent company. Conversation was her forte, something to be orchestrated and controlled; truth was relative and should not interfere with the grand design. The achievement of the right effect was more important to her than the precise fact. For the chosen young whom she liked to gather around her she did perhaps open windows which left to themselves they might not have known how to unlatch; at least that was what she believed when she took her godchildren and their friends on camping trips around the Aegean and southern Turkey in the 1950s.

The boys were to be the vehicles by which her beliefs would be transmitted to future generations. The girls had only to make suitable marriages and influence their husbands. The laughter this proposition evoked among the young women concerned was a disappointment to Freya, and signalled the withdrawal of her favour.[1]

What Freya actually did was always secondary to what was reported about her. This did not always go down well with people who in earlier, more humble days, had befriended her as a newcomer to the East; it was felt, in some obscure way, that her notoriety trivialised their own best years and this dismayed them. The gaiety and charm of her early work, and her unassuming approach to it, had earned her the enthusiastic appreciation of elderly admirers in London such as Admiral

Goodenough at the Royal Geographical Society, and Sydney Cockerell. On her first appearance on the London literary scene, at the beginning of the Thirties, Freya displayed many of the attributes of the popular fictional heroine of recent wartime – The Right Sort of Girl – trusty, sporting, perhaps a little old-fashioned, ardent and adventurous. Her feminine smallness, her delightful modesty, her air of brave independence, belonged to a period uncontaminated by the raffishness of the Jazz Age. The award to Freya in 1942 of the RGS's Founder's Gold Medal, its highest distinction, was pushed through by the Admiral's influence at a period when feats of scientific exploration were in abeyance because of World War II.

Perhaps her greatest achievement was her breaking through the sheer weight of prejudice she had to contend with as an unattached woman making her way in a closed society dominated by a particular male educational elite, very conscious of being the guardians of a unique inheritance. The English technique of reducing to impotence, either by ignoring, or by treating the outsider with patronising levity, was hard to withstand for one with a limited experience of the English social system; it was the resourcefulness and determination she showed on arrival in Iraq at the end of 1929 that made her interesting to more discriminating observers and earned her their friendship. Once launched as the acclaimed author of entertaining accounts of travel in remote areas of the Middle East, the charm of her writing and the liveliness of her wit did the rest.

The thing that strikes me now is the very makeshift quality of her first travels. She arrived in the East with the flimsiest awareness of existing political structures, and a total ignorance of the conventions of colonial rule, inspired more by the glamour of T. E. Lawrence's World War I exploits among the Arabs than by scholarly interest in other cultures. The giants of the 1914–18 Middle East theatre of war, Lord Allenby and Sir Percy Cox, presided in retirement over the Royal Asiatic and Royal Geographical Societies, whose endorsements of Freya's enterprise as a traveller launched her literary career. But to the general public she was by no means a household name. In terms of contemporary adventure she was already out of date.

Wartime developments of tracked vehicles enabled people to take Citroën cars into Central Asia, and to explore Libyan desert oases. When Freya was making her first modest journeys in Persia, Amy Johnson's daring single-handed flight to Australia had already made her a world heroine. Freya was never in that league. The most she achieved was a certain notoriety when she was airlifted into Aden by the RAF in 1935 for hospitalisation after an attack of measles in Hadhramaut.

Freya's motivation as a traveller came under discussion early in her career. Her rise to fame seemed to derive more from shrewd journalistic instinct than from intellectual curiosity; she was looking for copy leading to recognition by her own people and financial reward. Money was always important to her. She was careful of it, and reluctant to spend on general necessities more than was essential, though with success she became increasingly self-indulgent where her own tastes were concerned.[2] Dress was always a major preoccupation. Saving for a particular object was a discipline forced on her in youth, a habit that never left her. She was unsympathetic to others' financial difficulties. A young god-daughter, to whom a small yearly sum was sent to build up a travel fund, was kindly but firmly rebuked when she confided that she had spent ten shillings of it on a bow and arrows. The money was sent, Freya wrote, to be saved for the purpose of travel, which is expensive; it was not to be dissipated on random fancies.

It was the constraints of her own meagre budgets that gave her individuality as a traveller. As in a fairy-tale, the trials she endured in the pursuit of her chosen adventure turned to advantage; it gave her the awareness of humble life in eastern countries that made her experiences so intimate and enthralling to her readers. Freya's tolerant acceptance of local life and the foibles of her travelling companions impressed her compatriots, deeply imbued with a sense of the mysterious otherness – and distrust – of the native life over which they as Britons presided.

From both her parents, and growing up in pre-1914 Italy, Freya inherited an ease of communication with very simple people that was unselfconscious and natural. This was unusual among her fellow-countrymen in positions of authority in the

1920s and 1930s, and it gave her perceptions, in their eyes, their particular quality of originality and authenticity. It was as far as she could go. Her chosen stance was that of an observer, passing through landscapes and societies in inward isolation, yet drawing in stores of intellectual sustenance from the experience which would be transmuted by her talent into literature. It was what Graham Greene described as the essential chip of ice in the heart of the writer.

Freya's awareness of her own singularity in slipping through the net of conventional experience grew as her travels continued. It was the shedding of identity, the casting off, the loosening of holds that entry into the fluidity of native life promised her; an abandonment of self such as others find in the many varieties of religious experience. There is a dimension to Freya's journeys that differentiates her from more prosaic travellers. Her adventures are as much adventures of the spirit as records of toughness and persistence and it is her willingness to venture, to enter the unfamiliar, that earned her the recognition of men who had the imaginative resources, but perhaps not the opportunity, or the daring, to do the same.

Unlike her mother, she was not a feminist, nor a socialist; her instincts were conservative and she had no taste for bohemianism. Her ideas were not in themselves original; she was essentially a communicator, a populariser of others' findings, yet in herself she was an oddity – *une originale* – someone out of the ordinary whom many felt it a privilege to know. It was this that interested me; I wondered what particular mix of ingredients had produced the mythic identity.

The skill, fluency and charm of her early writing was a prime asset. Her early books are eminently readable. A reader could share vicariously in her adventures (a word she frequently used to describe her activities) without any taint of sordid brutality. There are no horrors, unless they are safely distanced by history. At worst, an animal is slaughtered, a bird tormented, a pet lizard dies; very rarely is there pity for another human. A stoic acceptance of fate and a turning away from the foredoomed is the chosen attitude.

The combination of travel in difficult country and the bringing back of photographic records of defunct empires, and of the people still living among their remains, became the hallmark of her particular experience. In this, as well as being a prototype of today's photojournalist, she was a lineal descendant of those early travelling artists in Asia and the Near East who recorded what they saw, first with notebook and measuring instruments, then with sketch-book and paint-box and eventually with camera. These men never had the romantic cachet attached to aristocratic wanderers such as Lady Hester Stanhope and the Blunts, who found in the desert solace for feelings and ambitions disappointed in their own society. Rather, they were the precursors of full-blown Romanticism, sturdy assemblers of information on which others could develop more individualistic interpretations. Travel increasingly became the means by which the writer's personality could be consciously displayed, so that the journey itself was the vehicle for self-expression.

Freya's lack of formal education was at first an advantage to her as a traveller, and gave her early writing a freshness which was its charm. She expressed with artless confidence perceptions evolved in isolation, but once she became a celebrity her work suffered. The lighthearted fun of the first books was lost in rather sententious uplift, so that many of her former admirers found her later books pretentious and unreadable.

She worked on a very circumscribed, personal scale, small journeys, small discoveries, small pleasures, and this gave her work its particular intimacy. When she attempted the grand sweep of historical narrative she was less successful; the excitement of her intellectual discoveries – for she read up the subject as she went along – never turned into the serious recognition she aspired to, and it is as an elegant descriptive writer that she is best remembered.

As an artist, she responded to words. The pinning down in exact phrases of a perception afforded her an almost sensuous delight, and she would work over her cadenced allusive evocations of time and place with the concentration of a scribe decorating a manuscript. In the 1950s a series of journeys in Turkey provided material for the travel books on which she depended for her living, but as conditions in the Middle East changed and freedom of movement for the traveller became increasingly restricted, she turned towards what she described as historical disquisitions, and padded the work out with musing and reflection, laced with literary quotations often found for her by her friends. Lots of people loved this, but others, tougher-minded, found it woolly and unsatisfactory. Instead of Political Agents and Consuls well placed to assist the recommended traveller, Freya now had to deal with suspicious local police chiefs not always susceptible to her charm or impressed by her credentials. There were some unfortunate episodes in which Freya failed to get her way. This encouraged her to give up travel and turn back into history.

Yet despite all this it was generally acknowledged among people who had known Freya during the war period that she made a good job of her old age. Something immature in her early personality mellowed with time into a serene acceptance of her own uniqueness and freed her of the compulsion to assert herself. This Indian summer of the personality was impressive. Her manner towards the suitably recommended young was perfect. Several men recalled how nice she had been to them, shy, awkward schoolboys, and how pleasant had been her interest and the attention she accorded them. Women were more inclined to have reservations, and it seemed accepted among the god-daughters that after the age of eighteen there was little room for them in their famous godmother's life. Yet 'Golden, quite golden,' was Elizabeth Monroe's recollection of her performance with an American post-graduate student who delayed her flight home on the mere chance of a meeting with the legendary personality.

She was by nature credulous, susceptible to flattery and charmed by attention. Her vanity was an aspect of her personality frequently commented on. On one level, that of wartime patriotism, she *did* believe in what she was doing, while her air of bracing optimism was a refreshing change from the hard-boiled attitudes of more jaded male colleagues. It encouraged confidence in the value of her pronouncements, as if some holy fool had entered the courts of beleaguered monarchs and with childlike simplicity was showing the way forward. That the emotional fuel for her convictions might derive from something other than pure patriotism was something that in those hurried, difficult times, robust, pragmatic British minds would not want to examine.

For hardened professional men so to underwrite her is a tribute to the heartening quality of Freya's patriotism in 1940. In a very bad patch of the war it earned her a lot of credit in the small but influential circle of Middle East policy-makers. One colleague, publishing his memoirs in 1970, likened Freya's efforts with her Brotherhood to the reunions of the early Christians in the catacombs of Rome, and attributed her success 'to the simplicity and sincerity of Freya herself . . . a remarkable instance of the persuasive power of positive good'.[3] Whether her insistence on the underlying affection for Britain among Iraqis and Egyptians – 'people who in their own hearts are already on our side,' she wrote – client states occupied militarily and held firmly to their treaty obligations with Britain, was a romantic misconception influenced by her own need to feel loved is mere speculation, but it paralleled Gertrude Bell's conviction in 1922 that she had obtained 'the love and confidence of a whole nation'. It was as if recognition from even the humblest and most volatile elements in the native population was enough to assure them that the capture of Arab gratitude and loyalty was a permanent thing.

The war years that promoted her worldly success were an increasingly arid experience. Her inner life, like some hidden river, disappeared under the sands of the encroaching desert, a dried-up watercourse from whose subterranean depths occasional draughts of refreshment might be extracted. Touring Kurdistan on Brotherhood business in 1942, she told her mother:

It has been glorious to see country I had been longing to reach for years, and there were mountain visions of pure joy . . . But to tell the truth I had only one little bit of *pure* happiness, when the car had to have its hood done and I walked on *alone* for twenty minutes with just the river gurgling beside me, and I had no-one to say the right thing to, no propaganda, no-one to make work . . . oh joy![4]

It was as if people were becoming secondary to her inner experiences and, in the manner of children who believe themselves neglected and misunderstood by those about them, she sought solace in her own feelings and imagination.

The post-war praise and recognition bestowed by 'old friends' reaching the climax of their official careers fostered a growing sense of her own uniqueness in Freya, and helped disperse the disappointments of her personal life. It enabled her to think of herself not as an individual, but as the witness of a heroic era, when wars were fought and won and generous ideals upheld against the wickedness of inhuman tyrants. It was a licence to promote her beliefs with energy and persistence, her individual identity subsumed in the stately march of history. As she had written to me on 28 August 1979, when I first entered into correspondence with her, she saw her life as a record, part of that heroic procession in which she had always walked, since she was first introduced to the Homeric legends at the age of eight. In having her Brotherhood publicised she would be preserving a lesson for posterity, not promoting her own personality; that was only something incidental to the greater vision. Freya's belief in the unique richness of her experience, spanning most of the twentieth century and documented by her books and her correspondence, led her to insist on its value as a historical record, and to consider the publication of her letters a self-evident right. Not everyone agreed with this.

Much of Freya's philosophic stance in old age derived from W. P. Ker's interpretation of the role in European culture of the sixth-century writer, Boethius, whose *Consolations of Philosophy* written in prison while awaiting execution had enormous prestige in medieval literature, and was the intellectual bridge between the worlds of ancient Greece and modern Europe.

'It is hardly possible,' wrote Ker, 'to mistake the character of Boethius . . . as above all others the preacher of Obedience in its most ideal form.' The attractions of such a mind in periods of accelerated change, of *fin de siècle* anxieties and the threat of another Dark Age encroaching on an ancient world are clear. Ker admired the *Consolations*, even though it belonged, he said, to the secondary order of books 'that are dependent on others, that are reflective, not imaginative or creative, that are informed by the soft, conciliatory graces of minds to whom obedience, appreciation, interpretation are the appointed task, rather than any original work in poetry or philosophy'. This seems to me to define Freya's status in the literature of her period.

Freya did not enter into generalised public interest until in her very old age, when she was approaching ninety. By this time her royalties were declining and concern about the cost of her financial upkeep was troubling her friends. Between 1977 and 1980 the BBC built two television documentaries around her legendary reputation as a traveller; against stunning backgrounds of desert and mountain landscapes the producers, one her godson Mark Lennox-Boyd, introduced to an amused public the small, stumping figure of an old woman discoursing with dignity and an almost childlike innocence on Death and kindred topics aboard a leaky raft on the Euphrates, and reciting passages from Matthew Arnold against a backdrop of Himalayan glaciers.

Thus, in her late eighties, Freya was moved from the private into the public domain, good-humouredly recognised as a genuine 'English eccentric' by mass audiences who had perhaps never read the books that in the 1930s earned her reputation as a traveller. It was a well-meaning attempt to raise funds by popularising a personality which had prided itself on its exclusivity, but Freya was happy to be involved in the experiment. She liked to feel she was forwarding her favourites' careers by lending herself to schemes which often originated in her own experiences. It generated a revival of interest in her, and paperback reprints of her early work soon appeared to supplement the *Letters* already on the production line.

In this last burst of acclaim the personality was still just intact. It was a source of irritated incomprehension to her at the age of eighty-six that livery stables, travel agencies, airlines, should fight shy of her custom, unwilling to accept the responsibility, or that local guides should decide for her what was feasible or not. Her last public role was as a performance artist. A stream of visitors, vetted and introduced by the manager of the Cipriani Hotel in Asolo, called to sample the famous personality, and to be photographed with her on her terrace overlooking the Venetian plain. Even at ninety Freya could still make small talk in three or four languages. What she said might not be very profound, or indeed very relevant, but she responded courteously to others' friendliness. The simplicity of her manner was touching and impressive. Her pleasure in the attentions she received was unfeigned, and many felt uplifted and reassured by contact with such a golden old age.

Freya's talent had led her into a wonderful world where wealth, privilege and high achievement were taken for granted, and one had to run to keep up. Perhaps she had entered it too late. When she first emerged from obscurity with *The Valleys of the Assassins* and landed, breathless, on its enticing shores, she was already over forty. The wonder of its acceptance of herself never quite left her.

So I thought one evening staying with her in Asolo. The classics master from the posh boys' boarding school was coming to dine and advise Freya on her reading. This weekly engagement was something of which she was rather proud, and she had already several times pointed out to me her achievements in the reading line. It seemed some sort of certificate of intellectual capacity. 'I read all these last year,' she told me, pointing to the left-hand section of a tall bookcase, 'and I'm halfway down these,' pointing to the middle section. The Greeks having been polished off, now it was the turn of the Romans. Next year presumably it would be the early Christian fathers. All were in the Loeb edition, which has the appropriate translation facing each page of text.[5] There was something a little studied in this parading of her scholarly credentials, as if awareness of her status as an extraordinary being required its meed of recognition. It seemed a harmless vanity.

Freya for this occasion wore her choker of pearls, her diamond watch and a knuckle-duster ring with a huge pale yellow stone in a modern claw setting, a present from Mrs Otto Kahn. She was surprised that my luggage, carried about from trains, boats and cars as I journeyed towards Asolo, did not contain some suitable little frock for the occasion, but having drawn attention to this deficiency, it was magnanimously passed over. She herself was clad in a bias-cut garment of some gauzy black material, threaded vaguely with beaten silver insets; it clung becomingly to her plump little figure, now much reduced by careful dieting in preparation for a pony-trek in Nepal with a BBC film crew. It gave her a sleek, avian appearance, as of some small bird, full breasted but shapely, a swallow rather than a domestic fowl.

She was pleased with my admiration. 'This is the first Arab dress I ever bought,' she remarked complacently, smoothing down the material. 'I got it years and years ago, on my first trip to Kuwait. My mother had it copied dozens of times – in silks from her workshop, you know. It's nice to be able to wear it again . . .'

The interest of Freya's appearance lay somewhere in the middle ground between eccentricity and convention. She retained the formalities of her upbringing in her clothes, ruled by a sense of occasion that discriminated nicely between morning, afternoon and evening, and dressed accordingly. Her rosy face, with its soft old-woman's skin, rouged and powdered and stabbed with bright lipstick, shone genially above the pearls. What came as a surprise was the pixie-hood fitting close over the ears and tying under the chin in a string bow concealed by the folds of flesh. Its only adornment was a small fringe of lace outlining the face.

In due course I observed that there were several of these hoods, of different materials and rather sombre colours, and I used to cogitate about them and their provenance. Now I think they were the residue of originals devised by Flora after her daughter's accident, to conceal the child's cropped and stitched head until the hair grew again. There was something of the shoebag about them, a home-made practicality; they made me think of Lady Blessington, the Italian Idler, but her lace caps were minor works of art, goffered and frilled to set off the pretty face in defiance of encroaching plumpness.

Freya's were not in that category. Rather they resembled that sketch of David's of Marie Antoinette on her way to execution, sitting upright on the tumbril, her arms bound, her head shorn of its locks, a plain cotton bonnet tied under her chin, to leave the neck bare for the guillotine's blade.

Such tragic associations were not in Freya's line. She rather liked her bonnets and wore them informally about the house and was interviewed wearing them in London, eye-catching emblems of eccentricity, eagerly recorded by the photographer. 'Pretty, isn't it?' she now murmured modestly, darting a sharp little look at me, challenging disagreement. Perhaps, after all, the personality cult was always something of a game to her. Did she enjoy hoaxing the unwary? I never could make up my mind about this aspect of her personality.

The classics master was a Marist brother, and wore ordinary clothes, not a *soutane*. A pale, thin, clever-looking man in his thirties, with glossy black hair and quick, lively brown eyes behind spectacles, his manner was decisive. Freya seemed to like that.

'No, no, you don't need to read the Elder Pliny, he's dreadfully dull, but you can the Younger – he's worthwhile . . .'

'Isn't he good?' Freya whispered admiringly, in an audible aside. 'He told me I didn't need to read Martial, he was too scandalous, and really, when I looked inside, I did see what he meant. So I thought I'd give him the copy. I don't suppose it can do him any harm . . .' she added, in a meditative tone, giving me a sly look of round-eyed innocence.

We seemed to be inhabiting some delightful eighteenth-century world, where courtly priests and erudite ladies amused each other with scholarly discourse, and the humble goings-on of life in the little town provided conversational relaxation over the dinner table after the intellectual athleticism of the reading programme. The schoolmaster was very sprightly and regaled us with exciting anecdotes of burglaries, deaths, accidents and other happenings of the district, while complimenting the maid, Floriana, as she leant over his shoulder to present the dish.

Now I understood where Freya got her fund of local gossip, always of a rather alarming character and mostly to do with enormities of conduct on the part of the local youth. It added an unexpectedly homely dimension to her general talk.

Roman history and its literature had been the menu for the evening, but we soon got on to poetry. We had a happy time, well mounted on a favourite hobby-horse. The schoolmaster leaped around the bookshelves and read now from this volume, now from that, expounding on the text in a schoolmasterly way. Perhaps it was the wine we had drunk at dinner that helped us dredge up favourite verses from our memory; it was the guest's familiarity with Keats' work that revealed to me his unanticipated fluency in the English language. Freya recited bits of Matthew Arnold and W. P. Ker's favourite passage from Dante, her clearly enunciated, fluting voice brought down to a measured cadence, pleasant to the ear. Our enthusiasm was of the innocent kind, self-indulgent perhaps, and uncritical, but it made the evening speed along, and left us in satisfied good humour, buoyed up by such a swig from the Pierian Spring.

So it seemed, as I watched Freya, flushed and rosy with exertion, clambering on a stool to find a particular volume on her shelves, the filmy folds of her dress falling about her strappy sandals. She was insistent on managing for herself. One failure of balance, Floriana's expressive eyebrows indicated, and what a fall there would be! But the hazard was discounted, the book retrieved, the page found, the passage read. Freya glowed. It was only afterwards that I wondered at this departure from the stately rationality of her drawing-room manner, and felt an illicit pang of relief at the escape.

That is how I like to remember her now. I see her breathless, eager, showing off, alert to others' enthusiasms and running to participate. The lively child, the romantic girl, the adventurous young woman were all there, responding to the measured unfolding of the spoken word. It was as if a truer personality peeped out, glad of recognition, a blithe spirit that whetted and clapped its silver wings among the trees of a poetic Paradise. That she might resemble Noël Coward's rather than Shelley's or Marvell's bird was incidental; the outer husk encased a spirit exalted and true, and this was what mattered.

Gibbon, when he came to the end of his great task, recorded his feeling on quitting the history on which he had been so long engaged; a work, he wrote on 27 June 1787, that whatever its merits, had amused and exercised nearly twenty years of his life. I cannot claim more than half that length of time for my immersion in Freya, and her story is set against a swifter decline of empire than that of Rome, but the amusement and interest she never failed to evoke in me bears some resemblance to what Gibbon felt for his subject, though the material is so different, and its scope so slight in comparison.

I last saw her at a small gathering in Murrays' famous room in Albemarle Street, where Byron's journal was burnt, on one of her last appearances in London. A select group of 'old friends' had been gathered to await her: an English duke, a wealthy marchioness of Sephardic Jewish extraction, an Ottoman princess, various ex-ambassadors or their widows, sundry godchildren, the middle-aged god-daughters now touched and softened, earlier storms and indignation put aside. Freya arrived late, escorted by her attendants, a small, composed figure, docile yet dignified, with an appearance of smiling, nun-like calm. In her 'good', quiet garments, a shallow, wide-brimmed, maroon-coloured felt set straight on her head, she might have been some very ancient exiled notability, dressed and brought out of retirement to be greeted deferentially by a now-dwindling group of friends and admirers.

Ensconced in a corner by the fireplace, a cushion embroidered with a coronet and a large B – on which Byron's dying head had rested – at her back, people were led up individually to sit with her and talk, trying to make contact amid the fluctuations of a now-childish mind. 'People are so kind, so very kind,' she murmured repeatedly as my turn came. 'Freya,' I said as I rose to go, 'I have a little something for you,' putting into her hand a minute packet of bon-bons I had bought for her in Fortnums on my way to the party. Freya loved such things, chocolates, petits-fours, whatever was delicious, hand-made and sweet. That her attendants would almost certainly confiscate the gift did not matter, I wanted to see her reaction. She did not fail me. Quick as a flash, her handbag snapped open and the forbidden treat disappeared inside it. It was like a sleight of hand.

I came away reassured; the shadow of Watts Dunton, Swinburne's 'Keeper' at the Pines, Putney Hill, receded. Despite appearances, the feral element in Freya's nature had not atrophied. The old mischievous instinct to circumvent, to deceive, was still there, and I was glad for her. Somewhere among the mists and confusion of second childhood the Life Force was holding its own.

APPENDIX A

THE LATER HISTORY OF THE BROTHERHOOD

The total costs of the Brotherhood in 1942, spread over three territories – Egypt, Palestine and Iraq – to include wages and all operational charges, was £18,000. Ten Britons were budgeted for but Freya was adamant in her rejection of conventional qualifications. No blue-stocking woman would be considered; what Freya sought in her assistants was charm and adaptability and good social connections. Understaffing was a constant problem; at the end of 1942 only eight posts were filled.

Lampson himself grew uneasy about the Brotherhood's snowballing growth in 1942 when direction of the Egyptian operation had passed into the hands of Christopher Scaife and Ronald Fay, and Freya had moved on to Iraq. He would not want it, he told Freya, to get too strong. The appearance of well-meaning amateurism which Freya had projected was difficult to sustain as the membership figure in Egypt expanded to about 40,000 at the end of 1943, with groups of 400 villages and 100 towns, spread all over the country.

In 1943 a budget of £25,000 was asked for, and getting his and Freya's accounts to tally was Christopher Scaife's priority in taking over the administration of the entire Brotherhood organisation from Freya that year.

Freya returned from her visit to the Wavells in India in 1943 to a final hectic tour of her Iraqi Brotherhood networks before handing over the organisation to Christopher Scaife in July and returning to London for briefing on her tour of America. This was to begin in October. Stung by the comments of her 'flightiness' in abandoning Iraq for two months to pursue notional schemes of expansion further east, she flung herself into an arduous round of visits to her committees in the course of which she traversed the country from north to south and east to west. Freya saw more of the Middle East as a government servant than ever she did as a private traveller. In the deadly heat of the summer there was something so punishing about this expenditure of energy that her superiors in Cairo were alarmed and begged her to keep something in reserve for her tour of America.

In her household it was believed the tour was a temporary assignment, but this round-up of committees and colleagues was the final act in her career as a propagandist in the wartime Middle East. The visionary element in her pronouncements was no longer practical politics for the men running the Middle East and with the movement of the war to Europe her usefulness ceased. The tide was turning towards victory for the Allies and, superficially, acceptance of a continuing British presence in Iraq returned too.

Lampson's foreboding about over-ambitious expansion of the Brotherhood was not without foundation as suspicious local minds saw in the spread of the organisation sinister evidence of British determination to hang on indefinitely to their treaty rights. The future of the British bases in the area was coming up for consideration and this was a factor in the decision to retain the Brotherhood networks.

Christopher Scaife recommended that the organisation move over from the purely anti-Nazi counter-propaganda of Freya's devising and be gradually adapted to a peacetime operation: training in citizenship and democratic practice to prepare for the difficulties of the post-war period in which the future of Palestine would certainly figure. In the ensuing discussions it was generally accepted in the Foreign Office that the Brotherhood was too useful a network to let go. Major Scaife produced ingenious calculations to show how *cheaply* the scheme could be run. The Brotherhood, he suggested, could be an established method of disseminating correct information and counteracting prejudiced and inaccurate rumours in Arab lands at small cost to Britain, which is rather where it had come in; only now it was no longer the Nazis that were the target but mysterious groupings of secret societies and outlawed political combinations at the very levels Freya had claimed she could reach. Sir Kinahan Cornwallis suggested the Brotherhood be absorbed by the British Council, 'as so far it had not developed into a viable organisation, depending as it did almost entirely on oral propaganda and personal influence'. It would be imprudent, he believed, to allow so efficient and widespread an organisation to pass out of British control. It would degenerate at once into local cabals, intrigue and personal chicanery, for which the British would be held responsible.

The trouble with this and other suggestions was that there were no takers for the organisation. It was as if people were wary of it. The Brotherhood, it was felt, reflected too narrowly the personality of its founder and was too individual and too difficult to incorporate in organisations which aimed at flexibility and exchangeability in their officers. The 'local expert' was now discredited, his paternalism regarded as a drag on progress and his established links with governing elites an unfortunate inheritance prejudicial to Britain's future interests. This shift in policy had a damaging effect on Freya's hopes of employment in diplomacy after the war.

By 1947, when Lampson had retired, the Egyptian Brotherhood had grown to 75,000 in 4800 committees. A virulent campaign was now launched against it in the local press on patriotic grounds. 'Rolls of Honour' were published purporting to show the numbers defecting and threats were received by staff and local helpers. A bomb was exploded outside the Alexandria office and the Beit es Sennari, the office in Cairo, was threatened with blowing up. About eight per cent of the committees were lost but the rest held firm.[1]

The campaign against the Brotherhood was set in motion by opposition to the existing Wafdist government, a party formed originally in the 1920s to promote democratic nationalist aspirations. Imposed by force on the young King Farouk under threat of dethronement and exile, since he was suspected of harbouring Axis sympathisers by Lampson in 1942, the party was now discredited in popular opinion as a tool of British imperialism. A likely theory is that the attacks on the Brotherhood were set up by the Egyptian Communist underground which later asserted that it was an organisation formed by the British in the war to incite the Egyptians against the Axis, and afterwards used against themselves.

The organisation was still being funded from the Cairo Embassy in 1950 but the end came in January 1952 when the Egyptian government outlawed it a few days prior to the burning and looting of the centre of Cairo by mobs from the slums of the city. A short while previously, the flat in Dokki of the Brotherhood's Embassy link, the Hon E. Gathorne-Hardy, had been burgled and the membership files of the organisation ransacked. The Embassy decided it was advisable for the Director, Ronnie Fay, to leave the country before being expelled and this added fuel to local suspicions. The campaign of vilification continued and blame for the burning of the city was attributed to, among others, the Brotherhood. Members were alleged to have been seen taking part in several of the criminal acts that took place on that day, including systematic attacks in the early afternoon on Jewish businesses and synagogues.

These events signalled the abandonment of the Brotherhood of Freedom in Egypt. The Iraq Brotherhood had already been closed by the Iraqi government as soon as the British military occupation ended. The Palestine Sisterhood, some 500 members recruited by Lulie Abu'l Huda, never developed further. Eddie Gathorne-Hardy moved from Egypt to wind up the organisation from Beirut where Christopher Scaife was now teaching at the American University.

Years later when I was researching this book I was told that traces of Ronnie Fay's networks were still to be found among the older Egyptian village people whose *Omdahs* or headmen had been the natural channel of approach for Englishmen of Fay's generation and training.

ASOLO

NOTES AND SOURCES

Foreword

1 They are among the ephemera relating to the Starks collected by Sir Sydney Cockerell.

2 Letter to Venetia Buddicom 25 November 1934. 'Now hope to write regularly to you again (and will you keep everything, as I shall write to you instead of a diary) . . .'

3 Conversation with author.

4 *Letters*, Vol V to Stewart Perowne, 21 August 1948, and see Chapter 17, note 1.

5 A letter of 'vicarage stiffness' declining the overtures of Brian Howard, noted aesthete and homosexual, when he came to Asolo in 1952 with a view to perhaps settling there, contributed to the deterioration of Freya's relations with Perowne after their mutually agreed divorce. He found her attitude odious.

Part 1 Image or Reality?

Chapter 1 An Enormous Reputation

1 The Back Memorial Prize is a bequest established by Admiral Sir George Back, RN, to assist in exploration. Its annual value is about £14, the interest on a legacy of £540 net, bequeathed by the Admiral on his death in 1878. He directed that the interest on this sum should be applied annually for the benefit of scientific geographers or discoverers. The first grant was made in 1882; Freya in 1933 was the third woman to have received it.

Admiral Back was a friend of the Victorian publisher John Murray, whose firm subsequently published many of the recipients' accounts of their travels; his portrait today hangs at 50 Albemarle Street, London.

2 See *Alan Moorehead*: Tom Pocock, Bodley Head, 1990, pp. 285–6. Lucy Moorehead, wife of above, was appointed by Freya to edit the mass of accumulated letters. Writing to a friend in Australia, she remarked that Freya, now in her eighties, was 'so full of her own opinions of the work in hand that she compares herself with Shakespeare, which makes literary discussion ticklish.'

3 *The Cornhill*, No 1062, 1969/70.

4 *The God Forsakes Antony: The Complete Poems of C. P. Cavafy 1863–1933* translated by Rae Dalven, The Hogarth Press, London, 1961.

Chapter 2 Visits to Freya

1 Now in the National Portrait Gallery.

2 Information from the archaeologist Mrs Hackforth-Jones (formerly Peggy Drower) of London University, assistant to Freya in 1942 and her successor in 1943.

Chapter 3 First Pieces of the Puzzle

1 Of Egyptian Department, Foreign Office: subsequently head of British Council in Egypt, and India.

2 For variation on the legend see *Cairo in Wartime 1939–45*, Artemis Cooper, p. 99: Hamish Hamilton, 1989. See also *Letters*, Vol VIII, 30 January 1964 to Sir Reader Bullard.

3 These documents, known to Wavell's staff as 'talismans', would speed the chosen recipient unchallenged to whatever destination Wavell had in mind. Their issue contributed to the sense of a private following responsive to a romantic chieftain. Wavell was known as Chief to his staff. See *Cairo in Wartime 1939–45*, Artemis Cooper: Hamish Hamilton, p. 84.

4 Letter to author.

5 *Of Generals and Gardens*, The Autobiography of Peter Coats, Weidenfeld & Nicolson, 1976.

Part 2 The Early Journeys

Chapter 4 The First Journey – Lebanon and Syria

1 Cockerell papers.

2 Conversation with the late Wilfrid Blunt.

3 Cockerell papers.

4 Information from the Misses Buddicom, second cousins of Venetia. Their brother Prosper was present at the shooting party when her father died.

5 *Letters*, Vol I, 17 February 1929 to Robert Stark.

6 *Letters*, Vol I, 28 February 1927 to Flora Stark.

7 Cockerell papers.

Chapter 5 The Decisive Step – Iraq and Persia

1 *Letters*, Vol I, 25 May 1929 to Robert Stark.

2 PRO: *A Pamphlet in Defence of Propaganda*, Freya Stark, 1944.

3 *Letters*, Vol II, 18 July 1931 to Flora Stark.

Chapter 6 Making Her Name

1 *Letters*, Vol II, 24 October 1931 to Flora Stark.

2 *Letters*, Vol II, 19 January 1932 to Herbert Young.

3 *Letters*, Vol II, 30 June 1932 to Flora Stark.

4 *Letters*, Vol II, 30 August 1932 to Venetia Buddicom.

5 *Letters*, Vol II, 31 August 1932 to Flora Stark.

6 Information from Mrs E. Hallett, Maxwell's daughter.

7 *Letters*, Vol II, 8 September 1932 to Flora Stark.

Chapter 7 Hadhramaut

1 President Royal Geographical Society 1930–3 succeeded by Sir Percy Cox.

2 *Letters*, Vol II, 13 October 1933 to Sir John Murray.

3 Cockerell papers.

4 Information from the late Lady Sanders.

5 *Letters*, Vol II, 2 September 1934 to Venetia Buddicom.

6 *Antonin Besse of Aden*, David Footman, St Antony's Macmillan Series, 1986.

7 *When the Going was Good*, Evelyn Waugh, Duckworth, 1943, pp. 152–7.

8 See *The Tombs and Moon Temple of Hureidha*, Gertrude Caton Thompson, OUP, 1944.

9 *Letters*, Vol II, 9 March 1935 to Venetia Buddicom.

10 *Letters*, Vol II, 9 March 1935 to Venetia Buddicom.

11 *Letters*, Vol II, 22 February 1935 to Venetia Buddicom from Shibam.

12 *Letters*, Vol II, 17 March 1935 to Flora Stark, pp. 273–4.

13 *Sheba's Daughters*, H. St J. Philby, Methuen & Co, London, 1939.

14 *Geheimnis um Schöbwa*, Hans Helfritz, 1935.

15 *Sheba's Daughters*, H. St J. Philby, Methuen & Co, London, 1939.

16 *Letters*, Vol III, 31 March 1936 to J. G. Murray.

17 *Letters*, Vol II, 3 April 1935 to Flora Stark.

18 Cockerell papers.

Part 3 Assertions of Identity

Chapter 8 Antonin Besse and Venetia Buddicom

1 *Letters*, Vol III, 9 July 1935 to Venetia Buddicom.

2 Conversation with author.

3 *Letters*, Vol III, 2 June 1935 to Venetia Buddicom.

4 *The Coast of Incense*, p. 96.

5 *Letters*, Vol III, 21 December 1935 to Flora Stark.

6 *Letters*, Vol III, 12 June 1936 to Venetia Buddicom.

7 Now at 50 Albemarle Street, London.

8 *Letters*, Vol III, 22 May 1936 to Venetia Buddicom.

9 *Letters*, Vol III, 31 May 1936 to Flora Stark.

10 *Letters*, Vol III, 12 February 1937 to J. G. Murray.

Chapter 9 Hadhramaut Again

1 *Mediaeval Rhodesia*, Dr Randall McIver, 1906.

2 *Letters*, Vol III, March 1936 to J. G. Murray.

3 Award of Founder's Gold Medal by RGS. Admiral Sir William Goodenough to Sir Sydney Cockerell, 11 June 1942.

I know how glad you will have been to see Freya was recognised by the award of the Founder's Medal of the RGS. I telegraphed to her and have a written reply. I see by it that she is much gratified. Apart from personal friendship and appreciation I was glad to be able to show that geography isn't all cartography and that the knowledge and description of peoples is as or more important as or than places.

4 *Letters*, Vol III, 18 October 1937 to J. G. Murray.

5 *Letters*, Vol III, 25 October 1937 to Herbert Young.

6 *Letters*, Vol III, 31 October 1937 to Flora Stark.

7 Information from Mrs Doreen Ingrams.

8 *Letters*, Vol III, 4 November 1937 to Flora Stark.

9 Gardner papers, RGS Library.

10 *Sheba's Daughters*: H. St John Philby, Methuen & Co Ltd, London, 1939.

11 *Mixed Memoirs*, Gertrude Caton Thompson, 1944.

12 *The Tombs and Moon Temple of Hureidha*, OUP, 1944.

13 Gardner papers, RGS Library.

14 *Letters*, Vol III, 28 July 1939 to J. G. Murray.

15 *Letters*, Vol III, 26 July 1939 to J. G. Murray. 26 July 1939 to Sydney Cockerell. 6 August 1939 to Sydney Cockerell.

16 *Mixed Memoirs*, Gertrude Caton Thompson, 1944.

17 *Mixed Memoirs*, Gertrude Caton Thompson, 1944.

Chapter 10 A London Winter

1 *The Tombs and Moon Temple of Hureidha*, OUP, 1944.

2 *Letters*, Vol III, 5 April 1938 to Sir Sydney Cockerell.

3 See *Letters*, Vol IV, 16 February 1944 to Flora Stark for Freya on Alice Delysia and the art of the Feminine.

4 Published *Royal Central Asian Journal*, Vol XXIII, Part 1, 1936.

5 Cockerell papers. Letter to Gertrude Caton Thompson, October 1944.

6 Information Ingrams papers.

7 *The Times*, 14 and 17 April 1939.

8 *Letters*, Vol III, 19 April 1939 to J. G. Murray.

9 See also *Letters*, Vol IV, 7 March 1940 to Stewart Perowne.

10 *Letters*, Vol IV, 9 June 1940 to Civil Secretary, Aden.

Part 4 Freya's Brotherhood

Chapter 11 Freya's War

1 *Letters*, Vol II, 27 August 1941 to Flora Stark.

2 *Letters*, Vol III, 2 November 1939 to Sir Sydney Cockerell.

3 Later Major-General Sir Walter Cawthorn.

4 PRO, E2029/2029/65.

5 PRO, FO371 Pol. Egypt General/ 1940/2464019.

6 *Letters*, Vol III, 20 November 1939 to Harold Bowen, Ministry of Information, London.

7 *Letters*, Vol III, 8 December 1939 to Sir Kinahan Cornwallis.

8 de Lotbinière diary.

9 *East is West*, John Murray, 1945, pp. 26–7.

10 *Letters*, Vol IV, 20 March 1940 to Stewart Perowne.

11 *Letters*, Vol IV, 25 March 1940 to J. G. Murray.

12 *Letters*, Vol IV, 20 April 1940 to Sir Sydney Cockerell.

13 *Letters*, Vol IV, 28 April 1940 to Flora Stark.

14 *Letters*, Vol IV, 26 May 1940 to Professor Rushbrook Williams.

15 Founder of Office of Strategic Services, later CIA.

Chapter 12 Birth of the Brotherhood

1 *Letters*, Vol IV, 21 May 1943 to Sir Sydney Cockerell.

2 *Spycatcher*, Peter Wright, Viking, 1987, pp. 158, 206, 207.

3 *Dust in the Lion's Paw*, John Murray, 1961, p. 68.

4 PRO, E2029/2029/6S.

5 Information from Mrs Doreen Ingrams.

6 *Letters*, Vol IV, to Sir Kinahan Cornwallis, 27 May 1943.

7 Freya Stark letter to Peggy Drower, 8 August 1943.

8 *Letters*, Vol IV, to Professor Rushbrook Williams 4 April 1941.

9 *Letters*, Vol III, 10 October 1937 to Flora Stark.

10 Information from Mrs R. Davies.

11 PRO, FO371/40078/10081, *A Pamphlet in Defence of Propaganda*, F. Stark.

Chapter 13 In the Cairo Swim

1 See Sir Kenneth Clark, *The Other Half*, John Murray, 1977, p. 17.

2 *Of Generals and Gardens*, The Autobiography of Peter Coats, Weidenfeld & Nicolson, 1976.

3 *Letters*, Vol IV, 7 September 1942 to Flora Stark.

Part 5 Mrs Freya Stark

Chapter 14 The Baghdad Siege

1 Later Sir Vyvyan Holt, KBE, CMG, MVO. HM Minister to Korea 1950, marched into captivity by North Koreans, believed dead. Released by Russians 1953. Died July 1960.

2 Information from Sir J. Marsh, late of Military Mission.

3 PRO, FO37/40078/10081. FO Registry No E2515/1099/93.

4 *Letters*, Vol IV, 14 November 1941 to Flora Stark.

5 PRO, Middle East files 4 June 1941 Cipher Telegram 500 to Sir H. Seymour.

6 PRO, Middle East (Egypt) file 17 June 1941 Sir Miles Lampson, HM Ambassador to Egypt, forwarded to Foreign Secretary Anthony Eden a report on Oral Propaganda signed by Freya Stark and Christopher Holme, on the need to rally Arab nationalism to British side by more positive, less defensive, approach to propaganda. Eden subsequently discussed with Freya in Cairo the existing use of broadcasting and how to improve its quality. Relayed to London, this news provoked Ivy Compton-Burnett to remark that Freya's must be 'the voice that breathed o'er Eden'.

7 *Dust in the Lion's Paw*, pp. 116–17.

8 Founder of American Office of Strategic Studies (OSS) later to become CIA.

9 *Letters*, Vol IV, 7 February 1941 to Stewart Perowne.

10 He tipped over the banister of a hill-station hotel above Teheran (while calling for his baggage to be brought up) where he had arrived for a short recuperative leave from the heat of Baghdad. He was killed immediately.

11 *The Interval*, Seton Lloyd, The Alden Press, Oxford, 1986.

12 Nigel Clive, *A Greek Experience*, Michael Russell, 1985.

13 Information from the late Christopher Scaife.

Chapter 15 A Soldierly Farewell

1 Sir Clarmont Skrine, *World War in Iran*, Constable & Co, 1962, p. 153.

2 Information from Lady Holman.

3 Information from the late Gordon Waterfield.

4 Information from Lady Holman.

5 *Dust in the Lion's Paw*, p. 148.

6 Drower papers, FS letters to Peggy Drower, 15 February 1943, 8 August 1943.

7 Lord Evans of Hungershall. Academic and Labour peer. Principal University College, London University; British Council, Cairo. Former student of W. P. Ker.

8 *Letters*, Vol IV, to Jock Murray, 6 December 1942.

9 *Dust in the Lion's Paw*, p. 129.

10 *Letters*, Vol IV, 12 April 1943 to Rt Hon R. G. Casey.

11 *Letters*, Vol IV to Sir Kinahan Cornwallis, 27 May 1943.

12 The later history of the Brotherhood is summarised in Appendix A.

Chapter 16 War End and Marriage

1 Office of Strategic Services, later CIA.

2 *Dust in the Lion's Paw*, pp. 212–14.

3 *East is West*, John Murray, published August 1945 – into four editions by 1947.

4 *Dust in the Lion's Paw*, p. 277–8.

5 *Letters*, Vol IV, 21 May 1943 to Elizabeth Monroe.

6 Wavell to Freya Stark.

7 *Beyond Euphrates*, Journal 21 January 1929, p. 45.

8 Freya Stark letter to the late Gerald de Gaury.

9 *Letters*, Vol V, 20 May 1945 to Moore Crosthwaite.

10 *Dust in the Lion's Paw*, p. 251.

11 *Letters*, Vol IV, 21 May 1943 to Sir Sydney Cockerell.

12 *Letters*, Vol V, July 1947 to Stewart Perowne.

13 Information from Sir Steven Runciman.

14 Information from the late Gerald de Gaury.

15 It seems that Perowne's original telegram suggesting marriage was followed up by a letter outlining the terms for the companionate arrangement he had in view. This was overlooked or conveniently forgotten by Freya when the marriage failed. Possibly the classical tag he employed to define the proposed relationship escaped her understanding, and no one had the courage to tell her the bald truth.

Part 6 Disinterring the Past

Chapter 17 Godparents and a Cousin

1 *Letters*, Vol V, to Perowne 21 August 1949 from Asolo. 'Am sorting out letters from infancy to 1927. Have already thrown away a whole basketful, two enormous drawers full of 1927–47 correspondence . . . will need three months to read through it all . . .'

2 *Secrets of a Woman's Heart*, the later life of I. Compton-Burnett 1920–1969, Hilary Spurling, Hodder and Stoughton, 1984.

3 In 1942 Sir Sydney Cockerell, following up the first draft of *Traveller's Prelude* sent him by Freya, wrote to the Ker family enquiring about any letters to the Professor which might survive. By now all WPK's generation were dead. His nephew replied that Ker's surviving sister had gone

through his papers before her own death and burned a great deal, so whether Ker ever kept Freya's letters is not known. Freya was disappointed at this news.

4 Information from Janet Adam Smith.

5 Conversation with Freya Stark.

Chapter 18 The Starkite Inheritance

1 *Devon & Cornwall Notes and Queries*, Vol XX, 1938–39; *Panorama of Torquay*, O. Blewitt, 1832.

2 Memoir of Robert Stark of Torquay, 1788–1854, edited by his daughter, Mrs Elizabeth Carne Wilkinson, 1858.

3 *Traveller's Prelude*, Chapter I, p. 5.

4 Information from the Archivist, Duchy of Cornwall, November 1988.

5 Taunton Public Library: William Cox & Co of Tancred Street, Taunton, owned a brass and iron foundry opened in 1811, while a son went on to develop an extensive general hardware establishment known by the name of the Tangier Manufactory from its site: its layout is shown in J. Woods' Map Plan of Taunton 1840.

6 R. S. Wilkinson gave up his London architectural practice in 1911 and joined a firm in Montevideo, Uruguay, where he was still working when he died, unmarried, at the age of ninety-two on 26 July 1936. His obituary in the RIBA *Journal* describes him as sociable, talented, lovable; eccentric in his working habits but reliable and fast when under pressure. No good in the morning, he worked best in sustained bursts of activity late at night; his

prize-winning design for the Asylum was prepared over a weekend.

Chapter 19 Asolo and Chagford

1 *Letters*, Vol I, 9 November 1928 to Herbert Young.

2 *Back to the Land; The Pastoral Impulse in Victorian England from 1880 to 1914*, Jan Marsh, Quartet Books, 1982.

3 *Traveller's Prelude*, Chapter 4, Roots in England 1893–1903.

4 *Traveller's Prelude*, Chapter 10, The Last of Dartmoor 1911–1912.

Chapter 20 Dronero and St John's Wood

1 *Letters*, Vol II, pp. 165–75. Freya entered St Andrew's Hospital, Dollis Hill, London just before Christmas 1933 for plastic surgery on the scars of her childhood injury in Dronero. This entailed a series of operations over a period of eight weeks. Discharged in mid-February, she went to Venetia Buddicom in Wales for a recuperation visit of some weeks.

2 Cockerell papers.

3 *Traveller's Prelude*, Chapter 7, pp. 86–7; Chapter 12, pp. 133–4.

4 Information from Mrs E. Hallett.

5 Information from Freya Stark's Canadian cousin, Art *Stark.

Chapter 21 Engagement and Aftermath

1 Ker papers. Letter to Olivia Horner.

2 *Secrets of a Woman's Heart*, the later life of I. Compton-Burnett

1920–1969, Hilary Spurling, Hodder & Stoughton, 1984.

3 *Façades*: Edith, Osbert & Sacheverell Sitwell, John Pearson, Macmillan, 1978, pp. 246, 248–9.

4 *Traveller's Prelude*, p. 264.

5 Information from Malise Ruthven.

6 *The Cornhill*, Winter 1969/70, No 1062.

7 Information from Hilary Spurling.

8 Information from Elizabeth Monroe.

Chapter 22 Dronero to L'Arma to Asolo

1 Information from his daughter, the late Lady Sanders.

2 *Letters*, Vol I, 15 April 1921 to Robert Stark.

3 *Letters*, Vol I, 26 November 1916; 24 April 1917, 11 May 1917 to Flora Stark.

4 W. P. Ker to Freya Stark, private correspondence.

5 *Letters*, Vol I, mid-July 1923, 3 August 1923 to Robert Stark.

6 Judge Eric Maxwell, holidaying on the Riviera with his family, called at this period on the Starks at L'Arma one morning with an introduction from Viva Jeyes. They were turned away by the servant as Freya was resting and on no account to be disturbed, and had to return in the afternoon, when she would be available to callers. Maxwell's daughter, then a young girl, recollects the atmosphere of hushed gloom and despondency surrounding Freya, occasioned, the Maxwells gleaned, by yet another disappointment in love. Cockerell in 1945, collating information on Freya, noted, 'Mrs Gray Granville today told me that it was to the Commendatore Bianchieri that Freya most lost her heart.'

The Bianchieris, a family of career diplomats, were connected by marriage to the Prince of Lampedusa in Sicily, to whom Freya was given an introduction when touring the island with her godchild Barclay Sanders in 1952. The Prince, his novel *The Leopard* as yet unpublished, seems to have made no impression on Freya, but in his diary Lampedusa, struck by the energy of their rapid sightseeing, refers to the two Englishwomen as 'the lionesses'.

7 *Traveller's Prelude*, pp. 326–7.

Part 7 Through the Looking Glass

Chapter 23 Mother and Daughter

1 *Letters*, Vol IV, 25 September 1942 to Flora Stark.

2 Information from Guy Nevill.

3 *Letters*, Vol IV, 25 October 1942 to Sir Sydney Cockerell.

Chapter 24 Father and Mother

1 *Letters*, Vol VI, 8 August 1948 to Stewart Perowne.

2 *Traveller's Prelude*, Chapter 7, p. 88.

3 Information from Art Stark.

4 *Times Literary Supplement*, 6 October 1950.

5 The *Observer*, Christopher Sykes, 8 October 1950.

6 *Letters*, Vol VII, 30 April 1953 to J. G. Murray. Freya suggests to Jock Murray that his family share Villa Freia with her – feels house is too big for her, she only wants her bed-

room and a little flat upstairs, so they would have plenty of room to spread. 'Have one or two people in mind with children, but would be very happy to see the children here now who are to take it over when I die, so that they might care for it just as I did . . . If you and Diana could manage it I would like in a few years' time to settle the house on whichever of your four seems most likely to enjoy it.'

Her letter of 14 May 1953 found her still urging this plan on Jock Murray. 'I would so like to have the feeling of continuity here while I am alive to enjoy it so do think hard, dear Jock, and don't be *too prudent*.' Other candidates for the inheritance at different periods were B. Sanders, the Taffy Rodd family, the Derek Coopers (she formerly Pamela Hore-Ruthven), Lennox-Boyds, Dulcie Deuchar, but nothing came of any of these suggestions which were still being promoted in 1963. One theory advanced to me by an early favourite was that Freya was so spiteful and malicious about any husband or male attachment who was part of the package that the men would not stand for it, and the schemes collapsed.

Freya's niece Cici had been given the L'Arma property at the end of the war under similar conditions to that suggested for the Villa Freia, but the outcome was unhappy and aunt and niece were estranged at the time of Cici's death in 1980. Freya was bored by Cici's bourgeois husband and disliked their Italian friends; they compared unfavourably with the more sophisticated English society to which she was now accustomed. That Cici might feel slighted by this discrimination seems to have escaped Freya; she herself told me Cici was

jealous of her successful life, but perhaps Cici, whose own young life was largely tragic, looked for warmer sympathy and affection than Freya could give when they were reunited after the war.

Chapter 25 A Blithe Spirit

1 Cockerell papers. Written conversation by Freya with Cockerell when latter temporarily stone deaf. Annotated by Cockerell February 1961.

> I am 68!! I have every meal out! And now busy with godsons, Simon Lennox Boyd, 'Skimper' Ruthven and all their friends . . . [Freya had ten godchildren, four boys, six girls.] I send a yearly present to be put aside for a journey at 18. I'm interested in three of the boys and only two of the girls!!'

2 The refurbishing of the Villa Freia at war's end, when Freya took possession of her inheritance, entailed ever-increasing expenditure, as central-heating, marble bathrooms and wash basins, furniture made by local craftsmen to her own designs, sent the original costings spiralling upwards. Writing to Gerald de Gaury on 29 October 1945 she told him 'am making a beautiful bathroom of green and white marble (to be one of three). Venini [a well-known Venetian glass blower] is doing the lamps – green glass, cherubs (the kind with legs and no wings) holding balls of light in their hands. You will never have seen such a beautiful bathroom, it will have a mirror with light all round twisted like a gold rope!' The saga of the Villa

Freia's improvements went on for years. On 7 November 1948 she wrote again to de Gaury. 'The bathroom is done, thank God! You never saw anything so like a compromise between Pauline Borghese and Caracalla. It is quite ravishing and I shall be in debt for years . . .'

Over the next twenty or so years Freya's alterations and improvements to her properties inevitably exceeded her own estimates, and recurrent financial crises were only arrested by loans or donations from well-off sympathisers. It was the early days at L'Arma all over again; people were sorry for her muddles and helped her out. The Villa Freia at last found a buyer, and the new villa at Montoria was completed. Freya philosophically accepted all the fuss and worry she experienced for the ten years of pleasure she had planning and planting her property. In the end it proved impractical for her, as her sales decreased and her income shrank, and difficulties with servants increased. Montoria was sold in 1972 for £80,000 to a local Italian family. Freya moved into a rented apartment in Asolo, which is where she was living when I visited her.

3 *Bright Levant*, Laurence Grafftey-Smith, John Murray, 1970.

4 *Letters*, Vol IV, 9 May 1942 to Flora Stark.

5 The complete edition of the Loeb Classics was a gift from Freya's friend and the object of her passionate affection, Dulcie Deuchar, who died in March 1976. As a young actress she had a successful career in Australia, until she contracted TB. Married to a wealthy sportsman twenty-two years older than herself, Tommy Deuchar, she was an important and generous patron of Freya for more than twenty years. Her death from leukaemia occurred just as Freya was departing on a visit to Yemen; she did not cancel her flight or rush back to attend the funeral, something she told a friend 'was like walking behind a used-up dress however loved.' (*Letters*, Vol VIII, 23 March 1976 to Edwin Ker.)

Appendix A

1 Letter from Ronnie Fay in May 1947.

FREYA STARK'S WORKS

The place of publication is London and the publisher John Murray unless otherwise stated.

The Valleys of the Assassins, 1934
The Southern Gates of Arabia, 1936
A Winter in Arabia, 1940
Baghdad Sketches, 1937
Seen in the Hadhramaut, 1938
Letters from Syria, 1942
East is West, 1945
Perseus in the Wind, 1948
Traveller's Prelude, 1950 (autobiography, Vol I, 1893–1928)
Beyond Euphrates, 1951 (autobiography, Vol II, 1928–33)
The Coast of Incense, 1953 (autobiography, Vol III, 1933–39)
Dust in the Lion's Paw, 1961 (autobiography, Vol IV, 1939–46)
Ionia: A Quest, 1954
The Lycian Shore, 1956
Alexander's Path, 1958
Riding to the Tigris, 1959
The Journey's Echo, 1963
Rome on the Euphrates, 1966
The Zodiac Arch, 1968
The Minaret of Djam, 1970
A Peak in Darien, 1976
Rivers of Time, a photographic collection, with Malise Ruthven, 1982
Letters, Vols 1–6, ed. Lucy Moorehead; Vols 7–8, ed. Caroline Moorehead, 1974–82, published by Michael Russell
Over the Rim of the World, Selected letters, ed. Caroline Moorehead, 1988, published in association with Michael Russell.

INDEX